BALES & SPIRES

Margaret Growcott

October 2021

· MARGARET GROWCOTT ·

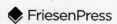

FriesenPress

Suite 300 - 990 Fort St
Victoria, BC, v8v 3K2
Canada

www.friesenpress.com

ISBN
978-1-5255-8433-6 (Hardcover)
978-1-5255-8434-3 (Paperback)
978-1-5255-8435-0 (eBook)

1. FICTION, ROMANCE, HISTORICAL, VICTORIAN

Distributed to the trade by The Ingram Book Company

Dedication

This book is dedicated to my husband, Robert Harry Growcott,
my violinist hero, who inspired, encouraged,
and cajoled me into writing it.

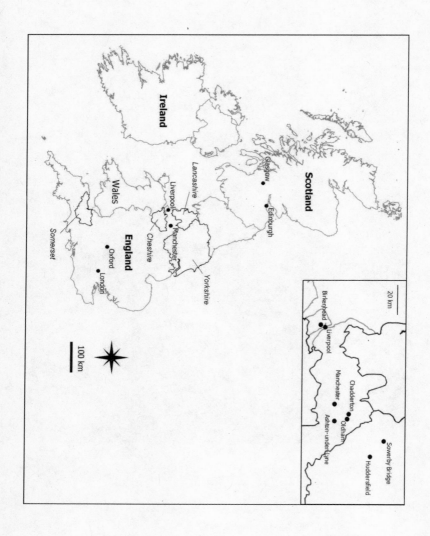

Acknowledgements

I am deeply grateful to the following:

Julian Growcott, my son who created the artwork for the cover.

Angela Hughes, my friend since Grammar School in UK, who was the first reader of my first chapter and said, 'this is quite good; carry on'.

Julia Turner, another friend in UK who was my first editor and 'laid it on the line'. I learnt a lot from her.

Derek Turner, for the map of UK showing where the narrative happened, 'because readers need to know'.

Sarah Macklin, my great-niece in UK who willingly and unhesitatingly took on the job of proof-reading.

Gisela Bangeman and Elaine Mantua, my two friends in Port Alberni who wondered why I was stuck to my desk all day and demanded chapters to read, convincing me I was on the right track.

Hardships often prepare an ordinary person
for an extraordinary destiny.

C. S. Lewis

Chapter One

1882

Jane was going home. She should be happy; she had dreamed of the day when she would see her mother and seven sisters after almost a year away. But her father had not said a word since they were on the train. Charles Kershaw seemed far away, looking out of the window. She put her small hand in his, but still he gazed out, at the disappearing cranes of Birkenhead, and then the green fields, with their cows and sheep slipping past.

Pa had been saying for the last three weeks it was time for her to go home. She was better now—no sign of tuberculosis. And today, he had said they must go home immediately.

She could hardly wait to see them all, especially her favourite sister, Kate, who, Jane figured, was now twenty-one. She loved them all, of course, but she had always been a little scared of Emma, the eldest. Then there was Eliza, nearly eighteen, in Jane's opinion the beauty of the family, with her straw-coloured hair and blue eyes. Mary-Rose and Mary-Anne, the twins, were next, aged sixteen. They always did things together and kept themselves to themselves. Jane smiled as she thought about Alice, the only redhead of the family. Would she still be as extrovert and dramatic, marching around the house, always reciting poetry whether anyone wanted to hear it or not? Next, only eleven months older than Jane was Amy, quiet and studious.

There was a brother, too, the oldest of the family, but he lived in London so they hardly ever saw him. When Jane was little, she had often wondered why her only brother, Algernon, lived in London. She had gradually learned that the whole family had lived in London before she was born and they had come to Lancashire as they were assured of finding work in the numerous cotton mills there. Algy had stayed behind in London, as he was fourteen with a good job at the post office. A few months after the move north, Jane had been born.

Jane was longing to see her mother. The last time she had seen her was when Jane had left home to go to Birkenhead. She remembered clearly: Ma had not been well that day and had been lying on the sofa by the kitchen fire, listless, hardly saying goodbye.

Hours later, Jane quickened her step beside her father as they alighted from the train in Chadderton, searching eagerly for sight of the house she had left so suddenly eleven months ago. They rounded a corner and there was Bower Lane, a narrow street of terraced houses, all exactly the same with their red brick exterior and front bay windows. The front door stood open. Jane jumped onto the big stone step, scrubbed with pipe-clay until it was white. Obviously it had been done that day.

But all was silent inside the house. The large kitchen and living space was empty. Jane thought they must all be in the front parlour. Perhaps Ma was taking her afternoon rest in there. But her mother was not lying on the sofa. She was lying in a coffin.

§

Only then did Jane understand why this homecoming had been so sudden. Tears stinging her face, she ran to her favourite big sister, Kate.

"Why didn't somebody tell me?" asked Jane, burying her head in Kate's apron.

Kate eyed her father critically, whilst hugging her little sister. Charles Kershaw shook his bowed head, taking off his topcoat and allowing Emma, his eldest daughter, to hang it up in the hall.

"So you're better, Jane," said Kate, holding her sister at arm's length and noting beyond the tear-stained face the rosy cheeks and the curly auburn hair that had not been tied up that day. She recalled the misery of that day all those months ago when Jane had left to go to Birkenhead with her father where he worked as a carpenter at the shipyards of Cammell Laird on the banks of the River Mersey. But now, at last, her youngest sister was home.

"But Ma's not better," said Jane. "Why did she have to die?"

"She had the consumption, like you," said Kate. "She wanted you to get better and that's why you went to live by the sea, with Pa, all these months, but *she* couldn't do that, could she?"

Jane had longed to see her mother for so many months. Was that really her lying in the cheap pine coffin in the cold parlour? She looked older than Jane remembered, the whiteness of her dead features almost as white as the satin which lined the coffin. It was just as well the weather was wintry for early April, as she would have to lie in the front room for several days. No fire could be lit in there.

"Aren't you glad to be home, Jane?" asked Amy.

"Yes," said Jane, through her tears, but no one was convinced.

"How old are you now? Ten?" said Alice. She noticed the city-bought shoes instead of the usual boots.

"Yes."

"So you'll be going to work half days at the mill, like me and Amy?"

"I suppose so," said Jane, turning away before Alice could start lecturing her on what was to come, having worked half days at the cotton mill for the past two years.

Emma managed to stop a comment that immediately sprang to her lips. How she wished her youngest sister, who had been such an ailing child a year ago, would not have to work in that environment. The damp climate was bad enough. It was, however, ideal for the textile industry as the delicate threads did not dry and break. Emma herself had worked in a cotton mill since they had come from London ten years ago when there had been a slump. It seemed this region at the foot of the Pennines in Lancashire would never stop attracting workers from all over the country who flocked to the seemingly limitless employment opportunities. And British engineers were constantly re-inventing the best spinning machines and looms that turned those raw bales of cotton Jane had seen coming off barges down at the canal into thread and fabric.

Emma could think of nothing but the funeral in three days time. She mentally checked all she had to do. Some of the girls had black dresses already; she would have to make sure the others had them and they would all have to wear them for many months. That meant a lot of sewing for her and Kate. Mrs. Burgess, their next-door neighbour was a seamstress. She would help with the sewing. Mrs. Kendal, at the village shop, had kindly offered to supply a ham for the special tea after the funeral. Then there was the baking; the older girls could help with that. And the next-door neighbours on the other side had offered to help with the refreshments.

Charles Kershaw, after fetching in a scuttle of coal and tending to the fire, eyed his daughters keenly as he had not seen them for almost a year.

Emma was twenty-three, tall, plain and practical, and ruled the younger ones with a harsh regime. She was in charge of everything as her mother had been bedridden for months. Kate, quiet and soft-spoken, was Emma's right-hand help, but she was much more tender hearted. Eliza, with her fair hair, was the only one to take after her father. The identical twins, Mary-Rose and Mary-Anne, had not much to say, except to each other. Alice, the twelve-year old redhead, was still as feisty as ever. Mr. Kershaw noticed Amy, with her head in a book as usual, the quietest of them all. He realized it would take Jane a while to settle back into this troupe, especially without her mother.

Kate, only just home from work was putting her shawl on again. "Come on, Jane. Want to come with me to Mrs. Kendal's? We need some butter and milk, and maybe some brawn." Jane, relieved at the opportunity to be alone with Kate, ran to join her. Kate rattled the coins in her pocket as they walked down Bower Lane to Mrs. Kendal's shop. Kate carried an empty pail whilst Jane clutched an old chipped cup to put the butter in.

The butter was in barrels, one either side of the front door of the shop. One of them was almost empty, the other full. Jane remembered she should go to the barrel on the left, where she would have to scrape her cup around the inside. It was more expensive to get butter from the full churn. At home, her job would be to pick out the bits of wood before the bread was buttered for tea.

Today they might have meat on their bread, even if it was only brawn, the type of sliced meat made from calves' or sheep's heads. Not much meat in it, but plenty of gelatine. Jane didn't care for it herself— she would eat her bread with nothing on it.

Mrs. Kendal, a sallow, middle-aged woman, appeared at the shop counter. "So you've got your little sister back, I see. What can I get you?"

"Butter from the cheap barrel and milk," said Kate placing the empty pail on the counter. "Oh, yes. Emma said to get some of that brawn we had the other day."

"Sorry love, there's no more of that 'til Butcher comes Saturday," said Mrs. Kendal, wiping her hands on the thick coarse apron which she always wore over her calico shift. "And there was no delivery from Dodds' Farm today, so I can only let you have two pints." There was a noise from upstairs and she raised her eyes towards the ceiling.

Kate made her usual polite enquiries. "And how is Mr. Kendal today?"

Mrs. Kendal's husband had been a boilerman at one of the mills, but an explosion a few years back had given him such severe injuries he was now either resting in bed or trying, inadequately, to help his wife in the shop.

"Oh, he's real bad. He's taken to bed 'til doctor comes."

The girls smiled at poor Mrs. Kendal who had the double worries of her husband and the shop always on her mind. Kate had heard snatches of conversation about Mr. Kendall who had been in the infirmary for a long time and still had to go back now and again. Although a profitable little shop, Mrs. Kendal was hard pressed to keep going on her own with her husband being indisposed. Their only son had married a girl from Manchester and gone to live over there. She always talked about Manchester as if it was some foreign country, not just seven miles away.

Kate held the pail while Mrs. Kendal ladled two pints of milk into it.

"Don't you want tripe for tomorrow? Don't you always have it for dinner on Thursdays?" reminded the ever-resourceful shopkeeper.

Kate hesitated. Emma had not mentioned the tripe, but it might have slipped her mind, with Pa and Jane coming home suddenly.

"Yes, we'd better take it," she said, as Mrs. Kendal put the lid on the pail.

Jane was grateful Emma insisted on the better quality "washed" tripe and not the "unwashed" green tripe which was much cheaper. At least Emma made it reasonably palatable by simmering it slowly in the oven with plenty of onions. But Jane would rather not have to eat the inside of a sheep's stomach, however much effort Emma put into it.

Kate began counting the coins from her pocket, frowning slightly. Did she have enough?

"You can have it on tick," said Mrs. Kendal kindly.

"Thanks, Mrs. Kendal," murmured Kate, as her cheeks turned red. "I suppose that will be all right." Maybe Emma had something else in mind for dinner tomorrow. She smiled gratefully at Mrs. Kendal.

"What's with that sister of yours?" asked Mrs. Kendal as she wrapped a generous amount of the flabby white pieces in thick brown paper.

"Which one?" asked Kate, as she handed over the coins. "There are eight of us, as you know, Mrs. Kendal."

"I mean Eliza, of course," said Mrs. Kendal.

"If you mean to ask whether she's going to the new mill once it's open, well, you know as much as we do, Mrs. Kendal," said Kate, gathering up their purchases.

"I didn't mean that. I'm talking about your Eliza and my nephew, Billy. Joe says they've been walking out together." Mrs. Kendal's brother, Joe, was the wages clerk, and knew everything that went on at the Glebe Mill.

"Joe should mind his own business," Kate whispered aside to Jane, but she shook her head implying it was all nonsense.

"Enough of that tittle-tattle," said Kate as they walked home. She was hauling the pail of milk while Jane carried the cup of butter and the parcel of tripe.

"Will you go to the new mill when it's finished?" Jane asked Kate, changing the subject. There had been much talk of the new big mill that was being built, called Textile Mill, which promised better conditions and higher wages.

"Just waitin' Jane," said Kate. "Just waitin' my turn. The Textile will ask me by and by—just you wait and see."

When they reached home, there was a pleasant surprise. Instead of the brawn that had been planned for tea, there were newly laid eggs brought by Mr. Critchley, an old friend of the family who ran a small farm on the edge of town. Mr. Critchley's farm, hemmed in by more and more newly built terraced houses, would soon disappear in Chadderton's rapid and dramatic evolution from a sparsely populated rural village into a Victorian industrial town.

At the tea table, Jane made sure she sat next to Kate.

§

Jane was the centre of attention as her sisters bombarded her with questions about her absence for the last eleven months. She remembered her first night in Birkenhead, hardly believing she had left home. Even though she was with her father at the lodging house, she missed her mother and cried herself to sleep, sleeping fitfully. She dreamt she was at home—happy, even though they were having tripe for dinner.

Jane hadn't liked the school in Birkenhead. It was so much bigger than the one in Chadderton. She had scarcely got to know any of the pupils, finding them distrustful and unfriendly and they spoke with a strange accent. If it hadn't been for Mrs. Kelly, landlady of the lodging house, she would have been very lonely when her father was at work. Mrs. Kelly had come from Ireland some years before. "When my man died I thought to myself, ships from Ireland take butter, eggs, pork and bacon to Liverpool, and they can take me too. Ah, but there's too many Irish folk in Liverpool. So I took myself on the ferry one day to Birkenhead, and here I am."

Jane had learned a lot about Ireland from Mrs. Kelly and thought some day she would like to go there. Another thing she liked about the lodgings was the piano, an old battered one that had yellow keys, some of which were missing. Mrs. Kelly's daughter had played it, but she was grown up and had gone back to Ireland as a nurse. Jane had found this instrument to be a source of fascination and occupied herself for many hours, picking out tunes she had heard the lodgers humming and often some hymns she remembered from church back in Chadderton.

Birkenhead, in the county of Cheshire, was a fairly big city, although, unlike Liverpool across the River Mersey, it had been spared most of the ravages of the Industrial Revolution. If you looked straight ahead, there was the Irish Sea, but if you looked in the opposite direction, you could see Liverpool on the other side of the river, with all its factories, docks and ferry boats. By contrast, forty-eight miles away, Chadderton was in Lancashire, on the River Irk and Rochdale Canal, near Oldham. Once undulating farmland, beyond the river there were still green fields to be seen, although more mills were being built owing to the huge demand for cotton production. Chimneys dotted the skyline in Chadderton. If Jane half closed her eyes, the church spire she passed on her way to school in Birkenhead looked just like the chimney of the Glebe Mill where four of her sisters worked. One thing she discovered, as her father had said she would, was that it was not as damp in Birkenhead as it was in Chadderton.

Now, eleven long months later, she was home again, but Jane almost wished she was back in Birkenhead. Ma was gone. She would miss her father and Mrs. Kelly with her excellent cooking, especially the Sunday roast chicken, something they rarely had at home, and the buns bursting with raisins Mrs. Kelly made on a Wednesday. And she already missed that piano.

"So you're better, Jane," said Alice, as they finished their tea. "No more of that nasty consumption. What was it like at the seaside?"

"It wasn't exactly the seaside. It was all shipbuilding, cranes everywhere. There was a lovely park though, with flower gardens and woods; and a lake with a bridge going over it. They called it the Swiss Bridge. I pretended we were in Switzerland when I walked over that bridge with Pa."

Alice was unimpressed by this account, but Amy was totally interested. Her favourite lesson was geography and she knew all about Switzerland. "That's where they send rich people to get better when they have consumption," she said, noticing that Jane had not coughed once since she came home. Her eyes sparkled and her plump cheeks displayed dimples Amy had never noticed before.

Alice continued her interrogation of Jane but wasn't interested in what she heard. She might have been more attentive if Jane had said she had been to Timbuktu or seen the Taj Mahal.

"I hear they're going to put up a statue of the Queen in Birkenhead," said Emma. She had often longed to see this royal personage although it was well known that Queen Victoria had been in perpetual mourning since her husband, Prince Albert, died in 1861, and that she always wore black. It would be disappointing if she couldn't be seen in her colourful royal regalia.

"I haven't heard about a statue but they're building a new town hall with stone brought all the way from Scotland," said Jane. She knew about this because one of the lodgers at Mrs. Kelly's house was a builder, employed to work on this great edifice. "Pa did take me to the seaside once, on my birthday. A place called New Brighton. It was grand; golden sands and a long pier where you could get ices and see a show at the music hall."

Alice was an aspiring actress and that finally got her attention. "Oh! I'd love to see one of those shows," she said.

"You didn't go to a music hall, surely?" asked Emma sharply, who had never been to one herself, but had heard plenty about them. "You're far too young."

Yes, at ten years old, Jane was far too young to see a music hall show which, of course, she had only heard about from Mrs. Kelly. But she wasn't too young to go to work at the mill from six o'clock till noon every weekday, and then become a child again and go to school for the afternoon. She would do this until she was twelve or thirteen and then she would work full time at the mill.

§

Jane could not get to sleep. It was strange sharing a room with Amy, Alice and Eliza instead of the little attic bedroom all to herself at Mrs. Kelly's.

There was Eliza brushing her long golden tresses, trying to ignore Alice who was grilling her about Billy Lampson. Amy was snuggled down at her side of the bed she now shared with Jane, trying to read by the flickering candlelight.

Eliza tossed her head. "I don't know what you're talking about. I don't care about Billy. How can you think about things like that when Ma's lying dead in her coffin?"

"Come on now, Eliza," said Alice. "I've seen you looking at him over your hymn book on a Sunday morning." Evidently Billy was very noticeable in church because he was in the choir, although some claimed he could not sing a note. He was in full view of everyone whether he was actually singing or not. "And the vicar has promoted him from sexton to verger."

Eliza continued brushing her hair, looking not the least concerned.

"What with his choir singing and his verger duties, it's a wonder he has time for girls," said Alice, "but I have to say, Eliza, he does look handsome in his choir robe."

"It's called a cassock, not a choir robe."

"And he's got tremendous muscles," said Alice. "Mary-Rose said Billy was stripped to the waist when she and Mary-Ann walked past the graveyard a few weeks ago."

Eliza could not ignore this. "He's not digging graves any more. Remember, he's now the verger."

"I bet you'd like to see Billy stripped to the waist," Alice continued. Jane could clearly see that Eliza was affected as a flush spread over her even features. She put the hairbrush down and got into the bed she shared with Alice.

"You'll just have to be satisfied seeing him in his choir rig. You can tell he's got great muscles under that robe." Alice would not let go. "And Abigail says he's quite a one for the girls." Abigail Burgess, aged fourteen, was the daughter of their next-door neighbours. She was, evidently, a fount of knowledge when it came to local gossip.

"Kate told me *she* likes Mr. Goodacre," said Eliza, changing the topic. Mr. Goodacre was one of the Sunday school teachers. "But Kate said he's above us all."

Whether she meant spiritually or of a higher class was not clear. "He's young and not married, so I suppose Kate can fancy him if she feels like it," said Alice. Kate, of course, had not been to Sunday school for years, but she still saw Mr. Goodacre at church.

Jane's curiosity was peaked, hearing all about the romantic notions of her older sisters. Evidently much had been going on while she had been away and she felt like an outsider, even though Amy was in bed beside her, still trying to read. Amy was a keen scholar now, by all accounts, but Jane would be able to show her a thing or two. In her eleven months away, she had missed the family but had become close to her father. She had done well at school even though she had never been accepted socially. She had written all the letters home at her father's dictation and had a round, neat hand with excellent spelling. Being solely in the company of adults, when not at school, she had acquired knowledge beyond her years, reading the newspapers every day and listening to all that was said around the table at Mrs. Kelly's. She suddenly remembered, two other lodgers, who were also employed at the shipyard, had told tales about all the great ships that had been built there. One man said his father had worked on the *Ma Robert*, a steam launch, built for Dr. Livingstone's Zambezi expedition in 1858. Jane had meant to tell Amy about this because she had a book all about Dr. Livingstone. But right now, Amy had blown out the candle and appeared to be asleep.

It was suddenly quiet in the bedroom. Jane was home, but it was not like it used to be. She eventually fell asleep and dreamed her mother had come to kiss her goodnight.

Chapter Two

"**I**t pleases God to take His servant, Sarah, to His kingdom," the vicar said at the graveyard.

Emma looked miserable. Kate dabbed her eyes. The other girls wept, all except Jane who was busy wondering why God was pleased, when no one else seemed to be. The only one who smiled was Vicar Whitely.

Jane watched her mother's coffin being lowered into the ground. She felt detached from the scene. How could this be? Her mother, inside the box, was only forty-five and now dead after being ill on and off for several years.

Emma's mind was on the upcoming wake, preparations for which had taken her mind off the sadness of the occasion. Was there enough food? She figured about nine or ten guests would come to the house in addition to their own family. People had been generous; even Mr. Leggate, the manager of the mill where Emma worked, had given her money, a couple of pounds, towards the feast that was always expected at a funeral. Emma was tired of preparing food—she ate hardly anything herself. She was so tired, of food, of sisters all needing care and attention, of the whole house that needed her supervision. She sighed, recalling the vicar, who had only recently said to her, "My dear, this situation will not go on for ever. You are the oldest and you are the one to look after the family, but in the fullness of time, you will, no doubt, leave to get married."

Yes, in the fullness of time, if her sisters didn't overtake her and get married first. Eliza always had men turning their heads to take another look whenever she passed by, but Emma knew, in spite of what Eliza said, that she still fancied Billy Lampson. She never had the hymn book open at the right page in church because she was too busy watching Billy. And then there was Kate, who had colour in her cheeks whenever she was in the vicinity of Mr. Goodacre, and you couldn't get a word of sense out of her. Oh, things would happen in the fullness of time, but would they happen to Emma? Good things, that is. Marriage seemed to be the ultimate goal of most girls, she knew that, but she wasn't sure if that was what *she* wanted. And certainly, there was no one she fancied.

"The Lord giveth and the Lord taketh away … … " How many more times would she be hearing this? Emma didn't much like the Lord at the moment. It was a big effort to get herself ready for church every Sunday. She must set a good example to the younger girls, but oh, she had no mind for it herself. The Lord had not given them much. He had just taken away. Emma was growing bitter about the Lord; he that took away and gave back nothing.

Emma looked round at her sisters in the dismal graveyard. Kate held their only umbrella but hadn't deployed it since there was only a sifting sort of rain. Next to Kate stood her father, lips pursed with his head hung low. Emma wondered what he was thinking. He was now a widower. But, had her parents been happy? Hardly likely, as they had lived apart for the last ten years, due to his work in Birkenhead. Alice was standing next to their father; Emma knew Alice would need taking down a peg or two. You had to be careful what you said in front of Alice—she hung on every word and repeated things at the most inappropriate time. Emma would have to keep an eye on Jane, too. Living away at Birkenhead for months, she seemed older than her ten years, with all sorts of knowledge of which the other girls had no idea. Then there was Eliza, unconscious as usual of how her striking good looks had an effect on people. She stared into the void where her mother's coffin was disappearing, strands of yellow hair straying from the black bonnet, her complexion flawless, as usual. Emma noticed Algy's wife staring at Eliza, and well she might. Lucy was a plain thing, no doubt about that, with her wispy hair and pinched features. But she was from London and wore fashionable clothes. Emma had a certain envy of her. She clearly remembered living in the Islington borough of London, before they had moved north to Lancashire. People were different in the South and their clothes were quite distinct. The whole family was amazed that their brother, Algy, had come to the funeral after not hearing from him for years. He had not sent word, but had just arrived by train that morning with Lucy. As Pa was occupying the small front bedroom, the couple had announced they would stay at a local inn. Emma could hardly believe they had that kind of money—cash they could waste away. Then there was Aunt Clara, Mrs. Kershaw's only surviving sister, who lived in London and who had also come up by train. The older girls had not seen her since they left London and Jane had never met her.

"That's what you get," Aunt Clara was saying as they walked back to the house. "Working in a mill around here." She was referring to the high toll lung diseases took on the residents of Chadderton. As far as Emma knew, London had bad air too, depending on where you lived. Who would have thought that living in Lancashire was so unhealthy?

"That's what you get," repeated Aunt Clara to emphasize her point. "It's a wonder no one else has got it." She shook her head, looking meaningfully around at her nieces, particularly Jane.

What choice did they have? Emma wondered. She was about to point out to her aunt that their mother did not get TB from working in the mill, but the general air and debility that was widespread in the region. In fact, her mother had never done mill work, coming north in her early thirties with eight children and giving birth to a ninth upon arrival.

Aunt Clara continued her diatribe as they marched back to the house for the funeral tea. Emma remembered her aunt's distinctive voice across all those years long ago. She still had a voice like a screeching railway engine.

"I told my sister not to leave London," Aunt Clara said to her brother-in-law, Charles. "You don't know what you're doing, I told her. It's not God's will. Poor Sarah might still be alive if she had stayed in London."

Sarah Kershaw had often told her daughters how Aunt Clara was apt to hold forth on health and religion although, as this was the first time she had visited them, they had not witnessed this before.

As if her poor father needed this sermon, thought Emma, trying to move between them. She could just about bear her aunt's preaching about the wicked and sinful, that happiness was reserved for some vague afterlife, and only for a few fortunate 'blessed' ones, but Emma felt her father did not need this kind of talk. In their household, there was little preaching and praying; it was reserved for their Sunday attendance at Christ Church, the Anglican place of worship in Chadderton. This day, however, a prayer would be said before the meal because Aunt Clara would expect it. And she made sure she was the one to do it when they got back to the house. Everyone was assembled in the front parlour, which now had more space since the coffin was no longer there. Aunt Clara said a lengthy grace while Vicar Whitely nodded his approval. The table fairly groaned with the refreshments, the likes of which the girls had never seen before. There was the ham—Mrs. Kendall had not let them down—and generous slices were placed on Emma's home-baked bread. There were sandwiches too: cucumber made by Aunt Clara, who had specially brought the cucumber all the way from London where they were plentiful and grown in glass houses. The other plate of sandwiches was fish paste, Pa's favourite. Other savouries were pork pies brought by Dick and Annie Leighton from next door, and sausage rolls, provided by the Burgess family from the other side. 'Neighbours are useful at times', reflected Emma. She wished she liked Mrs. Burgess and her daughter, Abigail, better. Mrs. Leggate had brought some of her celebrated jars of pickled onions and pickled beets, displayed next to the sandwiches on the one-and-only family heirloom—a silver-edged glass dish. Eliza was slicing the seed cake she had made under instructions from Jane, who maintained she had often helped Mrs. Kelly make one in Birkenhead. There were also spice buns, made by Kate. Aunt Clara had told them everyone had plum cake at funerals, but Emma had never made one and plums were not in season. Maybe they were easily obtainable in London where everything seemed abundant at all times of the year. She must remember to taste a sausage roll and thank Mrs. Burgess, specially. Cheese with water crackers sat on a marble platter along with red grapes, a great delicacy provided by Mr. Higginbottom, manager of Glebe Mill. On the mahogany chiffonier were two decanters, one of port and one of sherry. The decanters flanked the tray of funeral biscuits, small sponge-like biscuits, wrapped in white paper envelopes and sealed with black wax. These were for the guests to take home with them. Aunt Clara had shown the girls how to make them. It was something she had done for the funerals of her four siblings in London, but it was not such a well-known custom in Lancashire. The girls were intrigued and dutifully followed Aunt Clara's instructions. Jane had proved herself a dab hand at preparing the delicate envelopes to hold the small biscuits made from a long sponge cake cut into thin slices.

"Eliza, fetch some more sandwiches from the pantry," said Emma whilst putting the last of the cucumber and fish paste sandwiches together and handing her the spare plate.

Emma presided over the teapot, with Mary-Rose or Mary-Ann at the ready to fetch more hot water from the kettle in the kitchen. Aunt

Clara sat in the wingback chair as though it was a throne. Pa was between Mrs. Leggate and Mrs. Burgess on the narrow horsehair sofa, with Mr. Burgess and Abigail leaning against the wooden arm. Chairs had been brought from the kitchen, yet there still was not enough seating for everyone. But Emma and the other girls were on their feet, making sure everyone was served correctly.

"Don't lean against the wall," said Emma to Alice. "And go and fetch that other stool from the pantry, but put a cushion on it before you bring it in here."

Algy and his wife, Lucy, were squeezed together on the piano bench, a piece of furniture not owned by the Kershaws but on loan from the Church hall. Emma simply could not figure out Lucy, this standoffish girl, who had hardly spoken a word since she arrived at the house. Emma could not comprehend how, after being married for several years, there was no baby and not even a sign of one. Unknown to her, Alice and Jane had had much discussion about this and had shared their knowledge of how babies were born. They knew it was something to do with being married, and there would definitely be no bairn if you weren't married, but that didn't account for Lucy and Algy being childless. Alice had told Jane that babies were like the piglets she had seen being born at Mr. Critchley's farm. They came out down below, but how they got there in the first place was a mystery. Amy, who had read the Bible a great deal, said that it had something to do with seeds. But it was still a mystery. They daren't ask Emma even though she would be sure to know. She knew everything.

The fire in the parlour had been lit on this chill April day, but it wasn't the hearty warm blaze of the kitchen. Rarely used, it smoked and needed coaxing. Jane watched Emma take the poker, jabbing the obstinate coals. She looked at the hushed assembly. All there to celebrate the dead. Jane thought she might as well be dead. All she had to look forward to was working at the mill. She longed for that piano she had loved to play at Mrs. Kelly's.

But Emma tried to be optimistic. Now she might have more of a life of her own. She would go back to work full time at the Wharf Mill now that she didn't have Ma to look after any more. She liked it at the mill. She had worked at some of the other mills but had moved to the Wharf when she had become a weaver. Some of the mills had only spinning facilities. Mr. Leggate had always said she could go back to work full time as soon as she was able. She knew he had meant 'once her mother had died', Emma thought. He meant kindly though, she knew that.

When the second batch of sandwiches had disappeared and the ham was just a sliver left on the plate, Charles Kershaw rose to pour from the decanters. Only for the men, though. Algy took a glass of sherry and so did Mr. Burgess. The other men all chose port. Charles helped himself to sherry, and then changed his mind, on the refill of the tiny glasses. The women drank tea or elderberry cordial. Next, cheese and grapes were served. This signalled the end of the wake. Guests would soon be leaving, each taking with them a strange-looking small package containing a funeral biscuit, something they had not seen before.

Thanks were murmured and gradually the parlour became less crowded.

"Don't forget, Emma," said Mr. Leggate. "We'll expect you at the mill tomorrow." Well, that would be something, thought Emma. Work, but a different kind from what she had been doing the last few months. It would be good to get back to the mill, especially the earnings.

Mr. Leggate and his wife took their leave, shaking hands with all. Connie, a hoity-toity woman in Emma's opinion, had unexpectedly struck up a lengthy conversation with Aunt Clara and the two had promised to meet again. No doubt Aunt Clara found the mill manager's wife, who was originally from London, the most stimulating of the guests. She was not backward at coming forward when it came to striking up conversations, especially with those she considered a higher class than herself.

The Burgess family took their leave. Then Mr. Higginbottom left.

"Who would have thought that two mill managers would be at the funeral?" Aunt Clara remarked to Emma as they took dishes into the kitchen.

Emma, saving her breath as usual, refrained from telling her that it was customary in those parts for managers to attend funerals of their employees' families.

"Mr. Leggate brought his wife," said Aunt Clara. "I wonder why Mr. Higginbottom didn't bring his?"

"There is no Mrs. Higginbottom," Kate informed her aunt. "She was one of those killed in the Tay Bridge Disaster two years ago."

Aunt Clara nodded. Who could forget that dreadful night of December 28th 1879? The bridge over the River Tay in Scotland had collapsed in a violent storm and the train to Dundee and its seventy-five passengers had been flung into the deep, churning waters far below.

"His wife was from Scotland and had gone up to visit her mother in Dundee, with the new baby," continued Kate, eyes downcast. "Their bodies were never found, like most of the other passengers. Poor Mr. Higginbottom and the other three children suffered so." Kate shuddered whenever she thought of the tragedy. It was no wonder Mr. Higginbottom now had an aversion to rail travel. "At the mill, they say he refuses to go anywhere by trai n now."

The girls were all assigned duties to tidy up after the guests had left. But Jane stayed by her father's side. He would be going back to Birkenhead tomorrow and she wanted to be near him. She almost wished she was going back to Birkenhead too. But then she knew in her heart that home was best, especially as she had her beloved Kate. She would have to stay on the right side of Emma, though.

§

At half past five the next morning, Emma did her usual round of waking up the girls.

'Rise and shine', the same tune they had all heard before. Jane failed to see how you could shine when everything around you was dull and sad. But this day was different: Emma herself would be leaving the house earlier than the others to go to Wharf Mill on the Oldham side. The others all worked at the Glebe and they would be leaving later, taking their youngest sister, Jane. It was her first day at work and she would be going to school in the afternoon with Amy and Alice.

After the lavish spread following the funeral, it was back to basics for breakfast. A slice of bread with no butter, and a cup of strong, hot tea with no milk or sugar. The only one to have a variation from this repast was Aunt Clara, who came in from the Burgess house next door where she was being accommodated. Emma gave her aunt tea with milk and sugar, and a slice of buttered bread.

"I suppose you'll want me to be getting out of the way, now that your Pa has gone back to Birkenhead?"

Emma knew in her heart she could not deny it. If only their aunt were more like her dead sister. She was ten years older and it was hard to believe they were even related. Emma bit her lip, remembering her mother's motto: *Manners maketh man.*

"No indeed, Aunt. We haven't seen you for so long. Please stay as long as you like. Besides, little Jane has never met you before."

Aunt Clara sipped her tea. "She's not so little. She's ten years old and grown up enough to work at the mill. But she's a grand little lass, about the same age as my Sally's eldest."

"I know Pa's left already and Algy and Lucy caught the early train to London," said Emma. "But you can bide a while, surely Aunt?"

"Me and that Mrs. Leggate – Connie—we had a good chinwag. She did invite me to go to her house for tea on Thursday, if I'm still here. She's planning on having a ladies' tea."

Emma nodded. She knew Mrs. Leggate was famous for her tea parties. It was the sort of thing she did every now and again for some committee or social occasion.

Although she was busy organizing everyone's departure to work, Emma was still smarting at the conversation she had had with her father before he left.

"You'll come home again soon, won't you, Pa? Now that Ma's gone." Emma could hardly believe it herself.

"Nay, Emma. I'll come when I can, y'know that right well. But, but it's a fair distance and the train fare is mighty expensive. You'll manage well enough, like you've done the last few months. I'll still send you a bit of money every fortnight."

"But Pa, you could get a job here. I'm sure the mills need carpenters."

"Ah, but, my work's specialized, for ships, y'see." Pa was putting on his coat with his eye on the clock over the mantelpiece. "Dammit, Emma, you're not expecting me to give up me job at Cammell Laird's? I'll not get anything as well paid hereabouts."

"It would be good to have you home, to see to things. We could do with you here. I can't do everything. Please, Pa, think about it."

"Emma, you know as well as I do that I can't leave that job in Birkenhead. What's up with you? You've done everything up to now."

'I don't have Ma's patience," said Emma, envisaging what was ahead of her. "Alice is getting above herself and Eliza's always mooning about that boy. Ma understood—could talk to them. I can't do that."

"You can handle the girls, Emma. I'm relying on you. They'll toe the line with you." And then Pa was off to the railway station with a goodbye kiss for all of them, and a special hug for Jane, and words of encouragement for her first morning at the mill.

Emma was glad she was starting back to work. It would take her mind of things but she had a heavy heart as they all left the house.

§

Arms akimbo, Aunt Clara watched the girls depart, and decided she would bide her time. She was in no hurry to get back to London where she lived with her youngest married daughter who had four squawking infants. This stay up north, although a morbid occasion, was a respite for her, but she determined to do what she could to help out in the Kershaw household. First, there was some mending to be done and those curtains in the front bedroom could be taken down, altered and put in the back bedroom, which had none. She had thoughtfully brought some of her cast-off curtains thinking they might come in useful, and now she thought they would do for the small bedroom above the porch that she was going to occupy.

Next, she would send a message to Mrs. Leggate via one of the girls, saying she would indeed be able to go to tea on Thursday. Aunt Clara, who normally wanted to know all that was going on, didn't want to know much about the cotton industry but she was not averse to knowing who was in charge of it. She herself was more involved in the fruit and vegetable business, one of her sons currently a barrow-boy on a street corner in Islington, a district where most of her family lived.

§

Emma was back for a full shift at the Wharf Mill. Mr. Leggate had spent some time with her and asked her to tackle one loom for a while, instead of the usual two. He knew full well Emma was an experienced weaver and that she could have gone to any of the other mills that had weaving sheds—not actual "sheds", but long, low single-storey buildings with many north-facing windows and skylights. Weaving, because of the huge vibration of the looms, was not usually done in the multiple storey buildings of cotton mills, most of which did spinning only.

"You're getting back into the swing of things. Maybe take on another loom," said Mr. Leggate when he returned to see how Emma was getting on. She couldn't hear him, of course. The noise from the looms was deafening, but, like all the girls who worked there, she was good at lip-reading. She was contented in the cocoon of the mill discipline. Here she was in charge of two looms; it was better than being in charge of a house and coping with the seven sisters that went with it. But she knew she would still have to do that.

Emma was soon used to the clatter of the hundreds of shuttles racing backwards and forwards at high speeds. Keeping a close eye on the weft thread which had to be replaced at regular intervals, she occasionally had to lift out the shuttle when a weft thread broke, renew the spool and connect the thread again. It was all hard work and sometimes intricate, but at least now, she would be earning money—money she had been missing all those weeks at home. Her seven sisters, now including Jane, were all employed in different capacities in the cotton business at the Glebe Mill. Kate was extremely experienced at the spinning mules, but she wanted to get on into the weaving. The pay was higher, but she would have to leave the Glebe for they had no weaving capabilities.

On the way home at noon, Emma started thinking, as usual, about dinner. Then she remembered Aunt Clara had said she would prepare their main midday meal. Emma could see that her aunt, although distant in feelings towards them, had a good heart and had not wasted her morning in the house. They sat down to a dinner of liver and onions, with mashed potatoes and turnips.

While they were eating, Emma suddenly remembered that Amy would be going to Oldham that evening with their next-door neighbour, Mr. Burgess. He was a member of the Literary Club held at the Lyceum and once a month there was a lecture on some topic of interest. He had kindly offered to take Amy whose favourite lesson at school was geography. An Associate of the Royal Geographical Society had been engaged to talk to the members.

"Is tonight the talk on the Sahara Desert?" asked Emma.

"Kalahari Desert," said Amy, with her mouth full.

Emma knew it was some kind of desert. Sahara or Kalahari, it was all the same to her. Why on earth Amy wanted to hear about some dry desert she had no idea. Bearing in mind her mother's strict rule that no girl was to go anywhere without a chaperone, Emma was grateful that Mr. Burgess, the respectable teacher from next door, would accompany Amy. It had been suggested Alice should go along as well. This was bad news for Amy who would have liked to have Mr. Burgess to herself with his vast knowledge about everything. They often had great discussions when he popped round with a book or a newspaper, but Alice would be in the way on this outing to the Lyceum. She would monopolise the conversation with her non-stop chatter about everything and nothing in particular. Alice had only agreed to go because the lecture was at the Literary Club and she knew that they had poetry evenings there from time to time. She might be able to find out about those and maybe, at some later date, she would be asked to recite a poem, which she longed to do.

"I don't think Amy and Alice should be going out tonight, so soon after the funeral. It's not right." said Aunt Clara.

"It's been arranged for weeks," said Emma. "And Pa said it would be fine. 'Something educational like this is important' is what Pa said. Alice, Amy, you'll have to wear your best black tonight."

Alice appealed to Emma. "Do I have to? Mine is too big for me. I don't like it. It makes me look fat," she said, knowing at the same time there was not much alternative, for they had to wear black for at least six months and her only other dress was the one she wore every day at the mill and school which was also black. Kate, who had hurriedly made best black dresses for the girls, had been too generous in the one she did for Alice. Always allowing for blossoming figures, she had allowed too much for the thin, almost thirteen year old, whose girlish spurt of growth had not yet started. In fact, Emma was slightly worried as Alice had not started her monthly bleeding yet.

"Let's have a look at it," volunteered Aunt Clara. "I can take the bodice in a bit this afternoon and it'd be ready when you get home."

"Oh, would you, Aunt?" Alice was relieved. "That's so kind of you." She immediately began to like Aunt Clara even though she often gave the girls a look which was cold enough to chill the Sahara and the Kalahari deserts at the same time. But she was getting better all the time.

'I'm very impressed with those black dresses you made, Kate," said Aunt Clara. "You did a really good job."

"It would have been impossible if it wasn't for our next-door neighbour, Mrs. Burgess," said Kate. "She's just got one of those sewing machines and she's been so kind letting me use it."

"I read about sewing machines in that book by Mrs. Beeton," said Aunt Clara. "Lots of people have them now."

"It's been a godsend," said Kate. "It took a while to get the hang of it, but I'd love a Singer sewing machine."

"I'd like to go to the Lyceum as well," said Jane interrupting the conversation. A sewing machine was something they were never likely to have.

"Mr. Burgess can only take two guests," said hard-hearted Emma and everyone, except Jane, knew that no amount of pleading would change her mind.

"Why can't I go instead of Alice? We learnt all about deserts at my school in Birkenhead," Jane said to the retreating figure of Emma. "I like deserts more than Alice."

"You're too young and it was decided ages ago that Alice is to go with Amy," was Emma's final comment. Jane knew that was the end of that, even though she was sure she knew more about deserts than Amy and Alice put together.

The five older girls walked back to their jobs at the two mills; the three younger ones, Jane, Amy and Alice walked to school for their afternoon lessons. Emma carried a note from her aunt, to give to her boss to pass on to his wife, saying she would attend Mrs. Leggate's tea party.

Emma soon took over her second loom, gladly given up by a co-worker, who, married only five months, had a large protruding belly. Emma knew it was never likely to happen to her. She was not worried that she had no prospective husband. Marriage was something she had so far not envisaged for herself.

She was the last one to arrive home. High tea was ready, thanks again to Aunt Clara, but how Emma wished it was Ma instead. Her sadness was soon dispelled at the sight of Amy and Alice rushing through their food, hardly eating any bread and not much of the cream cheese and celery hearts which their aunt had brought in from Mrs. Kendal's shop. Mrs. Kendal always had cream cheese on a Tuesday. It was cheap and nourishing for the Spartan meals they had during the week.

'Please may I be excused?" asked Alice, already getting up from the table. "Must get ready, Mr. Burgess will be here soon."

Earlier, when she came home from school at half past four, she had done some of her preparations for her evening sortie. She had managed to procure something marvellous which she had been wanting for months—half a lemon which Abigail Burgess had gotten for her. With this priceless piece of fruit, she had secreted herself in the bedroom she shared with Jane, Amy and Eliza, and was in the middle of a certain treatment, lying on the floor with a strip of linen soaked with lemon juice over her nose and cheeks, when she was interrupted by Jane.

"What on earth are you doing, Alice?" said Jane.

"Mind your own business," said Alice, removing the pad briefly, then resuming her supine position, replacing the pad on her nose.

"If you aren't feeling well, I'll go to the Lyceum instead of you," said Jane. "I had a horrible morning at the mill. I hate it."

"Well, as far as I could see, you didn't do anything, except watch," said Alice. "It's always easy the first day."

"But can I go instead of you tonight? You can't be well, lying on the floor with that thing over your face."

"I'm perfectly well," said Alice, getting up. She still had to do her chore of scrubbing the front door step, assigned to her by Emma that morning. And it had to be done before Emma came home.

Alice was satisfied that the dress fitted better since the adjustments by Aunt Clara. She put on her pad of lemon juice for a few more minutes before Mr. Burgess called for her and Amy at half past six. They left with orders from Emma about not being late home and not talking too much to anyone. They were in mourning—as if they could forget.

Jane watched sulkily as the other girls busied themselves with various occupations for the evening.

"How can you and the others be content to work for the rest of your lives in a cotton mill?" Jane asked Emma.

"That's what we have to do," said Emma. "That's our bread and butter. The only escape is getting married." This with a sidelong look at Eliza, who ignored this remark.

"Of course, that's another form of slavery," added Emma. "You'll get used to the mill, Jane, just like Amy's getting used to it."

"I know Amy doesn't care for it either. We love our afternoons at school. Amy says it lifts her above the mill work and she thinks of all the things she loves to learn about. It won't lift me much, though. That carding room is so dirty, and stuffy and all those bits of cotton floating around. Amy says it's bad for you."

"Stop sniffling, Jane, and come and help me," said Emma as she prepared to wash the tablecloth they had used at the funeral along with some other linens. This was done at the large and only sink in the house which was situated in the scullery off the kitchen. Then the washed items would be hung out in the small cobbled yard. They would be ready for ironing tomorrow night. Kate sat at the table with her stitching—she was making a dress for a friend's infant. Eliza was darning a pair of stockings, gazing into the air several times between rethreading her needle. Aunt Clara was busying herself stoking the fire next to the oven. She had just popped in a loaf of bread and some Chelsea buns. She settled on the sofa with her Bible, appalled again at how little food there was in the house. She had had to visit Mrs. Kendal's shop twice that day.

The twins were studying their sheets of music at the kitchen table, learning the anthem they would be singing in church next Sunday. They had just been admitted to the choir as old Mrs. Hartidge, whose voice was now not much more than a croak, had finally been persuaded to step down. Emma had noted lately, when she stood next to Mary-Rose in Church, that she had a sweet voice. Mary-Ann's was not bad either. But if you let one twin into something, you had to let the other in as well. Emma was not going to lay down the law attempting to separate the twins. They could not seem to do anything without each other. Eliza said she would like to be in the choir too, but luckily, thought Emma, there were already enough female voices and it would place Eliza too much in the vicinity of Billy Lampson. Emma and everyone else knew he was only allowed in the choir, with his dubious tenor voice, because they were short of men.

§

At the Lyceum, the lecture on the Kalahari Desert was in full swing. The speaker, Major Talbot, had been introduced to the audience by a young man. Alice recognized him as one of the boys who had worked at the mill part time when she had first started there. She thought his name was Archie something-or-other. She would ask Mr. Burgess about him as he was obviously a member of this prestigious Literary Club. In the meantime, Alice could see that Amy was entranced by Major Talbot from the Royal Geographical Society. During the applause at the end of the lecture, Alice managed to whisper something to Amy, who was too busy clapping to hear her clearly.

"Amy! Do you see anything different about me?" Alice demanded again, in a louder voice.

"What are you talking about?" said Amy. "You look the same as ever."

"You mean I still have lots of freckles? Aren't they any fainter?"

"They look just the same," said Amy. "Freckles belong with red hair and that's a fact."

Leaving Oldham, it was decided they would walk the mile back to Chadderton as it was only half past eight. The train was not due for another fifteen minutes and it was not yet fully dark. Alice fumed at the unfairness of it all. She thought they might have started or finished with a poem, even if the lecture was about the dry, boring desert. It was supposed to be a Literary Club. She was resentful at how she had urged Abigail to persuade her sister to steal half a lemon from the kitchen of the Big House where she worked. Now Abigail would never let her forget that Alice owed her a favour. All for nothing. She still had freckles and she now knew they would never go away. Why was she the only one in the family who had red hair and freckles?

"It's a combination of our Pa's fair hair and Ma's dark hair," Emma had explained her theory. "You ought to be thankful. I wish I had red hair instead of this mousy brown."

Alice was also furious that she had been unable to find out about the poetry readings at the Literary Club. She had looked for that fellow, Archie, but she hadn't seen him again, and then she wanted to ask Mr. Burgess but all the way home he was talking earnestly to Amy. Alice had no idea how they found so much to discuss on the desert, which she found tedious. She was seething about her own affairs but when they got home, the house was in an uproar.

"Have you two seen Eliza anywhere on the way home?" Emma was flushed and angry.

Amy and Alice shook their heads in bewilderment.

"She's not in the house. She seems to have disappeared."

Chapter Three

"Thank goodness you're back," said Emma to Amy and Alice. She was getting ready to go out, but in her panic, she was having difficulty tying her bonnet strings. "Where on earth can Eliza be?"

"She might be in the privy," suggested Amy. Already the pleasant evening was a fading memory.

"If she is, she's been in there a mighty long time," said Emma.

"No, she's not in there," said Mary-Rose, who had just paid a visit to the outhouse on the alley.

"I just remembered," said Aunt Clara. "When you were out in the yard, that girl from next door, Abigail, came round and gave Eliza a note."

"Oh, she did, did she?" said Emma, tight-lipped, finally managing to tie her bonnet. "Who was it from?" She pointed this question at her sisters, realizing they would know better than her aunt.

"I don't know," said Aunt Clara, "but she went out of the room to read it."

"And then she was in the parlour a long time," offered Mary-Ann.

"Well, she would be. I told her to put all the best china away in the sideboard," said Emma.

"When I saw her, she was just staring out of the parlour window," said Mary-Ann. "But when I looked again, some of the plates were still on the table and she wasn't there."

"This is where we could do with a man about the house," said Emma, who found this was one of the rare occasions when a father figure was needed. She could lay down the law as much as she liked, knowing that it was unseemly for a young woman to go out unescorted, especially in the evening, but she was at a loss to know how to bring about a solution. There was no man about the house. However, there was Aunt Clara, and she was ready for action.

With a grim look on her face, Aunt Clara crammed her bonnet on top of her tightly coiled bun as if it were a military helmet. "I thought she was stretching out that darning, and then she goes into the parlour for goodness how long." She took her cloak off the hall stand and with a determined flourish, quickly had it furled around her stout figure.

"Come with me, Emma. We're going to the police station. Kate and Alice, you go to the other end of the street and wait there in case she comes back that way. The rest of you stay here."

But Emma and her aunt didn't get as far as the police station. They saw two figures coming down Bower Lane, walking slowly, close together but quickly separating once they saw who was coming towards them.

"And what do you think you're doing?" Emma grabbed Eliza by the arm and glared at her companion, Billy Lampson.

"I just went for a walk," said Eliza, biting her lip. "It was a nice evening."

"It was getting dark," corrected Emma.

"I don't see why Amy and Alice can go out and not me," protested Eliza, withering under Emma's scathing look.

Aunt Clara was taking a good look at Billy, whom she had only seen briefly at the funeral. She saw a well-dressed young man of about nineteen, and she also saw that he could go far with the lasses with his kind of looks.

"We can't be thinking of a wedding—we've only just had a funeral," she said, waiting for her words to take effect.

"Wedding?" said Billy. "Who said anything about a wedding?"

"I'll thank you not to take my niece out in the evening if your intentions are not honourable," said Aunt Clara. "Young men who go out in the evening, walking with well-brought-up young ladies, must surely know how it looks."

Billy reached out his hand, looking imploringly at Eliza who was snatched away by Emma.

Turning their backs on Billy, Emma and her aunt frog-marched Eliza back to the house, and then sent the twins to fetch Kate and Alice who were still on watch at the other end of Bower Lane

All the other girls waited silently as the trio entered. Everyone knew Eliza was in deep trouble.

"This clandestine meeting … ," began Emma. Most of the girls had never heard her use this word before, but they knew it must be bad.

"Did he … touch you?"

"He held my hand when we walked along."

"I mean, … did he touch you … anywhere else? Kiss you?"

"He might have touched my boot. One of my laces came undone."

"Remember: *Thou shalt not tell a lie*," said Emma, one of the few times she would call on the church to substantiate her rules.

The now-weeping Eliza was sinking under Emma's cross examination. The only one to openly come to her defence was Kate, who put her arms around the distressed girl. "We were so worried about you," Kate said, which was more comforting than what Emma and Aunt Clara had to say.

"I only went for a walk," said the condemned prisoner.

"Y'know you're not the only lass he takes for a walk?" said Emma. "Common girls, I've heard," she added for extra effect.

Eliza could not control her tears and Emma softened her attitude somewhat. She knew that many young men had been attracted to Eliza, but she, poor girl, apparently only had eyes for Billy.

"I think we should talk to the vicar," said Aunt Clara, her obvious solution for dealing with this kind of situation.

"What's *he* going to do?" asked Emma.

"For a start, he could stop Billy singing in the choir," said Aunt Clara. "Only God-fearing people should be in the choir. Not anyone with loose morals."

"That's not going to help," said Emma. "All it means is he'll be in the congregation." The cat among the pigeons, she thought. "Say nowt to the vicar. Won't do any good."

Like everyone else, she knew the vicar needed to encourage his parishioners to attend church. The surest way to shrink his flock was to dismiss someone from the choir. People could only leave of their own accord, like old Mrs. Hartidge.

"I think we should all have a cup of tea," said Aunt Clara, eyeing the mahogany tea caddy that, in normal circumstances, would not be opened until the next morning. "And then to bed, but I will say prayers first."

Emma shut her ears to her aunt's supplications to the Good Lord, imploring him to save them all from undesirables in the form of lustful men and any other bad things that came to mind. But tea in the evening was a rare treat and they all silently thanked Eliza for it. She hadn't come to any harm, but later, when they were trying to get to sleep, they could hear her sobbing.

§

Aunt Clara found the vicar in his vestry a few days later. He was a little more liberal minded than Aunt Clara could have wished for, defending Billy in a relaxed, carefree kind of way.

"Boys will be boys," he smiled. "Billy is high-spirited and adventurous and now he's just started his apprenticeship. He'll settle down. You'll see."

"I'll not be here to see anything," said Aunt Clara. "I'll be going back to London one of these days, but he'd better keep away from my niece unless he means to marry her."

§

Emma was beginning to think Aunt Clara was outstaying her welcome. Whilst appreciating the help and support they had been given, Emma could not help wishing her aunt would leave. True, she was keeping a good table although she was not contributing to the household in a monetary way. Whenever she went to the shops, she asked for some housekeeping money and this was agreeable to Emma as Aunt Clara was not idle and did some of the household chores as well as most of the cooking. Emma was now, however, finding the girls were not sure who to obey or who to turn to for advice—their oldest sister or Aunt Clara. Most evenings were spent with her giving a detailed account of her six grown children and how well they were succeeding in life; extremely well, if you could believe everything she said, thought Emma, but it was all too perfect. Also, in order to uplift her nieces' spirits, there was the daily dogma of readings from the Bible and prayers. Emma tried to turn a deaf ear to these but it was difficult to eliminate her aunt's piercing voice. Why didn't she have a gentle voice like Ma?

"This brisket is done to a turn, Aunt," said Emma, one dinner time towards the end of May. She had to admit that although it was good to have a hot meal on the table when they came home at midday, something she had always prepared during the weeks she had stayed at home looking after her mother, Emma was finding it more and more difficult to keep to Aunt Clara's discipline, which was even more rigid than her own. She was about to enlarge on the fact that it was time they were fending for themselves when Aunt Clara interrupted her, almost taking the words out of her mouth.

'I've been wanting to make sure my poor sister's girls are well looked after," said the aunt. "But, I think I should be getting back to my own family. My youngest, Sally, will be coming to her time with her fourth."

Emma did some mental arithmetic and calculated that this would be the fifteenth grandchild for her aunt who was much older than their dead mother. Her four girls and two sons were all long married and well settled.

"My girls were all married when they were younger than you, and my sons," said Aunt Clara, staring first at Emma and then Kate. It was a fact she didn't need to point out.

"It's a known fact; girls have more chance to meet husbands down in London," said Alice.

"Don't be ridiculous," said Emma. "Wherever did you hear such nonsense?"

"Amy told me once. She read it in the newspaper. It was something called statistics," insisted Alice.

"We've had little opportunity to meet young men," said Kate.

"Apart from her," said Aunt Clara, sniffing and looking sideways at Eliza.

"We have no brothers to introduce us to their friends. Apart from Algy, that is, and he's in London." This was a piece of honest truth from Kate, knowing full well that her girl-cousins in London had married friends of their two brothers.

"Let's hope at least one of you will meet a young man soon," said Aunt Clara. "There's never been any spinsters in our family."

Emma felt that her aunt's time was limited. If their father came for one of his rare visits, which occurred every few months, where would he sleep now that his domineering sister-in-law was occupying the small bedroom over the front porch? Aunt Clara had graced them with her presence for six weeks. Enough.

It was Jane who would steer the conversation round in Emma's favour.

"I miss Pa," she said. "We've not seen him since Ma passed away, and the funeral and all." What she meant was that she missed being with her father in Birkenhead where she had been a somebody. Here, she was smothered amongst too many others: sisters all competing for recognition. She also missed that piano. Would she ever get a chance to play again?

"I know I cannot compensate for your father and his ways," said Aunt Clara, knowing only too well that her brother-in-law was lax in regard to his daughters. What she had intended to say was that he was also lax in his religious beliefs, but refrained from mentioning that topic. "Perhaps I've stayed here long enough."

There was a murmur around the table that seemed to disagree somewhat with what she said, but she couldn't be sure.

The following day, Aunt Clara came home from tea at Mrs. Leggate's bringing a basket of bolts of heavy-duty red velveteen and some hanks of embroidery yarn.

"Mrs. Leggate says we need new cushions for the church pews," she said. "I told her you girls could make some. They need doing soon."

"Well, of all the cheek," said Emma, as she thumped the smoothing iron over some bed-sheets spread over the kitchen table. "As if we haven't enough to do of an evening without sewing for Mrs. Leggate."

"It's for the church, not Mrs. Leggate," said Aunt Clara. "I thought we could do a few each and it would soon be done."

"Speak for yourself, Aunt," said Emma. "I'm not spending my evenings stitching pew cushions for her. I've got plenty of sewing of me own to be done." The iron ran savagely up and down the sheets until Emma changed it for a hotter one on the hob.

"The Good Book says . . . " began Aunt Clara.

"Never mind what the Good Book says," said Emma. "I'm not working my fingers to the bone for anybody when I've been slaving over those looms all day."

As usual Kate was the one to try and smooth things over and provide a solution. "I could go next door and ask Mrs. Burgess if I could use her sewing machine. I could run them up in no time. And then we could each embroider a small cross on them."

She was silenced with a withering look from Emma. "Let Mrs. Leggate make the cushions—she's got nothing better to do than have tea parties, and her with a kitchen maid *and* a parlour maid." She slammed the iron down to enforce her words.

Aunt Clara made no further mention of the Good Book or the Good Lord and placed the material back in the basket.

"I'll return these to Mrs. Leggate tomorrow," she said. "And then, I'll be getting the train home to London."

In the morning, she kissed her nieces with individual fervour, muttering a few words of prayer before she released each of them.

"But rest assured, girls," promised Aunt Clara. "I will come and see you again soon."

They could hardly wait.

Chapter Four

It was November and Kate, modest as a violet and punctual as Big Ben, carried out her round of duties. She now worked at the new Textile Mill and was an expert on the spinning "mules", the huge machines that held the spindles. They did all the work of spinning the yarn. Kate was senior to most of the other girls who worked there. She was more or less an unofficial supervisor.

First, she had to see who were the "minders", workers operating a machine, and who were the "doffers". Doffers were mostly young "half-timers"—boys or girls who spent part of the day at school and the rest of their time in the mill. Although a menial job, "doffing" had to be done in a timely fashion, otherwise the mules would get jammed and the spinning would be halted. The mill manager would take a dim view of this. Any doffer not removing the bobbins as soon as they were full of finished yarn would be sacked. Speed was essential. The machine was shut off for a few seconds and the full bobbins were removed and replaced by empty ones.

Kate had to keep her eye on these doffers and also on the "piecers"—two children appointed to mend a broken thread in the mule. Breakage could happen several times in close succession and the "piecers" had to twist the threads together. It was tricky: they had to be extremely nimble and join the broken threads while the huge machine, the spinning mule, which carried on working ceaselessly, paused for a few seconds every time the carriage moved back and forth. Timing had to be precise, otherwise there were accidents. Kate had to keep her eyes on all the spindles in her area. Once the spindles were full, she had to shut off the machine so the full bobbins could be removed by the doffers. Also, the huge amount of fluff that gathered on the mule had to be cleared off at regular intervals. When the machine was stopped, a child would rush down the length of the mule, under the threads, to gather up the fluff. Kate hated to see these children working so hard, some of them malnourished and exhausted, but she knew it was ten times better than twenty years earlier. That was when better safety measures had been brought in following fatal accidents, most of which involved children. Now, mill owners had to obey the Factory Act, with its many rules, including fenced machinery. Then the Education Act of 1870 made full-time education compulsory until the age of ten, and part time until at least twelve.

Even while she was occupied each day with her work, Kate still gave a lot of thought to Mr. Goodacre. It was true, the only time she saw him was at church although he had no occasion to speak to her. But she felt she knew him fairly well. A few years previously she had attended Sunday school. He had been one of the teachers, even though only a few years older than his pupils. He spoke to her plenty then, she recalled. Now, it was a brief smile bestowed not just on her, but all her sisters as well.

Emma knew Kate still liked her Sunday school teacher, but not in that role any more. She had little to offer Kate in the way of advice, her own experience in the matters of the heart being rather limited. Surprisingly, Jane was the one who seemed to have the most knowledge on the matter, having lived for many months in a male-dominated household in Birkenhead. Jane seemed to be worldly wise about young men and would frequently regale Kate about the goings-on at Mrs. Kelly's.

"There was poor Sam who was lovesick. All he could think of was Bridget, the baker's daughter. She often came with her father when he delivered the bread twice a week. Sam was always asking Mrs. Kelly how he could go about courting Bridget. Mrs. Kelly told him, 'You just have to ask her Sam, but you might have to ask her father.' That should have been easy, as usually her father was the driver on his own baker's van. If the horse 'dropped', as it often did, the van would have to stay a bit longer while somebody got a bucket and cleared it up. As he was the one who had to fetch the bucket and shovel to get the manure, Sam didn't always have the chance to talk much. But Sam was so shy. He seemed to be struck dumb whenever Bridget was sitting up at the front of the van."

Kate knew the feeling. "What happened?"

"Mrs. Kelly kept saying he just had to ask. The worst that could happen was she would say no, but if he didn't ask, he would never know. He often ran out to get the bread for Mrs. Kelly, before Bridget got down from the cab. It was usually early and he was just off to work. Sometimes he nearly made himself late, making sure he was the one to get the bread." Jane smiled, obviously finding the situation humorous.

"Did he ask her … eventually?" Kate asked.

"One day, it was her brother up there handling the horse. He had a problem with the reins so Bridget got down to go to the back of the van to get the bread. Suddenly Sam found his courage and rushed round the other side, but in his hurry, knowing he was going to be late for work, he nearly collided with Bridget. She fell over and he pulled her up, and he sort of had his arms around her." Jane paused, enjoying this retelling of the event. There might have been a few embellishments. Who could tell?

"Well … ?" prompted Kate.

"He said, all in a rush, 'Bridget will you go a-courting with me?' and she said 'Oh yes, Sam!' She was almost swooning in his arms." That bit was definitely an embellishment, Emma thought as she came in upon the conversation.

"And how is it that you're such a know-all about these matters?" she asked Jane, who coloured up to the roots of her chestnut curls.

"I was there, at Mrs. Kelly's," said Jane. And to Kate, "See, he could have asked her months sooner. They could have been wed by now, at least by Christmas."

Kate reflected on this information, but it didn't help much. She had wanted to ask Jane if Bridget had given Sam any hint that the answer was 'yes', but Emma was hovering around and it was useless to have this kind of conversation within her earshot.

Former Sunday school teacher, Nathaniel Goodacre was the son of a tailor in Oldham. The small business had originally started up in Chadderton, but the business had grown. They had gone to grander premises in Oldham where they had lived over the shop and were now Goodacre & *Son*, Tailors and Gentlemen's Outfitters with a grand front shop window. They lived in one of those new villa-type houses on the edge of town. But they still attended Christ Church in Chadderton. Every Sunday, Kate saw Nathanial, accompanied by his parents and married sister and husband. They always sat in a side pew in full view of Kate and family. They nodded and smiled at everyone for a few moments outside the church door at the end of the service before being conveyed home in their carriage. The smile included Kate, but it seemed distant. As Nathaniel smiled, he often bid her good-day but he now called her Miss Kershaw, whereas five years ago, when she was in his Sunday school class, he had always called her Kate. This seemed like a regression to Kate, to be called Miss Kershaw. Why! There were seven other Miss Kershaws. How could he be so formal? Beyond being polite, he had certainly given her no encouragement at all.

Kate sighed. Passion was self-motivated and what was the use of that? If only she were a man. She could pick who she wanted to live with for the rest of her life and go ahead and ask away.

Kate hardly heard the bell above the noise of machinery and she had to be told by one of her co-workers that it was time to leave. The grey November day matched her spirits. She cheered at the sight of Jane on the way home. Jane had been sent to Mrs. Kendal's shop by Emma. They walked the last few steps home together. Kate smiled as Jane regaled her with tales of her afternoon at school.

"I don't much like needlework, though," said Jane. "We had to start sewing an apron this afternoon. Just think, if we had a sewing machine like Mrs. Burgess, I could have finished it in an hour. It's going to take me every needlework class from now till Christmas to finish it, what with the embroidery that we have to put on the pocket and all."

"Yes, it's a pity they don't have a sewing machine at school," said Kate. "But then, it wouldn't be fair. Which girl would they choose to use it? Only one sewing machine would be no good at all. And they are so expensive."

A sewing machine would be a wonderful thing in their own household, thought Kate, who had long been envious of Mrs. Burgess who had purchased the machine with money earned from her wealthy clients. She now had a Singer sewing machine, an American invention that had become so popular, it was now made in England as well. Kate was able to use the machine occasionally and found that working on the Singer was a lot easier than working at the mill and once you got the hang of the treadle, there was no knowing what you could do. You could even make a wedding dress, if you wanted to.

§

One evening as Christmas was approaching, when the herald angels were being harkened to, and the merry gentleman were resting, the girls were sitting around the kitchen table, having done their chores for the evening. Jane and Amy were reading. Kate was doing some embroidery; so was Eliza, but she kept putting her linen down to gaze into space. Emma was entering figures in her housekeeping book and doing additions. The twins were looking through their music. There would be plenty of singing for the choir over the Yuletide including some carol-singing parties when the girls could join in, going the rounds of the big houses up on the hill. Alice was the only one not sitting down, pacing round and round the table, mouthing silent words and throwing her arms about as if in an imaginary battle. She was learning the words to a poem she was to recite for the school concert at the end of term in two weeks' time. Then she would be leaving school and would be working at the mill full time. She didn't mind – the money would be good, even though she had to give it all to Emma, and would have to ask if she wanted anything for herself.

Pacing up and down in the kitchen, Alice was the only one to hear the knocking as she passed the hall door. She rushed into the hallway to open the front door which led directly on to the street.

Within two seconds, she was back in the kitchen. "It's Mr. Higginbottom. He wants to see Kate."

"Well, ask him in," said Emma, slapping down her notebook and removing her apron. "Show him into the parlour. He's probably come to ask if Kate will go back to the Glebe."

It was true. There had been rumours that Kate was sorely missed at the Glebe Mill because of her skill with the mule spinning, and her knowledge of the machines. She was already much valued at the new Textile Mill.

Jane knew it would take a lot for Kate to go back to Glebe Mill although she would dearly like it herself. She missed her older sister each morning when they walked together to work. This was time when she and Kate always talked – just the two of them. But for several months Kate had worked at the Textile Mill, which was in a different direction.

"Jane, go and fetch some coal while I light the fire in the parlour," said Emma.

Kate hastily smoothed her skirts and, with a quick glance in the hall mirror, patted her hair, tucking a few stray locks into place.

As Emma picked up the matches, she said, "Make some tea, Eliza. And use the best teapot."

Mr. Higginbottom was shown into the cold parlour just as Emma held a taper to the gas lamp, and then moved to light the ready-laid fire. A fire was only lit in there for high days or holidays, as Jane well knew as she came in with the coal scuttle. She was slightly nervous; it was not everyday that a mill manager came to call.

Tom Higginbottom stood with his back to the feeble output of the always obstinate parlour fire, and rested one arm on the mantelpiece. Emma ushered Kate in and they both sat on the sofa while Jane hovered behind them.

He was a small man, but stocky and well dressed. He had a good head of dark hair, with specks of grey at the temples. "I would like to speak to Kate alone, please," he said, frowning slightly at Emma.

"What you have to say to Kate can surely be said in front of me," said Emma. "Jane, you go back to the kitchen."

As Jane left the room, Mr. Higginbottom shook his head and turned to look into the fire which crackled faintly but could not compete with the loud ticking of the clock on the mantelpiece. Then, ignoring Emma, he said to Kate, "How old are you now, Kate? Twenty-one? I believe I may talk to you without your sister being present."

Emma stood up and with an exasperated look at Kate and then the mill manager, she too retreated to the kitchen, slamming the door behind her.

The girls all sat round the kitchen table, questioning each other silently, hearing one voice only from the room next door and then a faint, hesitant tone from Kate. In a few minutes, she came back into the kitchen, looking agitated, obviously needing Emma's help.

Emma, at the ready, rose and went to Kate's side. "You don't have to go back to the Glebe," she said. "You can stay at the Textile Mill if you want."

"It's nothing to do with that," said Kate. "He's asked me to marry him."

Chapter Five

Emma swept into the parlour closely followed by a dazed Kate. The older sister came straight to the point, facing Mr. Higginbottom like a drill sergeant about to give orders. "This is rather sudden." An understatement coming from Emma. "But you should have asked our Pa first." This was a delaying tactic and Emma well knew that her father would not have much input into any plans of marriage for Kate, although the etiquette of asking his permission was important.

Quick to the defence, the mill manager retaliated. "Seeing as your father is rarely here, I did not have a chance, but please be assured that I will remedy that at the first opportunity."

Emma nodded. Kate was flustered.

"Can I expect an answer by Christmas Eve?" he asked, trying to catch Kate's eye. "I'm sure your father will be home by then and I can talk to him."

This was reasonable to Emma. She didn't say anything more, but had a look of stern satisfaction. Kate had her hand to her mouth with downcast eyes.

Tom Higginbottom was a patient man. After all, he had been contemplating this for months ever since he had attended the funeral of
Sarah Kershaw and had noticed the second eldest daughter, Kate, in
a new way. He had observed her, not as one of his employees at the
Glebe Mill, but in a different capacity. He had perceived her quiet and
competent manner, her fine dark eyes and her smooth complexion.
He had missed her sorely when she left to go to the Textile Mill; not
just her competence at the spinning mules, but her general presence
about the mill. He had noted Emma too, at the funeral; two years older
than Kate, and a fastidious housekeeper. But Emma was rather plain
and at twenty-three, had the reputation of being something of a mar-
tinet. He had dismissed her early on as someone who could replace
his dead wife. Then there was Eliza, with her blue eyes and her hair
the colour of fresh straw—a striking beauty, but he knew she didn't
have the capabilities of Kate. He could not picture her as a wife or as a
mother to his children. She seemed immature for her eighteen years.
Kate was definitely the one. He had seen her calm way of dealing with
matters at the mill and he could just see her in his home. He didn't
consider the twenty-four years age difference as an obstacle to either
party. He had bided his time, knowing that he could not approach the
family while they were in mourning, but he had watched lately as the
black garb of the girls was slowly being phased out.

Mr. Higginbottom left, without any tea and the parlour hardly
warmed up. Back in the kitchen, Emma looked at the best teapot
sitting in the middle of the kitchen table. Although it had been
intended for Mr. Higginbottom, there was no point in wasting it. She
poured a cup and gave it to Kate who shook her head and silently
pushed the cup to Jane who was sitting beside her.

"This is something, eh, Kate?" said Emma looking round the table.
But no one appeared to be overjoyed by the happenings of the last
fifteen minutes. They were more in a state of shock.

As far as Emma was concerned there should be no question about
it. This proposal to her sister from such an eminent man was beyond

her wildest dreams. But for Kate, the whole situation was absurd. She could not think rationally.

"Fancy him wanting to get married again," said Mary-Ann.

"And him with his wife dead only two years," said Alice.

"Three," corrected Amy, who had a better memory of when the Tay Bridge disaster had occurred.

"He's got a grand house," said Alice.

"And three children," said Mary-Rose. "That's something to think on."

Emma seemed to be the only one who was thrilled at Mr. Higginbottom's proposal. She could already hear wedding bells and told Kate how lucky she was.

"He told me he had admired me for months, that he had formed the opinion I was the ideal wife for him. Then he said that I was beautiful," whispered Kate, in a daze.

"You *are* beautiful," said Eliza, the only girl in the family so far who had been told that.

"But I don't love him," said Kate.

"Who said anything about love?" said Emma. "Think about it! Being the wife of a mill manager."

Kate was confused. This sounded more like a promotion at work except she didn't work at the Glebe any more and he was no longer her boss. If love had nothing to do with it, was this just a step up in the world? But did she want it? Her heart ached. If only this proposal had come from Nathanial Goodacre. She knew she had been his favourite several years ago at Sunday school, but the more grown up she had become, the more reserved he appeared to be. At least, as far as she knew, there was no rival. The only women he kept company with seemed to be his mother and his sister, Deborah. Was he tied to his mother's apron strings? Was that why he had not come forward? He was known to be a successful tailor and "gentleman's outfitter", albeit in his father's business and according to some, affluence had come easily. But to others, it was indisputable that he was a master of the sartorial craft. Whenever she saw him, which was only every Sunday at church, he always appeared in an immaculate frock coat of well-cut broadcloth with silk lapels. His trousers were striped cashmere with knife-edge pleats and fitted his tall angular frame to perfection. His shirt was always of the finest cambric with plenty of cuff to complement his slim-fingered, strong hands. He usually wore a contrasting waistcoat of pale grey. She could go on dreaming about Mr. Goodacre for ever—his dark wavy hair with a lock that sometimes strayed over his forehead. His clean-shaven face. He didn't yet follow his father's be-whiskered look, which reminded her that Mr. Higginbottom, as other men of his age, favoured the fashion of the mutton chop moustache. How appalling to be kissed by someone with hair all over his face! She had two weeks to give Mr. Higginbottom her answer. The answer would be a definite 'No', in spite of Emma's eagerness.

But after a few days, on observing how miserable Kate appeared to be, Emma's initial enthusiasm for her sister's proposed new state in life diminished somewhat. Perhaps she should not encourage Kate in this momentous decision; she seemed so averse to the idea. Disinclined as she was herself to the thought of marriage, Emma asked herself whether she herself could submit to it. She didn't think so, not even to be a mill manager's wife. She resolved to think more about Kate and to leave aside her own desires and ambitions for her sister.

But Emma could not easily discard her practicality; she never wasted anything, whether it was food, clothing or coal. It was painful to think of a proposal of marriage going to waste, and Emma briefly harboured the thought that if Kate was going to turn Mr. Higginbottom down, he might consider one of her other sisters. Eliza was the only one of age but, like Kate, was always mooning after someone else; in her case it was Billy Lampson. The other sisters were still too young. If Mr. Higginbottom was prepared to wait a few years, there would be the twins, who were now sixteen. But that was ridiculous. He had obviously decided he wanted to re-marry; he would not want to wait for Emma's sisters to mature. Emma was so eager to take advantage of this opportunity; she even briefly contemplated herself as a candidate. But she knew she would not be able to overcome her general aversion to the thought of marriage even though the prospective husband was the manager of a thriving mill. She was still convinced love had nothing to do with marriage. She had formed the opinion that not many people found love in reality. Love was something you read about in books.

Some of the girls had their own thoughts.

"He's old enough to be her father," observed Alice.

"Surely Mr. Higginbottom is a fair bit younger than Pa," said Amy. "His oldest bairn is only nine."

"You know what I mean. He's far too old for Kate."

Jane's only acquaintance with Mr. Higginbottom was when she collected her wages each week and she saw him sitting at his desk. She had not taken any note of his age, but she knew that Kate's heart was set on someone else. It didn't seem right to Jane who observed that Eliza and Kate could not have what, or more precisely, who, they wanted in love. What hope was there for the rest of them?

Kate's tortured thoughts kept her awake at night. As she shared a bed with Jane in the same room as Amy and Alice, they discussed matters. Although Jane was ten years younger than Kate, she seemed to have a worldly-wise knowledge. That's what came of spending many months in a big city, in a household of men, run by a woman who was the complete opposite of Emma and her inflexible rules.

"Take no notice of Emma," whispered Jane. "You don't love him. You don't even know him, except he's the manager at the mill. You love Mr. Goodacre. I'm sure he loves you. But he doesn't know it yet."

"I hope you're right, Jane," said Kate, but her hope was low.

The thought of lying in bed beside Mr. Higginbottom, her boss, filled her with dread. He was a pillar of the local community, but as a husband, he ranked very poorly against Mr. Goodacre. She could only look upon Mr. Higginbottom as a kind man, a former employer. Nothing more.

§

The days towards Christmas sped by. On Alice's last day of school, there was to be a Leaving Day ceremony, a concert, and presentation of prizes.

Alice was to recite a poem; she was also to receive a certificate which she would take to the manager of Glebe Mill who happened to be Mr. Higginbottom, stating that, at almost thirteen years of age, she had completed enough education and that she could now work full time at the mill.

That evening, Alice and her sisters pushed open the heavy wooden doors and entered the school hall. There was a swirl of richly hued skirts and formal jackets, everyone in their Sunday best. Amid murmured greetings, the girls moved down the centre aisle.

"Don't sit on the front row," whispered Alice "You might put me off." Then she grabbed Amy's arm with cold fingers. "Except you," she hissed. Amy was clutching a volume of poems, her finger tucked in at the right page in case Alice forgot her words.

"You'll be fine," Amy said, though she looked a little anxious. "You've never forgotten your words before."

"You never know with Alice," said Jane, as she sat down on the front row with Amy, the others sitting behind. "It's so exciting, leaving school and getting her certificate. She might do anything. She might even recite the wrong poem."

The certificates were handed out with some words from the headmaster, and the concert began. Annie Birtwistle sang a song by Schubert, accompanied by her sister, May, on the piano. It was about someone called Sylvia. It made Jane wish she was called Sylvia. Then May played a tune by Beethoven, something with an unpronounceable German name. It made sense that these two, daughters of the church organist, should be performing, but Jane vowed she would be playing at the next end-of-term concert.

Jane's fingers itched to get on that piano which sounded infinitely better than the one at Mrs. Kelly's. It had been many months since she had touched those keys. She must pluck up courage to ask Emma if she might have piano lessons. She really must.

Then it was Alice's turn. Alice stood in front of the audience, raising her eyes to the rafters and holding her arms out in a theatrical pose, she began.

"Christmas in the Olden Time, by Sir Walter Scott."

Heap on more wood! – the wind is chill;
But let it whistle as it will,
We'll keep our Christmas merry still.

Each age has deemed the new born year
The fittest time for festal cheer.

And brought blithe Christmas back again,
With all his hospitable train.

Domestic and religious rite
Gave honour to the holy night:

On Christmas Eve the bells were rung;
On Christmas Eve the mass was sung;

That only night, in all the year,
Saw the stoled priest the chalice rear.

The damsel donned her kirtle sheen;
The hall was dressed in holly green;

Forth to the wood did merry men go,
To gather in the mistletoe,

They opened wide the baron's hall
To vassal, tenant, serf, and all;

The heir, with roses in his shoes,
That night might village partner choose."

Alice hesitated, shifting her gaze from the ceiling to Amy on the front row. Disconcerted, Amy dropped the book of poems with such a clatter on the bare floor, it seemed to put Alice back on track.

Amy picked up the book but before she could find the correct page, Alice continued:

"All hailed with uncontroll'd delight
And general voice, the happy night

The fire with well dried logs supplied,
Went roaring up the chimney wide;

The huge hall table's oaken face,
Scrubb'd till it shone, the day to grace,

Bore then upon; its massive board
No mark to part the squire and lord.

Then the grim boar's head frowned on high,
Crested with bays and rosemary.

The wassail round in good brown bowls,
Garnished with ribbon, blithely trowls.

There the huge sirloin reeked; hard by
Plum-porridge stood, and Christmas pie;

Nor failed old Scotland to produce
At such high tide her savoury goose.

Then came the merry masquers in,
And carols roar'd with blithesome din;

If unmelodious was the song,
It was a hearty note, and strong."

Alice paused, lowered her eyes to the front row, where Amy began to fumble in the book. Amy opened her mouth but before she could say the prompt, Alice began again,

"White shirts supplied the masquerade,
And smutted cheeks the visor made

But oh! What masquers, richly dight,
Can boast of bosoms half so light!

England was merry England when
Old Christmas brought his sports again.

'Twas Christmas broached the mightiest ale,
'Twas Christmas told the merriest tale;

A Christmas gambol oft would cheer
A poor man's heart through half the year."

There was a thunderous applause. Alice bowed, her long red hair falling over her shoulders. Then she remembered what she had been told and curtsied.

Kate hardly heard the poem. All she could think of was what she would say to Mr. Higginbottom in one week's time. There was only one word that she wanted to say and that was 'No'. But how was she going to say it? 'Thank you kindly, Mr. Higginbottom, for asking me to be your wife, but ...' or 'Thank you, Mr. Higginbottom, for honouring me with your wish that I should be your wife, but ...' or she could resort to flowery words which Alice had provided: 'Thank you for bestowing on me your kind and esteemed offer of marriage, but ...' or words from the Bible (Aunt Clara would like that): 'Entering into Holy Matrimony in the sight of God is something I do not ...'. How could she express in the nicest possible way, that she could never care for him in a million years? That he was too old for her? And that she would rather die than marry him?

As they walked home, all Emma could say was, "You did your recitation well, Alice. But it was a mighty long poem."

"I wanted to do 'When icicles hang by the wall' by Shakespeare, but Miss Partridge said everybody does that."

"You missed out a couple of lines in the middle somewhere," said Amy.

"Yes, and I saw you drop the book. I don't think anyone noticed."

"Amy, everyone noticed you drop the book," said Jane.

"I meant no one noticed I missed a few lines," said Alice.

"But I think your reciting days are over, Alice," said Emma. "There's not much call for that sort of thing at the mill."

Alice had her own ideas about her reciting days, especially as Miss Partridge, her teacher, had a fondness for poetry too. She had noted Alice's efficiency at spouting verse, especially Wordsworth and Gray. Miss Partridge had promised that they would go to the Lyceum in Oldham where once a month the Literary Club held a meeting which sometimes took the form of a poetry evening. Alice would make sure Miss Partridge kept her promise.

Poetry and school-leaving were forgotten as a surprise was waiting for them when they reached home.

"Pa!" Jane was the first one to be gathered into his arms. Then there were kisses and hugs all round.

"I thought I'd surprise you," he said. "This is a flying visit. I've to be back by Sunday."

He produced a bottle of Irish whiskey from his hold-all. "A little bird told me there's some big news hereabouts," he said, looking at Kate, who blushed and looked at the floor.

Emma suddenly knew why Pa had come home unexpectedly. She looked at Jane who was studying her finger nails. Jane was the one who wrote faithfully to her father each week. Even though it had been agreed that no one should know about Kate's offer of marriage until a decision had been made, Jane had taken it for granted that she could tell her father in her weekly missive.

"Jane, we said we wouldn't mention it to anyone," reprimanded Emma.

"Yes, but Pa isn't just anyone," said Jane. "I thought he needed to know."

Emma was silent. She had not thought to inform their father. Now, in her new role, she no longer looked upon him as the head of the house. She had only told Mr. Higginbottom his remissness in not asking their father first as a point of etiquette. Pa had never lived at home with the family since they had come to Lancashire from London. In Emma's opinion, he had contributed little to the lives of his children and it had never occurred to her to include him in any major decision-making.

"Mrs. Kelly said I should bring this whiskey and have a drink with my future son-in-law," said Pa, winking at Kate. "Is he coming along this night?"

Kate looked miserable, and they all shifted uncomfortably. To Kate's dismay, Pa seemed enthusiastic about the situation.

"No, he won't be coming here 'til next week—Christmas Eve," answered Kate. "But the answer will be No."

Pa looked puzzled. It had not occurred to him that Kate might turn down an offer of marriage!

"You mean, you've not given him an answer yet?" he said. "Oh, I see. You were waiting for your Pa to come home. To think a lass of mine has taken Tom Higginbottom's fancy. But I'm none surprised. You're a mighty handsome lass Kate, and canny too. There's no mistake about that. You're a credit to me and your poor mother."

At Kate's continued silence and miserable countenance, he realized there would be no celebration with Mrs. Kelly's whiskey. He saw a tear run down Kate's cheek.

"Nay lass, if you've not a mind to marry him, there's an end to it." As Charles Kershaw had met the unfortunate suitor only once, at the funeral earlier in the year, he hardly knew him, but he had to admit it was a disappointment. A mill manager for a son-in-law would be a mighty fine thing, but he could see Kate was unhappy. "I reckon you'll not be left on the shelf. Happen you've got someone else in mind?"

This was a wild guess on her father's part, but Kate wondered if Jane had been divulging too much in her letter writing. Had she told

Pa about Mr. Goodacre and how Kate felt about him? Jane was not one to hold things back, especially in a letter and Kate was always confiding in her, young though she was.

Kate looked keenly at Jane, who, knowing what Kate was thinking, shook her head. They would have a talk later, in their usual way, when they were in bed.

"You know how it is, Pa," said Kate. "It's just that I never dreamed of marrying Mr. Higginbottom. He was my gaffer at the Glebe Mill and I can't look on him any other way. I'd like someone nearer my own age." Some one, in fact, who was about five years older than her, thought Jane, giving Kate a little secret smile.

"Oh, Pa! Please be here early Christmas Eve and speak to Mr. Higginbottom. I can't face him. You talk to him and tell him the answer is No. Please say you'll be here when he comes, Pa." Kate was insistent.

"I'll be here, Kate, don't you worry. Aye, but I'm right proud of you. To think a lass of mine gets a proposal from the mill manager!"

Kate was relieved. "Tell him, I'm sorry. No chance. But thank him kindly for his offer, Pa, won't you?"

"Happen his nose will be out of joint, but he'll get over it," said Pa.

"Kate couldn't possibly marry anyone she didn't love, even if it does mean she'd live in a grand house and have servants," said Eliza. "I'd rather work six and a half days at the mill than marry a man I didn't love."

That seemed to sum up the opinion of all except Emma, who still thought her sister had wasted the proposal of the mill manager, something many girls would hanker after.

§

The next day, Saturday, all the girls worked the morning in the various three mills, Glebe, Wharf and Textile, meeting back at the house where they had dinner with their father. In addition to the bottle of Irish whiskey which stood unopened on the sideboard in the parlour, he had brought some buns and pies from Mrs. Kelly.

"Hmm! Does she think we can't do our own baking?" asked Emma. She was suspicious and a little in awe of Mrs. Kelly, whom she had never met, but she had heard plenty about from Jane.

"Mrs. Kelly bakes the Irish way," explained Jane. "Everything she makes is different but it's so tasty."

Emma sniffed and took a slice of soda bread, taking the tiniest bite as if it might poison her. Giving a slight nod of approval, she said, "But it's not proper bread – got no yeast in it." Then, scrutinising another kind of loaf, "Looks more like a fruit cake."

"It's called barmbrack and it's a kind of bread, but sweet, with spices and currants," said Jane. "Mrs. Kelly makes it nearly every week, and she makes soda bread because it's quicker than ordinary bread. The baker brings proper bread twice a week in his van. That's how Sam met Bridget." Jane looked at Kate meaningfully as they had discussed this romance thoroughly.

Speaking of Mrs. Kelly, reminded Jane that she would like to send a Christmas gift to that person who had been so good to her and was dear to her heart.

"Pa, please would you come with me up to Oldham Market this afternoon and help me choose a Christmas present for Mrs. Kelly."

"Nay, lass, she won't be expecting anything from you," said her father, although he was agreeable to getting out of the house.

"But I've saved the money from doing the letters for Mrs. Burgess, and I want to send her something. She was always so kind to me."

Over the last few weeks, Jane had been writing letters and doing the bills and receipts for Mrs. Burgess next door. Although their neighbour was an experienced seamstress, her reading and writing skills were sadly lacking. Mrs. Burgess was pleased to find that Jane was so efficient in this respect and, as it lent prestige to her modest dressmaking services, she paid Jane a penny for every letter, and a halfpenny for every bill or receipt she wrote in her fine Copperplate handwriting, a skill she had learnt at school in Birkenhead.

"Come on then," agreed her father, putting on his overcoat and turning up the thick collar. "But let's walk brisk-like, lass. Chadderton's a deal colder than Birkenhead. There's a harsh wind coming off them moors. That could mean snow."

"You could do with a scarf, Pa," said Jane, knowing full well that Eliza was knitting one for him as a Christmas gift.

"Aye, certainly for here, but not so much in Birkenhead." It was true; the climate was certainly a few degrees warmer on the coast. Chadderton on the edge of the Pennines was prone to freezing temperatures and flurries of snow which often turned into blizzards.

"Do you think Mrs. Kelly would like a scarf, Pa?" asked Jane.

"Aye, maybe a fancy one for Sunday best or walking round the park on a sunny afternoon."

"Yes, something like that would be perfect for Mrs. Kelly."Jane could just see it.

"At Birkenhead market you can get scarves made from Welsh wool or Scotch tartan and lace collars made in France."

"I bet they're not all real – genuine, y'know," Jane was sceptical about markets and what they sold.

"And if they're not, who's to know?"

"It doesn't matter in Birkenhead, but here a lace collar would not go down so well as a wool scarf or mittens, even if it *was* made in France."

They looked at every stall in Oldham Market but nothing came up to Jane's expectations and most of the merchandise was beyond her saved pennies which amounted to one shilling and nine pence. She reflected how kind it was of Emma not to ask for the money towards household expenses. Emma had been remarkably generous in this regard only taking the girls' mill wages and doling out what she considered they needed in the way of clothes and other personal items. If they were enterprising enough to earn extra funds, Emma allowed them to keep it.

"Aye, but it's not a patch on Birkenhead market," said Pa. "You can always get something special there, and right cheap too."

As they left Oldham Market and walked homewards, they found themselves outside the imposing shop-front of Goodacre & Son, Tailors and Gentlemen's Outfitters, and who should be in process of showing a customer out, but Mr. Nathaniel Goodacre himself.

"Good afternoon, Mr. Kershaw. Good afternoon, Jane," said Nathaniel, holding the door open after the customer had left, as if he wanted Jane and her father to enter. They did, more to get out of the cold than with the idea of buying anything. Jane could see that her pennies would not go far in this high-class establishment, obviously intended for the rich and affluent of Oldham and Chadderton.

"We're only looking for ladies' things," was Jane's bright idea, knowing full well that there would be nothing available in a place full of gentlemen's attire.

"Ah, we have a line of ladies' apparel; small items, you understand," said Nathanial, "for our customers' wives. My mother sees to that side of things. If you will step this way, please."

Jane looked at her father who nodded as they followed Nathaniel to the far end of the shop. "No harm in taking a look, eh, Jane?"

Nathaniel led them through the premises, past polished counters and mahogany-framed glass cabinets with displays of collars, studs, braces and all manner of men's accessories. He opened a large glass case on the wall and started to lay some items on the counter: scarves of silk and satin, woollen scarves with matching gloves, lace galore on collars and handkerchieves, fur trimmed muffs, embroidered stoles, leather purses and dainty dancing shoes.

"My word, I reckon there's everything you'd need for a wedding if our Kate should change her mind," said Pa, holding up a diaphanous shawl and draping it around Jane's shoulders. "She could still say 'yes' to that toff."

At the mention of Kate's name, Nathanial Goodacre spun round from the glass case on the wall as if he were being pulled by an invisible cord.

"Kate! Mr. Kershaw, did I hear you mention Kate . . . er . . . Miss Kershaw? Did I hear you say there's to be a wedding?"

"It's a moot point," said Charles Kershaw. "But I doubt she'll be getting wed any time soon."

"But it's not for want of being asked," added Jane. She turned her large brown eyes fully on Mr. Goodacre, wishing to convey her meaning, at the same time fearful that she might be overstepping the confidentiality that Emma had insisted upon.

'Oh?" said Nathaniel, with a quizzical look.

Pa realized they must change the subject quickly. "None of my girls is getting wed, not yet awhile."

The look of relief on Nathaniel's face was something Jane was relieved to see. He *did* care about Kate. Jane was sure of it. She didn't mind that her father had made an indiscreet remark, but Emma would have been furious.

The immediate problem was, of course, to get back to the task at hand, of choosing something for Mrs. Kelly

"How much is this?" she asked, selecting a small red velvet scarf, the sort a lady would tie in a bow or fasten with a brooch and wear under the collar of a jacket. It was narrow, not much wider than a hair ribbon. Surely it could not be very expensive?

Nathanial opened his book on the counter and ran his finger down a column. "That one is half a crown," and at Jane's crestfallen face, "It's an extremely fine velvet."

"Half a crown!" echoed Jane, mournfully viewing her pennies spread out on the counter which no way added up to two shillings and sixpence.

Seeing Jane's disappointment and that her father was obviously not coming to her rescue, Nathanial said, "Well, Jane, in view of my much-valued acquaintance with you and your sisters at Sunday school, I am sure my father would agree to the wholesale price of, say, one shilling and sixpence?"

Jane couldn't for the life of her think what buying a red velvet scarf had to do with Sunday school, but it might have something to do with Kate. Mr. Goodacre, in his anxiety to please, was making sure she could afford this item. Maybe he thought it was for Kate. He had heard her name mentioned.

The bargain was struck and Jane left the shop with the purchase wrapped in a neat parcel tied with coloured string.

"You *do* think Mrs. Kelly will like it, don't you Pa?" asked Jane on the way home. She was thankful that after all the searching at the market she had found something suitable in the most unlikely place, and was still in possession of three pence. Her father's secret thoughts on the matter of the scarf were twofold: it was obviously no ordinary scarf; it certainly would never keep a lady's neck warm, but it was obviously fashionable and therefore desirable to most women.

"Aye, she'll surely love it," said Pa. "I'll put it in my bag as soon as we get home. That way I won't forget to take it tomorrow."

The package was placed safely in father's hold-all with instructions from Jane not to give it to Mrs. Kelly until Christmas Eve, the day he was coming back to Chadderton, in one week's time.

Next morning, he caught the train to Birkenhead while the girls attended church. The service was much the same as any other Sunday, except there were some carols, and some festive greenery hanging about the pews. Some red candles had been lit in addition to the usual white ones. Outside, as usual, six girls waited for the two sisters in the choir, Mary-Rose and Mary-Ann. While they waited, they nodded and curtsied to everyone who passed them, all that is, except Mr. Nathanial Goodacre, who suddenly stopped in front of Kate even though his parents, sister and husband walked ahead.

"Miss Kershaw," said Mr. Goodacre. "I realize that you are hastening home for your Sunday dinner, but I wonder if I might walk along with you?" He replaced his hat after a stately bow, and Kate, unclasping her hand from Jane's, stepped out to his side with a perplexed smile.

Chapter Six

Once inside 54 Bower Lane, all were agog to know exactly what had happened on the walk home from church with Mr. Goodacre. Kate was all smiles and had to chronicle events to everyone immediately.

"He said he needed to speak to me urgently. Then we walked along without him saying a word, although he coughed several times, as if he was trying to speak. Just as we were getting to Bower Lane, he stopped and asked how I looked upon him."

Kate paused. She wanted to remember his exact words. "What could I say? I was wondering what he meant. He started to say something but seemed anxious. Then, as all of you girls overtook us and went into the house, he suddenly said, 'I must tell *you*, Miss Kershaw ... Kate ... I think the world of you and I would like you to be my wife.'"

Kate paused again while her words sank in. She looked round the table. All the girls were stunned. It was too exciting for words.

"And *then* what?" asked Jane. "What did *you* say, Kate?"

"I was flabbergasted. I couldn't say anything. I was shaking all over. I just smiled at him and then he said, 'I have been meaning to talk to you about marriage for a long time, but I was waiting for my father to clarify my prospects in the business. I wanted to have something more substantial to offer you. But I was afraid that some one else might beat me to it, so I decided I couldn't wait any longer.' Then he said, 'Please, please say, yes, Kate.'"

"I bet you didn't have to tell him you'd think about it, like with Mr. Higginbottom," said Emma.

"No, no, of course, I said yes. Then he drew my hand from my muff and he kissed it."

"So long as that's all he kissed – broad daylight and all," said Emma while peeling potatoes, but she was laughing in spite of her caustic remark. "Hurry up with those parsnips, Eliza."

"But of course, he wants to talk to you and Pa – do things right, you know," said Kate, remembering that propriety was always present in their household, even though she knew they would all take it for granted there would be no obstacles.

"Good for him," said Emma.

"He told me that his father always wanted him to wait until he'd reached thirty to get married, but he's only twenty-six."

"So what will his father have to say about this?" said Emma, frowning.

"Not much. Nathaniel is over twenty-one and he says he can do what he wants."

"But he knows which side his bread is buttered," Emma pointed out. "He doesn't want to go upsetting his father."

"His father has plans to give Nathanial control over the business in a few years. Nathaniel said he wanted to be able to offer me one of those new detached houses, up near his parents. But to start with we could live over the shop." Kate dreamily gazed into the fire. If Nathaniel had told her they were going to live in a cave, it would have been fine with her. She felt glowing all over as she helped prepare the Sunday dinner. Everything was turning out grand. It was a phrase her mother had used a lot, before she became so ill, in the old days. Everything would be grand again. Kate knew it.

§

At the Goodacre house, the conversation went a little differently that Sunday afternoon.

Nathaniel was biding his time until his father had finished reading the newspaper. It was the Saturday newspaper, but his father always saved part of it for Sunday afternoons.

After Kate's encouraging response to his proposal, Nathaniel was unprepared for his parents' reaction.

"Getting married? Kate Kershaw?" His father showed much surprise.

"Is that one of those mill girls we see at church, whose mother died some months ago?" enquired Mrs. Goodacre.

"Yes, Mother, you are well aware of who she is. She may be a mill girl, as you say, but she is a fine young woman, and comes from a good family."

"Didn't they come up here from London," asked Mrs. Goodacre who had a hankering for what she regarded as 'The Good Life' down south.

"Yes," replied her son, "but they've been here over eleven years."

"That's right. A lot of those from London were lured up here by the cotton trade, no doubt about that," said Mr. Goodacre. "But her father's not a mill man."

"Kate's father is an experienced ship's carpenter."

"Not much call for that around here," observed his father, dryly.

"You know as well as I do he works in Birkenhead at the shipyards."

"Why didn't they all go to Birkenhead?" asked his mother.

"The three oldest girls got jobs right away at the Glebe Mill and they also went to school, of course," said Nathanial. "And the housing here was easier than in Birkenhead, apparently."

Mrs. Goodacre said, "This girl likely thinks you're a good catch—that you were born with a silver spoon in your mouth?"

Mr. Goodacre looked at his wife sternly. "Caroline, have you forgotten those years of scraping, trying to save money, hardships, when I started the business. When we met, I had only just finished my apprenticeship at my uncle's Bespoke Tailors in Manchester. No lad of mine was born with a silver spoon anywhere about him. And we didn't always live in a house like this."

"I never thought my boy would marry a mill girl," said Mrs. Goodacre, looking round her home as though she was afraid it might be besmirched by these girls. "But, I have to admit, for mill girls, they are remarkably well turned when we see them at church."

She also marvelled at eight sisters and an older brother in London she had heard of. Caroline Goodacre's first three children had been taken by scarlet fever in 1857. Only her two youngest had survived, Nathaniel and his sister, Deborah.

But Nathaniel was saying, "Kate may be a mill girl, but she can turn her hand to anything. She is known to be an excellent seamstress, by hand or with the sewing machine. And I know that her mother could do embroidery fit for a queen and indeed, used to sew for some titled ladies in London. And the brother, who stayed in London, is on his way up in the General Post Office. Kate only works at the mill because there are few other jobs around here for a young woman, but she is superb at everything she does."

A thought struck Mrs. Goodacre: if Kate was such a good seamstress, she would be an asset to their business. Already thoughts were spinning in her head. A tailor's shop would always be a man's world. But visions of another department came into her head, something like exclusive, hand-made ladies' gowns. There were two rooms at the back of the shop full of boxes and materials. Mrs. Goodacre had often thought they could be utilized more efficiently. She didn't hold with wasted space. But she, herself, had no knowledge of the tailoring or the sewing business and didn't know one end of a bolt of cloth from another.

"Oh, so she has one of those sewing machines," Mrs. Goodacre said, marking that up as a factor in favour of this union.

Nathaniel ignored her, not bothering to inform his mother that the sewing machine belonged to the next-door neighbour, Mrs. Burgess. He was preoccupied, planning the official announcement of his engagement. He would have to buy a ring. He had his eye on one at the jewellers in Oldham. There would be an afternoon tea party or dinner party when the Kershaws would be invited to officially meet his family. But first, Emma would have to invite the Goodacres to their house. That was the protocol. It would be arranged. Nathaniel knew Emma would see to that.

Nathaniel came to see Emma the very next day although, in fact, he wanted to see Mr. Kershaw as well, but he, of course, was at work in Birkenhead.

"I hope I didn't speak out of turn," said Nathaniel. "Not asking you or your father first. I've been wanting to ask Kate to be my wife me for a long time but my father had made it clear I must build up the business more before I can marry."

"You'll have to speak to Pa, of course," said Emma, who knew her father would agree wholeheartedly with whatever she advocated. And Emma always insisted on doing things the right way. "He'll be here on Christmas Eve." Then she suddenly remembered the appointment with Mr. Higginbottom. "But he might be busy. I don't suppose it would be convenient to come on Christmas Day?" She knew it was just a formality, but it had to be done.

"Yes, Christmas Day," said Nathaniel, thinking it would be wonderful to get away from his staid household and see Kate on Christmas Day.

"My father will say yes, as like as not," Emma said, to reassure Nathanial.

§

It was Christmas Eve. As promised, Pa was home early from Birkenhead. Mr. Higginbottom had come for his answer as promised. All the girls were in the kitchen as their father ushered Mr. Higginbottom into the empty parlour. Pa came straight to the point.

"Well now, Mr. Higginbottom. You'll not take it amiss, I trust, when I tell you that my Kate cannot marry you."

Not one willing to easily admit defeat and wanting to explore the situation thoroughly, Mr. Higginbottom said, "Is there no chance she might change her mind?"

"Y'see, it's like this; she's going to marry somebody else."

Pa quickly regretted his abruptness. Kate had implored him to let the mill manager down lightly. At the look of astonishment on Mr. Higginbottom's face, Pa hurriedly turned to the decanter of Irish whiskey on the sideboard and made haste to pour two drinks.

"Isn't this rather sudden?" said Mr. Higginbottom, taking the proffered glass. He knew only too well why most girls were suddenly engaged to be married, when they had been nowhere near that stage a short while before. Frowning, he took a good draught of the whiskey.

"I reckon they've been sweet on each other for a long time, but with Christmas and all, and Kate out of her black, Mr. Goodacre must have suddenly plucked up the courage to speak out."

"Nathaniel Goodacre, eh? I was not aware that they were well acquainted." Mr. Higginbottom stood with his back to the fire which was behaving better than the last time he had been there. "Well, Kershaw, I cannot hide the fact that I am bitterly disappointed. I was sure Kate would give me a favourable answer, after due consideration."

"Hmm. You can't overlook the fact that you're much older than Kate and you with three bairns an' all. Maybe she wants someone her own age. Then they can start their own brood when they've a mind to."

"I am aware that three young children are a handful. But we have a nursery maid and kitchen help. Kate knows that." Mr. Higginbottom could see this line of reasoning would get him nowhere.

"I do have other daughters," Pa ventured to suggest, but did not pursue the matter on seeing the withering look he received.

"I wonder why Kate could not speak to me herself," said Mr. Higginbottom, attempting a last stab at justice.

"She's mighty sorry, Mr. Higginbottom, and grateful for your offer. She thinks highly of you, I know, but her heart is set on this other fellow. That's the way of things. She'll be out directly—she's mortal shy, y'know."

They drank in silence. Mr. Higginbottom took his leave as soon as his glass was empty. As he was putting his overcoat on in the hallway, Charles Kershaw knocked on the kitchen door and out came Kate, as previously arranged. She had agreed to end the painful interview although she felt nervous and ill at ease.

"Thank you, Mr. Higginbottom … I'm sorry, Mr. Higginbottom … Goodbye Mr. Higginbottom," she murmured with downcast eyes, not wishing to meet his reproachful look. He seemed inclined to speak to her but she kept her eyes averted. She quickly opened the front door. He stepped out after one more sorrowful glance at her. Kate watched as the pony and trap turned the corner of Bower Lane and disappeared. She ran back into the house, slammed the door and leant against it in relief. She raised her eyes to the topmost stair in front of her and said, "Thank goodness that's over."

§

This was the first Christmas without their mother. Everyone gave a great deal of thought to that, but they all knew Ma would have been pleased. Now, there was something to celebrate; Kate was engaged to Mr. Goodacre. It would be a merry Christmas.

"I always knew it would turn out like this, eventually," said Jane, provoking a look of exasperation from Emma, but she could not be annoyed for long and was as joyful as the rest of them. For once, she had relaxed her strict rules, allowing them to keep some of their earnings so they could buy small gifts for each other. And the extra funds Emma had set aside for the past few weeks were enough for the luxury of a goose for Christmas dinner.

However, there were certain formalities to be observed before the engagement could be officially announced. Of course, Emma would see to all that, with the help of the Goodacre family. They now had a wedding to look forward to in the summer.

And Pa had delighted them each with a gift of a small velvet scarf, some in crimson, some in royal blue; not the usual kind of scarf to protect against those freezing winter winds. They had enough of those. These scarves were narrow, the sort to wear under a jacket or dress collar and were the height of fashion. All the girls, except Jane, wondered how Pa had thought of such attractive, stylish presents. Of course, Birkenhead market had all the latest things.

All were in a fever of happiness. Kate was bright-eyed, joyous for Christmas and for the way things had turned out. Who would have thought that, after the proposal from Mr. Higginbottom, one would come from Mr. Goodacre a week later? It was unbelievable. It was sheer bliss!

The only one who did not enjoy Christmas was Mr. Higginbottom.

§

Everything was better than it had been for a long time at the Kershaw home. Even the mill did not seem so tedious. Alice, thinking of Kate and her engagement, found her first full days at the mill somewhat tolerable.

At least Jane had stopped saying, "It's six weeks since Ma died" or "It's three months since Ma died." Everyone was relieved that she didn't keep looking at the calendar and reminding them and remembering.

Emma had said "Thank you, Lord" in church. She meant Kate's engagement, of course. For once she considered the Lord had given them something, instead of the usual— taking away. At the Christmas service, the vicar was saying "Those that follow in the paths of righteousness shall find heaven." He said this at most services. Emma wondered whether she was doing something right, after all. She felt duly thankful to the Lord, even quite spiritual, but not so much that she failed to notice the cushions on the pews and the floor kneelers had recently been refurbished with new red and gold fabric. Some of them had embroidery on them. She vaguely wondered whose handiwork it was and remembered, with a pang of conscience, she had been quite sharp with poor Aunt Clara about this matter.

§

Nathaniel Goodacre, having received his permission and a blessing from Mr. Kershaw on Christmas Day, went ahead with his preparations for the engagement. He purchased a fine ring, a gold band set with a diamond and four small blue stones which he would present to Kate at the formal party given by the Kershaws for the Goodacres.

As arranged, the Goodacres arrived at Bower Lane at four o'clock on the appointed Saturday. Tea was served with delicacies made by the girls. All went smoothly. Introductions were formally done and the ring presented to Kate by Nathanial. Mr. Goodacre Senior was taken aside by Mr. Kershaw and given a glass of whisky. They talked in low tones and exchanged local news, while the ladies sipped tea and chatted. Nathaniel sat with Kate in the place of honour on the horsehair sofa. They hardly touched their tea and the scrumptious pastries were left untouched on their plates. They were too busy gazing into each other's eyes. Mrs. Goodacre was pleasantly surprised at the quality furnishings in the small terraced house. She was particularly taken with a handsome sideboard of bird's eye maple. She took good notice of everything else about her, noting that Eliza was the only one to resemble the father with his fair handsome looks. She grudgingly thought all the other seven girls were bonnie, particularly Kate, and noted that Jane was going to be a beauty with her large brown eyes and chestnut curls. Alice was striking too with her long red hair. She did have a face full of freckles though and looked too young to be working full time in the mill.

This was something that had been a source of worry to Emma for over a year. Alice was small and Amy was rapidly overtaking her. Alice showed no sign of development in her bust line and still no monthly bleeding. It was not something you could talk to the doctor about. You had to be seriously ill to talk to the doctor and otherwise, Alice seemed to be healthy.

Mrs. Goodacre, with a smile as frosty as the yard outside, complimented Emma on her refreshments. "And don't forget, you're all coming to our home in two weeks. You'll meet our daughter, Deborah, and her husband. We can discuss further details of the wedding. I think it's going to be in August."

Chapter Seven

1883

In January, about the time of Kate's engagement, there was a new teacher at Christ Church School. Giles Hunter was a handsome young man, passionate about his vocation and imparting his knowledge with a fiery enthusiasm. Indeed, he could hold forth for much of the afternoon without touching on arithmetic or spelling. Jane wished she could be there in the mornings too instead of having to work at the mill. She felt she was missing something vital. She had always loved school but never so much as now, and the time would be coming soon enough when she would have to leave the classroom, to work at the mill all day. Another year or so. She dreaded it. Mornings at the mill were long and monotonous amid the fluffy and stifling atmosphere of the carding room.

Mr. Hunter was from Bury, another cotton town a few miles north-west of Chadderton. He never failed to inform his class, and anyone else who would give an ear, that John Kay, the inventor of the flying shuttle, was from Bury. Eloquent with his descriptions, Giles

Hunter gave different versions of John Kay's wheeled shuttle in the hand loom.

"Just think, children", began one of his versions, "John Kay invented this in 1733 and it revolutionised weaving on the hand loom. Up until that time, it would take two people to operate a loom but after his invention, one person could do it." Hunter would then have two children come up in front of the class and he would demonstrate with pieces of string and chalk the actions of this amazing device, as well as drawing it, in detail, on the board. "The weft in the shuttle could pass through the warp threads at a much faster speed, and could make a wider piece of cloth. John Kay called it the 'wheeled shuttle', but it became famous because it was so fast, and people started calling it a 'fly shuttle'. Soon it became known as the flying shuttle."

Amy maintained that Mr. Hunter frequently got carried away and strayed from the lesson he was supposed to be teaching, which was the history of England and not the history of weaving. But Jane was enthralled. Mr. Hunter reminded her somewhat of her sister, Alice, who would recite from plays and poetry, eyes raised heavenwards, arms outstretched. It was no wonder Jane wanted her school days to last for ever. When Mr. Hunter embarked on his themes, the inventor of the flying shuttle, and other wonderful stories, Jane was not sure whether it was a geography or history lesson but she loved every minute of it. What did it matter? He had described Bury, the town across the moors, so well that now Jane felt she had been there and seen it all.

"That was over a hundred years ago and our weavers are still using the flying shuttle, but now in power looms, run by steam," he would say, flashing a smile at Jane as he knew her big sister, Emma, was a weaver at Wharf Mill.

Jane had excitedly told the family about Mr. Hunter's fascinating lessons.

"He's certainly not like any other teacher," said Amy, who still attended afternoon school with Jane. "Everyone listens and pays attention because he makes everything so interesting."

"Sounds quite the opposite of an ordinary teacher," said Emma. "Most of them are like what I read in the newspaper, 'An aging assistant to the headmaster, inefficiently teaching what he had, in his youth, inadequately learned'. No doubt one of the parents wrote that."

"Mr. Hunter is from Bury; that's about twelve miles from here. It's a famous town because someone there invented the flying shuttle," explained Jane to her audience at home. She felt sorry for them as they had missed this vibrant lesson on an important fact of weaving history. Amy, in the same class as Jane, had already heard it, of course, but the others found it interesting.

Emma, who had been to that other cotton town across the moors, was less impressed. "I thought Bury was most famous for their black puddings. Did Mr. Hunter tell you that an' all?"

"No. But he also told us that another famous man was born there. Sir Robert Peele. You know, he was Prime Minister once."

"Oh, indeed. Is that so?" said Emma, rolling her eyes. "Never mind a Prime Minister. Let's get on with these pastries." It was Saturday afternoon and as usual, Emma was supervising the weekly baking, helped by some of the girls.

Amy remembered something interesting whilst she mixed some cake dough. "Yes, Robert Peele was Prime Minister from 1835 to 1846. He also started the police force. If it wasn't for him, we wouldn't have those bobbies on the beat, protecting us all from robbers and cut-throats. I remember Pa telling us about him."

Mr. Hunter's zeal was unstoppable. "Yes, children, we must honour the famous people of our towns. And you should all be proud that you live in this wonderful time when you can have your education and can earn a living at the same time. John Kay had a difficult time and opposition from many people because, you see, although he invented the flying shuttle which helped the weavers, there was a slight problem. The weavers could produce cloth much faster, but the spinners could not produce yarn at that speed. The demand for yarn was unstoppable and there was total confusion amongst the workers.

Yes, our ancestors benefited from his invention, but in spite of all his brilliance, John Kay died in France, a poor man. Penniless, he was"

Jane was upset about this. She discussed it with Amy and Alice. "What is the point of being famous if you die penniless?"

They agreed. It was a tragedy. The three of them determined they would not die penniless.

"And if Mr. Hunter is so keen on these weaving stories, why didn't he go and work in the mill, instead of being a teacher?" Emma wanted to know, after Jane had regaled them yet again about the interesting lessons given by the marvellous Mr. Hunter.

"Mr. Burgess says he went to a high-falutin college in Manchester where they train to be a teacher," said Amy.

Mr. Burgess, although teaching at the other school in Chadderton, knew all about this college in Manchester, a new institute recently introduced for the training of teachers.

"I'd like to be a teacher," said Amy. "I'd rather do that instead of slaving away in that mill forever."

"If your precious Mr. Hunter's from Bury, why didn't he go back there?" Emma continued her cross-examination, sceptical about young men who ventured far from their home town when they could have been working in the local mill.

"I don't know." For once, Jane was lost for words. "Maybe they don't need any more teachers there."

Not only was this dynamic young man so proficient at his job, he was also devastatingly handsome, according to Jane. He was tall and lithe, with fair hair, a lock of which was allowed to stray over his smooth forehead. That seemed to be fashionable among young men nowadays, noted Jane with satisfaction. He was almost clean-shaven with a barely visible layer of flaxen velvet on his upper lip, like a dusting of down that could blow away on the faintest breeze, just like the fluff on a dandelion. He had a full mouth that could pucker with distaste but more often dispense dazzling smiles like bolts of lightning, electrifying, with one eyebrow jauntily raised when explaining something to his attentive class. Miss Partridge, another teacher at Christ Church School, looked upon him as charmingly refined and a welcome addition to the old school. Mr. Atkins, Headmaster, was more inclined to call him 'rakish'.

Jane sat mesmerized in his class; even the arithmetic was made interesting.

But one thing she had so far not mentioned to the family was that in addition to his teaching skills, Mr. Hunter could also play the piano.

Jane had been having spasmodic advice on the piano—you could hardly call it a lesson—from Miss Partridge. Because of the infrequency of the lessons, Jane's progress was rather slow.

"Mr. Hunter says he will teach me the piano," announced Jane one evening at the tea table.

"I thought you were learning from Miss Partridge," said Alice.

"I am, but she's too busy to give me a proper lesson. Mr. Hunter says I could be really good if I had regular lessons."

"And how is that going to help, if you don't have a piano at home to practise on?" asked Emma.

"I could practice at the church hall. That's where I'd have lessons," said Jane. "Mr. Hunter said he would arrange it."

Emma was rather sceptical about this arrangement. Then she thought of another objection. "And who do you think is going to pay for these lessons?"

"I have my money for doing the letters for Mrs. Burgess," said Jane, hoping this would satisfy Emma.

"That won't go very far and I think you've got enough to do – working at the mill all morning, and then school *and* doing the letters."

"Mr. Hunter says ..." began Jane.

"Shut up, Jane," said Emma. "We've all heard enough about Mr. La-di-dah Hunter. And take your elbows off the table."

§

Jane and Amy went to Sunday school every Sunday afternoon for one and a half hours, while their older sisters stayed at home doing their chores or reading or sewing. Jane, who had always found Sunday school to be rather a nuisance but something that had to be endured, was suddenly more interested in it than she had been hitherto. Mr. Humphreys, the Sunday school superintendent, was indisposed, and it was said he would be absent for several weeks at least. The vicar, not wishing to leave the children of his parishioners with nothing to do on a Sunday afternoon, needed a substitute teacher for these ministrations.

And who was ready to step into the breach? Giles Hunter, the new, young and dynamic teacher at Christ Church School who had not escaped the vicar's notice or anyone else's for that matter. He was not like any other Sunday school teacher in Jane's experience. He brought religion down to earth, to a level young children could grasp. Jane couldn't believe how lucky they were; they had Mr. Hunter every weekday afternoon at school and now, they had him on Sunday afternoons as well. And he lived up to his reputation for delivering lessons to remember.

"I *love* Sunday school now," said Jane.

On a warm June afternoon, Jane and Amy were in the front row of the Sunday school class. Old Mr. Humphreys was still away. Some said he would not come back as he had been in Oldham Infirmary for weeks and who knew what was wrong with him? The vicar had said everyone should pray for Mr. Humphreys as he was so ill. Jane was sorry for Mr. Humphreys but not so sorry she wanted him back at Sunday school.

"Yes, children, Jesus is all around us," said Mr. Hunter. Some of them looked around the large hall in a sort of holy and fearful expectation that he would appear beside them. Sunlight filtered in through the windows and threw slices of yellow light on the bare wooden floor. At the front of the hall, above the dais, was a large picture of the Son of God, in a large gold frame. It was the famous one, the same one that Aunt Clara had pasted into the front of her Bible. Jane knew it was called 'The Light of the World'. Jesus was knocking on a door, holding out a lantern and gazing out to something far beyond. The odd thing was, wherever you were in the church hall, Jesus seemed to be looking directly at you.

One little girl had fallen asleep in the heat of the afternoon, even on a hard Sunday school chair, the only kind they had in there. Mr. Hunter stepped on a small ladder and opened one of the windows to let in some air. He then gathered up the sleeping infant and walked around with her. Jane wished she was that little girl.

"Imagine, children, inviting Jesus to your home for tea," said Mr. Hunter, gently putting the awakened child next to Jane. "Wouldn't you like Jesus to come to tea?" he asked the little girl. This was going a bit too far, in Jane's opinion, but she went along with the general idea. "I'd give him a mince pie," said the small, drowsy girl. Jane wanted to say, 'Mince pies weren't invented then,' or 'Jesus didn't eat that kind of food,' but she didn't want to seem disrespectful, especially in the church hall, so she said nothing. Talk of mince pies had reminded Jane that she had a wrapped sweet given to her by Abigail that morning after church. She had not had a chance to eat it as Emma did not approve of such things. She always said 'think of your white teeth, and your beautiful smile,' and so on, but it was oh, so hard! Never to have sweets, like Abigail did.

Jane looked cautiously in her reticule. Yes, there was the boiled sweet nestling next to her prayer book. She unwrapped it carefully trying not to attract attention with the crackle of paper. She would slip it into her mouth while Mr. Hunter said the closing prayer. She must, however, try to ignore the compelling eyes of Jesus, always gazing at her from the large picture.

Mr. Hunter always finished his stint at Sunday school with a prayer and then a closing song or hymn. Usually there was another half an hour to go but he seemed to be finishing early. He gave the beginning note on the harmonium in the corner of the hall and then came to conduct the class in their chant.

> *Jesus loves me, this I know*
> *For the Bible tells me so.*
> *Little ones to him belong*
> *They are weak but he is strong.*
> > *Yes, Jesus loves me*
> > *Yes, Jesus loves me*
> > *Yes, Jesus loves*
> > *The Bible tells me so.*

Jane thought, 'Oh why did Mr. Hunter have to look at me?' Normally she would have liked that, but she had just popped the large sweet into her mouth. She knew she must not hold it in her cheek. She tried to mouth the words *Jesus loves me* but it seemed not only were the eyes of Jesus fully on her, but so were Mr. Hunter's. It was difficult to keep the sweet from bulging into her cheek or falling out. Trying to sing and suck at the same time was impossible. Suddenly her throat was racked, pinched. She spluttered and clutched her neck. She couldn't breathe and knew she must be choking to death. Amy's face was floating in front of her and a grey blanket seemed to be closing round her. She could hear the other children's voices ... *The Bible tells me so* ... becoming fainter and fainter.

When she came round, there was a sea of faces bending over her. She was lying on the bare boards of the Sunday school floor. There was Amy and Mr. Hunter, both looking worried. The vicar had been called from his house next door.

"We must get her home," he said to Giles Hunter. To Amy, he said, "and you tell your big sister she should get the doctor."

Jane was in a stunned silence and her throat hurt. Mr. Hunter carried her outside. Oh, if she hadn't been nearly dying, this would have been wonderful, she thought. She was put into a gig which had been waiting for the youngest Leggate child. Amy squeezed in beside her and they reached home in less than five minutes. The horse and driver were sent back to the Sunday school. And then the inquisition was begun by Emma, first asking questions of Amy as Jane was still gasping and clutching her throat. She was made to lie down on the sofa in the parlour. Kate tried to get her to sip some water. She was deathly pale.

Doctor Foster arrived. "Has she had anything like this before?" He knew this could be a symptom of epilepsy, a child nearby had this, and was prone to sudden attacks of dropping in a dead faint to the floor.

Emma shook her head. She was perplexed and extremely worried.

"Never been ill before in her life?" persisted the doctor. He was new and had not seen Jane before.

"She was ill with the consumption," explained Emma, "but that was over a year ago and she was sent to Birkenhead for the sea air and she got better."

They had almost forgotten that. But this sudden ailment had nothing to with TB. They all knew that.

"I'm all right," Jane finally managed to croak the words. At last she was able to drink from the glass Kate offered her.

After a thorough examination of the patient, the doctor left the house. "Keep an eye on her," were his last words.

Emma looked closely at Jane again.

A thought had suddenly struck her. "Were you eating something, at Sunday school?"

Jane knew Emma would get to the bottom of things. She nodded slowly. No use denying it.

"Could you manage a little of the broth from dinner?" asked the ever-caring Kate, trying to intercept what she knew would be a thorough interrogation by Emma. The bread and cheese they were about to have for tea would be out of the question.

"What were you doing Jane, when you were taken bad?" Emma persisted whilst something was stirring in her memory, something that had happened to her long ago when they lived in London. She had been eating a large boiled sweet while playing with Algy and Kate, hopping and skipping. She had been enjoying the treat, sucking and transferring it from one side of her mouth to the other. She had known she must not bite it. It was instilled in her not to crunch those sweets, or else woe betide her teeth. But something had happened whilst she was enjoying that sweet. She had swallowed it before it was a sliver and could easily slide down her throat. It had stuck in her throat and had been a nasty experience. She remembered it as if it were yesterday, instead of more than ten years ago. Algy had thumped her on the back whilst she crouched on the ground gasping for breath and everything had gone black. Oh yes! She had seen this kind of thing before, had experienced it herself. Emma looked hard at Jane. "What were you doing, Jane?"

Jane, now rapidly recovering, wilted under Emma's stern look, but she did detect something of a smile in her older sister.

Jane swallowed hard. Her throat was so sore and her chest hurt all the way down to her waist.

"Did that Abigail by any chance give you one of her sweets? One of those big boiled, fruit sweets? Did it go down the wrong way?"

Trust Emma to hit the nail on the head. "Just like Snow White, eh Jane? Somethin' stuck in the throat?"

Jane nodded reluctantly and Emma smiled. Yes, she was not so old and set in her ways that she did not vividly recall that childhood incident when she was younger than Jane was now.

"Sweets! We can't be wasting money on that sort of thing but Abigail always has a good supply. And *why* do you think we all have such good teeth and Abigail has a smile like a slit in a pie?"

Emma laughed and hugged Jane. "Remember, Jane. Thou shalt not eat sweets, especially in Sunday school."

Jane breathed a sigh of relief. For the first time she realized when Emma laughed, she looked a lot like Kate.

§

In August, there was the grandest wedding Chadderton had seen for a long time. Kate had heard of weddings where there was champagne and dancing in a grand hotel. But she was happy enough that, after the church ceremony, the wedding feast would be at the church hall. The Ladies' Committee, headed by Mrs. Leggate, put on a delectable spread. Kate had excelled in making her own wedding dress, with a little assistance from Mrs. Burgess and her sewing machine. Kate had always dreamed of a white wedding, a fashion set by Queen Victoria when she married her first cousin, Prince Albert, in 1840. Although not many brides of the Kershaw girls' acquaintance had adhered to this newer trend, usually wearing a new 'Sunday best' for the ceremony, Kate's dress was just as she had always dreamed, in ivory silk and lace with a long veil and headdress of mock orange flowers. Jane loved her bridesmaid's dress of sky blue satin. Ivory sashes complemented the ensemble with posies of white Gypsophila, more commonly called Baby's Breath, the same as the bride's, held by lace-mittened hands. Six sisters wore the same dresses, purchased from the emporium in Oldham. Of course, as Mrs. Burgess had so rightly said, "A shop dress is made for anyone who wishes to buy it, but beware; the sleeves may be too long or too short, and that goes for the hem too. And the waist could be too high. It is ready to hang on you but it might not hang just right, like a dress made especially for you. But one made to measure with tape and pins, that is completely different." But even so, even if the dresses for the six girls were not made to measure and were created in a factory, they were delightful and fitted perfectly in the end, once Mrs. Burgess and Emma had finished with them.

Their father had come up trumps with funds for all the wedding expenses. "Been saving for a long time for something like this," he had said. There had been some argument over Emma's role. "An older sister cannot be a bridesmaid," she had insisted. She had won, in the end, and was the Maid of Honour, wearing a dress of darker blue with a cream sash to finish off, like the other girls.

It was a wonderful wedding day. In the late afternoon, the couple were waved off at the railway station to their honeymoon destination of Lytham St. Anne's, a little seaside town on the coast. It was near Blackpool, but was much quieter than that bustling holiday resort, and was considered much more genteel, especially for honeymoon couples.

It was the loveliest wedding day anyone could wish for. It was also the day Mrs. Burgess was found dead—murdered.

Chapter Eight

The wedding bells had scarcely finished ringing, the guests and wedding party had hardly time to cast off their finery and bathe in the wonderful atmosphere of that day, when, at about half past seven that evening, John Burgess was in his shirtsleeves, waiting for his wife to come home in a cab. She had been to deliver a gown she had just finished making for Mrs. Applegate up at Springfield House. It was an urgent delivery as it was needed for a grandchild's christening the next day.

"How much?" John asked the cab driver, delving into his pocket for some coins he knew he had in there.

"The missus up at the house already paid me," said the cab driver, jumping down to see to his horse, which was whinnying and stamping its hooves. Some victualling was obviously needed. The driver reached for the horse's feed bag as John pocketed the coins and, as there was no sign of his wife alighting, opened the cab door. What he saw filled him with horror. There was Mariah on the floor of the cab, her dress blood stained. She was obviously unconscious or worse still, she might be dead.

The driver dropped the feed bag as soon as he heard John's anguished cry.

"What the devil?" he muttered, as they lifted Mariah out of the carriage. "I should'na have stopped."

"You stopped?" asked John, realizing that his wife appeared to be expiring. Her eyelids were fluttering and she was scarcely breathing.

"This fellow flagged me down, by the canal bridge. Said he had to speak to my passenger. Knew who it was, he said. I waited, and after a couple of minutes he got out and I drove on up here."

"Go and fetch the doctor, and the police," said John, carrying Mariah into the house.

The first person he encountered was Aunt Clara. She was back again for the wedding, having stayed with them for a funeral a year and half before.

"Lord, have mercy on us," Aunt Clara began as John carried his wife into the kitchen and laid her on the sofa. Aunt Clara was frozen to the spot, clutching the Bible that she had been reading. Pulling herself together, she ordered a bewildered Abigail to fetch some water. But looking at Mariah lying on the sofa, it was obvious to Aunt Clara and John that she was lifeless. Her lovely dress, the one she had made especially for Kate's wedding, was stained with blood, which was seeping through the bodice. She also appeared to be bleeding from a neck wound.

"Oh, Ma, Ma," wailed Abigail. "What's wrong with her?" she asked her father, who was trying to revive his wife.

The water lay untouched. Aunt Clara knew it was useless. The poor woman was dead. No amount of water would resuscitate her. She took up her Bible again, and holding it tight, started praying.

Abigail could not bear the scene. She ran next door to the Kershaw's, crying piteously.

The doctor arrived, but as John well knew, it was too late. What could have happened? Why had his wife been attacked so viciously?

"These wounds on the neck and breast are only superficial," said the doctor, examining Mariah thoroughly. "They would not have killed her." He did, however, pronounce her dead and continued his examination.

While they waited for the police, the cabbie came into the house.

"What was he like – this fellow who got in the cab?" asked John.

"Well, truth be told, I didn't notice," stammered the cab driver. "He looked much like anybody else hereabouts. Young, tall, wearing a cap. He had no jacket, just his weskit, it being such a warm day."

"And you never set eyes on him before?" asked John.

"No. Never. He must have been waiting, 'cos as soon as I drove round the corner from the Applegate's house, he flagged me down, like I said."

"I'm certain Mariah didn't know him. Maybe he thought it was somebody else in the cab."

By this time, two police constables had arrived. They did some preliminary questioning and made a thorough search of the cab. They noted the valise, the small suitcase in which Mariah had packed the gown. They found it lying open on the floor of the cab, empty, apart from a box of pins and a tape measure. The important item, the gown, must have been delivered safely and Mrs. Burgess was bringing back the empty valise.

"No sign of anything that could have caused those wounds, though," said the man in charge, who was Sergeant Wilkins. "But there *are* signs of a struggle. Her dress is torn." Turning to the doctor, Wilkins asked, "Would you say this neck wound and the one on her breast were made with a knife?"

"Yes, some kind of sharp, slim, knife, I believe," replied the doctor. But there was nothing to give them a clue. No knife was found. He reiterated that he did not think the wounds had killed her. He had in his mind that she could have expired from a heart attack, which further examination at the mortuary would reveal.

Thank goodness the happy couple knew none of this. By now they were safely in each other's arms at the Royal Hotel, Lytham St. Anne's.

§

The following day, the police questioned everyone who had known Mrs. Burgess—especially the next-door neighbours. All the girls had been asked to go down to the police station.

Emma was the one they questioned the most as she was the senior member of the Kershaw household. Charles Kershaw had already left for Birkenhead.

They would have liked to question Kate, of course, as she was the one who knew Mrs. Burgess best, often going next door to use the sewing machine. But Kate was away on her honeymoon and had no knowledge of this catastrophe. She would get a shock when she returned in a week's time. Jane was questioned closely about the letters, bills and receipts she did for Mrs. Burgess. "There was no money in the case or on her person," said Sergeant Wilkins, "but if there had been, that scoundrel could have stolen it. She had just made delivery of a dress to Mrs. Applegate. Do you think Mrs. Applegate would have paid her?"

"Mrs. Burgess always let the customer have the dress and insisted they wear it at least once to make sure it was right," explained Jane. "She never collected money on delivery in case the customer wanted an alteration. I always had to send a bill with a letter about two weeks later."

"We will, of course, be talking to Mrs. Applegate," said the Sergeant. "But obviously Mrs. Burgess was alive and well when she left there."

Emma stayed behind for some extra questioning.

"The doctor has established that Mrs. Burgess died of a heart attack, but nevertheless, it was obviously brought about by her being attacked by the man who got into the cab. Do you know anyone who might have something against this woman?" asked the Sergeant.

Emma did not, although she had never cared for Mrs. Burgess personally. Kate had got on with her much better. But even so, Emma would have given anything for Mrs. Burgess to walk through the door right now. Poor Abigail was so distressed they had to give her a sleeping draught. Her older sister, Frances, who worked as a kitchen maid at the 'Big House' Thornbridge Manor, had been sent for to help calm her down, although she, too, was beside herself with shock and disbelief.

Sergeant Wilkins hesitated before he asked Emma his next question. "Miss Kershaw, I have to ask something. It's . . . er . . . very . . . awkward, but I don't think I can ask her husband at the moment. He's too upset. You don't think she was carrying-on with anyone, do you? I mean, did she have a fancy man?"

Emma almost laughed out loud in her denial of this question. The idea was ludicrous. Everyone knew Mariah Burgess was no charmer. For all her dealings with rich clientele and fine gowns, in Emma's opinion, she would be as alluring to a man as a spider would be to Little Miss Muffet. Come to think of it, Mrs. Burgess had the characteristics of a spider. She was an odd little woman, small, wiry, with black hair and black, beady eyes. She had no social graces, was ill at ease in company and had difficulty conducting a conversation. Nevertheless, none of these shortcomings appeared to be a problem in dealing with her well-to-do customers and advising them on what styles, fabric and colour would suit them best. Emma had often wondered how someone who had received such a scant education had come to marry a school teacher. There was no doubt, however, that the community had held her in high esteem as an extremely skilled dressmaker.

"I'm quite sure she didn't have . . . an admirer, or anyone like that," Emma assured the Sergeant. "She wasn't the type."

Sergeant Wilkins said, "Rest assured, Miss Kershaw, we will do our best to catch whoever did this. We will constantly be on the lookout for him."

"But, Sergeant, I *am* concerned about him being on the loose."

"As I said, Miss Kershaw, we will be constantly vigilant for the suspect. Would you care to have one of my men escort you home?" Emma declined the offer. The last thing she wanted was to be seen walking through the streets of Chadderton accompanied by a policeman.

The police were not able to locate the man who had got into the cab. They were of the opinion that he might have been a drifter who, on hearing a cab approach, had come up from the canal where he could just as easily have slipped back down again and disappeared on one of the many kinds of craft that plied those waterways. A thorough search of the canal and bank had revealed nothing of consequence. Exhaustive enquiries at taverns patronised by canal workers had not revealed anyone answering the rather vague description given by the cab driver. And certainly, the knife that had inflicted the superficial wounds had not been found.

The police questioned the cabbie again. "Did he have an accent, this chap who got into the cab?"

"I hardly exchanged two words with him, and who's to notice an accent? Every Tom, Dick and Harry comes here from all over the country to work in the cotton trade."

"Did you not hear anything from inside the cab? Some kind of cry for help or scream from this woman?"

"Being a Saturday evening, there were lots of people about; other cabs coming and going. There was noise enough on the street. I could hear nowt from the inside of my cab."

"We cannot rule out the possibility of mistaken identity. This man might have intended to meet a completely different person thought to be in your cab," said the police sergeant.

Even Aunt Clara had not escaped the questioning, but she could not help much, even though she had been staying at the Burgess house. All she could think of was a decent Christian burial. She would stay on, of course, to help supervise the funeral for Mr. Burgess. She ignored Emma, who had automatically assumed she would be taking charge of things. Abigail, only fifteen, was of no help at all, and her sister, Frances, was not much better.

Then there was the inquest. Just when they should have been enjoying the aftermath of the wedding, here they were, steeped in sorrow at the death, possibly murder, of their next-door neighbour.

§

Algy had not come to Kate's wedding. He had sent a letter to his sisters explaining that although he realized this was an important family occasion, which obviously was going to be more enjoyable than the funeral he had attended the year before, he felt the need to remain in London with Lucy, his wife. Lucy's health was delicate with the imminent arrival of their first child. The girls were pleased to note this coming event as so far there had been no children in the five years Algy had been married.

All the sisters had enjoyed every minute of the wedding beginning with the ceremony at Christ Church with full choir and followed by the reception in the church hall. Even Billy Lampson had joined the singers, much to Eliza's delight. She had not seen him for over a year. Naturally the entire choir, in which Billy had been temporarily reinstated, was invited to the banquet and Eliza managed to seat herself next to him. Aunt Clara had taken special note of this, remembering her last encounter with this young man.

"I'm pleased to see that Billy appears to be an upstanding member of society," she said to Emma later, having observed him at length.

"Yes, he probably took heed of your penny lecture on leading girls astray," Emma had said.

Although sitting next to Eliza, Billy did not appear to monopolize her company and spread his charms around, talking equally to other guests.

Another choir member was also present at the wedding feast: the teacher, Giles Hunter. Possessing a reasonable tenor voice, he had been automatically granted access to the coveted membership of the church choir. He was, therefore, included as a wedding guest which pleased Jane, even though he had managed to seat himself between the twins which seemed the natural thing to do as he was in the choir with Mary-Rose and Mary-Ann, but Jane was consumed with jealousy and finally consoled herself with the fact that she *did* see Mr. Hunter every day at school, and also on a Sunday. She must not be so selfish. Let the twins sit betwixt the only two eligible young men in the room, she reasoned to herself.

"Who would have thought I would have come to a wedding, and a few days later there would be a funeral?" Aunt Clara said the next day, shaking her carefully coiffed grey head.

This sent Abigail into fresh floods of tears. Now, having only her father for company, she spent a lot of time next door. Poor Abigail's eyes were rarely dry and Jane felt sorry for her. John Burgess seemed bewildered and lost. His tall frame was stooped and he seemed to be silently grieving, immersed in his books. Abigail was receiving little comfort from him. Emma was the one she was leaning on. It would be good when Kate came home the following Saturday, but she would have a nasty shock when she heard the appalling news.

The main topic of conversation was, of course, the death of Mrs. Burgess. It was never ending. For the hundredth time poor Abigail asked everyone and no one in particular, "Who could have done her in?" No one knew but all agreed with the police; money must have been the motive and they still could not rule out the possibility of mistaken identity. The inquest had not turned up any new evidence and the coroner had declared an open verdict.

After the funeral and reflecting on the sad events again, Aunt Clara said, "I'm going to read my Bible now". That meant everyone had to be quiet. Emma said silent prayers to the Lord requesting that Aunt Clara would read the Good Book to herself and not foist it on to the sombre gathering. Emma missed Kate and also prayed that Aunt Clara would not stay as long as last time. Her prayers were answered the very next day.

"I hope to come to another wedding soon," Aunt Clara said as she was preparing for her journey back to London. There was no reply from any of the seven sisters as they gathered to bid farewell to their aunt while waiting for the cab to take her to the railway station.

There was a problem in the Kershaw household and Emma, as head of it, was forced to admit that, apart from their father, there was a shortage of the opposite sex in their lives. She wasn't thinking of herself, however, and she certainly wasn't about to mention this fact to Aunt Clara who had her own ideas of progress in this department.

"Eliza might get wed, y'never know?" were the final words from her aunt as she left the premises. She could see as well as anyone else that suitors were thin on the ground. "Maybe Billy will come up to snuff now he's an engineering apprenticeship. And that new teacher is promising. I like him." At the wedding reception, Giles Hunter had been chatting to everyone, dividing his time courteously between all the ladies. "It's pity he doesn't have a twin, then both Mary-Rose and Mary-Ann would be taken care of. They're nearly eighteen. My girls were all wed by that age."

§

After the funeral of Mrs. Burgess, things were quiet. The trail of the perpetrator had gone cold. It was no longer the main topic of conversation. The police had ceased their questioning. Frances had gone back to Thornbridge Manor. Abigail spent even more time next door at the Kershaw's where the girls' activities and lively conversations helped her to dwell less on the devastating events of August 18th, a day that had started so happily with a wedding and ended so tragically with her mother's death. Jane had noticed, however, that Abigail seemed to be taking an interest in a young man and had seen her more than once walking home from the Glebe with Bertie Dawson, a mill hand. Jane knew he had been a 'half-timer' like all of them had been once, and she had seen him frequently for he lived close by. But Abigail was not forthcoming to her neighbours about her friendship with the young man, and her father, still steeped in his grieving, saw no reason to interfere. However, Mrs. Kendal, who was as usual the fount of knowledge on local gossip, had plenty to say.

"That Abigail had better be careful," she told Jane on one of her errands to the shop. "I know Bertie's one for the girls."

"Just like Billy used to be?" said Jane, relieved for Eliza's sake that Mrs. Kendal obviously had switched her attention from Billy Lampson and his activities to another young man.

"I hear he's been walking out with that oldest Leggate girl, as well as with Abigail," said Mrs. Kendal. She had other things, however, to occupy her mind as her husband was once again in the infirmary. She was hard pressed between getting up there to visit him and also running the shop.

"I'm sure it doesn't mean much, Abigail walking home from the mill with Bertie," said Jane, who, herself, had even been walking along with both of them at times.

Their minds were relieved of such gossip when they received a letter from Algy, saying that Lucy had given birth to a girl. She was to be called Sarah. That was good news, thought Emma. A little newcomer, named after their dead mother.

§

1884

A few months later, shortly after Christmas, Jane arrived home from school to find there was a large delivery van outside their partly open front door. She knew there was no one home, the other sisters still at their mill jobs, but was surprised to see Kate appear on the front step. "What's going on?" Jane asked. It was unusual for Kate to be there when no one was at home.

Jane watched as Kate supervised the unloading of what looked like a large piece of furniture from the delivery van.

"Put it in the front parlour," were her orders to the two men.

Jane was transfixed as she saw something beyond her wildest dreams. A harmonium was being delivered to the Kershaw household.

"Yes, it's yours, Jane," said Kate hugging her youngest sister. "This will be grand, won't it? Your very own harmonium, so you can practise whenever you want, and you won't have to wait your turn at the church hall."

They followed the men into the parlour and Kate showed them where to deposit the instrument, first asking them to move the chiffonier along to the end of the wall. She enlightened Jane as to how it was that this marvellous item, which she had last seen at the Goodacre's residence, was being installed in their humble home.

"My in-laws have just got themselves a piano," Kate explained. "I told them that you're having lessons and have nothing to practise on, so they said they wanted you to have this. Isn't it wonderful? You do want it, don't you, Jane?" Kate was a swift as she was sweet and had not missed the opportunity to place the harmonium where it would be most appreciated. "Now you can play to your heart's content any time you like. So let's get a carrot for the horse and these good men can be off."

Jane could hardly wipe the smile off her face as she opened the casing and ran her fingers over the keys which she could tell had not seen much use. She had heard that society people were eager to follow the current fashion to put a piano in every parlour. They had even replaced the harmonium in the church hall with a piano. There was one snag, however, which struck her later, after Kate had gone. Grateful as Jane was, this instrument meant that she might see less of her music instructor, Mr. Giles Hunter. Not only did she have her regular lessons with him every Wednesday, but he often called in at the church hall after school to oversee her practice. From now on she would be doing her practice at home.

A worse snag, however, was that Emma, always the practical one, was wondering how far Jane's dwindling pennies for piano lessons would go now that Mrs. Burgess was dead and that source of income was gone. Jane had given much thought to this and had racked her brains to think who might want to avail themselves of her services as a scribe, but so far, no resolution had come to mind. Fortunately, rescue was at hand, after Emma had mentioned this problem to her married sister.

"I will pay for Jane's music lessons," said Kate. "I've discussed the matter with Nathaniel. We both agree it would be pointless for Jane to inherit Mrs. Goodacre's harmonium if she can't continue with her lessons."

Emma had to admit there seemed to be many advantages to being married to someone with high expectations. "And now, Jane, you won't be gallivanting off to the church hall to practise," was an after-thought from the Head of the House. She wanted to keep an eye on her youngest sister who had been spending far too much time outside the home.

Jane was completely enthralled with the harmonium. She could hardly keep away from it. She practised every spare moment she had. There was, of course, a huge difference between the harmonium and the piano. First, there was a slight difficulty with the pedals as Jane was only eleven, and had to sit on the edge of the stool to be able to just reach the pedals to do the pump action and it was a little tricky. But it was so convenient to be able to practise whenever she liked and therefore to impress Mr. Hunter, who was astounded at her progress. This love of music seemed to have rubbed off on other members of the family, and at times Jane had a hard time keeping the instrument to herself, constantly interrupted by Alice wanting to try it, or the twins who wanted Jane to play for their singing. But Jane was good at persuading one sister or another to put one foot each on the pedals to do the pumping. Emma was secretly rather proud of Jane whose fingers seemed to fly over the keys. True, it did not have the clarity of tone of the piano, but nevertheless, it generated a pleasing sound for the whole household to enjoy.

"Who would have ever thought there would be a harmonium in our parlour?" said Emma. "Pa *will* get a surprise when he comes home."

§

Amy had now left school and was working all day at the Glebe Mill, mostly in the carding room. Carding had long been done by machines, which disentangled and cleaned the fibres of cotton before they could be spun into yarn. The girls, or card hands as they were called, had to frequently change the rollers and there was always the monotonous work of sweeping up the residual fluff. A perpetual haze of dust caused a lot of workers to cough; it was called 'carder's cough' which could be dangerous if left unattended. Amy had heard some of the workers talking about a forward-thinking owner who had introduced more ventilation in the factories. Mr. Higginbottom, the manager of Glebe Mill, had told them that if workers would bind a handkerchief over their noses, the chances of that deadly lung disease would be minimised. Greatly feared, Byssinosis by all accounts was far worse than Tuberculosis. Amy made sure she always had one of her father's old, large handkerchieves with her.

Amy had finished school in record time when she had barely turned twelve years old. She reflected it was not always in one's best interest to excel at lessons, for if she had not succeeded so well, she could have stayed longer at school and delayed working full time at the mill. She missed her schooling, but did not go on about it the way Alice did.

"I might get a cough, and look how rough my hands are getting," were Alice's frequent complaints.

Amy quietly decided that she would enter into some further study. She had talked things over with Mr. Burgess who offered to teach her free of charge, being only too willing to pass on his knowledge to an eager student.

"I regret that my own daughters have such a lack of interest in further education," said Mr. Burgess. "Frances is content with her job at Thornbridge Manor, and Abigail doesn't seem to mind the menial work at the mill. Neither of them ever had any aptitude for classical studies. Your ambition to become a teacher is admirable, Amy. I think you could easily aspire to that. You should be able to find your niche if you study hard for a couple of years and then pass the examination to college."

"Yes, days at the mill will be bearable if I have something like that to look forward to," said Amy, even though Emma had pronounced her misgivings about Amy spending every evening studying and then reading in bed until the candle petered out.

§

Alice was enjoying her monthly visits to the Literary Club at the Lyceum in Oldham with her former teacher, Miss Partridge. Here, they became immersed in poetry and drama readings. Alice noted with interest that Archie Hawkins, the boy she had seen on that first evening at the talk by the Royal Geographical Society, was also in attendance at these evenings. They had exchanged a few notes about poetry and even the theatre where he said he had been to see a play. Alice fervently hoped that some day she would be going to the theatre in Manchester.

Life was improving all the time at 54 Bower Lane; no more tick necessary at Mrs. Kendal's. Charles Kershaw had been promoted at work and more money was coming from him; Emma's good, now steady, earnings as a senior weaver were a bonus and all the girls, except Jane, worked full-time at the mill. When Jane went for her errands to Mrs. Kendal's, she did not have to get butter from the nearly empty barrel.

No one would have to pick out woodchips any more. Their mother had been dead for almost two years, and although there were still few comforts in the home, Emma was able to make sure that the nutritional needs of the family were met. The doctor had recommended certain foods for Alice, who was on the small side for her age and still had no monthly bleeding. Amy and Jane had long overtaken her in height and puberty. But it didn't seem to matter to Alice who made up for her lack of stature with her powerful voice which she used to state her opinions strongly and also to recite poetry all around the house.

Gradually, Jane realised they had not had tripe for months. She hadn't missed it. Emma had finally admitted that none of them really liked it and it took hours to cook, so why bother? Soon there was a change in their usual Saturday fare. On one of Jane's errands to the shop, Mrs. Kendal recommended black pudding instead of the regular sausage supplies which had run out.

"Black pudding, eh?" said Emma, as she fried the rounds of black sausage with onions; cabbage and potatoes boiling on the side. "Is this the real thing? From Bury, maybe? I bet this is what your Mr. Hunter has many a time."

Jane thought she could detect a faint smile from Emma. Although uneasy about 'pudding' made from pig's blood, Jane had to admit, although in the same category as tripe, being cheap and nourishing, the black pudding was tasty and definitely preferable.

The family had always had the regular pork sausage when their mother was alive, the kind of sausage they had had in London where they were from. Habit as well as orderliness was the theme of Emma's life, and it was hard to deviate from old ways, but she was becoming more pliant in her orderliness.

"We'll have black pudding again," she said. "And we mustn't forget the tripe," at which Jane pulled a face, not detecting the wink Emma gave over her head to Eliza.

"Be thankful," said Emma. "If we still lived in London, we'd be eating jellied eels."

In her orderly fashion, as it was Saturday, she checked their monthly finances and noted, with satisfaction, there was now enough money for a headstone for their mother's grave. It was time to replace the plank of wood which had marked the spot for so long.

§

Jane spent almost every Saturday afternoon at Kate's new home over the tailor's shop in Oldham. The rooms were hardly recognizable from when she had first moved in. Furniture bought with the help of Pa and some good, unwanted items from Kate's in-laws had transformed the place. There were new curtains made from that marvellous new material they were making, rather like that soft, sheer fabric they were imitating from India. Jane had developed a taste for all things emanating out of India.

At school, Mr. Hunter always stuck to the curriculum and most days, after what he considered a suitable time spent on the three Rs, would turn to History or Geography. His uncle was in the British Army in India and the young teacher would now entertain more than teach with tales from the letters he received from the uncle he so admired. Corporal Hunter had written to his nephew about life in India: there were tigers in the jungle, and elephants that could do the work of ten men. Jane found it most fascinating.

"And don't forget, children," was one of Mr. Hunter's favourite themes, "our beloved Queen is Empress of India." He entranced them with the well-circulated story of Queen Victoria's son, the Prince of Wales, who had been on a Tiger Hunt from 1875 to 1876. Secretly, though, Jane was of the opinion that if it took a whole year to find and shoot a tiger, they couldn't have been as plentiful as everyone made out. She did think, however, Mr. Hunter would look splendid in a turban.

§

The apathy of Mr. Burgess, which had set in fast after the death of his wife, was finally thrown off later in the year when he popped round to see the Kershaws.

"Abigail and I will be leaving Bower Lane," said Mr. Burgess, with a rare smile, although his daughter looked miserable. "It makes sense as I've been offered a teaching position at the Blue Coat School in Oldham. We'll be living with my widowed sister near there."

"That's good news, about the teaching post," said Emma dutifully. "But we shall miss you, as next-door neighbours."

"I'll still come to give Amy her tutorial on Saturday afternoons, of course. By the way, would you like Mariah's sewing machine? It has sat untouched in our parlour since . . . my wife . . . died."

"We don't have the space now that we have that harmonium in the parlour," said Emma, sorry to turn this golden offer down. Thinking of who might want the valuable and useful machine, Kate immediately came to mind, as in Emma's opinion her sister had nothing else to do but keep house and sew, having left the Textile Mill as soon as she was married.

Mr. Burgess readily agreed to this arrangement and the machine was taken up to Kate and Nathaniel's home by carrier. Kate was extremely appreciative of this but the first thing she noticed was that some scissors, always kept by Mrs. Burgess in the long, narrow drawer of the table, were missing.

"This is odd as they were always stored in that drawer," said Kate to Mr. Burgess.

"There are some large, heavy shears on the shelf in the parlour."

"No," explained Kate. "I don't mean those. Your wife had some small, razor-sharp scissors which she kept in this drawer."

"Oh. Yes. Now I remember those scissors," said Mr. Burgess. "They're a special French style of scissors. Mariah bought them in Manchester when we went there a few years ago to get some special material for a dress."

Abigail was called upon to verify when she had last seen these scissors, but she had no idea as she had never used them or even touched the machine.

"I think these missing scissors might have a bearing on my wife's death" said Mr. Burgess to Kate. "Do you think she might have taken them with her to Mrs. Applegate's house when she delivered the dress?"

"She might well have done," said Kate.

"I must go and see the police. The case is unsolved and still active."

Like a terrier which had been given a whiff of the fox, Sergeant Wilkins was keen to resume the trail which had been eluding him since the previous August—a matter of almost one year.

First, Mrs. Applegate was questioned again. When she took delivery of the dress, did she try it on, as was usually the case? Did she notice if the scissors were in the valise?

"The dress was a perfect fit," Mrs. Applegate said, casting her mind back to that evening. "No adjustments were necessary and so Mariah left with the valise. I did not notice any scissors, but then, I scarcely looked in there."

Mrs. Applegate had settled the bill owing for the dress with Mr. Burgess the week following the funeral and that was the end of it. Almost. But the talk of scissors had sparked a conversation between Abigail and her sister at the 'Big House'. Mention of scissors had stirred something in Frances's memory.

"Scissors . . . "said Frances, casting her mind back to a year ago. "Mrs. Williams, she's the cook at Thornbridge Manor, said some of her knives and scissors could do with sharpening. And just about then, this tinker comes to the tradesmen's entrance, asking if we needed anything sharpening."

"When was that?" asked Sergeant Wilkins who lost no time in questioning Frances.

"The morning of the 18th August," said Frances, after checking with Mrs. Williams.

"That was the day of the wedding?"

"Yes. I remember it was, because I'd seen Abigail the day before and she'd told me all about the wedding dress Ma had helped Kate make, and the bridesmaids' dresses they got from the emporium."

"Tell me about this man who came to the door, looking for work."

"He was young, tall, and good-looking. Said he worked for the tinker and they would sharpen anything we needed doing. Mrs. Williams was going through her knives and then came out with them wrapped in a kitchen cloth. There were some scissors in there as well."

"And did he do them just then and there?"

"No. He said their grindstone was down at the canal on their boat and he would have to take them away and bring them back in the evening, or the next day."

"So, did he say anything else?"

"While he was waiting for Mrs. Williams to get the knives, I think he took a fancy to me." Frances, like her sister, Abigail, was not one to belittle her own charms. "He asked me my name, and I said it was Frances. Then he said his name was Francis too, but with an 'i', you know, for a boy. And then he said, 'but they call me Frank.'"

"When did be bring the stuff back?"

"*He* didn't. The gaffer did. The next day. Said Frank was off— not sure what he meant. But he gave me the cloth with the knives and scissors in and I paid him. I got into trouble with Mrs. Williams later as there was one knife missing and one extra pair of scissors in the cloth. She said I should have checked."

"I said she might be mistaken, and she said 'A good cook knows exactly how many knives and scissors she has in her kitchen.'"

"Then what happened?"

"Nothing. The tinker had long taken off and we didn't know how to get hold of him. Mrs. Williams said if I wasn't more careful next time, I would get the sack."

"So there were scissors that didn't belong to the house? What did you do with them?"

"As far as I know they're still there."

Sergeant Wilkins lost no time in fetching the scissors from Thornbridge Manor and showing them to Kate and Mr. Burgess. The small, French-style scissors were not the kind used in her kitchen, Mrs. Williams had said. They were more the sort of scissors used in dressmaking. Mr. Burgess was fairly sure and Kate was absolutely certain that these were the missing scissors.

After talking it over with the doctor, it became clear the scissors could have inflicted the superficial wounds on Mrs. Burgess, thus precipitating the heart attack.

Sergeant Wilkins was convinced this was the weapon, but this did nothing to assist the police in finding the man in the cab. They also needed to find the owner of the canal boat who had employed Frank. But Tinker Carberry was an elusive fellow, working on the waterways between Lancashire and Yorkshire, and sometimes, even further afield. Eleven long months had elapsed since the horrific incident.

"Couldn't they organise a special search of all the canals?" said Alice when she and her sisters were having one of their endless discussions about the case.

"Alice, it's Chadderton Police Station, not Scotland Yard," said Emma. "They simply don't have the manpower to do any more than they're doing at present."

But then, a few weeks later, some heartening news came. A diligent police constable had managed to locate Tinker Carberry on one of the many locks on the Rochdale canal as it rose over the hilly terrain of the Pennines to Sowerby Bridge in Yorkshire.

"Yes, I did have a fellow working for me called Frank Barrow," said the tinker, "but I dunno where he is now. He collected his money and took off just after those jobs I did near Oldham—said he was going back to London. Strange fellow. Made out he could speak French and could make gent's clothes, if you can believe that. I'd say he was a Jack of all Trades."

"How long was he working for you?" asked the Sergeant.

"About three weeks. He was useful, good at talking to the customers, getting jobs for me."

Sergeant Wilkins pondered on this information, but it didn't seem to help much. They needed to find Frank Barrow.

"Even if they do find him, it's not going go bring my mother back, is it?" said Abigail. "I don't honestly care. But I wish we weren't moving to Oldham, 'cos we'll be living with my Aunt Nan."

"What's *she* like?" asked Jane.

"She's a bit like Emma—very strict, only much older, of course. And she's . . sort of cold . . . distant."

"Well, it will be handy for the Blue Coat School where your Pa will be teaching," said Jane.

"Yes, but I wish we didn't have to move. I'll have to leave the Glebe. And I've lived next door to your family ever since I can remember. I'll miss you all so much."

Jane had never seen Abigail so miserable. Perhaps she sincerely meant it.

§

1884

On a sunny Wednesday in September, Jane came home from the Church hall after her piano lesson with Mr. Hunter and realized she had left her music behind. She walked back to the hall, hoping it would still be open, thinking more about Kate's baby, born that day—a boy. She would see him on Saturday. It was exciting to be an aunt. Of course, she was an aunt already—to Algy's bairn. But what was the point, thought Jane, if you had never set eyes on the baby, Sarah, who must now be more than one year old?

There had been some speculation as to the name of Kate's baby.

"They'll probably call him Charles, after Pa," Emma said.

"Why wouldn't they call him after Nathaniel's father?" asked Jane, wanting to be absolutely fair about this matter.

"Elijah? I don't think they would call him that. Kate would want him to be called Charlie." Emma had been positive about that.

Jane thought Emma may be mistaken, but on the ten-minute walk back to fetch her music, she was surprised to see Jimmy Leighton running towards her from the church hall. He was the youngest of the Leighton family, who lived on the other side of the Kershaws, and was about nine years old. He was running so hard he collided with Jane, knocking the breath out of her. She caught him and quickly saw that not only was he running hard, he was terrified, running away from something.

He looked so relieved to see Jane, but his face was bleeding and he was crying.

"Whatever happened, Jimmy?" said Jane as she wiped his face with her handkerchief.

"He came at me," said Jimmy in between sobs. "He's a ... a monster."

Jane held him by the hand as they hurried home. "Who is?" she asked, mystified.

"The teacher."

"Who? Mr. Hunter?"

"Yes. Him."

They walked on in silence, apart from Jimmy's snivelling, thoughts racing through Jane's head. What could have happened with Mr. Hunter? He seemed a fair and mild-mannered teacher and had never been known to raise his hand to a child.

As they reached Bower Lane and Jane prepared to deliver Jimmy to his house at No. 52, he pulled back, reluctant to enter.

"I dursn't go in. I think Pa's home. Jane, please let me go into your house. Please Jane. Please."

Silently Jane led him into their house and through to the kitchen. No one was home yet. She fetched a basin of water and a cloth and began to mop Jimmy's face which was starting to puff up. He had a cut on his forehead. His upper lip was also bleeding.

"Won't they wonder where you are?" asked Jane, looking at the kitchen clock. It was just past six o'clock and the other girls would be home soon.

"Yes. Please could you fetch Ma, but don't let on to Pa. He'll be going on shift just now. I don't want him to know."

Jane looked cautiously through the front parlour window and was relieved to see her sisters coming down the street, and at the same time, Mr. Leighton leaving for his evening shift at the Glebe.

Emma was the first to size up the situation. "Fetch Mrs. Leighton," she ordered. "Who did this to you?" She asked as she took off her shawl and bonnet and rolled up her sleeves.

"He said it was Mr. Hunter," said Jane reluctantly. "But I don't know why."

"He grabbed me here," said Jimmy, still trying to stifle his sobs, and pointing to his genital area. "Then he said I should take my britches off."

"What? In the church hall?" asked Jane, as though it might have been permissible anywhere else.

"No, I were up the tree in the yard," said Jimmy. "He told me to come down. He was nice and all, and then he dragged me behind the bushes. That's when he grabbed me and told me to take m' britches off. He was taking his belt off so I kicked him in the shins. Then he punched me in the face. I ran out and that's when I saw Jane. Thank goodness."

"Where's a Bobbie when you need one?" wailed Annie Leighton, Jimmy's mother, when she was summoned from next door.

"Nay, we've no need of police," said Emma, gently swabbing the fat lip and puffy eyes of the poor boy. She thought it more likely that the burly Dick Leighton, Jimmy's father, might take matters into his own hands if he knew the truth and then the police *would* be involved.

"Don't tell Pa. Please," begged Jimmy. "He'll give me another licking. Like he did when me and the lads took the money from the Poor Box. We only did it for a lark. I was all for giving it back, but

Reggie and Ned said no, and I got blamed for it. He walloped me with his belt and it hurt so bad."

"What are you going to tell him? You ran into a brick wall?" asked Emma.

"You fell out of a tree," suggested his mother and to Emma, "He's always climbing trees."

"I suppose that's as good as anything."

"But it weren't my fault, this time," insisted Jimmy.

Jane did think it unfair that the boy might get punished by his father when he might have been an innocent victim.

Emma was doing some thinking. "I reckon we'll sort this out ourselves. If the police come, they'll likely arrest that teacher. They might even put him in prison."

"And then the whole of Chadderton will hear all about it," said Mrs. Leighton.

All Jimmy could say, over and over, was that he didn't want his father to know what happened. He would get the blame again.

"I'll talk to that popinjay Hunter," said Emma. "If he knows what's good for him, he'll never show his face here again." She deftly attended to the boy's cuts. "There! You'll do," she said after applying some ointment. "Looks like you'll have a shiner for a week or two."

"Your Pa is working night shift for two weeks. You should be able to keep out of his way 'til you're mended," said Mrs. Leighton. To Emma, she sounded just as afraid of her husband as Jimmy was.

Jane was inconsolable. Here was her hero, the one she had always dreamed about. The one who had finally appeared in her life. Was he, in actual fact, the instigator of this beating? Had he truly tried to grab the lad's breeches? This young man was her idol in every way. She was only twelve years old, but she was in love with him. No matter that he had assaulted a young boy. Perhaps it was all a mistake. Jimmy could be making it all up. He had done things like that before.

She heard Emma and Eliza discussing it as she went to bed. "He should go and join his uncle in the army," said Eliza.

"Yes, the East Lancashire Regiment serving in India. Best place for him. He might even get some of his own medicine."

"Don't be so harsh."

"It's no more than what he deserves."

As she lay in bed that night, trying to sleep, Jane remembered, between her sobs, the music she had been to fetch was still sitting on the piano in the church hall. It made her cry even more.

Then she thought about Kate's baby which made her smile and she finally fell asleep.

Chapter Nine

1885 - 1886

A year later, when Jane came home from Mrs. Kendal's shop in the late afternoon, she had something in addition to the usual grocery items of milk, butter and flour. As well as a tin of treacle, a special treat to go on their bread, which Emma said she could get, Jane had purchased a copy of *The Cotton Factory Times*, a local newspaper which had just started publication. Printed in Ashton-under-Lyne, a neighbouring town, the front page announced it was a paper for workers in cotton districts all over the region. A copy was displayed on the notice board outside the shop and Mrs. Kendal had chalked on the slate next to it, "For Cotton Operatives. Put an order in to your newsagent today. Published every Friday."

As soon as Jane reached home and before she had time to open it, Emma snatched it out of her hand. She had heard about this new publication which had been discussed at the Wharf Mill and she was loath for her sisters to read it. Amy was far too interested in it for Emma's liking. In Emma's opinion, it could be inflammatory or even dangerous to take an interest in this press. After all, it was put out by trade unions. It was quite enough to read an ordinary newspaper, but one that was specially aimed at cotton operatives made Emma uncomfortable. She had seen a snatch of news, more like history, which mentioned the 'four-year cotton famine'. Why, oh why, did they have to rake up that awful event? Emma had recollections of that as a young girl in London. At the time it had been widely talked about all over England, but these days people still talked of all the mills that had closed; only a few had remained open in part-time operation. And here was this newspaper recounting the miseries of those dreadful years, when people were standing around on street corners, waiting for the soup kitchens to open, and speculating how long before bales of raw cotton would get through to Liverpool from America. And they all knew if those bales did make it, they would have been contraband for the present time. Then Emma had vivid memories of their family coming north to Lancashire in 1871 when the great cotton empire had recovered and was desperate for workers once more. These days, some folk seemed to have forgotten about the lean times and talked about going on strike for more wages. Many people had such short memories, reflected Emma.

"I bet I could write something for that newspaper," said Amy, who although a quiet girl, frequently commented on workers' conversations at the mill, and often made notes about them. She hadn't managed to read the *Cotton Factory Times* yet, as Emma was still monopolizing the precious copy.

Nothing escaped Emma's scrutiny and she often wondered what Amy was writing about apart from the Latin words and phrases she had been learning. While the others were reading or sewing, Amy preferred scribbling something in that little notebook of hers. Sometimes she showed what she had written to Jane, who also had a habit of writing things, mostly her weekly epistle to her father, or so Emma thought. For all she knew, Jane could have been writing to the Man in the Moon. Amy also had her nose in the Latin book a great deal, still being coached by Mr. Burgess. Emma wondered if Amy was turning into a "blue stocking", albeit she was a mill worker. As everyone knew, there was no need for Latin at the mill but Emma knew Amy hankered after going to college. Would it come to anything? Emma did not want to bolster Amy's hopes too much, but it was a lofty goal to aspire to. And then there was Alice, also often immersed in a book, sometimes reading out loud.

But another thought occurred to Emma. It had been almost a year since Giles Hunter had left Chadderton and Jane, now aged thirteen, was working full time at the Glebe Mill. The music lessons had stopped although Jane still played the harmonium most evenings.

"It's about time you were taking piano lessons again," said Emma. "I saw Miss Partridge the other day, and she said you were too advanced for her to teach and we should find you a proper teacher."

"I would love that more than anything in the world," said Jane.

"Pa said you must continue," said Emma, who was most impressed that their father set such store by music lessons. It was no secret, of course, that Jane was his favourite. "You'll have to go to that teacher we heard about."

Having decreed that, Emma immediately set about walking up to Oldham with Jane the very next Saturday afternoon. They visited, by appointment, a piano teacher with a high reputation, a Miss Lamont, recommended by Mr. Burgess who had made her acquaintance since his appointment to the Blue Coat School. She was highly esteemed and taught music at the school, the only woman to do so.

"From now on, you can't spend all Saturday afternoons at Kate's," Emma said. "As soon as you come home from the mill, you'll have to walk up to Oldham for your music lesson."

Jane knew there was no option. She loved her Saturday afternoons with Kate and little Charlie, but she also loved her music and knew she would not improve without further help. It was a pity she had to give up one for the other, but as Kate and Nathaniel would be paying for the lessons she would not quibble. She might still have time to call at Kate's before she walked home to do her Saturday afternoon chores set by Emma.

She had other things, more important, to think about. Miss Lamont, the new piano teacher, was a hard task master. She expected a lot of Jane, who found there was almost too much on her plate with all the scales, exercises and arpeggios, which she had never done before. Neither Mr. Hunter, nor Miss Partridge before that, had taught this way.

"This is classical study," explained Miss Lamont. Only when Jane was getting adept at these new exercises on the piano, exercises which she found difficult to execute on the slower, ponderous harmonium at home, was she allowed to progress to some Bach. Then there was that little Beethoven tune which she had first heard at school played by May Birtwistle. She now knew it was called "Für Elise", which she could soon pronounce perfectly and play proficiently.

After a few months, Jane was beginning to feel like Amy and Alice, imprisoned at the mill. There was not much outlet for her talents. She and Alice discussed this out of the hearing of everyone else who considered they should be contented with their lot.

But salvation was at hand. In the spring, Kate came with the news that Mrs. Goodacre was planning a musical soirée. Miss Lamont had been invited to play, but because she was already engaged at the Blue Coat School for that evening, she had highly recommended one of her pupils, Miss Jane Kershaw. Mrs. Goodacre was at first sceptical about this arrangement, but was assured by her daughter-in-law, Kate, that Jane was now no novice on the piano and would impress the guests at the evening entertainment.

"This will kill two birds with one stone," said Emma proudly. "Jane can show off her playing, and Mrs. Goodacre can show off her new piano to Councillor and Mrs. Nuttall."

At the evening's entertainment, at Rushbank, Mr. Nuttall and Mr. Goodacre senior puffed at their pipes and discussed their stocks in the Suez Canal Company. The younger Mr. Goodacre put down the latest issue of *Punch* to listen more attentively to his young sister-in-law. The ladies, including Nathaniel's sister, Deborah, sat closer to the piano and watched every move of the pianist. When Jane ran out of tunes to play, she offered the services of Mary-Rose, who sang the Schubert song, the one Jane had heard for the first time three years before, sung by Annie Birtwistle. They all thought "Who is Sylvia" entrancing. Then when all was quiet and expectant, Mary-Rose whispered something to the unofficial Master of Ceremonies, who appeared to be Jane. Jane nodded and introduced the other twin, Mary-Anne, who along with Mary-Rose sang the two-part madrigal "On the Plains".

"You could hardly have better entertainment if you went to the Theatre Royal in Manchester," declared Mrs. Nuttall as she sipped her blackcurrant cordial.

This was a presumptuous statement, in Mrs. Goodacre's opinion, as to her certain knowledge Mrs. Nuttall had never set foot in the Theatre Royal, or any other theatre for that matter. Still, she knew what the councillor's wife meant; the sentiments were those of everyone.

But that was not the finish. There was one member of the assembly who must be heard, and seeing the reception of the entertainment going down so well, Jane wasted no time in introducing her other sister, Alice, who although not a musician, was an expert at reciting poetry. Never one to miss an opportunity, Alice had something at the ready, just in case.

"The Boy Stood on the Burning Deck," she began. There was a rustle among the men and Alice thought she detected a look of boredom on Mr. Nuttall's face. She quickly changed her mind. "Would you prefer to hear something by Wordsworth?"

"If it isn't too long," said Mrs. Goodacre, who had heard about Alice's lengthy recitals.

"This is a poem by William Wordsworth, written after a visit to Scotland with his sister in 1803." She began, her eyes fixed on the highest point in the Goodacre drawing room: the newest and most up-to-date ceiling gas light.

"The Solitary Reaper . . .

Behold her single in the field,
Yon solitary Highland lass!
Reaping and singing by herself;
Stop here, or gently pass!
Alone, she cuts and binds the grain
And sings a melancholy strain;
O, listen! For the Vale profound
Is overflowing with the sound.

No Nightingale did ever chaunt
More welcome notes to weary bands
Of travellers in some shady haunt,
Among Arabian sands;
A voice so thrilling ne'er was heard
In spring-time from the Cuckoo-bird
Breaking the silence of the seas
Among the furthest Hebrides.

Will no one tell me what she sings? —
Perhaps the plaintive numbers flow
For old, unhappy, far-off things,
And battles long ago;
Or is it some humble lay,
Familiar matter of today?
Some natural sorrows, loss, or pain,
That has been, and may be again?

Whate'er the theme, the Maiden sang
As if her song could have no ending;
I saw her singing at her work,
And o'er the sickle bending; —

I listened motionless and still,
And, as I mounted up the hill,
The music in my heart I bore,
Long after it was heard no more."

The applause was short and polite as Alice came to the end and lowered her eyes, bowing solemnly to her audience. Jane had not heard this before and was, as usual, impressed with her sister's lyrical rendition. She could already imagine it transposed into a song with a piano accompaniment.

The evening was a huge success. Mrs. Goodacre was beginning to think that her son had married into a remarkably gifted family. She must do this again, and invite more people next time.

But this performance had gone to Jane's head. Emma had been afraid that her youngest sister might have delusions of grandeur. She was right. Jane announced to the family as they were going to bed, "I want to be famous."

"So do I," said Alice.

"The thing you'll be famous for is if you let someone see you in those curl papers," said Emma. who wondered why Alice bothered to try and curl her hair when it was a handsome red and shone like those altar cloths in the church. But Alice could not be told to do anything. Emma knew Alice would do as she pleased, famous or not, and Jane was beginning to be rather like that too.

§

Jane knew Alice was like her, discontented with their daily work at the mill as they made their way there one fine summer morning. Jane knew Amy, in between them, also hated the mill, but she did not go on about it the way Alice did. Jane and Amy walked sedately, but Alice was muttering things—sounded like lines from a poem or play—throwing her arms in the air as she went along. Alice was often whimsical and dramatic and even resentful, having to go day in and day out to the Glebe where they were ordered around; run here, run there, pick up this, pick up that and all that sweeping and pulling and stacking. They had always known they would work in the mill, just like Emma, Kate, Eliza and the twins, but there was a rebellious side to Alice. Amy was impervious to it but it seemed to be rubbing off on Jane who was also something of a dissenter. Nevertheless, Emma was fairly confident that Jane was still very much under *her* influence.

Amy was close to Alice in age, although not in temperament, and found her amusing, but also disturbing at times. It was a good thing Alice was not interested in what Amy had been reading in *The Cotton Times* newspaper. It was just like her to become involved in cotton workers' grievances and trade unions, something she knew little about, and she would be up there on the soap box. Alice had always fancied herself as an actress and in Emma's opinion it was becoming an obsession which was worrying. Alice frequently had something droll to say, mostly pertaining to her favourite theme. "The stage is the thing" was one of her pet sayings, or "All the world's a stage". Alice loved quoting from Shakespeare. Miss Partridge had often spoken about the 16th century bard and the present well-known actress, Ellen Terry, who was famous for appearing in Shakespeare plays. Also the actress, Lillie Langtry. Miss Partridge told Alice that she had seen this strikingly handsome woman in the play "She Stoops To Conquer" when she was in London a few years back. Alice was so impressed and so very envious. And she had read in the newspaper that Lillie Langtry was known to be a friend of Oscar Wilde, the Irish poet. Some sources said she was probably more than just a friend! All so fascinating and all too much for Alice who could not get the stage out of her head.

"A chaste and sober life alongside a poetic spirit" was what Miss Partridge advocated for Alice when she complained about the mill. Miss Partridge had lent Oscar Wilde's book of poems to Alice. She had also read the poem by William Blake, of the dark satanic mills. She knew what he was talking about only too well: the factories where human beings were forced to work on diabolical machines. Machines capable of killing them. She hated the mill and she knew Jane and Amy did too.

One evening after Alice finished an hour-long enactment, Emma said, "Alice we're sick to death of your speeches. We don't want to hear any more about the theatre or high-falutin actors. You work in the mill. That's where you'll stay. And don't you forget it."

Alice crossed her arms. "Not be on the stage? I'd rather stop breathing. As Shakespeare said . . ."

She was interrupted by Emma. "If you keep harping on about him, I swear I will . . ." She brandished the rolling pin. "Heavens! Don't you ever get tired of listening to your own voice?"

Alice shrugged and walked away.

"What about those apples you're supposed to be peeling?" Emma called after her.

Alice swept her shawl off the coat stand.

Emma continued, hands clenched in her apron pocket. "You're cursed with ambition, Alice. You and Jane, both. You both have delusions about piano playing and acting. I should never have let you go to Mrs. Goodacre's musical evening."

Alice opened the front door. "It's too late now, isn't it?"

"Where are you going? You can't just march off!"

"Oh, yes I can. I'm going to the library if you must know, where it's quiet," Alice flung back at her.

The door closed and she was gone.

§

Alice sat at the long table at the library. She angled her book away from the other patrons so they could not see the title: *East Lynne*. She might ask Miss Partridge, when she saw her next, if this novel was still considered as risqué as it had been in 1861. Miss Partridge would know. She was a bookworm extraordinaire. But a novel like this might seem shocking to her.

Alice read of how the main character, Lady Isabel, leaves her husband and infant children for an aristocratic rake of a man. Once abroad, she realizes he has no intention of marrying her, even though she has given birth to his illegitimate child. He soon cruelly deserts her. Certainly Emma would strongly disapprove of this story.

She wondered what Miss Partridge thought about it.

Miss Amelia Partridge, one of the four teachers at Christ Church School, was aptly named, for she herself was rather birdlike. But the name "Partridge", a game bird, similar in size to a grouse or pheasant, could hardly describe Miss Amelia. Alice did not know a great deal about the sport that upper classes indulged in, of shooting prize birds up on the moors for the fun of it and sometimes for the pot, but Miss Partridge definitely did not fall into that category. She came more into the class of a small bird, such as a sparrow or a finch, birds given to flitting here and there with a lot of chirping. Or perhaps she was more like a tropical bird, a parakeet or a canary or a budgerigar, birds kept by rich people in a cage in a conservatory. Miss Partridge cooed and preened her "feathers" – dresses, always of the colourful, frilly variety – and she was often tying and re-arranging various flounces and ribbons. On the whole, one could say Miss Amelia was an attractive woman, but so far, her looks had not caught her a husband, and now they were rapidly fading. She had, however, a quaint and delicious humour and the monthly meetings of the Literary Club at the Lyceum were entertaining when she was present, even though the stated program had offered little to her liking. Alice, Amy and Jane attended these evenings and Emma felt inclined to go herself at times, mostly in order to avoid the detailed commentary by Alice on her return. Emma also wanted to verify for herself exactly what took place.

Alice would have to wait for Miss Partridge's opinion of the book and she would also have to wait until next week on her next visit to the library to see what happened to the ill-fated Lady Isabel.

§

"Time to go to the Lyceum," said Alice one warm summer evening. "It's to be a drama this time."

"A drama? You mean a play?" Emma was immediately suspicious. In her opinion, nothing that took place on a stage could be considered worthwhile or even legitimate.

"There's bound to be something by Tennyson first," said Alice, whose favourite at that time was the Poet Laureate. "And then we're having an excerpt from a play, probably a bit of Shakespeare." Alice could hardly wait to get there. Jane had asked to go too, and so had Amy, although she was not normally interested in drama.

"Archie will be there," said Alice, hoping that Emma would consider this a good thing. Even though Archie Hawkins did not, in the same sense as Alice, work at the mill, he was connected through his book-keeping services.

"Birds of a feather," muttered Emma. "Just make sure you stay close to Miss Partridge."

Alice smiled. Certainly, Miss Partridge was a bird she was going to stay close to.

Archie met them at Hollinwood station where they caught the train to Oldham. He had some startling and exciting news for Alice, out of the hearing of Miss Partridge.

"I'm going to London," he whispered. "When I was in Manchester I met this actor fellow, and he says there are more theatres in London than there are mills here and they're always looking for new, young actors. There are plays galore being performed every night and some afternoons. It's a sure bet, this fellow says, and the pay is good. And it's not like it used to be; it's real respectable now, a proper profession."

That said it all as far as Alice was concerned, and for once, she was preoccupied and could not join in the lively conversation at intermission. She could hardly concentrate on the second half of the proceedings of the Literary Club. On the way home, she placed her penetrating look on Archie, pleading silently for him not to say a word in front of Miss Partridge. Alice knew Miss Partridge, so sensible and level-headed—she was a teacher, after all—would not approve of a venture the likes of which Archie had proposed, though to Alice it sounded like a veritable treasure trove waiting to be explored. And everyone knew the streets of London were paved with gold.

§

Alice bided her time before she made her announcement. A few days later after more cloak-and-dagger discussions with Archie, she let the bombshell drop.

"I'm going to London," she proclaimed to her six sisters. There was no point in beating about the bush. "I've given my notice at Glebe."

"You've what?" asked Emma. There was nothing wrong with her hearing but she needed to collect her senses.

"And I'm going tonight," continued Alice. "With Archie. We're getting the night train."

Jane could not believe what she was hearing and looked at Emma closely to see how this daring proclamation was being received. She could tell, for once, Emma was lost for words, but she wasn't sure whether it was anger or distress that caused her oldest sister to try and hide the tears she brushed away as she surveyed the unruly girl who only came up to her shoulder. Alice stared resolutely back, throwing a lock of red hair over her shoulder to emphasize her defiance.

At length, Emma found her tongue. "You're not old enough – you haven't even started putting your hair up yet."

"I'm nearly seventeen. And I'll put my hair up when I'm ready."

"Well, don't be looking to me for money."

At this point, Alice was not above a little begging, although still defiant. "You could give me last week's wages as I've not been here a full week."

Emma reached into the tin on the mantelpiece and slapped a few coins on the table. "See if that will pay your train fare!"

Alice scooped up the coins and put them in her pocket. "Archie's got money for the train. This'll buy us some food."

"Does he want to wed you? Is that it?"

"Nothing like that. We're just friends. We're actors. We're going on the stage."

"I never heard such nonsense in all my life. They'll never take you back at the mill, leaving all of a sudden like that."

"I'll never go back to the mill," said Alice. "If it was the last job in the world, I'd never go back."

Emma almost added, "And don't come back here either, you've really burned your bridges this time." But instead she said, "Wait till Pa hears about this."

But Alice was waiting for nothing. By the time Pa heard about this she would be far away.

Chapter Ten

1886

Jane couldn't sleep that night. On the one hand, she was filled with admiration for Alice, going off to London, just like that. On the other, she was confused and worried about her sister's decision. True, Alice had escaped the mill, which was what Jane desperately wanted to do, but Alice had also, at the same time, forsaken her home, and that was definitely not in Jane's scheme of things, unless of course, she was going to Birkenhead. She marvelled at her sister's bravery but knew she could never disobey Emma the way Alice had done.

Emma was distraught, more so than anyone else in the family, much to her own surprise. She had almost lost her self-control but she would never let the rest of the family see how Alice's waywardness had affected her. There was no one she could to turn to; Kate who had formerly been her help and confidante was now otherwise occupied in her role as wife and mother and living in Oldham. And as for her father; he would probably just shrug his shoulders and would certainly not understand Emma's matriarchal lamentations. She must face this alone. She had failed in keeping her family together. Recklessness she had always abhorred. It was something that could never be said about Emma and the rest of the girls, but certainly Alice now came into this category. Emma wondered where on earth Alice had got her outlandish ideas. She had certainly been born in London but transported to Lancashire when she was only three years old. She was a Northerner, not a Londoner. Emma herself had certainly never questioned the family coming north when she was about thirteen; except she remembered her mother saying a few times that they should have stayed in London. The older girls all quickly became employed in the local mills but then, nothing else was right. Ma had begun to suffer poor health after a few years and then, so had young Jane who was the only girl to be born in Lancashire. As Pa was a ship's carpenter he had had no option but to go to Birkenhead for work and he hardly ever came home. But, Emma also remembered, they had been getting poorer every day in London. "There was nowt for us in London and then we heard all about the cotton mills in Lancashire," she affirmed to herself. "People said it was like finding treasure up there." And so it had been, for a while.

And now this. Emma's protracted efforts to divert Alice away from her obsession with the stage had come to naught. Maybe she should tighten the reigns but she feared it would be like closing the stable door after the horse had bolted. So now, the only one she had worries about was Jane; but Emma knew Jane would be a pale imitation of Alice the rebel, and although Jane had tried to stand up to her oldest sister many times, Emma was also aware that Jane would do nothing to upset her father.

The only consolation for Emma was that Alice, so small and underdeveloped, was unlikely to get into trouble romantically and she was well able to stand up for herself in most situations. Nevertheless, she was worried about Alice in London, a city where she had been born but knew nothing about.

She was cheered up somewhat by the progress the twins seemed to be making in the area of suitors. Mary-Rose and Mary-Ann were now almost twenty and both had young men who were attentive and had come calling, with Emma's permission, of course. These potential husbands, Ben Huddleston and his pal, Davey Clothier, were new to the area and had come from Manchester to join Ben's uncle in his haulage business. Because Uncle William Huddleston was a staunch church-goer, both young men had started attending Christ Church with him on a Sunday. Of course, they were immediately roped into the choir since they were young and could hold a note, according to Mr. Birtwistle, the organist. It was only natural that they should become friendly with the twins who, along with Mr. Birtwistle's own two daughters, May and Annie, were the main strength of the sopranos in the choir. Emma certainly knew she had no worries concerning the twins, but in spite of her efforts not to, was constantly wondering about Alice and how she was faring in far-away London.

Her mind was relieved of this worrisome matter when her father came home a few weeks later. He was not alone.

§

When Charles Kershaw arrived home in August, accompanied by a fresh-faced young man, he was mildly shocked, but not surprised, that his third from youngest daughter had absconded to take up acting. Jane had had implicit instructions from Emma not to divulge this awful news to her father in her weekly letter.

"That's our Alice. Leave her be. Don't be going off looking for her. If that's what she wants, so be it. She'll find the error of her ways soon enough, Believe you me! Acting . . . Huh . . . Tomfoolery!" That echoed Emma's philosophy.

Pa had not come home since early spring. Ships were being built in record numbers and he was progressing well, now a senior foreman, so there was not much time to visit his family who, as usual, seemed to be doing all right without him. On this occasion, however, there was machinery shut-down for a few days and Charles Kershaw brought a stranger with him as an overnight guest.

"He's a good fellow, works at the shipyards," he told Emma. "He's had a sad life, lost all his family in that ship launching a few years ago. Remember? I told you about it. I thought it would take his mind off things to meet my girls." He winked at Emma. She knew what he meant all right.

"And I suppose there are no girls in Birkenhead he could meet?"

"You suppose right, not at Mrs. Kelly's. This is Robbie Cameron," said Pa, ushering in the young man, who, showing his good manners, immediately removed his cap, a sort the girls had never seen before. Pa told them later it was a Scottish 'bonnet', a tam-o'shanter. He was tall, about twenty-four years old with curly reddish hair, fair-skin and ruddy cheeks. He looked strong and healthy, and was extremely polite and respectful. Emma immediately felt sorry for him, as he had obviously felt the need to leave Scotland to come and work further south after the disaster had occurred.

Emma remembered Pa telling them about that tragedy. Up in Glasgow it was, about three years before, when the *S.S. Daphne* was being launched. Something had gone terribly wrong; the port anchors had failed to stop the ship's progress; strong currents had caused it to keel over just as it left the dock's slipway on the Clyde. Right there, in front of hundreds of horrified spectators, the ship immediately sank in the deep waters. One hundred and twenty-three lives were lost. Seventy had been saved, but unfortunately they did not include the father and brothers of this young man.

"Robbie and his three brothers were on the ship, waiting to get to work as soon as she was afloat," their father had explained. "His father was on there too, of course, as he was one of the bigwigs. Robbie was one of the few to make it to shore. After a major inquiry, the shipyard owners were held blameless. Robbie had stayed on with his mother, but she died last year, so he had decided to come on down to Cammell Lairds at Birkenhead."

Cameron bowed formally on introduction and then spoke with a deep, resonant voice, although with a peculiar accent. "Good day to you, ladies. Pleased to make your acquaintance." He seemed somewhat reserved, but gave a hesitant smile to Charles, then shook the hand of each girl as he was introduced, uttering a polite remark to each one.

Jane was the one to speak to him first. "So you're Scotch?" she said, recalling a teacher they used to have at school who had pronounced words in that odd way.

"If you mean, am I from Scotland, then the answer is yes. And, young lady, it's Scottish, not Scotch. Scotch is a drink – whiskey." He was becoming more at home but smiled awkwardly.

Everyone could tell Eliza had made a big impression on Robbie. After tea, he spoke to the most talkative and unreserved of the girls, Jane, but he kept looking in the direction of Eliza once they had all retired to the parlour. Jane, as usual, was asked to play something. She was now tall enough to play the harmonium and work the pedals without assistance. Robbie moved to stand by the harmonium and offered to turn the pages for her. He had a good view of all the girls, but in between his page-turning, his eyes strayed to Eliza.

"My mother used to play, up at the kirk. We had no piano or anything like that at home, but she was canny at the hymns. Everybody said so." He seemed to smile to himself, and then regarded the assembly: Mr. Kershaw puffing at his pipe, the girls, only six of them now, variously occupied; Amy's head in a book; Jane tinkling on the keys and the twins warbling in the background. Robbie found them all charming, but his eyes dwelled a little longer on Eliza, busy with her crochet work. He had heard all about Alice who had gone off to London only a few weeks ago and she not quite seventeen. They all seemed worried about her, but nothing was being done about it, for now.

"Stop worrying about Alice," Mr. Kershaw had said for the umpteenth time to Emma. "You know as well as I, she can look after herself. You mark my words; she'll be home soon enough when the novelty wears off."

Emma had to admit that Alice seemed to be doing all right if she believed what she said in her letters home. But Emma was an expert at reading between the lines and the last letter was not quite so optimistic, or splendid, or so full of news. Did she detect a tiny speck of homesickness in Alice's words?

As they prepared for bed that night, Amy and Jane, whose room was now also occupied by Eliza since Alice's departure, exchanged views of the visitor. The three of them chatted and giggled about Robbie, a guest, a friend of their father, but much younger and, therefore, rather interesting. Jane was full of admiration for the newcomer, good-looking, tall and well-built, rather like a certain school teacher she had admired a year ago.

"Robbie the Riveter," said Jane. "He fancies you, Eliza. I can tell by the way he kept looking at you." She glanced sideways at Eliza who seemed oblivious to this remark.

"Don't be ridiculous, Jane. He's only known her a few hours," said Amy recollecting only too well Jane's romantic disposition with regard to anyone who could read music and turn pages at the right time for a keyboard player.

"Pa likes him a lot."

"He brought him here just because he's sorry Robbie lost his family. That's all."

Emma and the twins also exchanged words in the next room.

"Seems a fine young man," said Emma,

Mary-Rose and Mary-Ann both agreed he was, but neither was interested. They were both otherwise occupied with thoughts of Ben Huddleston and his friend, Davey Clothier.

But Robbie, like someone before him, had immediately fallen for the stunning Eliza. Before he and Charles Kershaw left the next morning, he managed to get Jane alone and ask, "Is Eliza spoken for?"

He was encouraged by Jane's vehement shake of the head.

In fact, he was so encouraged, he made his mind up to return as soon as possible and ask Eliza to marry him.

Chapter Eleven

Alice wondered whether she could call herself an actress. She had been in London for five months and had landed a small part in the stage adaptation of the novel *East Lynne*. Being of petite stature, she played the part of a young boy and only appeared in one scene with just two words to say: "Yes, Mama." It was amazing how many different ways you could say "Yes, Mama."

Having read the book by Mrs. Henry Wood several times, which she had not been able to put down, she found the play irksome in spite of its fame as a scandalous Victorian melodrama. It was a wonder to her the theatre filled night after night. But it did.

Accommodation was provided nearby. There was a theatre-owned boarding house for girls and one for boys and never the twain would meet, it seemed. Alice had hardly seen Archie since they arrived, although they had both been employed by the same company. He was certainly never at the theatre. She had looked for him each evening before she walked back to the lodgings but the constant stream of hansom cabs, landaus, and four-wheelers coming and going to the theatre meant she might have missed him. What wages Alice was earning in this play went straight to the mistress of the house. In that respect it was just like being at home, Alice thought, except at home, she could at least ask Emma now and again for some money for herself. Here, it was made quite clear that they were actors 'in embryo' and had to toe the line in respect of behaviour and rules of the house. Alice knew how to behave. They had had it drilled into them by their mother and later by Emma. "Never forget your manners, no matter how you are treated." And no man was ever to touch them anywhere, except on the hand or arm. They had all heard the story of Aunt Clara who, as a young woman, had broken off her engage-ment because her fiancé had playfully grabbed her ankle through the banisters as she was going upstairs. She had eventually given in to his apologies and the engagement had proceeded. But that's how it was. Alice had to admit it all seemed rather extreme, even for those days. But then, Aunt Clara was that kind of person, and Emma had said it was quite right that the engagement had been called off—she would have done the same, not that it was ever likely to happen to her. She was adamant about that. Alice didn't think she would have reacted in quite the same way. After all, it had only been meant as a bit of fun.

But what Alice was experiencing now was far from fun and not what she was used to. An aging thespian, Mother Marishka was the proprietor of the boarding house for girls. Anyone less like a mother Alice could not imagine. A Mrs. Kelly she was not, she reflected ruefully, remembering the jovial, kind and caring landlady in Birkenhead, described fondly many times by Jane. It seemed this hostelry was run strictly for the benefit of the landlady, and she, by all accounts, was a retiree from the stage where her talents, if she had ever possessed any, were no longer required. Alice conceded Mother Marishka's looks might have been good once. One of the girls said she had been a gipsy and with a name like that, it seemed likely. Her hair had been frizzed so much over the years it was almost gone, with just little corkscrews left sprouting here and there from under her lace cap which she invariably wore. But what she lacked in hair, she made up for in colour and volume, unstinting with the rouge as if she were still on stage, and showing a tremendous cleavage that would have made a parson look the other way, not that Mother Marishka ever had anything to do with parsons. Strangely enough, that was something else that Alice was missing—the Sunday church attendance. No one from this house attended church and there was no mention of it. Alice thought Mother Marishka might have attempted to give some semblance of hospitality instead of being so greedy and grudging. And the other thing she wondered about was the lack of evidence of a husband or a "Father" Marishka.

Alice shared a room with eleven other girls. They were not friendly and they kept to themselves, treating Alice like the outsider she was. Didn't she come from somewhere up north, which to them was as foreign as the Steppes of Russia? There were no comforts and no good food except what Mother Marishka kept for herself: the best pieces of meat and the milk before it soured, and the companionship, most nights, of her small flask of gin. Alice compared her cramped and crowded room to the one at home which she had shared with Amy, Jane and, sometimes Eliza. Alice had not appreciated it at the time, but it was sheer luxury compared to what she now had to endure. Still, that is what you had to put up with in order to be an actress, she assured herself.

The current production had come to an end after several months and now, Mr. Downhan Shaw, the company director, needed another boy for their next play. It seemed fortuitous that he once again chose Alice to fit the bill. Unfortunately, when the fledgling actress had to say more than "Yes, Mama," her Lancashire accent came through, loud and clear. Mr. Shaw had said that was definitely not what they wanted and she was coached to improve her dialect. But something strange was happening: since she had come to London, she had noticed a change in her young, immature figure. She thought it could be the different air, or even diet, but Alice at last had the beginnings of some curves, and was beginning to look less like a child and more like a young woman. She had just experienced something all her sisters had been having for a while—that monthly bleeding they all talked about. Now, she was just like the rest of them, but at the moment, she found it not to be a blessing, which announced her entry into womanhood, but a downright inconvenience.

Downham Shaw had also noticed a change in this member of his cast. His young star would not be able to play the role of a boy much longer.

"Our boy is getting titties," he announced to the entire cast. "Better get some corsets on her," he said to the wardrobe mistress.

He might be an actor, and director of the theatre, but in Alice's opinion he was the rudest man she had ever met. She was humiliated by his bellowing when she was sure the whole of London, not just the theatre, heard what he said. She had refused to go on stage that night.

After that she was told she was no longer needed.

"Come back when you've got rid of your Lancashire accent," yelled Mr. Shaw. "Elocution lessons might be a good idea."

Elocution lessons? Her short acting career was now over and so was her stay at the boarding house. When not engaged in a production, girls were not allowed to remain there.

"You've got two shillings and four pence coming to you, my girl, and you can thank me for getting you that. When actors get the sack, usually they get nothing." Mother Marishka shoved the money into Alice's hand as she left with her few belongings packed into her holdall.

Her first thought was to try and find Archie. He could probably help her; find her somewhere to stay, or even get her another job, acting at another theatre. Perhaps he was like her, out of work and wandering the streets of London. For a start, she made for the nearest railway station but as she feared, she did not have nearly enough for the fare up to Manchester and on to Chadderton. But then, she didn't want to go home just yet, in defeat, as it were. Surely something would turn up, if only she could find Archie to help her. She felt so alone and disoriented. She needed some direction.

It was now late December. The weather was turning cold. The stale, warm air of the London streets was being replaced by sharp, gusty winds and the nights were nippy. She knew it was her own fault she had been turned out of the theatre. Was her illustrious theatrical career already over? She didn't miss the scent of the grease-paint; it had made her feel sick, but she had endured it because it hid her freckles. If she had swallowed her pride when Mr. Downham Shaw had humiliated her in front of the whole company, she probably would still have a job, in spite of her accent. Now she noticed the smell of a soap factory and also a leather-tanning factory nearby, all mingling with the smell of rotting debris in the river. She felt nauseated. The foggy, damp air of Chadderton, often chased away by gusts of wind from the Pennines, would be like wine compared to this. At home in Chadderton, if you walked a few minutes in any direction, you could see the mist-shrouded moors. She had walked for over an hour and seen nothing except more derelict buildings, more squalor, and more rude and unfriendly people than she could have believed possible.

She remembered what she had been told at Sunday school: if she prayed, her soul would awaken to a new and nobler life in the spirit world. But did that mean you had to die first? Alice thought she *might* die in London if she didn't get something to eat soon. She had bought one of those Penny Pies, the sort they sold on street corners. It was stale and dry, but it was better than nothing. She began to feel sorry for herself as she remembered Emma's mouth-watering pies and all the other things she had taken for granted at home. She had not set eyes on a bale of cotton since she had left Chadderton. There were plenty of chimneys, though, of all shapes and sizes, but none of them like the ones in Chadderton. As Alice walked on, clutching her warm cloak around her, tears stinging her eyes, she regretted consenting to let the wardrobe mistress cut her long red hair for the part in the play. It was not a good cut and hung unevenly just below her ears. She knew she looked like a street urchin from the shoulders up which did not match the rest of her attire. Her one and only bonnet had disappeared at the theatre so she needed some kind of head attire to hide her shorn hair. She might as well dress as a boy, but then a horrible thought struck her: supposing a debauched young man, or any man, for that matter, should fancy her, as a boy, just as Giles Hunter had fancied Jimmy Leighton? It did not bear thinking about. It did not occur to her that she was far more noticeable and in more danger as she was, a girl, alone, wandering about the streets of London.

She asked herself: "Was it better to die starving in London or coughing in the mill?" And everywhere was crowded, throngs of ne'er-do-wells, brushing against her; depraved citizens with their crazed jokes and so-called camaraderie. Compared to these, Alice thought her family in Chadderton was like royalty. She noticed signs, especially in the shops and markets—holly boughs and mistletoe and colourful ornaments. This caused her to start thinking about Christmas at home, but she firmly put it out of her mind. She had now been away six months. In the first weeks of her arrival in London, she had written to the family using some headed notepaper she had managed to obtain from the theatre. She knew this would impress everyone at home, well, everyone except Emma from whom she had received a stiff, stilted kind of return, just what Alice would have expected, typical of the 'gospel according to Emma'. She had also received a letter from Miss Partridge to whom she had written in glowing terms of her "situation" in London. Miss Partridge must have foreseen what could happen so soon to a budding actress and had reproached Alice for her 'foolhardy and impetuous step, leaving her family so abruptly' and had entreated her to return home 'to seek more orthodox methods and careful preparations for her advent on to the stage, a most precarious career at the best of times'. Alice had been upset at Miss Partridge's views of her actions. She didn't think she had been impetuous. After all, she had considered Archie's proposition for a full three days before leaping into the desirable but unknown world of London and its theatres. Now, as Alice walked on, aimlessly, she knew that Miss Partridge, and Emma were absolutely right. Of course, she would never admit it to them. Never.

Chapter Twelve

December 1886

In Birkenhead, Robbie Cameron felt he had been encouraged, not by the girl he had suddenly fallen in love with in August, but by the opinion of her younger sister who had more or less told him he stood a chance. He started making plans. But first he thought it prudent that he ask his co-worker, the father of the girl in question.

"With your permission, Charlie, I'd like to ask your daughter to be my wife."

"And which one would that be?" was the lackadaisical reply, given as though someone proposed to his daughters every day.

"Eliza, of course. Emma is too old for me. And the twins have gentlemen friends. The others are too young. But do you think Eliza will accept?"

"Well, lad, it's not for me to say."

"I have means - I have a house up in Scotland. If she was agreeable we could go up there. I'm sure I could work at the Stephens' ship-yard again."

"I can't speak for her, lad. But Scotland—I'm not sure she'd like that."

"I'd just as soon stay here, but she'd have to live in Birkenhead if we didn't go up to Scotland. But then, we wouldn't have a house in Birkenhead. And then ... Eliza might want to stay here, with the family." Already, Robbie was thinking it was an impossible hope he had been nurturing. "She might not have me."

"Eh, come on, lad. Faint heart never won fair lady," was the reply. "Ye'll not know if ye never ask."

§

As soon as the family returned from the Christmas morning church service, the tantalizing aroma of the goose, which had been slowly cooking all morning, made them scurry to their tasks. The table was set, finishing touches to the roast potatoes, parsnips, sprouts and bread sauce were carried out by the girls who all had their instructions from Emma.

Robbie contemplated the family at the table. He was sitting opposite Eliza. He smiled across at her, a special smile. She smiled back, but it was just the same smile she had for everyone else. Nothing special about that, he thought. Should he propose a toast at the table, after the Christmas pudding, rum sauce and port, and then announce that he wished to marry Eliza? That was a bit precipitous, he realized. After all, he had only met her once before. He should somehow contrive to get her alone. In a family of this size, it was a difficult task.

Perhaps an afternoon walk, he pondered, as after the remains of the feast had been cleared up, most of the family gravitated to the front parlour where Jane was playing the harmonium and the other girls were singing and dancing.

"Would you care to take a walk?" asked Robbie of the girls, but his eyes were on Eliza. "It's a wintry afternoon, but it's dry and there's a pale sun trying to show itself."

Eliza was the only one to volunteer. Emma made sure of that as she could see the ardent look in Robbie's eyes.

After a few comments on the fine afternoon and by the time they had reached the end of Bower Lane, Robbie launched into his speech, which although rehearsed many times, was not delivered precisely as he had intended.

"Eliza. You are a beautiful girl. I have admired you since the first day I set eyes on you. Would you marry me . . . please?" They stopped walking. Her face was flushed but she looked straight ahead. She tried to say something but no words came out.

At her stunned silence, he continued. "Of course, I'm not expecting an immediate wedding. I'm prepared to wait, but I'm a Scot, and I know what I want." Eliza still did not look at him, but seemed to be gazing into the far distance. At her continued silence, he continued. "I'm much impressed by you, and indeed your whole family. I've never met anyone quite like your Emma—so efficient." He knew he had an ally in her. "And there's the sister I haven't met; the one who ran away to London." He admired Alice before even meeting her. "And your Pa and I get along well."

He had been preparing his proposal during the intervening months since August when he had first set eyes on Eliza. He found his ardour started to quickly cool, however, at the frosty response he received from her.

"Thank you, Robbie, but I can't marry you. I hardly know you. And, you see, I don't . . . love you. It's no use."

It was a short walk back to the house. And a silent one.

How was Robbie to know her heart was set on another? Emma explained to him later about Eliza's long-held infatuation with someone else.

"I'm so embarrassed," said the dejected suitor. "How could I have had the nerve to approach Eliza?" He could not believe he had taken such an impulsive step. He, who was usually so staid and level-headed. But then, love did astonishing things to people.

With a heavy heart, Robbie left the next morning.

"Don't take on so," advised Charles Kershaw on the train to Birkenhead. "You hardly know her. Give her time. She might change her mind. Girls often do, y'know."

§

January 1887

Eliza thought about the proposal Kate had received three years earlier from Mr. Higginbottom. It was just the same sort of thing with this Scotsman. Impossible. And what of Billy Lampson? Eliza fretted yet again. He had never said he loved her. He might have said he was fond of her, and yes, he had looked at her in a certain way, but he had never uttered those magic words 'I love you'. And where was he? He must have finished his apprenticeship by now. She had heard via Mrs. Kendal, his aunt, that Billy had been sent to Ashton-under-Lyne to train with the new, higher pressure boilers. Since the beam engines were being replaced by horizontal engines, and as Chadderton and Oldham had not adopted this new trend, Billy was in Ashton. But it was only a few miles away. Eliza wondered for the hundredth time why she had not heard anything from him. Maybe he had met someone else there. She reflected upon the unfairness of love which, it seemed, could come upon an unsuspecting person at any time, without invitation or will by the recipient. Love could come on suddenly and could leave again just as suddenly. In her case, love had not left; it had played a wicked trick on her, had intended her to love Billy, whether she wanted to or not, had given her no hope that it was reciprocated, but had never ceased to torment her despite other young men at work showing an interest in her. And now this young Scot had asked her to marry him. Was love always one-sided like this? But no, she had seen that was not the case with Kate and Nathaniel. And there were others she knew who, so it seemed in many cases, had married not for love, but for convenience. That would not do for Eliza.

It hardly seemed fair. Love could come and go as it pleased, trifle with some one's feelings, and go on to do the same, again and again.

And yet, she wanted to marry. She had witnessed Kate's happiness, but feared that sort of love was not for her. She was not as fortunate as Kate who had married the man she had long been in love with.

Eliza began to think she would have to be like so many other women; she would marry, not for love, but in the hope that love would eventually develop with someone who loved enough for both of them. However, Robbie's proposal had opened a door that seemed to have been denied her so far. Even though she had given him a resounding no, maybe she should consider it? After all, he was a friend of the family and she did like him. She wondered if that was how love started. She would talk it over with Emma and also with Kate, of course.

§

On a cold January day, when Emma and Eliza came to Kate's home above the tailor's shop, there was a cheerful atmosphere with a grand fire. Emma wondered what they must have done to the chimney to get such dancing flames. It was as good as their kitchen fire at home, but she had long given up on the one in the parlour. Pa had said it was time to call in the chimney sweep, but Emma had insisted it was not necessary.

The object of Emma and Eliza's visit was to discuss the sudden proposal of marriage from Robbie Cameron. Although Eliza had given him a definite refusal, Emma thought it merited further consideration. But for once, Kate did not agree with her.

"It's just like the proposal I had from Mr. Higginbottom." said Kate. "Eliza, you can't possibly accept it. You're not in love with Robbie, in fact you hardly know him."

Eliza nodded. "I knew you'd understand, Kate." Tears came to her eyes. "I will get married one day . . . I hope. But not to him."

"You can't pick and choose," said Emma, her mind briefly resting on the absent Billy. Then she reflected on the bizarre coincidence that two of her sisters had had proposals of marriage they didn't want. Society had always dictated that the heart should not rule your head. Money, yes. Social standing, yes. But affairs of the heart? Never. "You'll likely not get another offer. After all, you're twenty-three, Eliza. It's time you were wed."

Eliza bridled at this. "And what about you, Emma? Why aren't you wed, then? You're nearly twenty-eight."

"Chance would be a fine thing, and I've not been asked," said Emma. "Anyway, I've never had a mind to marry. You know that."

"You follow your heart, Eliza," was Kate's advice, ignoring the exasperated look on Emma's face.

Eliza nodded. "I can't— I won't marry Robbie. Absolutely not!"

§

Kate and Nathaniel were soon going to leave the flat over the tailor's shop and were moving into a new house that had been built next to the Goodacre's at *Rushbank*. It was a smaller version of Caroline and Elijah Goodacre's house, but had all that a happily married young couple would need, especially since Kate was now expecting a little brother or sister for Charlie.

Jane and Amy had enlarged their theories on babies by now.

"It has to do with being married and lying down. Babies will definitely come that way. It doesn't work if you are standing up – not even if you're married," Jane said, having listened to gossip at the mill. She had never plucked up the courage to ask Kate more about this topic. She had often thought it might have helped if they had had brothers. However, their education on the mysteries of conception was about to be expanded again with the arrival of Abigail on their doorstep one evening in late March.

Abigail was beating about the bush, asking to speak to Emma alone. It soon became evident that something serious was amiss.

"Something that should have happened a month ago, hasn't. And again this month. There's no bleeding."

In Emma's limited knowledge, this was a bad sign if you were not married. Some explanations were in order. To her questions, there was no answer, except Abigail's floods of tears.

Emma automatically assumed the role of a parent, knowing Abigail's father was probably unaware of his daughter's activities since they had moved a while ago to Oldham to live with John's sister. She ran the house like a camp for Spartans; it was cold and comfortless because most of her time was spent at the Catholic Church or at the priest's house where she was housekeeper. It was clear to Emma that Aunt Nan would not be one to sympathize with Abigail and her condition.

"Are you going to tell me, or what?" demanded Emma, trying to find out the name of the perpetrator of this dire situation. "You turn up here all of a sudden, saying you're in the family way, and expect me to help you. A bit of explaining wouldn't go amiss."

Abigail's fixed her gaze on the tiled floor. "I had no one else to go to."

"I won't hold me breath, but you need to tell me soon, as there's got to be a wedding."

"No, no," pleaded Abigail. "Not a wedding. Pa wouldn't like it. I went to see Frances up at the Big House, and she told me what to do. Drinking gin will do the trick."

'Tell your Pa, Abigail. Please do. He's so kind and understanding. Look how he bore up when your mother was so brutally . . . er . . ." Emma's voice trailed off.

Abigail shook her head vehemently. "I'm not telling Pa."

Emma studied her closely. Then. "Ah, I see. So, whoever it is can't marry you? That's why you're so against your father finding out! Heavens, don't tell me this wretched man is married already?"

Abigail shrugged. At this Emma pushed away an ungracious thought that Abigail, given her move from one town to another, must have got to know this man quickly.

Abigail still studied the floor. "Gin?" she whispered.

She might as well have said "Gold" for the effect it had on Emma, tossing her head impatiently. She had heard of this kind of remedy before from a girl at the mill, but no one had ever stipulated exactly how much gin was needed, or equally important, how they were to have access to it.

"And even if you knew how much to take—gin—I've heard it doesn't always work. What then? It's probably an old wives' tale." But Emma did not totally reject the proposed remedy, much to the relief of Abigail who cheered up a little with this ray of hope. Emma was obviously of the opinion that getting rid of the baby was an acceptable solution. She knew it was no good approaching her aunt, who, according to Abigail, was much like Emma's Aunt Clara, and would not tolerate such a drastic measure. But mercifully, Aunt Nan had no knowledge of her niece's plight. Not yet.

The gin method did not work. Abigail was back two days later with thanks to Emma who had procured the gin with great difficulty. But Abigail had to report that, unfortunately, the situation was just as bad as ever. "I should have bled and the thing gone away," she said, as if she were referring to an unpleasant caller at the house. With Emma on her side, she didn't seem perturbed at the seriousness of her situation.

"We should know who the father is and ask Parson if he'll get you wed," said Emma, even though earlier it had seemed that the man responsible for Abigail's condition might already be married. But maybe he wasn't.

Abigail looked uncomfortable. This was a resolution she had not envisaged. She blinked and fluttered her wet eyelashes looking round at the six assembled girls who now knew her terrible secret and wondered what was to be done. Abigail seemed to be mulling something over in her mind while Emma glared at her, waiting for an answer, wondering if there was going to be a wedding. It would not be a full, carefully planned wedding like Kate's, but a hurriedly planned one with Abigail in her best, plain blue dress. No orange blossom posies, no bridesmaids. Just a small group in the Church.

"Was it that Bertie fellow you met at the Glebe?" Emma, as usual, was not giving up on her questioning tactics.

"No … No. Not him," Abigail faltered.

But Emma *was* sure of one thing. She would have to talk to Mr. Burgess at the first opportunity. First, though, she would have to get the truth out of Abigail.

"Well, who was it?" Emma persisted.

Abigail fiddled with the tassels on her belt, all the while studying the kitchen tiles, with an occasional glance at Emma who was looking at her as if she were a criminal.

"I couldn't help it," she said in her own self-defence.

"What d'y mean, you couldn't help it? Did he attack you? Did he take advantage of you? D'y mean to tell me you didn't encourage him, whoever it was?"

"It was … Billy Lampson." Abigail bit her lip, knowing what a devastating effect these words would have on one particular member of the assembled girls.

The colour drained from Eliza's face. She could not believe what she was hearing She felt faint and leaned against Jane. This was too, too painful. Seeing how upset Eliza was, Emma ushered Abigail out, hoping it was yet another of her lies.

"There will have to be a 'marriage of necessity'," said Emma, once they were out of the room. "I shall have to go and talk to your Pa, maybe tomorrow."

Abigail looked defiant, but knew there was no stopping Emma in what she intended to do.

Chapter Thirteen

London – December 1886

Alice had begun to dislike London when she was forced to leave the shelter of the boarding house. No amount of wheedling with Mother Marishka would have allowed her to stay. One final time, she made her way back to the theatre in the hope of seeing Archie, but as usual there was no sign of him and no one seemed to have heard of him.

She had almost decided little was to be gained searching for Archie. He had obviously found his own niche in London. Or he could be just like her, wandering around, forlorn and lost in the labyrinth of a strange and vast city. She wished she had Jane with her. She was the one Alice missed the most. Jane with her piano playing would have been a passport to all sorts of opportunities in this vast metropolis.

She eventually made her way to the boys' hostel, which had been strictly out of bounds to her whilst residing with Mother Marishka. She was met with hostile looks but then, suddenly, there was Archie, just coming out of the side entrance.

"Oh, it's you," he said, obviously surprised to see her. "Where've you been hiding all these months?"

"The same place as when you last saw me, at the Young Ladies' Boarding House," she reminded him.

"I've called there several times and that old hag always said you were out and the last time, she told me you'd left," he said. "Thought you'd up and gone home."

"I wish I could," said Alice, reminding herself again how untrustworthy Mother Marishka was. How could she have told such a lie? So Archie had been seeking her out. That was some consolation. "Where're you been? Haven't set eyes on you for ages."

"I've been working at a music hall. I'm now a conjuror's assistant, the art of illusion, you know."

Alice was not quite sure if that was a step in the right direction career-wise but at least he seemed to be faring better than she had done at the theatre that had so callously cut her off.

"I had to leave that boarding house today, and I need somewhere to stay," she told him, thinking that the small amount of money she had received from Mother Marishka would only allow for one or two night's accommodation in the cheapest kind of hostelry. Archie looked well-to-do, wearing a fashionable jacket. His light brown hair, curling over his collar, fluffed in the stale London breeze. It was evident he did not follow the fashion of using Macassar oil. He seemed confident, self-assured.

"There's a place called Dr. Barnardo's I've been hearing about from a lad here. They look after waifs and strays at a place in Stepney, a huge house—lots of homeless boys and girls." He realized that she didn't fit into this category, being dressed reasonably well and knowing she had a home, although over two hundred miles away. "You could try that until something else comes up." He had a certain bravado which Alice had never noticed before; it was something common in theatre folk. But he seemed genuine in his efforts to help, unlike most people she had met in London.

"If you know the way, perhaps you could show me where this place is."

He took her bag and they set off through the streets of London, from the affluence of the London theatre district towards the East End, where ragamuffins roamed, and unkempt people outnumbered the ones decently dressed. They passed enormous, dirty warehouses, squalid homes and taverns, various merchants, some behind grimy shop windows, some selling directly from a barrow or a cart.

"How much further is this place?" asked Alice after they had walked for nearly an hour. She was hungry. Her boots, long in need of soling and heeling, and which had become too small, were now hurting.

"I told you. Dr. Barnardo's is in Stepney," said Archie, changing the hefty bag from one arm to the other. "I reckon it'll be another twenty minutes or so. We'll stop for a bite if you like." He suspected she didn't have any money, unaware of the two shillings she had been given by the landlady.

Alice trudged bravely on until they stopped at a tavern where Archie paid for a hunk of bread and some cheese to share, a mug of ale for himself and some milk for her. She ate and drank silently, hardly believing she had come to this state of affairs. They resumed their trek into the East End. Alice was grateful she was not alone. But for all she knew, she might yet be thankful for nothing. Where on earth was Archie taking her?

"Here, I told you, didn't I?" said Archie as they stopped outside number 10 Stepney Causeway, a large, rather shabby grey house. "I reckon this is it. I'll wait for you here."

After two timid knocks, the door was opened by a stern-looking woman wearing what looked like a nurse's uniform.

The woman noted Alice's well-worn, but good quality cloak, a hand-me-down from Emma, which certainly did not broadcast the fact that she was a waif or stray. If she hadn't been dressed in a rather stylish gown of cream and brown calico, the Matron could almost have taken her for a boy with that kind of hair cut.

"I'm the Matron here," said the woman, in answer to Alice's query. "Step in for a minute. How old are you?" She felt certain that Alice was older than she looked. "We only take girls up to fourteen, and in any case, this house is just for boys. Our girls are at Barkingside."

"I'm a bit more than fourteen," admitted Alice, biting her lip. What a stupid idea it was to allow Archie to bring her here. He obviously knew very little about Barnardo's.

"How old are you?" repeated the Matron. "And where are you from?"

"I'm seventeen and I'm from Lancashire. I came down here to be on the stage," Alice stated grandly, but soon faltered. "I *was* in a play . . . at Drury Lane Theatre . . . "

The Matron looked rather dubious. "The stage? Hmm. For one so young and far from home." She didn't need to elaborate.

"But I was born in London," Alice told her. "I have relatives here."

"If you have any relatives at all in London, I advise you to seek them out," was the Matron's advice. Alice told her of a brother, Algy, she had seen only twice since she was five years old, and Aunt Clara, that old battle-axe who at times was irritating and sometimes unbearable, who had stayed with them twice and laid down the law. In truth, Alice did not want to seek out her brother or Aunt Clara and she had to confess, she had no idea of either's address.

'If you don't know where they live, can't you contact those at home for the address?" asked the Matron.

Alice had no intention of writing home for Aunt Clara's or Algy's address. Emma was the last person who should know Alice had nowhere to stay.

"Nevertheless, they are your kith and kin and should be able to help you." insisted the Matron, surveying Alice's clipped hair, which was straggly and uneven and was neither fitting for a boy or girl. "But we must find you a bonnet. You can't go about in that state. What would your Aunt say? You certainly must find her or your brother right away. But you have no address for them?"

"All I know is my brother works at the post office."

"Which post office?"

"The big one, I think."

"You mean the General Post Office?"

"I suppose so." Alice really had no idea.

"Then the Good Lord has a refuge for you. You must find your brother for he will surely not turn his sister away, even though he has not seen you for such a long time."

"I last saw him and his wife at my sister's wedding a few years ago, but still, I don't know him very well."

"Nevertheless, the Lord is pointing you in that direction," stated the Matron emphatically. "Surely he will provide for you? But first, you must have something to put on your head. We don't have any girl's clothes here, but sometimes people drop things off and I'll see what we have."

Alice looked gloomily around her whilst the Matron left, in search of something appropriate. She knew she needed to look more respectable and that she looked neither woman, nor child. She wanted to be on her way and her usual vivid imagination told her this was not a place where she might like to stay. This was supposed to be a haven for homeless boys. The girls' home might be just as cheerless. She could hear no sounds that would signify that there were any young people about. She left the large barn-like Barnardo home, wearing a simple grey bonnet and with a half-hearted intention to take the advice she had been given.

"It's only half past four," were the Matron's final words. "If you go straight away to the General Post Office, it should still be open, and you'll be able to find your brother." To Alice's amazement, a shilling was pressed into her hand from the woman who must have had a kind heart in spite of her austere manner. "Take a hackney cab and you'll get there in no time."

"Wouldn't they let you stay?" On the pavement outside, Archie pushed himself away from the railings, picked up Alice's bag and fell into step beside her.

"Well, it's like this. They don't take girls here, and I'm too old anyhow. That woman in there said I'm not really homeless. I have a home, but it's a long way off so I'm to find my relations here in London."

"And where might they be?"

"I don't know where they live, but I know my brother works at the post office."

"You mean the General Post Office? That huge building on St. Martin's-le-Grand?"

"You know where it is?"

"I might, if that's where you really want to go."

"Well, I suppose I do. I haven't much choice."

She hailed a passing cab and jumped in while he was pushing her bag in beside her, uttering words about when he might see her again. "Come and see me at the Variety Theatre one night," he yelled as the cab pulled away. Alice paid no heed. She was too busy worrying about what she was going to say to her brother. If she found him.

§

The cab dropped her off outside an imposing building. Alice knew there were other post offices in London, but this must be the main one. Hadn't Algy said he worked there when he came to their mother's funeral four years ago?

The General Post Office, where sorting and delivering was done, along with mail guards, an armoury, and administration facilities was a huge, grand structure. And so it should be, in Alice's opinion; it was the residence of the Post Master General and the Royal Mail. It looked like one of those Greek buildings she had seen in Amy's Book of the World, and she was impressed, having only ever seen the insignificant post office in Oldham and the red pillar boxes dotted about the countryside and on street corners. Upon enquiring for her brother, Mr. Algernon Kershaw, she was told that there were hundreds of people working there. "Go and see Miss Hardcastle, secretary to the Post Master General."

There was a clatter of typewriters all through the hallway as she was directed to Miss Hardcastle who turned out to be most helpful. Maybe she wasn't from round here, thought Alice.

"Let me see, now …. Mr. Kershaw." Miss Hardcastle ran her finger down a list of names in a ledger. "Here it is. He's now in charge of the new sorting machines."

At last Alice seemed to be getting somewhere. But she was a little apprehensive about meeting her brother. She had hardly spoken to him at their mother's funeral. He probably thought she was still a little girl.

§

Algy was aloof, for a brother, thought Alice. But then, as they had not grown up together, it was hardly unexpected. He was surprised, but not overjoyed, to see his sister. He could hardly believe the story she told him, how she had left home suddenly to come to the great city of London with such a nebulous ambition as acting.

"I suppose you'd best come home with me," he had said grudgingly. "Lucy won't mind, just for a day or two. But you'll have to go back home as soon as possible. You should never have left in the first place."

But all Alice could think of was that if she did return to Chadderton, the only avenue open to her would be the mill. She had vowed never to work there again, and she meant to stick to this even though she knew Emma would insist otherwise.

Somewhat annoyed at having a young sister suddenly foisted upon him, Algy knew he would have to deal with the situation in a brotherly way, otherwise he would have to deal with another sister. Even though far away, Emma was someone to be reckoned with and

Algy was well aware of this. Even though brotherly love was not high on his agenda, he reluctantly welcomed Alice but it was mostly in deference to his dead mother who had implored him to go to Lancashire with the rest of the family when he was fourteen. He had refused to leave London, with no feeling for his anguished mother, and alienating his father, but a job at the Post Office had seemed to him, at the time, better than one in the cotton industry. It still did.

Algy had just had a brilliant idea seeing Amy's reluctance to go back to Chadderton. "You could be a nursemaid to our little Sarah, and then Lucy can get a job, like she used to have before we had the baby. Lucy used to work at a sub-post office."

Alice mulled this over. She supposed being a nursemaid to her little niece was better than working at the mill. But you could hardly call it a career. Besides, she knew she wouldn't get paid, just her room and board would be provided, and she would be tied down day and night to that bairn. Nevertheless, it would give her time to take stock of her situation, maybe even make some enquiries at another theatre.

Algy's wife saw in Alice a way of salvation—an escape from a life of boredom. But little did Lucy know Alice was no candidate for this kind of occupation. However, an arrangement was made—a bargain struck. Four-year-old Sarah was to be the charge of her seventeen-year-old aunt, Alice, who could see that the frosty relationship between her and Lucy was likely to thaw to some extent. At least, this job, if you could call it that, would mean she wouldn't have to face those at home and it would give her time to forget the wounds dealt to her pride. She was fascinated by her brother and his wife with their London ways and their accent which she worked hard to imitate. The spirit of the actress had not been totally knocked out of her. She recalled painfully the cutting words of Downham Shaw at the theatre. Elocution lessons indeed!

Chapter Fourteen

January 1887

At the first opportunity, after she finished work at the Wharf Mill, Emma walked to Abigail's aunt's home where the Burgesses now lived. She was racking her brains to determine how to resolve Abigail's dire situation and, more importantly, how to gently break the news to Mr. Burgess. She knew the reticent, even-tempered man would be extremely upset.

She walked quickly as she left the mill, rehearsing the words she would use, arriving at the house about half past six. She had hoped to find Abigail and Mr. Burgess home, but to her dismay the only person there was the aunt, Mrs. Smythe. Emma had never met her before but she fitted Abigail's brief description: cold and distant.

"My brother is detained at the Blue Coat School; he may be late home," was her reply to Emma's inquiry. "Abigail's not back from the mill yet, but that's nothing unusual. That girl's never home." There was a pause while Emma was kept on the doorstep. "She said she was at your house yesterday." The aunt raised her eyebrows, obviously wanting some confirmation from Emma. She was evidently used to some kind of subterfuge from her niece and didn't believe what she had been told.

"She certainly was at our house yesterday, but I was rather hoping to see Mr. Burgess and Abigail together," said Emma not wanting to divulge the nature of her business to the taciturn aunt. From the way she spoke, she obviously knew nothing of Abigail's affairs, much less her condition, and Emma certainly could not discuss the matter at hand without the presence of Abigail or her father.

"Seems she spends more time at your house than here, with what-ever she finds to do there."

So that was it—innocent visits to Bower Lane had been given as excuses for Abigail's absence from the dismal place she was now expected to call home. Emma could hardly blame her. Likely Abigail had been telling her aunt she had been at the Kershaw's when, in fact, she had been on other escapades, resulting in this pregnancy. But Emma was not surprised at this deviousness. It was typical of Abigail.

It occurred to Emma that Mr. Burgess was due to visit them in two days time for his weekly Latin tutoring for Amy. Could the discussion regarding Abigail wait till then? It might have to. "It doesn't matter," she said. "I'll probably see them on Saturday afternoon."

"If you'll excuse me," said Mrs. Smythe, "I have to go to the priest's house. When I see my brother later this evening, I'll tell him you called."

They left together, the aunt stepping into the house next door where she was the housekeeper. Emma knew it was the house attached to St. Mary's Roman Catholic Church. She didn't doubt for a moment that it was more welcoming than the house they had just left.

The long walk home gave Emma ample time to reflect on the problem. She mentally berated Abigail for her foolhardiness and for her expectation that Emma would resolve matters. It was after seven o'clock when she reached home and as soon as Emma opened the door she nearly collided with Jane who was running downstairs with an armful of towels. The house was in an uproar, Amy carrying a huge bowl of water from the sink and spilling most of it. Eliza was kneeling by Abigail who was lying on the floor, inert and deathly pale.

"Thank goodness you're here," said Eliza. "Abigail came about half an hour ago, said she wanted to see you, and then she fainted. She's bleeding something terrible."

Emma knelt down by Abigail's motionless body, a feeling of panic almost immobilizing her, but she knew it was up to her to deal with this. Abigail's eyelids fluttered as Emma patted her cheeks and tried to rouse her.

"Abigail, wake up, wake up. What happened?" Emma already knew the answer by the amount of blood that was slowly seeping onto the floor.

Eliza handed Emma some towels. "I knew you wouldn't be in for a while, so I sent Mary-Rose to fetch the doctor, and I've tried to stop the bleeding, Did I do right?"

"Yes, you certainly did," said Emma, lifting Abigail's skirts to remove the blood-soaked swathes of cotton cloth, packing fresh towels tightly between Abigail's legs. Emma marvelled at the resourcefulness of Eliza especially after the revelation that her beloved Billy was, according to Abigail, the cause of this upsetting state of affairs. "You did indeed do right, Eliza. She *is* going to need the doctor. Get some more cloths, towels, sheets, whatever you can find. We must pack them up tight."

Emma was still wearing her street clothes. Throwing off her shawl and pulling off her gloves she called to Jane while she rolled up her sleeves and put on her thickest apron. "Try to wake her. Shake her, poke her. She mustn't sleep."

Sleep was what Emma was afraid of. She remembered a girl at the mill a few years ago who had been in the same predicament. No one knew, though, until she had fallen asleep at her post and bled to death.

Abigail uttered a low moan when Emma knelt on the floor and tried to turn her over. "What happened?" said Emma. "What did you do?"

Abigail eyelids fluttered open and she smiled wanly at Emma. "It's gone," she whispered. "Good riddance."

Emma lifted the skirts again but the blood was still seeping through, slowly, inexorably. The other girls stood to one side in open-mouthed horror, holding towels, sheets and whatever cloths they had been able to find.

"I might have known she would try something like this," said Emma shaking her head. "What did you use?" she asked again, packing the cloths tight between Abigail's legs, trying to piece together the fragmented information coming from the girl who was slipping into unconsciousness.

At that moment Mary-Rose brought in the doctor, the same young doctor who had attended Jane when she had choked at Sunday school. Jane was petrified with fright and all she could think of was that Abigail looked like one of those white marble statues in church-yards. They were always dead, of course.

The doctor leaned over Abigail and asked her to say her name. She could not. He looked grimly at Emma then proceeded to examine Abigail while the girls averted their eyes.

"You have done very well, Miss Kershaw, but she will have to go to the infirmary."

"Oh, can't she stay here? We'll look after her, if you tell us what to do," Emma assured the doctor.

"I don't think you realise how serious this is. She has lost a lot of blood and there's always the risk of infection," said Dr. Foster. "She's critically ill. She'll probably die if we don't get her to hospital."

"Is it like a … sort of …a ruptured appendix?" Emma who knew that was something you could die of, and hoping the doctor would not broadcast the real cause.

"Miss Kershaw, you know as well as I do this is a botched abortion. I have seen it before. What did she use? Did she tell you?

"A knitting needle," said Emma who had managed to extract this information from the patient. It was no use trying to hide the facts any longer.

"That means certainly the uterus has been punctured and God knows what else as well. This could lead to peritonitis. Help me get her into my carriage," instructed the doctor. "And please come with me. Your sister may need you."

"Oh, she's not my sister," Emma assured him. "Just the girl who used to live next door. But please, don't tell anyone. Her father doesn't know yet."

The doctor shook his head. "If she dies, there will have to be an inquest. The truth will have to be told."

"And otherwise?" pursued Emma, thinking to spare Abigail's father the painful truth.

"If she lives, the least said, the better."

§

Mr. Burgess did not come to give Amy her Latin lesson on Saturday afternoon. He was needed at his daughter's bedside at the infirmary.

During the weeks that followed, he thanked the Kershaw girls and especially Emma who had looked after his daughter so well pending the doctor's arrival. He had been told Abigail would pull through and make a slow recovery from the peritonitis. That is what the doctor had called it, being kind enough not to mention the real cause with a little persuasion from Emma. But, Emma wondered, did Mr. Burgess guess what had caused his daughter's nearly fatal illness?

Although Eliza was still hurting about Billy, she was learning to accept the fact that the young man she had thought fondly of for the last few years was a rake and a bounder. Emma's heart went out to Eliza who showed no outward signs of heartache and despondency. If Emma had asked Jane, she would have told her that Eliza wept in bed every night and often talked in her sleep about Billy and Robbie; a jumbled hotchpotch of words.

Of course, they could not discuss the matter of Abigail's illness and her subsequent weakness. The mill workers and acquaintances of the Burgess family knew Abigail had been seriously ill but none knew the exact cause. Anyone could get peritonitis, couldn't they? Emma had known several people who had had that awful sickness, and more than one had died of it. And for that matter, Emma also knew anyone could find themselves in the same predicament as Abigail if they were as irresponsible as she had been. She still nursed the hope that Mr. Burgess did not know the real cause of his daughter's severe illness. If he did, he certainly didn't discuss it with anyone. As for Abigail, she was a model of Victorian respectability and stayed at home during her long convalescence. After some weeks it was deemed that mill work would be too strenuous for the now delicate girl and therefore she stayed at home occupying herself with simple domestic chores and occasionally helping her aunt at the priest's house. Her only social outings these days were restricted to Saturday afternoons when she accompanied her father to give Amy her Latin instruction. She made polite conversation with the girls, about the weather, what had been going on at the Glebe Mill since she had left and so on, but her recent illness was never referred to.

Eliza, although desperate to find out more about Abigail's relationship with Billy Lampson, could not bring herself to ask anything, and there was certainly no information forthcoming from Abigail herself. She seemed to have rejected men altogether and was 'holier than thou' in Emma's opinion. How long this would last was difficult to foresee, knowing what Abigail had been like in the past. But of one thing they were all certain; this situation would not occur again as Abigail, in her attempts to abort the foetus, had almost certainly rendered herself infertile.

Any thought Abigail might have had about entertaining the opposite sex seemed to have been completely knocked out of her head. After her ordeal, the once meddlesome, voluble, devious girl had been transformed into a sombre young woman; a shadow of her former self.

Emma was rather sceptical about the transformation in Abigail, because, as it said in the Bible, a leopard cannot change its spots. But this appeared to have happened in Abigail's case. But then, not only had Abigail killed her bastard child, she had almost killed herself. That was enough to make anyone undergo a drastic change. Emma stopped debating the transformation in Abigail for, when all was said and done, it was a vast improvement.

Now, more cheerful matters were afoot and their minds were taken up with the arrival of a baby daughter to Kate and Nathaniel in June. This little girl would be called Caroline, after her paternal grandmother, much to Mrs. Goodacre's satisfaction. Mrs. Goodacre was extremely satisfied these days. She had a dutiful, hardworking son in Nathaniel, and an elegant, capable daughter-in-law, Kate, who had provided her and Mr. Goodacre with first, a sturdy son, two-and-a-half-year-old Charlie, followed by a healthy baby girl. In fact, Mrs. Goodacre was disposed most kindly to the family her son had married into. Her musical soirees, with Jane and the twins being the main performers, were becoming the talk of the town. People were begging to be invited to these social evenings.

"We'll have to enlarge our parlour, or else find a more spacious venue," she said to Jane, her chief entertainer. "Councillor Nuttall mentioned the Town Hall in Oldham."

"My word," said Jane. "That would be something. I hear the Town Hall has a grand piano."

'It's a pity your Alice isn't available to recite some poetry," said Mrs. Goodacre.

But she was pleasantly surprised to welcome a young Scot; an occasional visitor to the Kershaw household and a friend and co-worker of Mr. Kershaw. Robbie sang some Scottish ditties with Jane's piano accompaniment. Caroline Goodacre and her guests were enchanted by his affable countenance and his flair.

Although 'enchanted' was not how Eliza felt about Robbie Cameron, she now looked upon him as a possible husband. True, she had turned him down firmly at first, but as Jane kept reminding her, it was her prerogative to change her mind. He was, after all, a strong, likeable lad, even though he sometimes wore that strange cap and trousers made of a kind of woollen check material which Pa had said were 'plaid trews'. She had finally given up hope for Billy Lampson who, no doubt, had been responsible for Abigail's near-death experience. But Eliza said to herself she must not dwell on it; she must look to new pastures and perhaps encourage the attentions of Robbie Cameron. That is, if he were ever to approach her again. They all found him an admirable guest and companion on the few occasions Pa brought him home. Jane loved the way he always said, "Och, aye" to confirm something, and "Pairrr-fect" when he found something to his liking, which he often did. Emma thought he was an altogether likeable lad with a pleasing personality, in spite of his bereavement. He had told the girls his mother had died of a broken heart after his father and brothers died in the Glasgow shipyard disaster. Jane thought it cruel. Even though his mother had lost her husband and three of her boys, why did not the one who had survived, Robbie, keep her alive?

§

1887

Eliza had reluctantly promised, at Emma's urging, that the next time Robbie came to visit, she would engage him in conversation and try to win his attention once more. With her natural reserve, Eliza was rather averse to this kind of behaviour for did it not smack of something akin to flirtation? This was according to Amy, but that's what Amy would be inclined to say. She was always immersed in her books on Latin or English grammar. Amy had no time for romance at all, intent instead of striving to get into college. But, according to Emma, simply talking to a young man could hardly be called flirtation, especially as most of the household was always present, including Pa. Jane, however, had other ideas and strongly urged Eliza to seek out Robbie, whereupon she, Jane, would make sure that other people left the room. Emma heard whisperings about this plan and firmly scotched the idea. And as for Eliza's reservations about accepting Robbie's proposal, that is, if he did ask her again, she tried to accept Emma's philosophy that 'you could love any man if you put your mind to it'.

However, an opportunity did present itself. There was to be a picnic on August 1st, the day of the Summer Bank Holiday. The family from Bower Lane would meet up with Kate and Nathanial and their two children for a picnic in the grounds of Chadderton Hall. The Hall was now unoccupied, the nobility there having died out a few years earlier, but the grounds were open to the public. It was the social event of the summer; to take a picnic, explore the gardens, the arboretum, boating lake, and even the meadows beyond. On the Bank Holiday, the Chadderton Brass Band would be playing. A rowing regatta and games of croquet and lawn tennis would be amongst other attractions. It had been arranged that Pa and Robbie would attend because all large factories and shipbuilders were expected to be closed for the day, it having been the date set for the overhauling and replacing of machinery and equipment.

On Monday, August 1st, Pa and Robbie arrived early on the train from Birkenhead, so by noon they could accompany the girls in a hired cab over to the hall, where Kate, Nathaniel and little Charlie were waiting. Pa and Robbie carried two large hampers of food while other smaller baskets were carried by Emma, Amy, Jane, Eliza and Mary-Ann. The only one absent from this outing was Mary-Rose who had been whisked off to Manchester to meet her future in-laws, the Huddlestons. Her fiancé Ben, and his friend Davey Clothier, had planned the event, but to Emma's dismay, Mary-Ann had suddenly and unexpectedly decided that she did not want to meet Davey's parents. She had absented herself from that expedition and was now eager to join the party going to Chadderton Hall.

"Just because Mary-Rose is going to marry Ben, doesn't automatically mean that I am going to marry Davey," explained Mary-Ann to an annoyed Emma, who had taken it for granted for some time that the twins would marry these two eligible young men. Why was Mary-Ann being so awkward? wondered Emma. It reminded her of the behaviour of Alice, not doing things according to what was planned. This thought caused Emma to start thinking and worrying again about Alice, far away in London.

It seemed that the whole of Chadderton was there at the hall, but that could hardly be possible; it was common knowledge that many mill workers had taken a daytrip to Blackpool on the cheap excursion train. The Kershaws walked about with their heavy baskets, seeking a place to set up their picnic. Emma decreed it shouldn't be on the lawns where the band was playing – it would be too crowded there. Mr. Kershaw wisely suggested a spot in the surrounding meadow. The day was becoming very warm but a large tree offered shade and they settled under it.

Little Charlie wanted to pick cowslips while the picnic was being set out. They had done so on a previous expedition to Chadderton Hall.

"It's too late for cowslips. They don't grow in August," Jane had explained. "When we've finished eating, we'll have a wander around and find what wild flowers are growing up the hill."

This was the perfect event, in Emma's opinion, where Eliza could socialize with Robbie. Emma hung on to the hope that Robbie's earlier ardour would be renewed and that he would propose once more to Eliza. Emma had carefully choreographed the gathering to make sure that these two were seated next to each other. Eliza was well aware of the arrangements and of course, made no objection, smiling demurely at the tall, muscular Robbie as he seated himself next to her, gallantly placing two plaid cushions by her as his way of assuring her comfort on the wool blankets strewn on the hummocky grass. Eliza, as usual, warmed to his gentlemanly greeting and his immaculate manners. His looks were pleasing, with his curly hair and his angular jaw. He had the nicest way of saying things, rolling the rs slightly. Jane thought he was pretty much 'pairr-fect' and had already told Eliza this several times. No one could promote a suitor better than Jane.

Jane had heard Aunt Clara say that the way to a man's heart was through his stomach. If this were true, Jane thought, it was a wonder Emma had not won a man's heart by now. The picnic baskets were a sight to behold. They made your mouth water just to look at the contents. The cloth was spread. Luckily, it had hardly rained all summer and the grass was bone dry. The men set the baskets down, lifting the covers carefully.

There was Emma's game pie, created over two evenings with two separate sessions in the oven and, finally topped that morning with the hot-water crust followed by another hour in the oven. Emma had never made a game pie before, but she knew a picnic pie had to be done in stages. Done slowly, it would hold its shape and not fall apart. But Emma's pie pastry was not the same kind of pastry in the lemon curd tarts Kate had brought. Tart pastry was meant to melt in your mouth and Kate had ensured the blend of lemon and fluffy flakes hardly needed to be chewed. Somehow a whole tart just slipped down, as easy as the draught of Dandelion & Burdock or the damson cordial which was corked and stoppered in amber glass bottles. There were gooseberry tarts as well, made by Eliza the day before. And only an hour ago, she had made delicate watercress sandwiches which she had wrapped in cold cloths to keep them as delectable as possible. And there were ham sandwiches too, made by Jane. These were not as delicate as the watercress ones; Jane was not adept at cutting thin slices of ham or bread, and although Emma had rolled her eyes as usual when she saw something that wasn't quite what she had ordered, everyone knew Jane's ham sandwiches would be delicious and the men, especially, would appreciate the more robust slices. To follow, there was a sultana cake, and a Victoria sponge with icing sugar sifted over the smooth top and freshly-made plum jam in the middle. Everyone gasped when Nathanial set down his contribution—strawberries galore, in a gigantic pudding bowl. Mrs. Goodacre had brought these round that morning to Kate and Nathaniel's house, next door to hers. Grown in Somerset, the strawberries had been shipped through Manchester to arrive in time for the picnic. The berries were a different variety from the ones the family were accustomed to sampling from Mr. Critchley's farm. His farm, once in the country, was now surrounded by rows and rows of houses and huge mills, their chimneys all spitting out black smoke. This was not good for strawberry growing, and not much good for growing anything else either. But the Somerset strawberries were large, firm and flavoursome and there was a cup of the finest castor sugar for dipping. In exchange for the strawberries, Mrs. Goodacre had scooped up baby Caroline and had excused herself from the event. Kate had nodded her approval.

All eyes were on Emma as she took her sharpest knife and sliced deftly into the game pie amidst exclamations of approval from everyone. Not even the tiniest morsels of grouse, partridge or rabbit fell from the confines of the redcurrant jelly inside the hardcrust pastry and as the slices were placed on Kate's second-best plates and handed round, the shape remained perfect. It was a pie of which fables were made—a true masterpiece.

The refreshments were fit for a queen. Afterwards most of the family mingled, and chatted and strolled about the gardens. Amy curled up on the blankets with her books.

Charlie soon lost interest in wild flowers and after exploring the arboretum with Jane, took much interest in the band. They were splendid in their dark blue uniforms with silver buttons flashing in the sun, playing all the latest tunes in the open-sided pavilion.

"Why aren't you playing, Auntie Jane?" asked the three year old.

"Well, you know, Charlie, I play the piano. They don't have a piano here. Just trumpets and tubas; that's what they have in a brass band."

"Why don't you play the trumpet?"

"What? And blow my cheeks out like a puffing Billy? That wouldn't be very ladylike, would it? And anyway, there are no ladies in the band."

Jane sighed, wishing she could be in that bandstand, playing the piano. But she was content to be in charge of young Charlie. Now on their exploration of the other side of the hall, they found a croquet game in progress. It was all Jane could do to stop her little nephew from running over and joining in.

Oh, yes! They all had a grand time at the picnic. Everyone was exhausted as they left Chadderton Hall and waited for the cabs to take them home. Jane had loved every minute. Robbie was positively glowing with his success with Eliza in her blue muslin that matched her eyes. She had shared a plate of sultana cake with him, and then had walked with him down to the lake, taking an occasional peep at him under the edge of her parasol. Mary-Ann was sure she had had a better time than if she had gone to meet the Clothier family in Manchester. Emma was proud at the success of her pie, certain that the famous Mrs. Beeton would have been gratified with the success of her long and complicated instructions for this culinary tour de force. Although Emma was still miffed at Mary-Ann's change of plan, it was gratifying to see that Robbie and Eliza seemed to be progressing in the right direction. And Amy? Amy was a scholar, albeit still a mill worker, and she could have studied just as well at home, but the sun and fresh air were good for the brain. Emma approved of this refreshing break, especially for Amy, as she would be taking her college entrance examination the following week.

It had all been so enjoyable.

And tomorrow they would all be back at the mill.

Chapter Fifteen

The summer continued hot and dry. Towards the end of September, Emma was slightly worried as they had not heard from Alice for three weeks. Although she knew that Alice was safely occupied at Algy's house, she looked everyday for a letter with a London postmark. Instead, when she got home from the work on a Friday evening, there was a letter for Amy. It bore the crest of Victoria University in Manchester.

All eyes were upon Amy as she opened the letter. Everyone was seated at the kitchen table but tea had not yet started. The letter was far more important than the evening meal although they were ravenous, as usual, after work.

"It's from the Office of the Dean," said Amy. A smile lurked at the corners of her mouth which immediately put the minds of her audience at rest. Jane stood behind her and started reading out loud, over Amy's shoulder.

"The University is pleased to award you a Scholarship of Merit ..."

"Thank you, Jane. We'll all read it for ourselves," said Emma as Amy handed her the letter. A smile as broad as the Rochdale Canal spread over the face that looked older than its twenty-eight years as Emma slowly read the news they had all been waiting for.

Everyone read the letter in turn, passing it on, hugging and congratulating their clever sister who had not only passed with high honours but who would now receive her tuition absolutely free with the scholarship that had been awarded her. This was more than Emma had dared to hope for. Much as she wanted her sister to pass the entrance exam, she had been secretly worrying about funds Amy would require and her accommodation at the Residents' Hall. But their father had said all along that if Amy was clever enough to get into university he would pay most of the fees. Now, he could pay for the accommodation instead.

Amy would begin there in January, instead of the usual start date of the following September, as a place had become unexpectedly vacant. She would have to make up the time missed and work hard catching up but it would not be a problem for Amy as Emma well knew.

Another event that pleased Emma was that Mary-Rose and Ben Huddleston had set the date for their wedding the following spring. Mary-Ann had not become engaged to Davey Clothier, although she still saw him on occasion as a foursome with her twin sister and Ben.

"You know, Mary-Ann, you shouldn't keep the poor boy dangling," said Emma. "You should either see Davey with a view to marriage, or not at all."

There was a murmur of agreement from Mary-Ann; she wouldn't dare say anything to contradict Emma. Emma, the matriarch, was right in most matters, and the matriarch laid down the rules accordingly. And where on earth would they be without her?

"She's the highest wage earner and the oldest of all of us," reasoned Eliza. "It's reasonable that she rules the roost."

But Emma always had something to worry about. At the moment, it was Jane who was seldom home, going straight to Miss Lamont's for practice or lessons most days as soon as she finished at the mill. This was all in preparation for the upcoming Harvest Festival concert at the church hall where she would play a solo and also accompany the singers. Emma had been lenient in releasing Jane from many of her household chores to devote time to her piano studies. Though Emma did think her youngest sister should spend more time at home.

"You can't play Chopin on the harmonium," said Jane.

Emma didn't see why not. The look she gave Jane clearly said that.

"The harmonium is only suitable for hymns," said Jane.

"Oh, looking a gift horse in the mouth now, are we?"

"The harmonium was good for a while, but now, I have to use the piano all the time if I'm to get anywhere".

While Emma was wondering where it was Jane wanted to get to, she made a note to herself that after the concert at the church hall there would be some curtailment of these frequent odysseys into Oldham. Emma had heard rumours. Although she was at the Wharf Mill, news had travelled from the Glebe where five of her sisters worked. She would not hear it from Eliza, from the twins or Amy, of course, but it had leaked out that Mr. Higginbottom had found it necessary to have words with Jane about her work. According to Emma's source, he had reprimanded Jane for not paying enough attention in the carding room. Apparently, he had hinted there was too much diversion in her private life and it was affecting her concentration. Emma knew only too well from her time, many years before, in the carding room, like any part of the mill for that matter, that it was the last place for daydreaming. The cleaned cotton had to be straightened on a machine, the lap being fed by rollers against a wire cylinder with rows of teeth that straightened the tangled fibres and removed the short undesirable ones. Operatives could not take their eyes off the machines for a moment even though there were over-lookers. Emma resolved to speak to Jane about this, maybe after the concert whilst being reminded that the person reprimanding her sister could have been their brother-in-law, if matters had gone the way Mr. Higginbottom wanted. Emma relived the moment when Mr. Higginbottom had come to their house five years ago and asked Kate to marry him. Why would he have words with Jane? She surely couldn't be that careless at work?

That was something else to worry about and, of course, it would be up to Emma to sort it out. In her opinion, Jane was getting above herself with all this piano playing. She must be reminded not to forget her 'bread and butter' provided by her job at the Glebe Mill. But, in her heart, Emma knew Jane was not interested in bread and butter. Apart from her attachment to Kate's little boy, Charlie, Jane occupied a different world, mostly of her imagination; one of soirées, piano recitals and sophisticated society.

§

Concerns about Alice receded to the back of Emma's mind with all this worrying over Jane and her misdemeanours at work, about the progress of Eliza and Robbie, about the lack of progress of Mary-Ann with Davey, and Mary-Rose's spring wedding in just over four months time.

But these matters were put firmly out of her head upon receiving a letter from Aunt Clara in late October. According to the aunt, all was not well in London regarding Alice. In spite of Algy and Lucy's good intentions, they had come to the end of their benevolence towards Alice. She had not done well in her career as a nursemaid. She insisted she had tried, but Lucy was invariably critical of her and this had undermined Alice's relationship with little Sarah. Besides, according to Alice, she was virtually a prisoner or at best, an unpaid servant, with just a bit of pocket-money from Algy. After all, Alice had invited herself to stay and he, as a brother, could hardly have turned her away.

Alice had complained to Aunt Clara that she was expected to carry out an endless list of household duties and always had Sarah in tow. And, according to Aunt Clara, Lucy was not doing so well either in her job as sub-postmistress in a small haberdashery shop. Before her marriage, Lucy had worked in the General Post Office – that's how she had met Algy – but, according to Post Office rules, married couples could not be employed, so Lucy had been compelled to leave after the marriage. However, the wife of a GPO employee would be allowed to work in a sub-post office. Four years at home with young Sarah had evidently taken toll of Lucy's clerical abilities and she was finding it difficult to run the post office counter in the busy shop as well as serve other customers.

As Emma read on, she had to smile. Aunt Clara said things had been reversed. Lucy was now at home, having quit her job in the haberdashery shop and Alice had gone to work in the General Post Office. This was quite a change from an acting career, but evidently, Alice had excelled herself and after some preliminary training, was holding down a good position as a clerk. According to Aunt Clara, Lucy had become the green-eyed monster. Trying to ignore his wife's ill-concealed dislike of his sister seemed impossible for Algy and in order to keep the peace with Lucy, he had told Alice they would prefer it if she moved elsewhere.

That is where Aunt Clara had come in useful, allowing Alice to come and stay with her two weeks ago to relieve the situation at Algy's house. But a career girl, especially one as outspoken as Alice, did not fit in there either. There was Aunt Clara herself, and also her youngest daughter with a husband and five children. Definitely, Alice was surplus to their capacity for any length of time. Aunt Clara had felt she had returned what hospitality she had received up in Lancashire and done her duty by her dead sister's child, but enough was enough!

So, the long and short of it was, Alice was coming home! Emma smiled some more. It was just about fifteen months since Alice had run away 'to the stage', and now, here she was, coming home. Aunt Clara would be bringing her, insisting there would be no more unchaperoned journeys for her niece.

§

The arrival home of Alice was, in Emma's view, the Return of the Prodigal, and not before time. No matter that she was accompanied by Aunt Clara; Emma was so relieved and delighted to have Alice back by whatever means, she was would have welcomed Aunt Clara and her whole family.

Emma took a good look at Alice. She was dressed simply but fashionably in a high-waisted jacket of dove grey with a skirt to match. A business-like white blouse showed at the neck and cuffs. Buttoned gloves, and a saucily angled highwayman-style hat completed the outfit. If Emma was impressed she didn't show it, giving Alice a peck on the cheek as if she had only been absent a few days instead of many months. Emma tried to wipe the smile off her face as the other girls clustered round Alice giving her hugs and exclaiming their glowing approval.

"Alice, how you've grown, and your hair up too."

"Your hair is not as red as it used to be." Alice had wondered about this too, but it was probably due to the rough and stringent treatment her hair had been subjected to in an effort to promote fast growth from that boyish cropping she had suffered at the theatre. It was only in the last few weeks her hair had been long enough to scrape into a bun at the back of her head.

"What happened to all those freckles?" That was good news to Alice.

Alice also had luggage, not the simple holdall she had left home with, but a large leather suitcase which she referred to as her 'portmanteau'. And there was a leather briefcase too. "There are important documents in there and letters of reference from my employer." Everyone was impressed by this. Jane could hardly wait to try out the hat; one like that had never been seen in Chadderton before.

Yes, Emma thought, Alice was matured almost beyond recognition. But she was still Alice all right. She still had that attitude, something that Emma had strived to stamp out, but which Emma now knew would be a feature of Alice forever. And Alice talked in an airy manner. Her accent was more like Aunt Clara's—cockney style—but with an occasional lapse into Lancashire dialect. It was a bit of a mix, Emma had to admit, but she was sure it would soon revert to normal kind of talk.

"There's no post office hereabouts, so I reckon you'll be looking for a job at the mill?" said Emma. However, the look Alice gave her totally denied this and moreover, Alice had a trump card up her sleeve. If Algy had done anything right by his family it was to introduce his sister into employment at the GPO.

Here, Aunt Clara took over some explanation while Alice unbuttoned her gloves and removed her jacket, carefully hanging it on the hall stand.

"Alice has had some good training," explained the aunt who secretly admired her niece after the apparent fiasco of the theatre. "Oh, yes, our Alice has an excellent good career at her fingertips. Why, that Mr. Sutcliffe, her boss, he as good as told her she could go as high as she wanted in the Post Office." That began Emma wondering, why then had Aunt Clara encouraged Alice to leave.

"And not just in London," Aunt Clara enlightened Emma, "but anywhere Alice wants to be. And Mr. Sutcliffe also said she just learns things so fast, as if she were born to it. And ... meeting all those bigwigs Algy knows in the post office ..."

Oh, yes, Emma could see it all, Alice hovering around Algy whenever she wasn't required at her desk. He had a senior position, in charge of the sorting machines. After all, Algy had worked at the post office since he was twelve years old. Emma could see as vividly as if it were happening in front of her eyes: Alice flitting about the halls of the great Post Office building in London, striking up conversation with whoever she happened to bump into. Emma knew there was no end to the bravado of Alice. Everything would rub off on to Alice, and she would absorb everything, just like those poems she used to recite so well.

"Algy is so important at the Post Office, and his sister did not go unnoticed," continued Aunt Clara.

Margaret Growcott

"Why didn't she stay there, then?" asked Emma, who was amazed at Aunt Clara's high opinion of Alice, especially as she was the one who insisted Alice should come home.

"Hasn't she told you?"

"Told me what?"

"I'm to open the new sub-post office in Chadderton," said Alice, coming to join the discussion.

Emma's face was a sight to behold: disbelief, wonderment, elation. But for once, Emma was lost for words.

"They asked me in London if I could think of any small shop that might like to expand their horizons and devote some of their space to a post office. Of course, I could indeed imagine such a place. But it wasn't exactly imagination. It was Mrs. Kendal's shop here in Chadderton. And as there's no post office here, they wrote right away to Mrs. Kendal asking her. And she said yes! Because she had been thinking of it already, like the one down at Failsworth. They have post offices all over the place. Many a little shop has a sub-post office in the corner and stamps are being sold alongside eggs and butter."

Jane could already see Alice established in Mrs. Kendal's shop. She smiled, just seeing her sister at the counter. Fancifully, she could just hear Alice asking customers, "Would you like a helping of poetry to go along with those stamps?"

Emma was delighted, after her initial shock. This, in her opinion, would be the end of Alice's misguided fixation with the stage.

Many things had changed since Alice had last lived at Bower Lane. Kate now had another baby, Caroline. Mary-Rose was engaged to Ben Huddleston and they would be getting married in the spring. Jane was excelling at the piano and was being asked to play here, there and everywhere. There was a new young man they were all talking about, a Scot, who had been brought home from Birkenhead by Pa and he was sweet on Eliza. Amy had been studying hard with Mr. Burgess and had passed the examination to enter the Victoria University in Manchester.

178

Talking of Mr. Burgess, Alice started wondering about his daughter. "How's Abigail?"

There was a deathly silence. Jane was about to say something, but the look on Emma's face told her not to.

"Abigail has ... not been well," was Emma's answer.

"So what's wrong with her? Has she got the cotton disease or something?"

"She had peritonitis, and she's still weak."

That didn't mean much to Alice although she vaguely remembered hearing of it.

Naturally, it wasn't long before Jane supplied some details when they were alone, supplemented by Mary-Ann. No mention was made of Billy Lampson, supposedly the father of Abigail's illegitimate child. Eliza had told them never to say his name again.

Alice thought it deliciously scandalous but was sworn to secrecy as it appeared no one else, least of all Abigail's father, knew the true cause of her serious illness from which she had only partially recovered.

"It's a bit like *East Lynne*," said Alice who thought a whiff of scandal was so entertaining. "Trust Abigail to get into trouble. It's just like her. Those kinds of things happen all the time in London." Alice had never heard of them in Chadderton, but then Emma had never told them about some of the goings-on she had heard as a senior weaver at Wharf Mill.

Alice could hardly wait to go to Mrs. Kendal's shop, but she had to wait, to ride out the bleakness of Sunday in a northern town. On Sunday, everything was closed, except the church, of course. It wasn't at all like London, thought Alice. She was not used to it, but there was something comforting about being back among the restraints of a Sunday in Lancashire. There was something to be said about it—not like the decadent behaviour she had come across in London. Mind you, Alice said to herself, she wouldn't want it to be Sunday every day. But she remembered vividly not being able to pass a church in London without an ache, like a certain longing, or a type of acute nostalgia. In church, she looked along the pew. Aunt Clara was next to her, then Emma, sitting on the end near the centre aisle, and there, at the other end was Jane with Amy and Eliza. And there were the twins, up in the choir stalls. It was just like it had always been, apart from Kate, of course, who now sat with the Goodacre family since her marriage.

Aunt Clara praised the Lord diligently. Once again, she had been in a position to help her sister's family, having been instrumental in uniting them. During the sermon she took a good look at everyone, then placed a lace-gloved hand on the pew cushion to her side, and examined the embroidery with her practised eye. It came up to her expectations— but only just. Everything seemed to be in order at the Kershaw home. She had informed Emma that she would not be staying long; just long enough to go with Alice to Mrs. Kendal's shop to make sure all things were in order for the start of the sub-post office. Of course, Alice had said this was not necessary, but Aunt Clara had had her orders from Algy to accompany his sister on her first day. After all, Alice was only eighteen, young to be handling such business matters.

"I wouldn't mind staying a little longer," said Aunt Clara, "but my chilblains are much worse up here than in London." Emma thought that was absolute nonsense but kept her silence.

"But I would like to see my friend, Mrs. Leggate, before I leave," Aunt Clara informed Emma. "I've not seen her since Kate's wedding." Emma recalled that her aunt had first met the mill manager's wife at their mother's funeral and although they had met again at Kate's wedding, Emma thought Mrs. Leggate could hardly be considered a bosom friend. The way Aunt Clara referred to her, you would think they had been in constant correspondence. In fact, she was no more than an acquaintance in Emma's opinion. Emma wished her aunt would leave soon, and then they would be relieved of those never-ending prayers and Bible readings. But still, she was grateful to Aunt Clara for chaperoning Alice. The next one who would likely

180

need some chaperoning looked to be Jane, but Emma would see to that herself.

§

Alice was a true fount of knowledge on everything to do with the post office and Mrs. Kendal could not have managed without her. There was a certain amount of diplomacy to be observed, though, as Alice could clearly see. Mrs. Kendal was a slow learner and once Alice had explained something to her, she wanted to reinforce what she had learned by referring to the post office manual and that took some time. She was adept at selling the eggs, the flour, the potatoes and everything else in the shop but when it came to post office matters, she was extremely slow.

"I must remember not to keep telling Mrs. Kendal what to do," said Alice to Emma at the end of the third day.

"Just keep that mouth of yours tight shut, and you'll manage," said Emma. "Or at least take the words out of your mouth first," suggested Amy.

It was arranged that Alice would stay for a few weeks to assist Mrs. Kendal and then, if all went well, might find that the GPO had another position awaiting her to open another sub-post office. Everyone had to admit that Alice appeared to be extremely efficient in her new vocation. It was hard to believe she was now employed in such a down-to-earth capacity after her obsession with the stage.

But Emma didn't take kindly to being told by Alice that she should not keep all their money in a tin on the mantelpiece. The sojourn in London had certainly widened Alice's horizons and she had stopped constantly harping on about the stage, and now was harping on about Emma's method of saving money. However, Emma felt her present method of saving money was adequate, as it always had been.

"You should open a post office savings account," was Alice's advice.

"I'm not such a fool! I don't keep all our money in the tin," said Emma, her eyes straying to the over-mantel where the item in question was positioned behind the clock. "I've got a safe place where I keep the rent money and savings," Emma said. "There's only money for food on the mantel-piece."

She scooped up the laundry she had just brought in from the yard and Alice knew that was the end of the matter for now. Strangely enough though, Emma, for once, was going to take Alice's advice. She had heard about the Post Office Savings Bank where money was safe and soon accumulated if weekly deposits were made. Following the collapse of many private financial schemes, the Savings Bank had been started by the General Post Office as a safe way for ordinary people to save. Alice could see that Emma was coming round to the idea.

§

By the time the year ended and Christmas festivities were upon them once more, Robbie came to Chadderton again with Mr. Kershaw. He had seen Eliza once since the picnic in August. That was at the Harvest Festival concert at the church hall. Robbie and Eliza had sat together and she had seemed to genuinely enjoy his company which was encouraging. Now he thought the time was right to approach Eliza again on the question of marriage. She had given him every indication that he might not be turned down this time.

There was no need to ask Eliza's father. Robbie had known from the first time he had proposed to Eliza a year ago that his friend, Charles Kershaw, would approve.

Emma had almost given up waiting for the magic words. But then, at last, she heard them on Christmas Eve.

"Robbie and I going to be married," said Eliza. She showed everyone the elegant gold ring with its circle of small diamonds and appeared, if not ecstatic about being engaged, reasonably contented.

This was the first time Alice had met Robbie although she had heard much about him. She knew about his first proposal and the rejection, and knowing how keen on Billy Lampson Eliza had always been, Alice was surprised Eliza had changed her mind. But she *did* know from Jane and the others that it was forbidden to talk about Billy Lampson in the Kershaw household.

Emma immediately started making plans for a second wedding to be held in the summer. There was to be Mary-Rose and Ben's wedding just after Easter and then, in September, Eliza and Robbie would be wed.

But Eliza could not give her mind to planning a wedding. Let them get on with plans for Mary-Rose's wedding. She was already having misgivings. She had done what everyone had wanted, including Pa, but deep down, she knew it was no use. She remembered the words clearly from Kate's wedding ceremony "With my body I thee worship." How could she, in all consciousness, say such a thing to Robbie? Her mind was in turmoil. She could not, now or ever, believe this could happen with Robbie, likable as he was—a great companion for an afternoon picnic or a discussion on Scotland versus England. Anything more intimate, more to do with his body, was out of the question. She could not in any way "give herself to Robbie". She took into account Emma's thoughts on marriage which she had heard many times. To Emma, marriage was more of a business than a matter of the heart. It was not Eliza's way of thinking at all.

She had tried talking to Kate about it, and whilst Kate could understand, to some extent, Eliza's ignorance of the physical aspects of matrimony, and how it would happen between her and Robbie, she could only reiterate what she had said before. All Eliza heard were some profound statements "when love abounds, all things come naturally" and so on. It didn't help her predicament one bit.

"I will marry him, though," determined Eliza, eventually. "No matter what. He is so nice, and Pa likes him so much." Her responsibility to her family seemed to be surmounting her own future happiness. She reasoned with herself: Robbie was such an agreeable and likeable young man with good prospects. How could it not be right to marry him?

"The wedding is not for months," was Kate's final advice. "You'll feel different. Something will happen."

§

Something did indeed happen. On New Year's Day, there was a knock on the door and to everyone's amazement, Jane ushered in a well-dressed, prosperous-looking young man, who removed his Derby hat and bowed to all the girls. But his eyes were on Eliza. He started to unbutton his fashionable top coat with its astrakhan collar.

"Well, of all the nerve," said Emma, but relieved him of his coat.

Billy Lampson approached Eliza who backed against the wall. She was red to the roots of her fair hair. She was confused, not knowing whether to take his proffered hand or turn her back on him.

Emma was sorry that Pa was not there. She could have done with a man to drum this bounder out of the house. "How dare you show your face here, after all this time and after … after what you did." Emma was fit to be tied.

Billy looked confused at this hostile reception, but still looked appealingly at Eliza who was shrinking away from him.

"Oh, Billy, why have you come … why? Why now?" Her eyes glistened with unshed tears.

Billy looked in exasperation at the six girls, Mary-Rose being the only one absent as she was out visiting with her fiancé, Ben. Emma could see that Billy wanted to be alone with Eliza but she was not going to co-operate. Trying to stop a torrent of words, she gathered her troops around her: Eliza, immediately to her right, was hanging on to Mary-Ann. On the other side was Alice, looking as though she had plenty to say, but was daunted by Emma's angry glare. Then there was Jane, also standing to attention. Amy remained seated at the table with her book as though nothing unusual was happening.

"I couldn't come before," he said, moving close to Eliza, trying to catch her hand, but she snatched it away. "Now I've got something to offer you. My prospects are excellent. We can be married"

"Oh, no you can't," said Emma. "You're too late! Eliza is engaged to somebody else!"

Chapter Sixteen

1888

Billy looked shocked, but his eyes were still fixed on Eliza who was shaking her head and trying not to spill those tears.

"Engaged? Who to? Why didn't you wait for me?" Billy looked from Eliza to Emma, waiting for the explanation which he knew would take some time.

As Eliza strived to find the words, Emma had plenty to say.

"You come in here, strutting like a peacock, without so much as a by your leave, and expect Eliza to be available when you want, without a word for nigh on four years."

"I wrote to you." Billy tried to ignore Emma, and looked beseechingly at Eliza.

"She got no letter," said Emma, seeing that Eliza was still gasping for words.

Billy was puzzled. "I sent you a letter explaining everything, asking you to wait for me." Then his face cleared. "I was going to the post office in Ashton to get a stamp, and then I saw Abigail Burgess coming down the street. You know what she's like—a right busybody. She stopped me and saw the letter and said she would give it to you. She lives next door, doesn't she?"

"Not for the last four years. She lives in Oldham now." At last Eliza found her voice.

"You mean you never got the letter? I explained everything, about my job prospects and me working in Ashton and going to night school. No?"

Eliza shook her head. "I've not seen anything of you since Kate's wedding. How was I to know where you were or what your intentions were?"

"I couldn't say anything to you before. After seeing your sister's husband and *his* good prospects, how could I compete with that? How could I ask you to wed before I had made something of myself? Remember? Emma and that aunt of yours, so pernickety. They told me not to hang around unless I had marriage in mind."

"You went off to the back of beyond, never getting in touch. What was I supposed to think?"

Billy would not have called Ashton-under-Lyne the back of beyond; it was only six miles from Chadderton, but he knew women were given to exaggeration, especially when they were upset. However, he had other matters to straighten out with Eliza.

She certainly had to straighten out matters with him. "What about Abigail?"

"What about her?"

"What you … gave her?"

"I only gave her a letter."

"According to her, you gave her more than a letter." Eliza was suddenly finding her voice.

"I don't know what you're talking about," Billy looked bewildered. "I only saw her that once in Ashton."

Emma thought quickly. No one, except the Kershaw girls and the doctor, knew that Abigail had been expecting a child. Even Abigail's father didn't know the real cause of Abigail's severe illness. Emma hoped he did not. And then she remembered that Abigail had been evasive to Emma's questioning about Billy. Perhaps he wasn't the father, but now was not the time to sort it out. She tried to steer the conversation away from Abigail. "Whatever happened, Eliza never got any letter and now you've got the cheek to suddenly turn up after all this time."

Clearly, some explanations were needed all round, but Emma could hardly wait to get rid of Billy. She could see, however, that he had had such an effect on Eliza that it seemed unlikely that Robbie would stand much chance now. Even though Billy's reputation was tarnished in Emma's opinion, she was willing to admit there was some possibility that Abigail had been making things up as she had done many times in the past. One thing was uppermost in Emma's mind: her sisters had been so traumatised by Abigail's experience; it would never happen to them. She had always worried about this kind of thing, though. She had known mill girls who had either married in a hurry, if that was possible, or had disappeared for a while. It wasn't as if Emma and the other girls cared so much about killing a baby— they didn't care about that, not like those Roman Catholics up at St. Mary's—but they did care about the trouble Abigail had caused for herself and for others close to her.

Billy tried again, the smooth touch. "But Eliza, sweetheart. Now I have something to offer you."

"Don't you 'sweetheart' me." Eliza was still putting forth her protests but her defence was beginning to wear down. "I can't forgive you for what you did." Her voice said that, but her look gave another message. Her eyes met Emma's and she knew too, that it was unlikely that Billy was the father of Abigail's child.

Billy was beside himself. He even knelt on one knee, looking imploringly at the agitated girl. "Please, please, Eliza. You know I love you. I've waited all this time. I can't live without you."

"I'm sure Eliza would not want to be the cause of your death," said Emma, finding Billy's outpouring somewhat cloying. "But you'll have to go now." Eliza was silent, trying to ignore his beseeching. She turned her back on him, dabbing her eyes with her sodden handkerchief, but sneaking a worried look in Emma's direction.

"Come back when Pa's here," said Emma as she handed Billy his coat, signifying an end to this painful meeting. She was fully aware that she and Eliza could handle this situation themselves and Pa would go along with whatever they decided, but it was a useful ploy to terminate this intolerable situation.

"Yes, I'll be back, very soon," said Billy as he buttoned up his topcoat with the astrakhan collar. "And tell your Pa I'm now the engineer at Whitelands Mill in Ashton. Think on that." This information was intended mainly for Emma's benefit and he knew he had hit the mark.

§

Eliza regretted that Emma had encouraged her liaison with Robbie. And, come to think of it, Jane had egged her on too. Now, by breaking off the engagement, Eliza would not only upset Robbie, but her father, Emma, and probably the whole family. Why had she listened to Emma and Jane? They knew nothing of such matters. Of one thing she was sure, no matter what dealings, if any, Billy had had with Abigail, it had not quenched the feelings she had for him.

But now, at twenty-four, she was confident about the man she wanted to marry. Once she had recovered from the shock of seeing Billy again, she knew, for sure, he was the one for her. Even though she hated the thought of upsetting Robbie, the agreeable young Scot, she knew it had to be done. It was no good pretending any longer. But she would have to face Robbie, and it would have to be soon.

§

It was done. Eliza and Robbie were alone in the parlour sitting yards apart. She had said her words, although they had not come out quite the way she had rehearsed them. She drew the ring from her finger and laid it on the small table between her and Robbie. She produced the pretty little box from her pocket and also laid that down.

"Ye dinnae care for me at all?"

"Oh, but, I do Robbie." She fixed her blue eyes steadily on his face, wondering how she could choose the words to let him down lightly. "I *do* care for you. And everyone in the family loves you. You know that. But that's it—I care for you like . . . like … a brother. That's it. I'm very fond of you. I'm so sorry."

Fondness was not what Robbie wanted at this moment. Nor did he want a sister. He leant forward, elbows on knees, head in his hands. The only sound came from the ticking of the mantelpiece clock and a faint sputter from the fire. Finally, he got to his feet.

"Well then, Eliza, I'll say fare-thee-well." He made for the door.

"Oh, don't forget the ring, Robbie," she said, picking it up with the box and following him out.

"Nay. I ha'e no use for a thing like that." Robbie went into the kitchen where all the girls and their father were sitting, solemnly reading or sewing. They all knew what had been going on in the parlour.

"Good day to ye, ladies." He put on his tam-o-shanter, the cap that had so amused them all at first.

"You're not leaving are you, Robbie?" asked Charles Kershaw. "Ye'll stay the night as usual?" "Nay, I best be getting back to Birkenhead. I'll not be stopping the night."

"But I had a surprise for you, and a treat," said Alice. "I know it's Robbie Burns Day soon and I prepared one of his poems to recite to you. I know you're fond of his poems."

There was a faint smile on Robbie's face, the first one all day, at this diversion by Alice. Eliza was grateful to Alice who could always be counted upon to save a dull or bad scene.

"Well, let's hear it, Alice, and then I'll be off," said Robbie, sitting down next to Emma, careful not to look at Eliza. He couldn't bear to look at her. He was already learning, painfully, there was no easy path for getting out of love. It was easy, oh, so easy, to fall in love, but to do the opposite seemed impossible.

Alice began the poem.

"O, my love is like a red, red rose
That's newly sprung in June.
O, my love is like a melody
That's sweetly played in tune. ..."

She faltered, seeing Emma's thunderous expression and Jane on the verge of tears. That poem was not what Robbie needed to hear right now.

He was soon on his way back to Birkenhead.

§

Bolstered by her success in breaking off her engagement to Robbie, Eliza had no hesitation in telling Emma that she was going to marry Billy.

As arranged, Billy came back to the house a week later, to speak to Mr. Kershaw. Again, the parlour was the scene for this interview and all the girls were in the kitchen, Eliza sitting to attention, waiting to be called in.

"So you're the reason my Eliza wants to jilt poor Robbie," said Pa, lighting his pipe. "Took ye time coming forward, didn't ye?"

For once the confident Billy was at a loss for words. He felt uneasy at the knowledge he had made the other young fellow miserable, but he was not going to be made to feel guilty. He shifted uncomfortably from one foot to the other.

Mr. Kershaw made an unhurried business of sucking on his pipe and then waved it in the air. It seemed to indicate some kind of agreement to Billy who remained silent, yet hopeful.

"I hear you've gone up in the world with your night school and all." Another wave of the pipe.

"Yes, indeed, Mr. Kershaw. I'm now the engineer at Whitelands in Ashton-under-Lyne."

"So you'll be setting up home in Ashton?"

"Yes, sir. I already have a house I've been living in for a while. Eliza will surely love it."

"Happen she won't be doing mill work any more?"

"No, indeed, Mr. Kershaw. Eliza will never want for anything," Billy was proud to inform his future father-in-law. He hadn't been asked to sit down yet and would not do so until invited by his host. This invitation did not seem to be forthcoming so Billy stood to attention, looking slightly uncomfortable, even in his fine broadcloth suit.

Mr. Kershaw puffed away at his pipe. "I have to say, I want my Eliza to be happy, and if she wants to marry you, so be it."

Billy gave a sigh of relief knowing that this signified the end of the interview. Although this was scant encouragement, he was satisfied, knowing that he was not the first choice as a son-in-law, because Mr. Kershaw had favoured his young Scottish co-worker. Obviously, he had now relinquished the idea of having Robbie in the family but he didn't seem too displeased. Mr. Kershaw opened the door and called in Eliza. She looked at her father who gave a nod of assent, and then she rushed over to Billy who enveloped her in his broadcloth.

"Oh, Billy," breathed Eliza, knowing their first kiss would have to wait a while. And there was yet a pressing question she had to ask her new fiancé although she knew the answer. She was sure she did.

It had to do with Abigail.

§

1888

In February, to Emma's surprise, Mr. Higginbottom came to call. He had an envelope in his hand which Emma eyed with some suspicion as she showed him into the parlour. She recalled vividly the time he had come five years ago, with his proposal to Kate. She still didn't like him particularly, but put it down to his sombre attitude, probably due to the death of his wife years ago in the Tay Bridge disaster. Those three children were still motherless. Obviously after Kate, he had not found a potential wife to his liking, but Emma had heard that the nursemaid he had engaged was a treasure and the children were well cared for and much loved by her. He stood to attention in his well-pressed suit, perfect with not a crease out of place. His hair had a few more flecks of grey, and so did his handlebar moustache, and Emma had to admit he wasn't bad looking, though short and stocky. She towered above him. She couldn't forgive his harsh treatment of Jane, chastising her in front of all other workers in the carding room although Emma had to admit that he was within his rights and, being the manager of Glebe Mill, he could discipline whoever he wanted to. But he had been upsetting Jane for months and therefore Emma had her protective defences in place, although she knew how annoying and wilful Jane could be. She was thankful Mr. Leggate at the Wharf Mill was her boss and not this priggish, wooden-stick of a man.

Mr. Higginbottom did not waste his words, striding purposefully to the table by the window and laying down the envelope, indicating that Emma should open it.

When she made no move, he said, "I'm sorry about your Jane, but you know as well as I do that she isn't cut out for mill work. And not only that, she's a bit of a trouble-maker, being, as you know, militant, and always quoting from that newspaper. I don't like my workers reading that stuff."

Emma made no reply, feeling sure Mr. Higginbottom had not paid a special visit to 54 Bower Lane just to apologise for Jane's shortcomings and that he would get to the point soon. She was proved right as the manager continued.

"She's just asking to be sacked, with her ideas about conditions at my mill and talking to everybody about it. It's a wonder she hasn't had an accident, her being distracted so much with things that aren't her business. But Amy, so different, nice and quiet, and so clever too; she didn't seem to mind the work and was good at it. I'm right sorry to lose *her*. That's why I'm here."

He proceeded to open the envelope as Emma had not touched it. "This is a gift from some of the mill workers, and from me. Now that Amy's a university lass and living away from home, she'll likely need this."

Emma peered into the opened envelope. There were coins, five pound notes and some ten pound notes in there, lots of them. A generous gift indeed from a boss and from Amy's co-workers, but Emma knew the majority would be from the mill manager and the owners.

"Thank you kindly, Mr. Higginbottom," said Emma. "Amy will be so grateful to you and all the mill girls." She didn't tell him that owing to Amy's scholarship, this was more like a bonus and not essential for her university education. Still, it would be a windfall that Amy could spend as she saw fit, perhaps on some extravagance. Emma knew, however, that like her, Amy was a thrifty soul and the majority of it would be saved, probably in one of those accounts at the post office that Alice was always talking about.

Mr. Higginbottom prepared to leave, but Emma, as usual, was not going to let him escape without putting things in perspective.

"It's so very kind of you to bring this money for Amy, Mr. Higginbottom and so generous of everyone. She'll be most grateful." A slight pause. Then, as Mr. Higginbottom led the way out, she continued, "I'm sorry Jane is proving to be such a poor worker, but you haven't mentioned my other sisters. There's Eliza and also the twins. Are you not satisfied with them?"

"Oh, indeed, Miss Kershaw. Your other sisters are exemplary workers. Eliza is one of my best mule spinners. She has a most responsible position, and Mary-Rose and Mary-Ann are also extremely conscientious employees."

Of course, Emma knew this full well. She just wanted to hear Mr. Higginbottom say so.

§

At the rehearsal of the annual spring concert of the Blue Coat School, the boys were in confusion and somewhat intimidated by the arrival of a girl, a pupil of their piano teacher, Miss Lamont. She had been invited to play at their concert and they wondered why; there had never been an outsider before, much less a girl, taking part.

A senior boy, Jake Higgins, always played at these concerts, and was usually the star. But now, he had to admit, he was totally eclipsed by Jane Kershaw, as brilliant in looks as in her performance on the pianoforte. She had suddenly appeared amongst them and she threatened to outshine them all. Not yet sixteen, she was younger than most of the senior boys who performed, either on the piano or violin or in the orchestra. Most of the boys, Jake included, felt overshadowed, and unnerved by her as she was so talented. She was also extremely pretty with her soulful brown eyes, and dimples in her fresh-complexioned cheeks; not old enough to put up her curly auburn hair which strayed over her shoulders as she leaned over the keyboard. Jake was relieved he was playing his Scarlatti sonata early in the programme so there would be little comparison of him to this virtuoso.

At the evening concert, Mr. Burgess, Deputy Headmaster announced, "We are proud and honoured to introduce a young lady of outstanding musical ability. Miss Jane Kershaw from Chadderton is our esteemed guest this evening and will play Sonata Number 11 by Mozart."

The audience, composed of impressionable boys and their parents or guardians, wondered how this girl could be such an accomplished pianist as it was rumoured she spent most of her time in a cotton mill. They watched, enraptured, as she played the Mozart sonata, all seventeen minutes of it. The applause was thunderous as Jane left the stage, but she was not satisfied.

"I made a mistake in the Alla Turca," she whispered to Alice who was waiting just off stage to accompany her down to the hall where she could watch the remainder of the concert with her sisters.

"No one would know," said the truthful Alice, who knew about the tricky Turkish movement. "It sounded perfect."

Jake marvelled that this girl had played the piece effortlessly. He had volunteered to be the page turner for Jane, but she had hardly glanced at the music so ingrained was this sonata in her musical repertoire. There were other pieces she could have played, but she had only been asked to do one, so Miss Lamont had stated that in her opinion this would go down the best because, as far she knew, none of the boys would be playing Mozart.

At the end of the entertainment, Jake Higgins had managed to finagle a conversation with Jane as she was preparing to leave. "Well played, Miss Kershaw. What sonata was that again?" he asked, curious to know. "Is that Köchel No. 331?"

Jane rolled her eyes. Trust a Blue Coat boy to ask such a question. "I believe it is," she said but, in fact, had no idea. She just knew it was number eleven. Then, as she had the music in her hand, and with Jake gawping over her shoulder, was able to confirm, "Yes, it's K. 331."

"I just wanted to know so I can get it from our music library," he explained. He had attempted a Mozart sonata once and found it extremely difficult, but this guest artist had played it as though it was a nursery tune. The beginning sounded easy enough, but this sonata had some extremely difficult passages. He looked at Jane's small and delicate hands. How could they have executed those difficult octaves and huge crescendos in the variations? He had performed his Scarlatti sonata without a mistake, but it had lasted only three minutes and could not be compared with Jane's performance.

"Is it true that you don't have a piano at home?" was the next question from Jake as Jane was moving away. Miss Lamont had told him about this private pupil who not only had lessons but spent what little spare time she had practising at Miss Lamont's because she had no access to a piano. Miss Lamont had also told him Jane was the best pupil she had ever taught, better even than any of the boys she had at the Blue Coat School.

"No, we don't have a piano at our house yet," was Jane's reply. She was loath to impart this information to a stranger, especially as so many folk now had their own piano in their own parlour. However, she knew that this impertinent boy, who, she had to admit, she rather liked, was a boarder like all the boys at the school, so he might not have a piano at home, just the one provided by the school. She also knew that the majority of the boys were orphans—that is why the school had been started. He probably had no more access to a piano than she did. "We just have a harmonium," she added.

Jake Higgins knew how little use that would be to a girl with Jane's aptitude. He couldn't help a grudging admiration for this seemingly deprived yet marvellous young lady.

Chapter Seventeen

A t the grocery shop with its sub-post office, Alice was now in charge. Mrs. Kendal was preoccupied with her husband who was once again at death's door in the infirmary.

"I cannot give my mind to this post office business," said a confused Mrs. Kendal. "Where are those forms you use for the savings bank? Mr. Humphreys was asking me about those."

Fortunately for Mrs. Kendal, Alice had everything at her fingertips and smoothly skirted round Mrs. Kendal, trying not to be annoyed at her perpetual forgetfulness about post office procedures.

"That reminds me," said Alice, handing Mrs. Kendal the forms. "I should take some of these home for my sisters." They didn't know it then, but Mary-Rose, Mary-Ann, Eliza and Jane would soon be persuaded to start a post office savings account. It didn't take much persuasion when Emma showed them how her one shilling a week had accumulated so quickly. And there was Amy, a wealthy young lady in her sisters' eyes, who had already been persuaded by Alice to deposit her unexpected gift of money from Mr. Higginbottom into a post office savings account.

Alice realised Mrs. Kendal relied on her and she appreciated this trust. She knew she was proficient with every procedure of the sub-post office, even with the groceries, which were almost a secondary matter now. And Alice had persuaded Mrs. Kendal to finally dispense with the almost empty barrel of butter. Hardly anyone came anymore with an old chipped cup, to scrape around and get the dregs. And if they did come with their pathetic little cup, Alice let them have butter from the one and only full barrel at a bargain price. She remembered only too well that for years the butter they had had at their table was the kind that had often contained wood splinters.

It was relief to Emma that Alice had settled down so well and there was no more talk of an acting career. But it was Jane who most appreciated having Alice home. Her admiration for Alice knew no bounds, as she had had the courage to defy Emma and go off to London all by herself. Jane wished she had that kind of courage; not so much to leave home, but just to rebel against Emma. Instead, she had to be content to bend Alice's ears about London.

"Opera is very much in vogue. People in London seem to like it better than a play," said Alice, who had already told Jane everything about the theatre where she had graced the stage.

"What about the Royal Academy of Music?" asked Jane.

"I don't know much about music in London," Alice was honest and for once, was unable to embellish her scant knowledge in this area.

"What I'd like to know," said Emma. "Did you see the Queen when you were in London?"

"No. Sad to say, I never saw the Queen."

"It was Queen Victoria's Golden Jubilee last year. We read all abut it in the newspapers. There was a national holiday on June 21st. We all had the day off work. Surely you must have had that where you were?"

"You don't get days off in the theatre," said Alice.

"They said that princes and princesses came from all over the world to see the Queen, and she was taken all over London in a golden carriage," said Emma.

"Well, she may have done, but I didn't see any of it."

"There's not much point in being in London if you've never set eyes on the Queen," said Emma. "I'd like to see her, just once, even though she's so old."

And then Emma's line of questioning changed as she wanted to know all about her brother and his wife.

"What kind of house do they have? Is it by the River Thames? Is it grand?"

"I wouldn't say grand, exactly," said Alice, puckering her brow, trying to find the right words to describe Algy's residence. "A terraced house in Bethnal Green, but big, with four bedrooms, and a huge parlour that you could dance in. It was a bit of a walk to the river. The theatre where I worked was near the Thames, though."

Emma ignored that last remark. She didn't want to hear any more about the theatre. "And Lucy? Is she a good housekeeper ... cook?"

"She knows how to cook a stew, same as me, but she can't do parsnips like you, Emma. And there's no pleasing that one," said Alice, proceeding to demonstrate what she meant. "It's either 'these potatoes aren't peeled properly' or 'you'd better learn to make gravy better'. And then she goes on about Sarah: 'you're spoiling my little girl, don't give her so much attention'. Don't do this, don't do that," imitating to perfection Lucy's high-pitched Cockney accent. There was much flourishing of arms to further demonstrate what she meant, much to Jane's amusement. But Emma was not amused, and was still curious about Algy's house.

After some further elaboration from Alice, Emma was once again convinced that her sister-in-law was stand-offish, and gave herself airs and graces. Misplaced delusions of grandeur, Emma thought.

"I'm sure you're thankful to be safely back in Chadderton, Alice," said Emma. "London is a terrible place for goings-on. And somebody gets murdered every day, so I hear."

"We had a murder here, remember?" said Alice. "Mrs. Burgess. I don't think the police did much to find who did it, and now the trail's gone cold."

Then she reminded them of something she had on her mind. "When Eliza marries Billy, we'll all be related to Mrs. Kendal."

"Hardly a relative, Alice," said Emma. "She *is* his aunt, true, but you don't count that as a relation to us."

"So we won't be calling her Auntie Bessie?" said Alice, relieved that Mrs. Kendal would remain an employer and not an aunt.

"Certainly not."

"If she's his aunt, and he's got no mother, shouldn't she be invited to the wedding?"

"No. We'll have his Pa, and his sister and husband from Morecambe, and that's enough from that side."

At this point Alice recalled that Mrs. Kendal had mentioned that she had known the wedding of her nephew would be coming about. That was before the announcement of the engagement. Alice's curiosity was aroused. How did Mrs. Kendal know Billy and Eliza would be getting married?

Then Alice remembered Mrs. Kendal had said something about forgetting to give Eliza a note from Billy. That was months ago. Alice didn't reckon much to Billy's method of communication. First, a letter had gone astray because he had had the mistaken notion that Abigail would deliver it safely, and then, he had asked Mrs. Kendal to give a message to Eliza.

"I'm right sorry," said Mrs. Kendal. "My husband was so bad again, and I completely forgot the note Billy gave me. I don't know where I put it, but I thought Eliza was hearing regular from Billy and they were going to wed."

"Well, there you are!" said Emma clinching in her mind the opinion that Mrs. Kendal had too many worries to concern herself about their family. "And Billy is far too careless about his letter writing. Why did he leave it to his aunt to deliver his billet-doux? He surely couldn't have been that busy. And how could he have given that other letter to Abigail. How stupid is that?"

But Emma was relieved to see Eliza blissful, busy planning her wedding with the help of her sisters, especially Kate, now married for five years.

But before Eliza's nuptials there would be the wedding of Mary-Rose and Ben Huddleston. It was to take place the week after Easter. Mary-Ann, who was not going to be married along with her twin sister, which is what they all had wanted, watched from the wings, as it were, and wished she could go along with her family's plans for her. But she could not bring herself to do so. She still saw Davey Clothier and although he had reportedly asked her to marry him, she had declined. Emma was disappointed, as it did not fit in with her plans.

The wedding of Mary-Rose and Ben was the second in the family, and Emma was making arrangements similar to those that were made when Kate was married in 1883. Were they all going to be bridesmaids again? There was Amy at university in Manchester. She only came home on occasional weekends but she wanted to be included, naturally. Emma declared *she* would be Maid of Honour, and Kate would not be a bridesmaid, just an important guest, now that she had a well-connected husband and two children.

"I don't want to wear a pink dress," said Mary-Ann. "Why can't we have the same colour we had for Kate's wedding?" Of course, they had all long since outgrown or outworn those charming blue satin dresses from the Emporium, and Mary-Rose had definite ideas about what colour she wanted for the bridesmaids. That was pink, the palest pink possible and once again, they would come from the Emporium in Oldham. Everyone acquiesced with these carefully-laid arrangements. The only girl not in accord with these plans was Mary-Ann who, surprisingly, seemed not to be interested in her twin's wedding. This was most unusual as they normally planned everything together. Emma supposed if one twin was getting married, the other one would automatically feel excluded, but secretly she wondered if Mary-Ann was sickening for something. She had not been singing in the church choir the last few weeks. She said singing made her cough. Unusually quiet and indifferent, Mary-Ann was behaving as if a stranger was getting married, not her twin sister.

§

Emma still wanted to talk to Abigail. Delicate though she was these days, she still had some explaining to do. Now that Eliza was officially engaged to Billy, Emma wanted the truth and nothing but the truth. It was now a year since the abortion. Abigail had named Billy as the father of her child and even though it now seemed unlikely, Emma wanted the matter clarified, for Eliza's sake.

Emma acknowledged reluctantly they had no idea who the father was and you could hardly expect Abigail to divulge his name willingly. She was not, after all, a sister, in which case Emma would have insisted on her telling the truth. Emma's sense of fairness overcame her scruples and she determined to get to the bottom of this once and for all. She also wanted to demand of Abigail what had happened to that letter. It would exonerate Billy in Emma's mind. Naturally, Billy was already totally blameless in the eyes of Eliza. Emma would take much more convincing.

Emma found it difficult to talk to Abigail alone, but an opportunity presented itself when she came with her father to see Amy, who had come home from Manchester for a bridesmaid's dress fitting. Mr. Burgess, particularly, wanted to know how Amy was getting on at university so Emma saw the chance while he was chatting to his protégé. Emma, having tried to speak to Abigail for months, managed to get her into the parlour on the pretext of talking to her about a potted plant that Abigail had brought from St. Mary's Church Bazaar.

"I thought you'd like this plant," said Abigail. "It's called an aspidistra and they come from China, originally, you know."

"Thank you, Abigail," said Emma, pleased with this unexpected offering. "I've seen one of these at the Goodacre's. All the posh people have them."

They both knew there were other words that could have been said, and they also both knew the gift of the plant was an unspoken, 'Thank you, Emma. That's the end of that, Emma. Don't tell anyone, Emma—not my father, not my aunt. Please Emma'.

Instead Abigail said, as she perceived Emma swirling round, plant in hand, seeking the best place for it to thrive, "You don't need to water it much, and it's not bothered by the gas. It's very good-natured."

The aspidistra, with its pert, straight, green leaves so perfectly arranged, neat and orderly, just like Emma, was a welcome gift. Even so, she was not going to let Abigail escape the interrogation she had in mind. She may not be a sister, but in Emma's opinion, Abigail had caused too much misery to be let off the hook.

The chill parlour with its smell of wax polish was the last place Abigail wanted to be. She had come to see her friends, the Kershaw family. But were they her friends? She was plain scared of Emma and had never liked Eliza, jealous of her fair hair and blue eyes, inherited from her father, looks that stopped people in their tracks. It was the same with Jane, although four years younger than Abigail, she was far more accomplished and prettier too. Abigail tolerated the twins, and quite liked Amy because she was a quiet one, never saying much. But Abigail really liked outgoing Alice who, with her job at the shop and post office, always had something interesting or important to say, and knew first-hand about the goings-on in Chadderton.

Emma closed the parlour door firmly after placing the aspidistra on the table in front of the window. Abigail gazed past it, out to the street but the heavy net curtains obscured whatever might be going on in Bower Lane. There was just a faint clatter of horses' hooves on the cobblestones. Nothing else. In the uncanny silence of the parlour, even the usual ticking of the clock had ceased. Jane must have forgotten to wind it up on Sunday. The harmonium on the opposite wall was closed and shuttered with not even a sheet of music to show it had been used lately.

"And now, Abigail," said Emma, relieved she had finally got the girl alone in the parlour, "you've got to tell me about ... what really happened ... you know."

Abigail feigned ignorance. "What do you mean?"

Although patience was one of Emma's virtues, tolerance was not and she came directly to the point of her interview with the wayward girl.

"You know very well what I mean. First of all, you need to tell me who was the father of that ... child ... so Billy can be let off. It would mean a lot to Eliza. And before that, what happened to that letter you were supposed to give to Eliza over a year ago?"

"I can't name the father," said the wary Abigail who had thought this matter had been swept under the carpet some time ago. "I'm glad you like the plant," she added.

Emma's mind drifted for an instant. It was a clear, unspoken message from Abigail: 'Let it go'. But Emma was not so inclined although she had been appeased somewhat by Abigail's offering.

"Why can't you tell me the name of the father? It wasn't, after all, like the Virgin Mary—Immaculate Conception and all that." This was an attempt at light-heartedness on Emma's part but it seemed to disturb Abigail who blushed crimson.

"I was sworn never to tell."

"Don't you think it was most unfair to blame an innocent man? Why did you say it was Billy?"

"I can't name the real father. I only said Billy because I knew Eliza was so gone on him. It was to tease her, y'know."

Emma would hardly call this a teasing matter. She pursued her line of questioning. "Come on Abigail. For once in your life, tell the truth."

Abigail stroked her belly as if to signify to Emma that she had suffered enough. "Even my own sister, Frances, has never spoken to me like this. It's too much." She edged towards the door and her escape.

"And, in any case, I swore I would never tell. He said it would be a mortal sin if I told anyone."

Emma grabbed her by the arm. "Who said that? You've got to tell me, Abigail, for Eliza's sake and for Billy's too. You can't let an innocent bloke take the blame like that."

"It wasn't Billy. You know that, but I can't tell you who it was," insisted Abigail.

"Behaving like a trollop, and blaming others for your trouble is no good," continued Emma, who like the proverbial terrier was not going to let go once she had got this far.

"I didn't want to ... do what he wanted ... really I didn't ..." Abigail shook her head vehemently.

"You didn't want to, but you *did*. You lifted up your petticoat and let him get into your drawers."

Abigail was shocked; anyone would think Emma had done the same thing herself the way she spoke.

"He said it would be a mortal sin to tell anyone," repeated Abigail as though this would satisfy Emma, but the terrier would not let go.

"It's a mortal sin to tell a lie, and you know it, Abigail. It's also a mortal sin to let a man take advantage of you. That's two mortal sins."

That should have been enough to put the fear of God into any church-goer, but unfortunately, as Emma well knew, it was not enough to make Abigail fear eternal damnation. She had never been a devout Christian. At least Abigail had assured her that Billy was totally blameless. That was the most they could ever hope for and Eliza would stop fretting. But then there was the question of the letter. Before Emma released Abigail from the inquisition, she still wanted to know what happened to that.

"And the letter?"

"When I got home that day, I put it in the cubby-hole, to save till I saw Eliza. Then I forgot about it. Maybe it's still there."

"Cubby-hole!" said Emma, knowing full well that any cubby-hole would be just about as safe as placing the letter on the mantelpiece.

"Make sure you look when you get home. It's caused a lot of upset for poor Eliza. And also, do you realise it's an offence to keep a letter intended for someone else?" She had got this from Alice who knew all the rules of the Royal Mail. But the information wasn't absolutely accurate, as Emma well knew.

Alice had enlarged upon the rules and regulations. "It only applies if the letter has a stamp on it. That letter didn't."

"It almost did, if Billy hadn't bumped into Abigail," Emma had said.

Abigail's thin, pinched face, so like her mother's, began to pucker as she realized her adversary had not finished, but Emma knew she had lost the line of questioning for now. But Emma considered Abigail had been let off lightly. After all, there was no baby to look after or to foist on to someone else, and she *had* recovered although she was not strong.

It was getting dark in the parlour and so instead of lighting the gas lamp, Emma led the way into the kitchen. But something Abigail had said made Emma think that now there was a clue to the philanderer, the one who had put Abigail in the family way. Abigail had used the words "mortal sin" several times. Wasn't that something they said all the time in the Roman Catholic Church, the one where Abigail spent much of her time helping her aunt clean the brasses and dust the statues? She also spent much of her time at the priest's house assisting her aunt in light duties since her severe illness had left her too delicate to continue mill work. Emma had a theory, but did she still need to know? She was now finally convinced that Billy had never been involved with Abigail.

"Why don't you just let sleeping dogs lie?" had been the advice of Eliza, who was contented with the scant knowledge they had of Abigail's terrible secret. All that mattered to her was that Billy had had nothing to do with it.

Emma had never been one to let sleeping dogs lie, but resolved to let this one slumber peacefully, for now. She did wonder, though; Abigail frequented the Roman Catholic Church now, where they had a bazaar selling those potted plants that were the latest rage, where the congregation chanted in Latin, where the priest was not married and where the rule said you must eat fish for dinner on a Friday. So different from Christ Church, the familiar Anglican place of worship, where they had a Bring & Buy Sale, where they used the Book of Common Prayer in English, where the vicar was white-haired, portly and short-sighted, with a wife to match.

"And don't you forget to look for that letter," were her parting words to Abigail.

§

In the spring of 1888, shortly before Mary-Rose's wedding, Mrs. Goodacre's dream had finally come true. A ladies' department at the Goodacre's shop was shortly to be opened and it was to be supervised by Kate. It had taken some time, nearly four years, from Mrs. Goodacre's first dream of such an addition to the tailoring shop. The delay had been due to the unwillingness of Elijah and his son, Nathanial, to relinquish some of their precious space. The two downstairs rooms at the back of the shop that Mrs. Goodacre originally had in mind were, as her husband pointed out, necessary for them to store the many bolts of cloth, equipment and other important items relating to the business.

It wasn't until Nathaniel and Kate vacated the upstairs accommodation to go to their new house next door to his parents that it was finally agreed that the whole upper floor could be utilised for ladies' apparel.

And now the boss and his son had had to surrender part of their downstairs front window to show that ladies were now catered for, with a sample or two on display. To Mrs. Goodacre's chagrin, this event had taken another six months to accomplish.

Kate approached the project with great interest though considerable trepidation and soon realised there would be little help from her mother-in-law who knew only how to wear fashions, not how to make them. Kate could devote time to the business only on a very part time basis because of little Charlie and baby Caroline. The business would need a seamstress as well as another person who could be in the shop at all times to deal with the customers. A smile came to her lips as she thought of the perfect person for this—her sister, Alice, but it seemed doubtful that she could be pried away from Mrs. Kendal's shop as she was, without a doubt, *the* postmistress. Jane was the next candidate in Kate's mind. She probably would be eager to step in because she hated the mill so much. Kate was fully aware that Jane might consider a position in the new ladies' department as a temporary one, as she had set her mind on a career in music. Such a career would require access to fine gowns and the occasion to wear them—at a concert hall in Jane's dreams. Kate was sure Jane would be interested enough to help out in the new department.

Jane had recently reported to Kate. "I hate Mr. Higginbottom! He's always picking on me. He threatened to give me the sack."

Neither of them was too upset about this, knowing she was needed at Goodacre's once the new department opened, but the threat of dismissal was nonetheless an injury to Jane's pride, even though she relished the thought of leaving the unhealthy, noisy mill.

"Every time he passes me he finds fault," said Jane, smarting at the indignity of it all. "He accuses me of not doing what I'm supposed to be doing. He says things like, 'Come on now, Lady Jane, time to get those pianist's hand mucky' or, 'You're not sitting at the piano now; get to it'. I'm sick of sweeping up and changing those rollers. I was doing that when I was a half-timer. I can't stand the sight of Mr. Higginbottom!"

"The sight of him is something you won't have to put up with for much longer," said Kate. "We'll also need a good seamstress. Somebody like Mrs. Burgess. She was excellent." She was a little worried about the enormity of the task before her.

But help was at hand when Mr. Burgess came into the downstairs gentlemen's shop for a new suit.

Kate paved the way by making enquiries about how his dead wife had been such a skilful dressmaker.

"My wife was trained by a French tailor when she lived in London, before coming to Chadderton."

"I had no idea that Mrs. Burgess was originally from London. Come to think of it, though, she didn't have a Lancashire accent, not like everybody else around here." Kate smiled as Mrs. Burgess never did have a lot to say. Who was to notice her accent? Kate wanted to ask Mr. Burgess more about the intriguing matter of Mrs. Burgess and her earlier life in London, but more pressing right now was the need for a seamstress in the new department.

"You should pay a visit to the big haberdashers store in Manchester," was the advice of Mr. Burgess. "They train and employ lots of dressmakers there. Maybe one would like to come and help out here, away from the big city and all."

"But would she want to come to Chadderton, where wages are less?" Kate was doubtful.

But Mr. Goodacre Senior didn't need Kate or Mr. Burgess to tell him where he would find a suitable employee. He already knew he should go to Manchester to find who he wanted since he had been trained there himself in the tailoring business as a young man.

"I'll accompany you if you go to Manchester," Mrs. Goodacre said. "I don't know a lot about dressmaking, but I pride myself on my ability to judge a person's character and potential." She would be the one to choose the seamstress, not her husband.

§

Jane could hardly believe she had just worked her last day at the Glebe Mill. And she was triumphant that she had left of her own accord, not waiting to be sacked by Mr. Higginbottom. Drudgery was a thing of the past and she was now assistant to Kate at Goodacre's Ladies' Fashions. As Kate was only there for an hour or two each day, it was almost like being your own boss, Jane reflected. It was like something out of a storybook—escape from the mill, followed by a new career, although Jane realized that as much as she loved this new opportunity, it took precious time away from her piano practice and studies down at Miss Lamont's, only a few streets away.

Jane soon learned all she needed about the business, but she was a little worried. The arrival of clientele was slow; Goodacre's was not besieged by ladies wishing to have custom-made gowns.

"It's early days as yet," said Kate. "We'll get Alice to put an advertisement in that newspaper they sell at Kendal's, and another one up on the wall by the counter."

It was so quiet that Jane wished they had a piano up in the ladies' department. Then she could practice while waiting for the onslaught of customers, which she and Kate were confident would soon set them all so busy they might even have to hire another seamstress. The large room which had formerly been Kate and Nathaniel's parlour was now transformed into a spacious and elegant salon with pictures of ladies' gowns on the wall and a smooth mahogany counter where a book of dress designs reposed. The shelves above the long and gleaming counter displayed fashionable accessories which had formerly been located in a corner of the main shop downstairs. And racks of walnut and steel shafting displayed different kinds of fabric from linen and bombazine to velvet, muslin, silk and satin. Mirrors were plentiful so Jane was well able to view herself in her new frock with which she had been provided as befitted her position as receptionist and clerk at the new establishment. She had chosen a simple, yet elegant plain dress of grey silk with a small neat collar of white lawn. This gown had been made by eighteen-year-old Millie Bradshaw of Manchester, hired by Mrs. Goodacre. Only two years older than Jane, Millie, a skilled seamstress, had been keen to move to Chadderton where she could work unsupervised and, conveniently, take lodgings nearby with some relatives.

"You should tell Mr. Goodacre and Nathaniel to remind all those gents who come in for suits they should bring their wives as well," said Emma. "While the men are having a fitting, the ladies could look through some patterns you have up there."

In truth, she was somewhat sceptical about this new department. As usual she didn't keep her thoughts to herself. "It's not going to be easy now, since more than ever they have all those ready-made frocks at the Emporium. And there's the home dressmaker too."

"This is supposed to be an elite business," Kate reminded her. "We're providing the sort of clothing that can't be made at home. And it's much more exclusive than the Emporium. Those gowns all look the same. With us, ladies can choose their own design and material." Even so, Emma remained a doubting Thomas.

"These will cost a pretty penny, much more than the Emporium," Emma reminded her.

"But the wives of our gentlemen customers will be able to afford it," insisted Kate, mentally making a note to herself to remind her mother-in-law that business was slow and to bring along some of her acquaintances. Kate was still a little in awe of Mrs. Goodacre, and in reality, would not be reminding her of anything. But Mrs. Goodacre would see for herself when she came in on her weekly visit.

Jane, at sixteen, was too young and too inexperienced to disagree with her older sisters, but she was optimistic. She knew nothing about sewing machines or fabrics, but she was the best person they could possibly have to welcome customers, and they would hopefully soon be arriving in droves.

Apart from making Jane's new shop dress, Millie had not been set to work. But Kate's theories about the exclusivity of the shop were born out by their first customer, a niece of one of Mrs. Goodacre's friends. But they had not bargained for something so exclusive. Miss Alicia Birch, who had lately arrived from Shropshire, didn't want a new day dress or an evening gown; she wanted a cycling dress. This set Jane and Millie in a panic, rushing to the pattern book on the counter. Was there a design for such a thing as a cycling outfit? To their relief, at the end of the book there was a pattern for those forward-minded enthusiasts who followed the latest trend of cycling; an outfit with a high-cut jacket and full skirt in a suggested material of gray plaid. A wide band of leather would be sewn round the bottom of the skirt to prevent it flying up in the wind and there was even a military style cap to match.

"I'm not sure about gray plaid," said Miss Birch. "I'd like something more colourful, like the Highland tartan Queen Victoria's been wearing."

But in any case, Millie would have to send for the material as plaid was the one kind of cloth Goodacre's did not have in stock and it was not produced locally. There was some discussion about what colour or shade would be agreeable.

"I wish Robbie was here. He'd know—with his tam-o'shanter and tartan trews," said Jane, but they hadn't seen him since Eliza had broken off the engagement; it was unlikely they would see him for some time, if at all.

After some debate, and with Millie's expertise on material and colour, a resolution was reached on what would be the ideal fabric for this most unusual dress. The bolt of cloth would soon be dispatched from Manchester. Miss Birch would have her outfit in a couple of weeks and she would be up and away, cycling on the moors with her friends.

It had been mooted by Mrs. Goodacre that Mary-Rose's wedding dress might be made at this new department, but Mary-Rose had been engaged to Ben since last summer, and her wedding gown was almost finished.

§

Mary-Rose and Ben's wedding was a splendid occasion, almost as wonderful as Kate's had been, thought Jane, although that was becoming a dim memory. She loved her pale pink satin dress even it did come from the Emporium and was not custom-made like those gowns they would be creating at the ladies' department of Goodacre's, her new place of employment.

Mary-Rose was resplendent in her dress of white brocade with silver-thread embroidery, done by Eliza, on the points of the sleeves and at the heart-shaped neck. The exquisite gown had been made with the help of everyone in the house, even Kate who had taken sections of it back to her house in order to do some of the work on her sewing machine. But most of the dress was hand-stitched by Mary-Rose herself.

Her twin sister had given little help and seemed to be distant from all the pre-wedding fuss and general commotion. If Mary-Ann felt excluded from her twin sister's nuptial bliss, she was to feel even more so at the end of the reception in the church hall. After the ham sandwiches, sausage rolls, pork pies, punch and ale, the magnificent cake was cut. Speeches were made, but there was a shock in store for them all when Ben stood up and made his bridegroom's speech.

He spoke at length of his love for his sweet bride, of his attachment to the Kershaw family, his thanks to his beloved parents, his adored sister and to the uncle who employed him. Continuing on, just as the guests thought he had said everything a bridegroom could possibly say, he made an astonishing announcement: "And in a few months, I shall be stealing Mary-Rose away from Chadderton." Ben made a significant pause. "We'll be off to America."

Emma was fit to be tied. Indeed, they were all too shocked to speak. Mary-Ann started to cry. Mary-Rose's eyes were riveted on the table, that section of which was covered by a damask tablecloth from her home in Bower Lane. Her face was flaming pink. She must have known about this bombshell, Emma was sure. Why, oh why hadn't she told anyone?

Ben drove his point home. "Yes! The New World is the place for us. I can drive a cart just as well in America as I can here. But that's not what I'll be doing. I'm going to work for my mother's uncle. He owns a whaling station. In New Bedford, Massachusetts."

Chapter Eighteen

Stunning news, in Jane's opinion. In the aftermath of the wedding, all talk of the big day paled in light of Ben's announcement that he and his bride, Mary-Rose, would be leaving England for America in mid-August. The S.S. *Roman* had been sailing regularly from Liverpool to Boston since 1887 and, according to Ben, was an everyday occurrence. If this was so, Emma could not see why they had to depart before Eliza's wedding in September, but Ben had planned this for some time and was adamant they had to go when there was available passage.

There was much discussion and mounting excitement about the young couple's plans, but Jane had her doubts. "I don't think I'd like to sail on a Roman ship," was her opinion.

"It's just the name of the ship," said Ben. "It was built by Cammell Laird's in Birkenhead and it's just as British as you and me."

This comforted Jane somewhat but she didn't like the thought of Mary-Rose sailing so far away. A funeral—that was always the end of life, final. But a wedding was usually the start of something— a new life with someone you loved, and in the case of Mary-Rose, the start of a journey to the unknown. But for Jane, this seemed like the end. Would they ever see Mary-Rose again? Ben had said it might take two weeks to get to Boston. A fast ship would take only six days, but he wasn't sure of the speed of the S.S. *Roman*. Mary-Ann showed no interest in this matter. If she was upset that her twin sister was going to leave the country, she did not show it.

"For all I care, they can travel on a ship made in Birkenhead or Glasgow, and they could be going to Africa instead of America; it's all the same to me," she said. But Jane knew different. She could tell, deep down, Mary-Ann was hurting at the secret Mary-Rose had kept from them all, that she was leaving England for the 'New World' as so many people called it.

Emma took an extremely dim view of this whole situation. Why anyone in their right mind would want to go to pastures new, especially ones so far away and unknown, was beyond her comprehension. According to Ben, it was not going to the 'unknown', as he had been in correspondence with his great-uncle in America for many months. He knew all about the life out there; especially the whaling industry and was sure that was what he wanted to do. They would sail to Boston and from there would they would take a train to New Bedford where his great-uncle lived.

Naturally, a little bit of an inquisition was not above Emma and she wasted no time in grilling Mary-Rose.

"How could you go along with all this … this talk of going to America, and never saying a word to any of us?"

"Mum's the word. That's what he told me," said Mary-Rose. "I wanted to tell you, but Ben said, 'No! Wait 'til after the wedding'. That's what he said."

"Oh, he thought we'd talk you out of it, did he?" said Emma, hurting again at what she perceived to be a great deception on the part of Mary-Rose.

"He wanted to announce it at the wedding. To be a big surprise," said Mary-Rose, squirming under Emma's everlasting questions.

"What kind of a job is that? A whaler?" Emma was critical. "I've heard those whaling ships are gone for months, sometimes years, and those sailors—some of them never come back. How are you going to manage if that happens?"

"Oh, Ben won't be going to sea," said Mary-Rose, laughing at Emma's misinterpretation of the facts. "He'll be working directly for his great-uncle, in the company warehouses, right on the docks. He's a big-wig, his Uncle Albert. And we'll have a house of our own too, in the best part of town."

"You might as well be going to Timbuktu." Emma was still in shock and reluctantly dismissed the matter, for the time being. There was nothing she could do about it, of course. Mary-Rose was now married so that was the end of that.

At least when Eliza married Billy in September, she would be living in Ashton-under-Lyne. It was only six miles away. That was a relief to Emma.

§

In late May, Miss Estelle Lamont was not well. Increasingly, she had asked Jane to postpone her twice-weekly lessons and had not been able to make them up. She had even asked Jane if she would take over lessons for the younger boys at the Blue Coat School.

"In any case, there is no more I can teach you, my dear Jane," said the frail sixty-four-year-old piano teacher. "It's time you furthered your musical education. You should be going to a music school in Manchester, or even London. Yes, London would be better." Miss Lamont had herself graduated from the Royal Academy of Music in her youth. Jane still had a few months to go before her seventeenth birthday but Miss Lamont was right; she should be thinking ahead. Much as she liked Goodacre's, she did not want to stay there forever. The first obstacle would be Emma. She would have a large say in this matter but then, she had not objected to Amy going to university. Why then should she not be in agreement with Jane going to music college?

"For a start, where would you live if you went to London?" was Emma's first question. "If you went to Manchester, maybe you could stay at the same place as Amy."

Jane knew immediately this would not work out as Amy was in the Residents' Hall at Victoria University and anyone not attending that university would not be able to stay there. And in any case, she had a mind to go to London, not Manchester. She wanted to go where Alice had been. Tales of Alice's exploits in London had enthralled Jane. The rest of the family knew that some of these accounts had been embellished to some extent, thereby making them more exciting, but Jane found them endlessly entertaining. She had just discovered Manchester had no official school of music at that time. The conductor of the Hallé Orchestra, Sir Charles Hallé, had tried to initiate one, but so far there were only rumours and requests. Waiting for the possible start of a music college was no good to Jane. In any case, she desperately wanted to go to London.

"I could stay with Aunt Clara," she suggested, to placate Emma, "for a while." Secretly, this was the last thing she wanted, but she would consider anything to get Emma to agree, always supposing she could get into the Royal Academy of Music, Miss Lamont's alma mater.

"And there's Algy," added Jane, as there was no reply from Emma, who was busy ironing sheets. Jane knew that Aunt Clara's or Algy's would not be suitable for more than a few weeks because neither domicile possessed a piano. She would need to practice at her place of residence and not rely on available practice time at the college which might keep her out late.

"First, you'd better see if you can even get in there," said Emma. "And don't forget; there's the fees."

"I have money saved," said Jane with pride. "I've not been working at Goodacre's for nothing you know. And don't forget I'm also teaching those little boys at the Blue Coat."

Emma was fully aware that Jane had been saving hard, putting most of her wages from the mill and now at Goodacre's into a post office savings account. But as usual, Emma put forth her objections. "That's all very well while you're earning, but you won't be earning anything at a music college."

"Miss Lamont said I could probably find a few beginner pupils, like she did, when she was a student there. That would help towards fees. And Pa will surely give me some money. He's keen on me doing music."

This was true, so for now Emma concurred with the plan, even offering to accompany Jane down to London for the college entrance exam which would be in September. If successful, she would start the following September by which time she would be just eighteen.

"There may well be a waiting list; the sooner you apply, the better." said Miss Lamont. "But you'll have to pass the entrance examination." She was, however, a little worried as Jane had left school at twelve years of age, and that could mean her education was by no means up to college entrance standards. Miss Lamont determined to mention this to Jane as she knew that her sister, Amy, at college in Manchester, had been tutored by Mr. Burgess to make sure she had been up to the mark. Hopefully, Jane would be able to do the same. Still, it was something that should be attended to without delay.

Whether there was an entrance examination and a waiting list as long as the Doomsday Book, Emma had no doubt that if Jane wanted to get into the Royal Academy of Music, that's what would happen. She had long known that Jane had been born with charm along with her aptitude and good looks, and no door would be slammed in her face. Nevertheless, she deemed Miss Lamont's idea of tutoring for Jane to be necessary and sensible, ensuring Jane would not be lacking in her general education. Emma determined to speak to Mr. Burgess about it.

§

"It's all a question of scales—the backbone of music," insisted Miss Lamont who, although far from well, was lying on the couch in her music room, supervising Jane. "The fundamentals are scales and arpeggios. If you know them inside out, you can't go far wrong. You'll be asked to sight-read a piece of music as well as play one of your own choice. There may be a set piece as well. You should study all the Beethoven sonatas. They love to trot some of those out for the sight-reading. Mozart too, but you know quite a few of those."

Now came the question of who should take Jane's place at Goodacre's as she was taking up an unofficial part-time job as piano teacher to junior boys at the Blue Coat School. What about Mary-Ann, the only other eligible member of the family?

But Mary-Ann had had a sudden change of heart. More and more recently, she couldn't bear the thought of her twin sister going so far away and the likelihood she would never see her again.

"I've told Davey Clothier I'll marry him," said Mary-Ann to an astonished Emma. "He's going to America with Ben and Mary-Rose, so if I marry him, I can go too."

Emma, not one for hurried weddings, took this piece of news with bad grace. If Mary-Ann was to go with Davey, there would have to be another wedding soon, before the sailing date in mid August. She was already highly annoyed that Ben and Mary-Rose's departure date was only two weeks before Eliza's wedding. They would miss it.

"I must say, you're a dark horse," observed Emma to Mary-Ann's unexpected change of mind. "Why didn't you marry Davey at the same time as Mary-Rose married Ben? It would have saved a lot of trouble."

"I didn't want to get married back then, but with Mary-Rose's wedding and everything and her going away, I've decided that's what I want to do. And as for Davey, he's over the moon about it."

"A mighty strange way of going about things," observed Emma. "You'd best be talking to vicar and setting a date." Emma's favoured way of 'going about things' as everyone well knew, was taking a long time, with meticulous planning well ahead. "How are we to make arrangements for another wedding so quickly? What will everyone say? We're only just getting over Mary-Rose's wedding in April."

For now, though, they would all go along with the new arrangements and hasten to arrange the wedding.

"Goodness," said Jane, "That's three weddings this year. Mary-Rose's in April, then Eliza's still to come in September and in the meantime, Mary-Ann has to get wed before that Roman ship sails off to America."

Being practical, and in the interests of economy, Emma suggested Mary-Ann should use her twin sister's wedding dress.

"I am *not* getting married in a second-hand dress, even if it was Mary-Rose's," said Mary-Ann. "Davey says we're above that. He wants me to have a day dress. You know, something stylish, and have it made by Millie at Goodacre's."

§

In early June, arriving home from Goodacre's, Jane had some interesting news for Alice. "Archie Hawkins is back from London. He came into Goodacre's with his mother for an evening gown to be made, and he's paying for it."

Alice was burning with curiosity, fairly itching to find out how Archie had fared in London since she last saw him, and if he was still an actor.

"Oh, yes, certainly he is," said Jane. "He's come back up north and he's been taken on at the Theatre Royal in Manchester. He told me he's going to be in a play that's being put on by some fellow he knew in London."

Alice had pangs of jealousy, just for a few moments. Hadn't she wanted to do well on the stage? Why couldn't she have met someone influential like that before she was forced to leave her acting career?

"Don't you go hobnobbing with that scallywag again," warned Emma. "He led you astray, and don't you forget it. You're settled now with a good job."

"He did not lead me anywhere. I went of my own accord." Alice had fleeting moments of regret and then reflected on her good job and how much more reliable it was than one on the stage.

At this point in Alice's life, there was no danger of her being led astray, or wanting to meet Archie again. The only thing she was curious about was how he had succeeded on the stage, unlike herself. Apart from this question, Archie was the last person Alice was interested in. She had other matters crowding her mind; new, disturbing and confusing matters compared to the erstwhile straight-forward opinions she usually held. Alice could not get the thought of a certain someone out of her mind, even though she had met him only a few times. She hadn't seen him for months. And even then, he had hardly noticed her. At the time, he had been engaged to Eliza.

She could not stop herself thinking about Robbie who had not been to visit them since the broken engagement in January. She began to fear these thoughts, and for the first time began to understand what had ailed girls like Eliza or Kate, when all they could think of was one young man in particular. Alice was in love for the first time in her life.

"When's Robbie going to come and see us again?" she asked her father when he came home in late June, once again alone.

"I reckon he's still moping after our Eliza. He'll be coming, by and by. Just you wait and see. Robbie told me he doesn't want to run the risk of bumping into her. Get her off to Ashton and he'll be a-visiting us again. Just you wait and see."

"Eliza's wedding is still over two months away. Will we have to wait till the middle of September for Robbie to come and visit? Pa, you've got to bring Robbie with you, next time you come home," said Alice.

"He's still getting over Eliza," said the worldly-wise Jane. "But he should realize the next best thing to Eliza is Alice. I wish I could talk to him. I'd soon convince him."

"Don't meddle in affairs that don't concern you," said Emma. She was amused at Jane's attempts at match making, and silently commended her young sister for her efforts. She seemed to be as ambitious as Emma herself for the family to be happily settled. Some were settled, like Kate, the twins, and Eliza. There was still Amy, but she was busy at college in Manchester—far too busy to think about getting married. "And what about you, Jane? Don't you want to get married, some day?"

"That sort of thing is for others, not for me. I'm married to music and that's that."

§

Mary-Ann's wedding was only three weeks away when Emma came home from work one day and was surprised to find the house empty. Usually, Mary-Ann was the first one home as she worked at the nearest mill, Glebe. Goodness knows where Jane was—either at Goodacre's or the Blue Coat School or practising at Miss Lamont's. Alice was due home from Kendal's shop at any moment. But, where was Mary-Ann?

Emma started preparations for high tea. It had been a cool and rainy day for early July. She hoped the weather would improve for the wedding. Putting on her pinafore and going to the pantry, she was interrupted by an urgent knocking at the front door. It was Mr. Higginbottom. He looked worried.

"Come quickly, Miss Kershaw. We must get to the infirmary right away. I'm afraid I have bad news for you."

"What is it? Why the infirmary? Emma remained composed. "It's Mary-Ann, isn't it?"

"I came as soon as I could. Your sister collapsed at the mill about half past three this afternoon. We had to send for the doctor and he took her to the infirmary right away."

Taking off her pinafore and replacing it with her light summer shawl, she rushed to follow Mr. Higginbottom out to the street.

"Oh, just a minute. I'd better leave a note for Alice and Jane." After scribbling a message which she left on the kitchen table, Emma held on to her bonnet strings and ran outside to where Mr. Higginbottom was waiting in his pony and trap.

"Is it ... B ... the cotton disease?" Emma could not bring herself to say the word, but he knew what she meant.

"Yes, the doctor says it probably is Byssinosis." Mr. Higginbottom uttered the dreaded word.

They threaded their way through the busy streets where hordes of mill workers were hurrying home, their clogs and boots clattering and their voices raised in animated chatter. Emma clutched the side of the trap and wondered why, out of all these workers, did Mary-Ann have to get this dreadful disease? That would account for her cough these past months and her listlessness. Why had she, Emma, not taken heed of it? Why had she not insisted that her sister see the doctor?

Mr. Higginbottom said, "I'm sorry about this, I . . ."

"Are you? Truly? Then why dock wages when someone is ill? Why fire them? You work people to the bone then punish them for the illness that your mill causes."

Higginbottom snapped the reins over the pony's back. "She never seemed ill. Not a bit. Just a cough. Everyone coughs. It comes and goes. Especially after the weekend. I thought it was just the 'Monday' disease."

On arrival at the Royal Infirmary in Oldham, Emma found her sister in a room by herself. Seeing her motionless form, Emma felt that familiar feeling of panic whenever anything was amiss in her family. She stopped a nurse who was hurrying along the corridor.

"Why is she isolated? It's not contagious, is it?"

"We are not yet absolutely certain what it is. The doctor still has to give us a firm diagnosis," said the duty sister.

Emma approached the bed. All she could see of Mary-Ann was her long brown hair strewn over the pillow. Her face was hidden and she was sobbing, saying what sounded like 'I'm dying, I'm dying,' over and over again.

"Pull yourself together, Mary-Ann," said Emma, recovering her composure and lifting the sheets under which her sister was buried. "You are *not* dying."

Emma recalled, like Alice, Mary-Ann was sometimes given to histrionics. But, she had to admit, this situation was serious.

"Then why am I here? Can I go home?"

"Obviously not, at present, anyway," said Emma looking around for the doctor. She wanted to speak to him.

"Only young Dr. Foster has seen her so far," said the nurse. "He wants our senior doctor, Dr. Farraday, to see her."

"What did Dr. Foster say?" asked Emma, leaning over the bed, straightening the covers and tidying Mary-Ann's hair. She raised her sister's head, dabbing the tear-stained face and turning the sodden pillow over. Mary-Ann grabbed Emma's hand as if it were a lifeline.

"It certainly seems to be her lungs," said the nurse. "But you'll have to wait for Dr. Farraday. He's been out all afternoon on calls. He's due back soon."

"She's getting married in three weeks," said Emma, trying to extricate herself from Mary-Ann's iron clasp of her hand.

The look on the nurse's face, as she tossed her head as if to say 'nonsense' made Emma panic again, especially when Mary-Ann was suddenly overcome by a paroxysm of coughing. She was also extremely flushed with two high spots of deep colour on her very pink cheeks. She had a fever; that was certain.

But even so, Emma did not believe that death was near, not with that vice-like grip of Mary-Ann's.

About half an hour later, Alice and Jane arrived at the infirmary, having read Emma's hurried note on the kitchen table. The two girls approached the bed apprehensively, silently.

Mary-Ann roused herself a little and gave a wan smile to her two younger sisters, whilst still holding firmly on to Emma's hand. The room was hushed as the three girls gathered round their sister, silently hoping and praying it was not as bad as it looked. There was plenty of activity in the corridor with the clacking of heels on the bare floors, but all footsteps passed their door, till a nurse eventually came in to say "Dr. Farraday has still not arrived. But Matron has sent along something to strengthen the patient. She's very weak."

"Matron said to try and eat this," said Emma, offering Mary-Ann a cup of thin gruel, which no doubt was nourishing but looked unappetising. Emma was offering it to the patient as if it were a tasty morsel, thought Jane, but Mary-Ann turned her head away. "Nay, I can't eat anything."

"You should try and get some of it down you," said Alice. Looking at the clock on the wall which showed a quarter past seven o'clock, she thought it opportune to remind her sister of something, even though she did appear to be seriously ill. "Jane and me, we've not had our tea yet, nor has Emma."

"Doesn't matter," said Emma whose appetite always disappeared in a family crisis.

"Can we go home now?" asked Alice, having ascertained from her own observations that Mary-Ann was not going to quit this world immediately.

"Yes, you two go on home," ordered Emma. "I'll wait on the doctor."

§

It was late when Emma reached home that night, having waited and waited for the senior doctor to come and examine Mary-Ann.

"It's just what Dr. Foster thought," said Emma. "Mary-Ann has cotton disease and she must stay in the infirmary for a week or two, then she can come home. But she mustn't work in the mill again."

"Maybe she could go to Birkenhead, like I did, for the sea air," said Jane.

"That was for T.B., not Byssinosis," said Emma. "Doctor said nowt about sea air. He just said to stay away from the mill."

"Everybody knows sea air is good for the lungs, no matter whether it's the cotton disease or the tuberculosis."

"All right, Doctor Jane," said Emma. "We'll ask the physician, but so far he says she's never to set foot in the mill again and must go up on the moors for fresh air. Only when it's fine though. Not when it's misty or foggy."

"It's nearly always misty or foggy," said Jane. "She'd be better off at Birkenhead with the sea breezes."

"Well then, Miss Know-All, I'll see about reserving her room at Elm Street," said Emma, talking idly to bolster their mood. "Mrs. Kelly might like to have a young lass staying there again."

But as they all knew, it was idle talk. Jane had been only ten years old when she had stayed there. A child was one thing, but it was certain that there would be no provision for a naïve, twenty-two-year-old girl in lodgings for working men.

Emma felt relieved. Although Mary-Ann's diagnosis had been severe, Dr. Farraday and Dr. Foster both had said with her young age, Mary-Ann stood a good chance of recovering to some extent. "I have known a few die from it, but they were old and frail," is more or less what one of the doctors had said.

"What about the wedding?" asked Alice, the only one to mention this important event. "Will she be all right to get wed?"

"Doctor said we'll see in a week, how she is. The wedding may have to be postponed." Emma secretly worried about the ramifications. If Mary-Ann did not get married, she would certainly not be able to go to America. But what was more important was Mary-Ann's recovery from the dreaded disease, although the seriousness of it meant that it would take some time.

Davey had been to the infirmary to see Mary-Ann and staunchly had said that no matter what, he and Mary-Ann were getting married on the appointed day.

But Emma was more practical. Two things were abundantly clear to her. First, the hastily planned wedding might have to be put on hold and second, the imminent sea voyage to America for Mary-Ann and Davey would likely have to be cancelled.

Then Ben put Emma's fears into words. "If Mary-Ann has any kind of illness, there's no way she'll be allowed to board ship at Liverpool on August 15th, married or not. And we all have to be there the day before, for the medical exam."

"What medical exam?" asked Mary-Rose who suddenly saw yet another obstacle being placed before her wildest dream that had seemed to be coming true, that her twin sister was going with them to the New World. That dream was rapidly fading as she despondently listened to her husband.

"They're not going to let us on board without finding out first if we're all healthy." Ben struggled for the right words, from that pamphlet he had read so many times. "They want to make sure we aren't taking something nasty over there. They want immigrants, but they want 'em fit as a fiddle."

"I read somewhere they sometimes put you in a disinfectant bath and they fumigate your baggage," said Davey.

"They won't do that, seeing as we're not steerage passengers," explained Ben, who was proud of the fact they were all going third class. "But as like as not they'll give everyone's chest a good listen to. There's either a doctor from the steamship company or an American doctor. You can't expect them to let you on board ship willy-nilly."

This worried Emma as Mary-Ann's major symptom was the cough accompanied by the wheezing in her chest. Any doctor would be sure to detect that right away. There was also the intermittent fever.

"I heard that one voyage got as far as Queenstown and they put a lad back on shore because they found he had epilepsy. That was the last stop before the long voyage over the Atlantic, and the poor fellow had to get himself all the way back here from Ireland." Ben had heard variations of this tale.

"Isn't that just tittle-tattle?" queried Emma, hoping that's what it was but, also, wasn't she secretly cherishing the thought that Mary-Ann would stay in England? "You don't think they'd do that with Mary-Ann?"

"No! They would discover it before the ship even sets sail. She probably won't pass the medical." Ben was certain about that. "And then when we get to Boston, we've got to go through another medical exam with the doctor there, just to make sure, like."

"That would be a bit daft," said Emma. "If they found something wrong then, what would happen?"

"Go into quarantine or send them home on the next ship," said Ben.

Emma tried to put this from her mind even though Mary-Ann was so pale and sickly-looking when she came home from the infirmary a week later. No one could possibly mistake her for her identical twin sister. Immediately, she was made to lie on the sofa by the kitchen fire, the place her mother had occupied for many weeks when she had been so ill, six years earlier. However, the doctors said Mary-Ann had improved beyond their expectations. She was perking up considerably, although still desperately weak. Emma was hoping the weather would improve so that they could take her out for some fresh air, but she was still not well enough to leave her make-shift bed.

Everyone was kind and generous, sending Mary-Ann the greatest delicacies but she was not a good patient, hardly taking a bite of anything except when Davey came to visit, putting on an act for him, according to Jane. He brought some calf's foot jelly for the invalid and was trying to tempt her with it when Alice stormed into the kitchen.

"Oh, that Mrs. Kendal," said Alice as she flung off her cloak on to the sofa almost on top of Mary-Ann. "She wouldn't let me order those forms for the post office a month ago. Oh, no! And now we've run out. I really need them. How can I manage if she does this all the time?"

"It's the maid's day off," said Emma, picking up Alice's cloak. "You know where this goes."

Alice's problems at work were the last thing on Emma's mind. The wedding in one week was going ahead at Davey's insistence. It was going to be a quiet affair with just the two families in attendance and, after the ceremony at Christ Church, there would be a modest spread at the house. Then, barely a month after that, the bride and groom would sail away from England, along with Mary-Rose and Ben.

Emma had to confess, this wedding was not to her liking. After the splendid affair of Kate's and more recently Mary-Rose's nuptials it was rather disappointing. Jane also had to agree they were used to a wedding on a grander scale with the bride in flowing white instead of the simple, but stylish, dress of lavender silk with matching hat due to be worn by Mary-Ann. And whoever heard of bridesmaids wearing their Sunday best? But that is what Emma, Eliza, Alice, Jane and Amy had to do. It was what Mary-Ann and Davey wanted.

The bride looked lovely, though frail, in her dress made by Millie at Goodacre's, the Alexandra Bodice with its narrow, simulated waist-coat and centre buttons making her look thinner than ever. There was the hint of a bustle which had made a come-back over the last two years and was clearly visible as Mary-Ann walked up the aisle on the arm of her father. She walked back down the aisle on the arm of her new husband, pale and shaking, but she did not cough, not even once, during the ceremony.

§

It was a blustery day when Emma and Jane took the train to Liverpool to observe the departure of the twins and their husbands who had made their way there the day before the scheduled sailing of the S.S. *Roman*. Emma and Jane thought they were the only ones who would see the travellers off but they were delighted by the appearance of their father who had taken the ferry over from Birkenhead.

Emma waited patiently at the dockside with Jane and their father, hardly believing they were saying goodbye to some of their family, losing two sisters all at once. The dwindling family that took up occupancy at 54 Bower Lane was still all right in Emma's mind, so long as they were legitimately placed or were residing in the vicinity where she could still see them and exert some authority when needed.

Emma scanned the bustling quay for the twins and their husbands. Perhaps they were still at the inn where they had spent the previous night? It was all so hectic, throngs of people traipsing up and down the main gangway of the great ship S.S. *Roman*. Emma had been firmly told that they could not board—only passengers or VIPs who had been given special permission to embark briefly before the voyage could do so. Countless people of all classes crowded the quay. It was impossible to tell who were passengers and who were relatives seeing them off. Finally, Emma discerned members of their family approaching.

Mary-Ann was pouting whilst Mary-Rose was in tears. Ben and Davey looked like thunder.

"Just like I said," Ben was saying. "Mary-Ann would never get on that ship. Doctor says she's too ill. Didn't I say so?"

Emma had to agree that although Mary-Ann was much improved since her stay in hospital a few weeks ago, she was obviously far from well.

"That ship's doctor doesn't know what he's talking about," insisted Mary-Rose. "Dr. Farraday said she's much better and will get better still."

Emma knew this was true, but also knew from Dr. Farraday that Mary-Ann would never completely recover from the dreaded Byssinosis. So long as she kept away from the mill, she might maintain a reasonable level of lifestyle, but she would never be completely cured. Whilst she was sorry at the news, the thought of Mary-Ann staying behind was a mixed blessing. But Mary-Rose was devastated because her twin would not be going with them.

"And what about you, Davey?" asked Emma. "You're not still going, are you?" According to her firm beliefs, Mary-Ann and Davey should stay together now they were married.

Davey looked confused and could not look Emma in the eye. "I have my job waiting for me."

Ben voiced his friend's fear. "If you don't go, Uncle Albert could give that job to somebody else. Then when you finally arrive, you'll be like all those other fellows setting foot ashore—waiting in line every day till something turns up. That doctor says Mary-Ann can come later, when she's better."

Davey looked gloomy. "Nay, I can't go without my girl. But will I get me old job back at your uncle's in Oldham?" he asked Ben.

Ben sombrely contemplated what Davey should do. It was true. As soon as they had left Huddleston's Haulage Company, their jobs had been taken by other young men.

"I think you should come with us, and let's hope Mary-Ann can come in six months or so. That's what the doctor said." Ben was adamant about this. Davey wished he could be more decisive like his friend. But then Ben was not leaving *his* wife behind. Nothing was going to plan at all.

Davey was torn. He would lose the money he had so far paid for both of them to emigrate, quite substantial, even though part of the cost of the passage was government assisted. Should he go, at Ben's insistence, or should he stay at home for goodness knows how long, till Mary-Ann was fit enough to travel? The house they had lived in for such a short time in Oldham was now rented out to someone else. It was difficult to find good lodgings. And they certainly could not stay, as a married couple, at 54 Bower Lane. Time was of the essence; the ship was due to sail within the hour.

Emma, too, was confused. She had never known any member of her family to take things lying down. "Have a bit of gumption, Mary-Ann," she said to her sister. "Didn't you tell that ship's doctor that Dr. Farraday said you weren't contagious and that you would soon be better with rest and good, fresh air?"

Mary-Ann swirled her bonnet strings whilst examining her toes. "Didn't make any difference," she said, biting her bottom lip. "That doctor said I had a fever and my breathin's all wrong. Said I have a bad cough, and all."

She rushed over to Emma, burying her head in the folds of her sister's cloak. She was shivering violently as she raised her head from Emma's bosom.

"And he chalked somethin' on my back."

They could all see this clearly and knew the letter P stood for 'Pulmonary', the sign that meant a potential passenger had a lung disorder. Poor Davey looked perplexed and worried, his large capable haulier's arms folded across his chest in abject despair, his broad stocky figure braced against the stiff breeze that was strong and fresh from the Irish Sea upon which he was hoping he *and* his wife would soon be sailing.

Could it be, wondered Emma, as she contemplated these troubled waters, that Mary-Ann's reluctance to fight for her right to depart on this ship was that, deep down, she didn't want to leave her family after all? She fancied that Mary-Ann was not truly heart-broken at being left behind. Was it that she did not love Davey as he loved her? After all that work for a hurried wedding which she had insisted on?

"I'll go. And as soon as Mary-Ann is better, she can come and join me, in six months or . . ." Davey knew it would be longer than that, and his dilemma was obvious.

"Ben is right; you can't run the risk of losing that job in New Bedford. His Uncle Albert has a business to run and he's been good enough to offer you a job," said Emma.

Ben, his legs astride, his back to the bustling quay, looked anxiously at the ship. Mary-Rose, convulsed with tears, sat on the black cabin trunk, the one Mary-Ann was supposed to take with her, but which had been removed from the ship.

Emma sat on the cabin trunk and put her arms round Mary-Rose, and said with conviction, "You go with Ben and Davey. Mary-Ann will join you. It won't be long."

She did not fully believe these words herself and she also didn't voice her fear that even if Mary-Ann could go at a later date, how on earth was she to undertake the journey alone?

Charles Kershaw stood on the side-lines of the unhappy group, puffing on his pipe whilst contemplating his family with their sighs and tears as if they were no more important than the bird's eye maple bunks he had just completed on the latest vessel being built at Cammell Laird's. He did, however, offer some advice to Davey who seemed to take heart.

"Eh, lad, you surely know which side your bread's buttered? You *must* get yourself over there to that new job in America," Charles Kershaw emphasized to the confused and dejected young man. "Ye'll be mighty busy and before you know it, ye'll have Mary-Ann over there with you, mark my words."

The ship's whistle pierced the air. The S.S. *Roman* was ready to sail. Sailors ran among the people on the quay calling "All aboard! All aboard!" After a few more hasty embraces, Ben and Mary-Rose jostled with others up the gangplank. With a heavy heart, Davey reluctantly followed them, immediately going below deck so he would not have to look back at the receding coastline of the country he was leaving, where his wife remained.

It was a day of mixed emotions for Emma and Jane. Instead of two of their sisters, only one had left. Sweet, indeed, it was to keep one sister, but at what cost? Jane could hardly believe it as Mary-Ann waved vigorously with hardly a tear in her eye whilst she and Emma wept into their sodden handkerchieves as the ship sailed on the early afternoon tide.

Chapter Nineteen

Mary-Ann travelled home with her sisters on the train to the confines of the small terraced house in Chadderton from which she had had a brief respite but to which she seemed relieved to return.

It was just as well that another wedding, Eliza's, was to occupy the minds of Emma and the remaining girls at home: Mary-Ann, Eliza, Alice and Jane. A month had passed since Mary-Rose had gone away on that great ship. There had been many tears on both sides and promises to write every day and a promise to return if all was not well in New Bedford. And to come back for a visit, if they ever had the opportunity. They all knew it was unlikely. People just did not do that. Once they were off to America, that was that. Jane was sure of it; sure she would not be seeing her sister again. And then there was the likelihood that Mary-Ann would go too. She was to try again in six months. Jane shed a few silent tears, but thank goodness, her favourites were still at home; Alice, whom she was close to these days, and of course, Kate and her two adorable children in Oldham, where Jane called at least twice a week. She had to grudgingly admit it was just as well that Emma was still at home. What on earth would they do if she decided to go away or get married? One never knew these days. Who would have thought that only five sisters would be at home, when not long ago there had been eight of them? And Eliza would be off soon, immediately after her wedding, to her new home in Ashton.

Eliza's wedding was the third this year, but by far the best, as far as Jane was concerned. She, Alice, Mary-Ann and Amy were bridesmaids with Emma, the Maid of Honour. The wedding was quite different from the other two that year. Billy, the bridegroom, had long been in a brass band in Ashton-under-Lyne in which he played the tuba. The band had insisted on performing for the wedding, so after the short, solemn ceremony at Christ Church, the wedding guests had been treated to a fine selection of music at the reception in the church hall. For once, Jane was not required to provide the music for the festivities; the band did that instead. And, for further entertainment, Eliza had requested Alice to recite a favourite poem. During the long winter evenings, they had all been entertained by Alice reading the epic poem "The Song of Hiawatha" by the American, Henry Wadsworth Longfellow, written in 1855 and based on stories and legends of American Indians. It contained stanzas pertaining to "Hiawatha's Wedding Feast", a fascinating and lyrical account of the marriage of Hiawatha and Minnehaha. It was a favourite with all the girls, so the band had a respite from playing and could enjoy the refreshments. Although, in some cases, their attention was not fully on the poem, some of them enjoyed watching the girl reading it. Hardly glancing at the book, she was clutching, Alice recited flawlessly with expressions to match the words.

You shall hear how Pau-Puk-Keewis
Danced at Hiawatha's wedding
How the gentle Chibiabos
He the sweetest of musicians

Sang his songs of love and longing
How Iagoo, the great boaster
He the marvellous story-teller
Told his tales of strange adventure
That the feast might be more joyous
And the time might pass more gaily
And the guests be more contented.

Sumptuous was the feast Nokomis
Made at Hiawatha's wedding
All the bowls were made of bass-wood
White and polished very smoothly.
All the spoons of horn of bison
Black and polished very smoothly.
She had sent through all the village
Messengers with wands of willow
As a sign of invitation
As a token of the feasting.
And the wedding guests assembled
Clad in their richest raiment.
Robes of fir and belts of wampum
Splendid with their paint and plumage
Beautiful with beads and tassels
First they ate the sturgeon, Nahma
And the pike, Minskenozha
Caught and cooked by old Nokomis.
Then on pemmican they feasted
Pemmican and buffalo marrow
Haunch of deer and hump of bison
Yellow cakes of the Mondamin
And the wild rice of the river.

And when all the guests had finished
Old Nokomis, brisk and busy

From an ample pouch of otter
Filled the red stone pipes for smoking.
With the tobacco from the South-land
Mixed with bark of the best willow
And with herbs and leaves of fragrance.
Then she said, "Oh, Pau-Puk-Keewis
Dance for us your merry dances
That the feast be more joyous
That the time may pass more gaily
And our guests be more contented."

The handsome Pau-Puk-Keewis
Skilled was he in sports and pastimes
In the merry dance of snow-shoes . . .
He was dressed in shirt of doeskin
White and soft and trimmed with ermine
All inwrought with beads of wampum
He was dressed in deer-skin leggings
Fringed with hedgehog quills and ermine
And in moccasins of buck-skin
Thick with quills and beads embroidered
On his head were plumes of swan's down
On his heels were tails of foxes
In one hand a fan of feathers
And a pipe was in the other.
From his forehead fell his tresses
Smooth and parted like a woman's
Shining bright with oil, and plaited
Hung with braids of scented grasses
As among the guests assembled
To the sound of flutes and singing
To the sound of drums and voices
Rose the handsome Pau-Puk-Keewis

And began his mystic dances.
First he danced a solemn measure
Very slow in step and gesture,
In and out among the pine trees,
Through the shadows and the sunshine
Treading softly like a panther,
Then more swiftly and still swifter,
Whirling, spinning round in circles,
Leaping o'er the guests assembled . . .
Then along the sandy margin,
Of the lake, the Big-Sea-Water,
On he sped with frenzied gestures,
Stamped upon the sand, and tossed it
Wildly in the air around him . . .
Thus the merry Pau-Puk-KeeWis
Danced the Beggar's Dance to please them,
And returning, sat down laughing
There among the guests assembled,
Sat and fanned himself serenely
With his fan of turkey feathers.

Then they said to Chibiabos,
To the friend of Hiawatha,
To the sweetest of all singers,
To the best of all musicians,
"Sing to us, O Chibiabos!
Songs of love and songs of longing,
That the feast be more joyous,
That the time may pass more gaily,
And our guests be more contented!"
And the gentle Chibiabos
Sang in accents sweet and tender,
Sang in tones of deep emotion,

Songs of love and songs of longing . . .
Sang he softly, sang in this wise:
"Onaway! Awake, beloved!
Thou the wild flower of the forest!

. . .

And Iagoo, the great boaster,
He the marvellous story-teller
Jealous of the sweet musician,
Jealous of the applause they gave him,
Saw in all the eyes around him,
Saw in all their looks and gestures,
That the wedding guests assembled
Longed to hear his pleasant stories,
His immeasurable falsehoods,

Very boastful was Iagoo;
Never heard he an adventure
But himself had met a greater:
Never any deed of daring
But himself had done a bolder:
Never any marvellous story,
But himself could tell a stranger:
Would you listen to his boasting . . .?
No one ever shot an arrow
Half so far and high as he did:
Ever caught so many fishes,
Ever killed so many reindeer,
Ever trapped so many beaver!
None could run so fast as he could,
None could dive as deep as he could,
None could swim so far as he could,
None had made so many journeys,
None had seen so many wonders,

As this wonderful Iagoo
As this marvellous story-teller!

Thus was Hiawatha's wedding
Such the dance of Pau-Puk-Keewis,
Such the story of Iagoo,
Such the songs of Chibiabos:

Thus the wedding banquet ended
And the wedding guests departed
Leaving Hiawatha happy
With the night and Minnehaha.

Jane loved this poem as all the girls did, having listened to Alice's animated reading many times before. She smiled to contemplate that the feast at Hiawatha's wedding was vastly different from the repast they were having at the church hall. Haunch of deer, hump of bison and roast sturgeon indeed!

Instead, the main items were dainty sandwiches of ham, some of Mrs. Kendal's best, and also cucumber, watercress and cream cheese sandwiches. Sausage rolls were also plentiful and small cheese and onion tarts, made with the best crumbly Lancashire cheese. Morecambe Bay potted shrimp, with small rectangles of buttered toast, was something new and delicious, brought by Billy's sister. There were date and nutmeg scones, lemon tarts and Eccles cakes. Eliza, besides sewing her wedding gown, had made the magnificent wedding cake with its ornate crisp white scrolls and carved orange blossom, all from royal icing. Emma, in spite of being busy with last minute adjustments to Eliza's dress, had managed to find time to produce her famous game pie, the one from Mrs. Beeton's book, which had been such a triumph at the picnic last year. Although Jane did not consider it to be on the same scale as Hiawatha's Wedding Feast, she was relieved they didn't have anything like pemmican. She had found out it was a kind of paste made from meat and fat.

Looking around at the guests, Alice voiced her disappointment that Robbie did not attend.

"You could hardly expect him to come to Eliza's wedding, when he wanted to marry her himself," reasoned her father. Nevertheless, Alice was dejected. When would she see him again?

Mr. Burgess and his quiet, brooding daughter, Abigail, were among the guests. It had rankled Emma to invite Abigail as she had caused much suffering for Eliza. Every time Emma saw her, she felt like slapping Abigail's face. As far as Emma knew, Mr. Burgess still had no knowledge of his daughter's waywardness. Eliza seemed to have forgiven Abigail since she had found the missing letter and given it to Eliza with copious apologies.

Mr. Burgess, seated next to Emma at the wedding banquet, chatted amiably, explaining to Emma how Abigail, although recovered from her serious illness from a year ago, was still not strong. "She seems to be fairly well occupied," he continued, "helping my sister do the cleaning at St. Mary's Church and the priest's house."

Mr. Burgess was unusually talkative. He had not seen the Kershaw family much lately, apart from Jane. He had been tutoring her at the Blue Coat School each day when she had finished supervising the piano tuition of the younger boys.

"And you probably heard that my other daughter, Frances, is now married," continued Mr. Burgess. "She's done well, you know, married to the head gardener at Thornbridge Manor. And they've got a cottage on the estate. Of course, our Abigail didn't approve of the marriage. He's a widower and a good deal older than Frances, with two children. But then, you can't have everything the way you want now, can you?" Emma had to agree; young, handsome husbands tended also to be penniless ones and in the case of Frances, her husband, who was not quite old enough to be her father, had a good job, was kind and honest and the ready-made children were obedient and well-behaved. What more could a girl ask for? Yes, Emma had to agree with Mr.

Burgess. Frances had done well. But what about Abigail? Emma could still hardly bear to look at her.

Eliza was a breathtaking bride, thought Jane, and took pride that she had helped, just a little, with the dress, sewing the Guipure lace on the sleeves. Kate's son, four-year old Charlie was the page boy, dressed in a dark blue velvet suit with knickerbocker breeches, white hose and buckles on his patent leather shoes. His task was to hold the bride's train and prevent it from sweeping the floor. He did a good job and the floor was hardly swept at all.

The bridesmaids had new dresses despite the fact that they had been in this same role only a few months ago, at Mary-Rose's wedding. No pale pink this time, as they had worn at Mary-Rose's nuptials, but instead a deep sapphire blue to match little Charlie's outfit.

Emma enjoyed this occasion more than she had the wedding of Mary-Ann. Eliza's wedding was a more leisurely, planned affair down to the last detail, whereas the one of Mary-Ann's had been hurriedly put together and not up to Emma's sartorial or culinary standards. Mary-Rose's earlier wedding at Easter had also met with Emma's approval.

§

September was a busy month. The week after Eliza's wedding, Jane was to go to London to sit the entrance exam to the Royal Academy of Music. Of course, she had to go along with Emma's plans to accompany her. There was no way Jane would be allowed to travel to London alone. Emma had been firm on that.

Emma had made her arrangements carefully, taking two days off from the Wharf Mill. She had written to Aunt Clara well in advance, ascertaining that she and Jane could stay for two nights. The exam was on September 21st, a Friday. They would travel on the Thursday, stay the night at Aunt Clara's, and after the various exams taking up most of Friday, they would stay another night and return on Saturday. As a senior weaver at the Wharf Mill, Emma had had no problems making arrangements with Mr. Leggate, the manager, to take the whole of Thursday and Friday off. She privately considered her lack of wages for two days went against her general principles, but accompanying Jane to London was more important.

Jane was fascinated by the scenes of grandeur alongside poverty in the great capital, and wondered how Alice had managed to survive on her own for a year and a half in this strange, unfriendly city. Her admiration and respect for Alice knew no bounds and for once, Jane was thankful that Emma was with her. It was sixteen years since Emma had left London and she did not remember a lot, except the house where Aunt Clara and her family lived in Islington, a tall, grey, terraced house with four floors, one of which was occupied by her daughter and family. It was nowhere in the vicinity of the Royal Academy of Music which was situated at Hanover Square, but it was still a bonus for them to be able to stay there.

Emma and Jane took an omnibus to the academy early on Friday morning. The first part of the day went well with a written paper on the rudiments of music, and another on general knowledge. Jane was able to answer all the questions, grateful to Mr. Burgess for his careful coaching during the last few months. Next was a short essay on a composer of her choice. Jane's choice was Chopin. She loved delving into his history, with his delicate and then failing health culminating in death at a young age. His romantic entanglement with Georges Sand made Jane's spine tingle but, of course, was not included in her essay. Thankfully, there was no arithmetic, something a music college did not require, and Jane had banked on. Mathematics was a subject she abhorred and for which she had no aptitude.

She had been told to wait outside Salon No. 3 for the next session when she would be asked to play her choice of music, which was the Beethoven Appassionata Sonata. Students brushed past her, voices echoed and then disappeared and there was silence except for the occasional distant sound of piano or strings. For the first time since they had left home, Jane became nervous and afraid in this hallowed, hushed, mysterious building. Where was Emma? She must find her. She suddenly longed with all her heart to be back in Chadderton where life was sometimes unpleasant, hard, but familiar. These echoing corridors were not where she belonged. She began to doubt her own proficiency. Playing the piano should just have been a hobby, a pleasurable pastime, performing at Mrs. Goodacre's, not trying to enter this cold, intimidating environment. She felt ashamed that Emma had put all her faith in her, had helped her prepare for this nerve-wracking event, when in reality, there was no chance. Anger overtook her nervousness, anger at herself. How could she have persuaded Emma, who knew nothing about music, to think she might be skilled enough to enter into this alien world? She felt mortified, even embarrassed at her own confidence which had suddenly dwindled to nothing. She stood there, numb with despair, almost fear. She did not belong here. She had been born to work in a cotton mill and at best in a ladies' dress shop. She shuddered, but for all these feelings, she knew deep down, she still wanted it, but she was afraid it was not for her. She wandered down the corridor, blindly, knowing she must find Emma and they must go home.

A tall gentleman, in scholarly apparel, approached her. "Are you Miss Kershaw? We're waiting for you. Please come this way."

She was shown into a hall which was panelled in dark oak with matching benches and would normally hold an audience. The gallery at the far end, opposite the Steinway piano, held more benches where a huddle of distinguished-looking gentlemen was seated. Jane, who had never played for any audience other than her immediate family, the Goodacres and the Blue Coat School, was intimidated by the officials of the Royal Academy. The setting and the small audience of examiners were daunting. But once seated at the piano, she forgot time, forgot where she was and played the Beethoven flawlessly. The five examiners showed no expression, neither dissatisfaction nor approval. They put their heads together and then asked her to wait in the next room where in a little while she would be asked to play for another panel of examiners—a piece of their choice. That meant sight-reading. There was a boy waiting to come to the piano bench as Jane vacated it. He looked about the same age as her, almost seventeen, but appeared confident, assured. He swept past her, placing his music on the piano with a flourish.

In the next room, she waited at yet another piano. After what seemed an age, another five, learned-looking men, entered the room and sat at the other end on a small dais. This room was a smaller version of the other, but with the same dark panelling.

Once Jane was seated, a stern-looking gentleman who was wearing a gown similar to the ones she had seen at the Blue Coat School came over and thrust a sheet of music on to the piano. Jane looked at it apprehensively. Her doubts swept in again and once more, she wished with all her heart she could find Emma and go home.

"Well, get on with it, we haven't got all day, y'know," said another fellow in the group. They were severe and obviously not used to putting their quarry at ease. Jane felt they were a kind of jury and she was on trial. The man who had spoken took his watch from his waistcoat pocket at least twice and was doing so again. Did it mean her time was up? She stared at the keys as if in a trance. She finally took a grip on herself and took a close look at the music which was the sight-reading test. It was a Schubert sonata and although she had never played it before, she had heard Miss Lamont play it several times. Her sight-reading was fairly good, but her unfailing ear was her best asset as she started slowly and then played without hesitation as if she had performed the piece many times before.

Halfway through the first movement, the man with the watch said, "That's enough." The others were writing things down. "Before you go, we would just like to hear a few scales and arpeggios, starting with the G major scale."

Jane unerringly executed all the scales one after the other, without a break. Then she started the arpeggios, but suddenly the gentlemen started to leave before she had even finished. She concluded that the test was over although she had not expected it to end like that. She quietly left the empty, oppressive room.

Emma was waiting in the main hall of the college when Jane joined her and without a word to each other, they left the building. Emma was on tenterhooks to know how her sister had fared, but she knew better than to question at this point. It would all come out, eventually, as Emma well knew. They made their way back to Aunt Clara's where the family were polite, but distant, not asking too many questions, except one, which had been on Aunt Clara's mind for a while.

"If you *do* get in to this music school, when will you start and where will you be staying?"

"I won't hear for a few weeks," said Jane, wishing those few weeks had already sped by. "But if I *do* get in, I won't be starting till next September, a whole year away, and by that time, I will have found a place to live. It will have to be somewhere that has a piano."

Aunt Clara breathed an almost imperceptible sigh of relief. Much as she felt responsible, to a degree, for her dead sister's child from up north, it was quite another thing for Jane to be living with Aunt Clara's household for more than a few days. Yes, indeed, that was what she had feared.

The next morning, Emma and Jane took their leave, making their way to Euston Station for the train back to Manchester. Emma had their return tickets, but had temporarily mislaid them. The ticket collector waited patiently while she looked through her reticule again, during which time Jane struck up a conversation with him, having recovered from her apprehension of the previous day.

"So you're off back home to Manchester?" enquired the ticket collector.

"Oh, we don't live in Manchester," said Jane with an imperial wave of her hand to stop Emma interrupting her. "*We* live at Chadderton; that's out in the country, you know?" The way she said it made it sound as if they lived at Buckingham Palace. She did not want the ticket collector to think they lived in Manchester, which all

Londoners knew was an ugly, industrial city. She was forgetting the fact that Chadderton was now becoming as industrial and ugly as Manchester itself.

"I've never been out of London myself," he had to admit. "And Manchester is so far north." The way he said it made Jane laugh, as if Manchester was in another hemisphere.

"But, we'll be coming to London again," she assured him. Emma, having found the return tickets looked at Jane quizzically, wondering what she was going to come out with now.

"In about a year's time," continued Jane with assurance. "My mother was from London, you know. She was embroiderer to the Queen."

Emma, fastening up her reticule, looked at her incredulously, while the ticket collector looked impressed.

Once in their third-class compartment, Emma took her sister to task, although she had to laugh as Jane, having got over her nervousness which had been apparent for two days, had reverted to her usual telling of tales. Very tall tales.

"Embroiderer to the Queen? Our mother?" said Emma, laughing at Jane's usual inclination to exaggerate. "What are you talking about?"

"I know she did embroidery for Lady Musgrave, and *she* was a lady-in-waiting to the Queen." As far as Jane was concerned that was tantamount to the same thing. "I remember Ma telling me about it."

"That was when Ma was young. Before she was married," said Emma. "She never did that once she was married and had us children."

For the hundredth time she wondered why her mother had consented to come north. She obviously had no idea what was in store. Hundreds of people had been enticed to the Lancashire cotton mills with promises of steady work. There was little mention of the nature and harshness of the work they were going to. And there had been the prospect of steady work for their father at what was termed as the nearby shipbuilding industry, but it turned out to be over forty miles away which had meant they would not be seeing much of him.

Emma was relieved they were on their way home. As the train rattled past arched embankments, endless grimy houses, bridges and canals, Emma was thinking if Jane did not get into the college on her ability to play the piano, she certainly could take the prize for inventing fantastic stories. They talked about everything except the exam and the ordeal Jane had been through.

"Thank goodness I don't live in London any more," said Emma. "Lancashire is better; the countryside is better, and the people, too. They might be opinionated, and sometimes downright sour, and a bit suspicious of strangers, but they are good-hearted and hospitable."

That could not be said about Aunt Clara's house, which they had been thankful to vacate. Whilst appreciating the free accommodation, both girls had felt oppressed by the sternly religious and forbidding atmosphere in the house. There was no light-hearted banter amongst the family and the only books to be found on the premises were three: a giant-sized Bible, a small, thin Bible (the sort that could be put in a reticule) and a rather battered Bible (obviously, the grandchildren had ready access to that one). The parson had visited while Jane and Emma had been there and he had conducted a prayer meeting for the welfare of one of Aunt Clara's grandchildren. The child had suffered severe hearing loss after a protracted illness and was unable to go to school. The prayer meeting continued for twenty minutes and when the parson had left, Aunt Clara, always handsomely and impressively dressed in black silk, had conducted a second prayer session of her own. In fact, there was altogether too much praying, thought Jane. She was used to going to church on Sunday, and to saying her prayers kneeling by the side of the bed before she leapt into it, but this prolonged praying before and after each meal and at other times was too much. And those jellied eels they were so fond of—Jane had not been able to bring herself to even taste them. The sight of them was enough to put her off this Cockney delicacy. But her fears were eclipsed; she still had a desperate wish to return to London and the Royal Academy of Music.

As the countryside zipped past on their way north, Emma had another thought on why she didn't like London. "There's that Jack the Ripper who's been terrorizing the Whitechapel area. Six gruesome murders, all women. I'll never have a moment's peace if you go to live in London."

"I'm not worried about Jack the Ripper," said Jane

But Emma always had something to worry about. Now she was worried about how Jane had fared in her exams. Even if she had played like Franz Liszt himself, it didn't necessarily mean that she would get a place at the prestigious music college. Emma had no ambition for herself, but for her sisters it was limitless. In spite of her fears of Jack the Ripper and a dozen other things, Emma could hardly wait for that slim envelope which they knew would soon be delivered by the postman. Whether good news, or bad, the letter would surely arrive within the next two or three weeks.

Chapter Twenty

Emma knew that Jane would be in painful suspense until she heard the result of the entrance examination to the Royal Academy of Music. Stoically, Jane made no mention of her agonising wait; she kept herself fully occupied with three hours a day at Goodacre's followed by her commitments at the Blue Coat School. Emma was anxious too, but other things also filled her mind. She was ambivalent about Mary-Ann's return to 54 Bower Lane. Emma had to admit it would have been preferable if Mary-Ann had gone with her husband to America. As things now stood, the convalescent girl was at a loose end most days, in spite of Emma giving her light chores to do about the house while she, Jane and Alice were at work.

"You're only supposed to go walking up on the moors when it's fine, not in this fog," said Emma one day when she arrived home from work to find Mary-Ann had just come in, wet and bedraggled.

"It was sunny when I set off," said Mary-Ann, trying not to cough, as she shed her damp clothes and put them on the clothes horse in front of the kitchen fire.

Emma was somewhat perturbed about Mary-Ann's persistent cough but her appetite was better and she didn't look quite so sickly.

"Did you finish that ironing left from last night?" asked Emma, and then saw the scones on the kitchen table which was set for tea. "Oh, I see you did some baking." Although used to Emma's stringent rules, Mary-Ann did not feel she needed to strictly adhere to them. Wasn't she now a married woman? She felt slightly superior to Emma.

"There's a letter," Mary-Ann said, knowing the effect this would have on Emma, who rushed out into the hall and pounced on the vellum envelope. But it was not the one they were anxiously waiting for, or more aptly, what Jane was waiting for. It was, however, a welcome surprise for it was the first letter from Mary-Rose across the ocean in far-away New Bedford, Massachusetts.

"Still no post?" asked Jane when she came home, and although disappointed that her longed-for letter had not come, was placated by the arrival of the letter from Mary-Rose. They all considered this long overdue, although it was only six weeks since the sailing. Taking it in turns to read the letter, they devoured news of the different kind of life their sister now led in America. Ben was busy working for his great-uncle Albert, with a brief portrayal of the latter, a hard taskmaster but fair and understanding. Then followed a detailed description of the house they had, which sounded like a huge, barn of a place, near the harbour. Mary-Rose enquired about her twin sister and said that a letter was on its way from Davey and they all hoped Mary-Ann would be joining them in the spring.

§

Jane's eagerly-awaited letter from London arrived the day Charles Kershaw came home for the first time in two months, bringing Robbie Cameron with him. The young steelworker had finally been persuaded to visit the family again, although he was still despondent about the girl he loved who had broken off the engagement in January, nearly ten months ago. He had told Charles that he could never come to the house again on account of Eliza and the agonizing reminder of her rejection. However, Charles prevailed upon the young man's good nature to try and overcome this episode since Eliza now lived in Ashton.

"I think she drops in to see her sisters quite often," said Charles. "But she's not likely to be there on a Saturday or Sunday."

Robbie's visit was toned down somewhat by the arrival of that important letter for Jane. The postman had hardly put it through the letterbox when it was snatched up.

"I've passed, and I'll be going to London," said Jane, and then took to dancing and singing around the kitchen table applauded by the audience of her sisters, father and Robbie. The words echoed round the house for hours, "passed, going to London, passed, going to London, next year, next year, next year . . .".

Emma, practical as ever, read the letter herself and pointed out that although not a full scholarship had been awarded, there was a fairly decent one. And it came with extra money attached, from a patron of the academy who was a relation of Miss Lamont.

"That's what knowing influential folk does for you," said a satisfied Emma.

"Influential folk be damned—she more likely did it on her own merit, with *her* gift," said her proud father. "Jane, you've passed with flying colours. Whatever else is needed, I'll provide."

"Where will you be living?" was Alice's question, the memory still fresh in her mind of her stay in London, and the problem with lodgings she had experienced.

"I've got a whole year to find out," said Jane, "I'll find something suitable long before next September."

Some celebrations were in order that day, as Charles Kershaw insisted on Emma not going to the trouble of making high tea, although of course, it had been planned.

"We'll live it up a bit today," he said, as he and Robbie went to the fishmongers.

They brought back the best fish and chips, and on the way home, they picked up a bottle of wine and some beer from the pub.

A joyful party ensued, with speculations of what was in store for Jane in London and where she would stay, which was most uppermost in Emma's mind. They all repaired into the rarely used front parlour where Jane was asked to play the harmonium, something she had not done for over a year.

Robbie seemed to be cheerful and entered into the family celebrations, trying not to think of the absent Eliza and his sorrowful parting earlier that year. He took no special notice of Alice, much to her mortification. But he certainly admired all the girls. Of Jane he thought "She's a canny lass, and musical" and of Alice "the entertainer". With her endless recitations and her acting out of them, he had been thoroughly taken out of himself.

"Do you not think Robbie is so divine?" asked Alice of Jane when they were going to bed. Alice waltzed round the bed she shared with Jane, rapturously dwelling on every word he had said all evening, although he had said nothing in particular to her.

Divine was not quite the word Jane would have used for Robbie. In her mind, the word was connected with the church, but she had to admit Robbie was dashing, with his muscular build, and his deep voice with that oh-so-attractive accent.

Alice tossed and turned in bed. Jane would be going to London, well not for a while, but she would be gone by next year. That meant only she and Emma would be at home, since Amy would still be in Manchester and Mary-Ann would surely have gone to America by then.

She noted with some chagrin that Robbie had been pleasant and friendly to them all, but not particularly to her. She was just another Kershaw girl to him. How was she going to make him single her out, the way that he had singled out Eliza?

"Tactics," she thought. "Tactics are what's needed here." She needed to isolate him, like soldiers did during battle. That would surely lead to success. But how was she to get him on his own? The family was always present and Robbie and Pa always walked together to the railway station at the end of the visit.

She gave thought to her successfully married sisters. First there was Kate; she had received a proposal she did not want from Mr. Higginbottom, then suddenly Nathanial Goodacre had stepped forward. All the family had known Kate had always been sweet on him ever since he had been her Sunday school teacher, but tactics had definitely not been employed in that scenario. They all knew now that Nathanial had an inkling that Kate had received a proposal which prompted him to step forward. And there was Eliza herself, with Robbie falling in love with her as soon as he set eyes on her. But Eliza obviously had never loved him; that's why he was thrown over as soon as Billy, her first and true love, reappeared. Alice had not much knowledge of the courtship of the twins, only knowing they had met Ben Huddleston and Davey Clothier through the church choir.

But this passion was consuming Alice and she had no power over it. She thought back to her other male acquaintance, Archie Hawkins, who had persuaded her to go to London. But she had never been in love with him. There had definitely been no ardour like this one that was controlling her life. She could not confide in Jane, for there was no knowing what that lass might do to escalate matters and Alice did not need that. Jane's ways were not Alice's. She finally decided that she needed the help of Eliza. She might know what to do as Robbie had fallen for her, and they had been engaged for a short time. Alice had to find out what Robbie was made of.

§

Alice thought Eliza's house would be the perfect place to discuss some strategy in the area of romance, if only Billy was not around. Eliza had been married for a few weeks, and Alice had only been there once, in the company of her sisters.

She carefully planned her outing to Eliza's. For the six-mile journey, it involved a walk to Hollinwood station to join the train from Oldham to Ashton-under-Lyne. This gave Alice plenty of time to ponder on what she was going to talk about to Eliza. She had already told Emma that she would be going straight to Eliza's as soon as Kendal's closed on Saturday.

Of course, Emma, being what she was, needed to know the nature of this outing. Alice had given a plausible enough explanation: that she needed Eliza's advice on her red, unruly locks which had still not recovered fully from the scalping she had received in London. Emma was puzzled at this agenda as Alice normally did not take an interest in hair fashion, but Eliza was the acknowledged Queen of the topknot, whether it was the modest chignon or the latest pompadour. Her stunning flaxen tresses were always immaculately coiffured. Emma, with her innate sense of something impending, knew there was more to this than a new hairstyle, but she decided to say nothing. For once, she overlooked the fact that Alice was travelling alone in the evening, something she did not normally sanction, but she was not unduly worried about the dangers of a fifteen-minute journey on public transport.

On the short train ride to Ashton-under-Lyne, Alice was surprised to find that Abigail was also a passenger. They hardly saw each other nowadays since Abigail had gone to live in Oldham.

"Going to see your Eliza?" asked Abigail.

"Yes, and why are *you* going to Ashton?" asked Alice, even though her fanatical sense of purpose and her imminent conversation with Eliza pre-occupied her.

"I'm going to instruction," said Abigail.

"Instruction? What for?" asked Alice,

"To be a Catholic, of course," said Abigail, pulling on her gloves after popping a pear drop sweet into her mouth and offering one to Alice. "I'm going to classes."

Declining the large boiled sweet, Alice thought it was a strange time to hold classes of religious instruction. Saturday evenings were usually a time for social activities, but then, she knew nothing of the mysteries of the Catholic church.

"I'm doing it to please Aunt Nan," offered Abigail, sucking on her pear drop.

Alice thought that whatever it entailed, it suited Abigail who seemed mighty pleased and looked healthier than she had done for a long time.

"And what about your father? He's Church of England."

"Oh, he doesn't mind. He's too busy with his teaching."

They both alighted from the train at Ashton, Abigail making her way to St. Ann's Church leaving Alice to walk on slowly and dwell upon the matter in hand— that of Robbie Cameron and how Eliza could help her.

The newly-weds' house was on the outskirts of town and was a newer, and larger residence than the Kershaw's house in Chadderton. The tiny front garden was bursting with Michaelmas daisies with a bay window protruding over them. Alice hesitated at the front door with its brass letter box, and then gently tapped on the matching brass door knocker, her eyes on the spotless white door step.

"Why, Alice, how nice to see you," said Billy, the perfect husband and host as he opened the door. "See who's here, my love." He ushered his sister-in-law into the kitchen where Eliza was preparing the usual evening meal of high tea.

Eliza was surprised yet delighted to see her sister. "You can't have had tea yet?" she asked as Alice had clearly come straight from Kendal's shop.

"No, er . . . thank you, Eliza. Not had tea, but I don't need any. I just wanted to talk to you."

Eliza was not wrong in assuming it must be something important and personal for Alice to come alone and without prior arrangement.

They both knew there were some formalities to be gone through before the nature of Alice's visit would be revealed.

"You will have some tea, won't you? We're just about to sit down."

Alice demurred; she wasn't hungry. Lovesick, the normally sanguine girl had lost her appetite.

In the dining room, after the ham, pease pudding, and lardy cake, the polite conversation lagged. Billy came to the rescue, as they both knew he would.

"I'm sure you lasses have things to talk about. I'll go into the parlour and read the *Cotton Factory Times*. Very good of you to bring it, Alice." Alice breathed a sigh of relief for the newspaper and was thankful she had remembered to bring this week's edition which she had not yet read herself. Billy left the room with the newspaper and a cup of tea.

Alone with her sister, Alice launched into her topic with practised ease. "It's about Robbie." There was no point in beating about the bush. "When you were engaged to him, you talked to him a lot, didn't you? What he likes and doesn't like. Where he would like to live, if *he* was married. You know what I mean, Eliza."

Eliza was somewhat taken aback. She had not expected this line of conversation.

"You mean, you're setting your cap at Robbie?" Eliza burst out laughing. Alice failed to see what was so funny about it, and blushed deeply.

"Oh, sorry, Alice. I shouldn't laugh. I never thought of such a thing. You're obviously serious about it. You want Robbie!"

That was putting it mildly. "Well, *you* didn't want him. Why shouldn't I have him?"

"No reason at all," said Eliza, slowly, trying to hide her amusement and think how she could help her poor sister who was evidently pining for the attention of her own former fiancé.

"He probably still thinks you're the only girl in the world," said the lovesick Alice despondently, but then her fighting nature superseded this thought; she was not one to give up easily. Clutching at straws, she suddenly remembered the engagement ring Robbie had given Eliza last January.

"Where's that ring he gave you? I want to see it."

"What on earth for? It's no good to you."

"What are you going to do with it?"

"Nothing, it can just stay where it is."

"Where is it?" Alice was insistent.

"In the drawer of the chiffonier, right at the back."

Alice quickly drew out the small box and surveyed its contents: a gold ring with a dainty circle of diamonds.

"What a waste," said Alice, taking the ring out of the box.

"He wouldn't take it back," said Eliza, remembering that painful occasion.

"What are you going to do with it?"

"Nothing."

"Such a waste," repeated Alice, trying it on for size. It fitted perfectly on the third finger of her left hand.

Eliza, like Alice, had been brought up to waste nothing. It had always been Emma's mantra. 'Waste not, want not.' But this was not in the same category as a plate of food, or a gown that was fraying at the hem.

"But what would *you* do with it?" asked Eliza.

"I'd ask Robbie if he would like to give it to me," said Alice, relying on her knowledge that Scots, like Lancashire folk, did not like waste either.

Eliza was shocked. "That's a bit brazen, isn't it?"

"I wouldn't do it right away, of course. I would choose the right moment," explained Alice. "I'd wait till he notices me more and wants to go a-courting, y'know. Then I'd show it to him."

"What would he think of me if I gave it to you? No, I couldn't do that. Give it back. It stays here for now."

Reluctantly, Alice removed the ring from her finger and allowed Eliza to replace it in the box and stow it carefully away in the chiffonier drawer.

"That was a very silly idea," said Eliza. "Honestly, Alice, you've got a lot to learn. If you ever did get engaged to Robbie, I could mention the ring to him, but I don't think he would want to be reminded of it. He's a good wage-earner. He could buy another ring if he wanted to."

Eliza didn't have much else to offer except to remind Alice to be just her own true self and if their father brought Robbie home more often, he would be sure to notice her and maybe single her out. "You know he's from Glasgow," she said. "Go to the library and get a book on Scotland so you can learn more about it, then you can talk to him about it. He'd like that."

Alice had to agree, that was a start.

"And don't forget, he's Scottish. He's annoyed if you say he's Scotch."

Alice nodded, scintillating conversations with Robbie already springing into her mind.

"And you know what? He's been to Edinburgh, where there's a great granite statue in memory of Sir Walter Scott—you love his poems, don't you? Well, the monument has two hundred and eighty-seven steps to the top and Robbie's climbed them several times."

"Two hundred and eighty-seven steps," said Alice in awe, thinking of how she would surely love to skip up those steps, in the company of Robbie, of course.

"You probably could marry him, if you played your cards right. But tinkering about with that engagement ring is not the way to go about it. It'll just take time."

Not like when he met you, thought Alice ruefully, when he had immediately fallen head over heels in love with Eliza.

Alice looked so wistful, Eliza wished she had something more to offer, but then, she reasoned with herself, things might turn out the way Alice wanted, eventually. And knowing Alice, she might even change her mind and fall in love with someone else.

Alice wanted to take her leave, even though it was only half past seven, but then she remembered the excuse she had given Emma for the purpose of the visit.

"What about my hair," she asked Eliza.

"It's all right," said the faithful sister. "Just keep up the brushing. It's getting longer now and you can do more with it."

"Jane said I should have barley curls,"

"She *would* say that; it's easy for her with her wavy hair." Eliza was dubious about the long thin ringlets. "It would mean winding your hair in those long linen strips at night which is probably worse than those curl papers you used to try. But you could just do it now and again,"

"When Robbie's coming," they both said, at the same time, and burst out laughing.

"I best be getting on home." Alice did not relish the journey back and she was not sure what time the train left, but the timetable said they ran until nine o'clock. "It's been a lovely visit," she said politely to her sister, although she secretly thought it had not been beneficial to her main purpose. But she was thankful to see Eliza so happy.

As she was leaving, there was a knock on the front door. It was a messenger from the Whitelands Mill for Billy, requiring his presence. Calls like this were frequent for the young and upcoming engineer, who was an expert on the new horizontal compound as opposed to the beam engines which had been in constant use until then.

"Oh, so those Wolstenholme and Rye engines need my attention, do they?" said Billy, putting on his topcoat. "Alice, I'm going up to the mill in this gig. We'll ask the driver to drop me off, then give you a lift home. It's slightly out of the way, but it'll still be quicker than the train."

Alice gratefully took him up on his offer and squeezing in between Billy and the driver, figured it would only take her half an hour to get home as she wouldn't have that walk from Hollinwood station.

As they drove past the Catholic church, Alice looked for Abigail but there was no sign of her.

§

Jane was still in her euphoric state a month after the precious letter had arrived from the Royal Academy of Music. Plans and ideas crowded through her head as she mindlessly carried out her duties during her daily four hours at Goodacre's. She allowed herself to come down to earth at the Blue Coat School in the afternoons where she did what she liked most in the world: playing the piano or at least standing close to it, listening to her pupils. Miss Lamont had recovered her health somewhat and was back to teach the senior boys.

"Congratulations," said that Blue Coat boy, Jake Higgins, who had heard from Miss Lamont about Jane's successful entrance exam to the Royal Academy of Music.

"What are you going to do to do when you finish school? asked Jane, knowing he was in his last year at the Blue Coat. She could only envisage a career in music, but knew Jake had no aspirations in that direction although he still played the piano.

"Science is my favourite subject," he said. "Manchester University has a Faculty of Science and Engineering. That's what I'll be doing, starting next September, same time as you'll be going to London."

"Then you'll work in a mill, when you're qualified?" asked Jane, who believed that's where all engineers would be employed.

"I suppose I could," said Jake, "but what I really want is to get in to a big engineering firm, like Wolstenholme & Rye. They've already said I can apprentice there when college isn't in session."

That name rang a bell with Jane, and she knew from hearing Billy's conversation that he worked on Wolstenholme & Rye engines. "My brother-in-law's an engineer at Whitelands Mill in Ashton," she told him. "They have the latest horizontal compound engines."

"But no mill for me," said Jake, impressed with Jane's superficial knowledge. "I'll study engineering and then I'd like to go to

Canada eventually. They have hydro power there, and that interests me greatly."

Jane looked at him incredulously. She started thinking about her sister, Mary-Rose, in far-away New Bedford, Massachusetts. She wondered how close that was to Canada. She knew one thing, for certain; she would never leave England, except to visit Europe to see where the famous pianists had performed in the great salons and recital halls of Paris, Vienna and Prague. And there was that dream of hers, that she herself might give a recital in one of those picturesque European cities. Then there was London, a city famous for concerts with international musicians. This was a hope that was attainable; not beyond the bounds of possibility, to play in London since she would be studying there for at least two years. She bid Jake Higgins farewell, and lapsed into her dreaming.

When she reached home, Alice had some encouraging news for her. She had bumped into Miss Partridge who had been their teacher at Christ Church School in Chadderton.

"I was at the library, and who should be there, but Miss Partridge. I haven't seen her since before I went to London."

"Oh, how is she?" asked Jane, thinking fondly of her first piano teacher.

"She's fine, still at our old school. She was asking after everybody, particularly you, Jane. I told her about your scholarship and how you'll be going to music college in London."

"Oh, yes, and what did she say about that?" asked Jane, still hardly believing it herself that she would be starting a different life altogether.

"She said 'Well done' then wondered where you'd be living when you're there. I said we had no idea yet. After all, it's not until next September, nearly a year to go"

"The academy will have a list of possible digs," said Jane, "and . . ."

"To start with, she'll be staying with Aunt Clara," Emma put in firmly, noticing the pained look on Jane's face.

"Yes, Emma," said Jane rolling her eyes behind Emma's back. "To start with, perhaps . . ."

"Miss Partridge says you are to go and see her, because she has relatives in London and they might be able to help out with a place for you to stay." The look on Jane's face said it all. Relief, joy—a solution to a nagging problem? But Emma knew Jane had a bonfire of ambition burning in her, not to be dampened no matter how many problems arose.

"I'll go and see her tomorrow when I finish at Goodacre's. I should just have time before I go to the Blue Coat."

Jane was in high anticipation although Emma, as usual, had her reservations. "Better not count your chickens before they're hatched," she warned. But she, too, was hopeful. She had worried a good deal about Jane going to London. But then, she reasoned with herself, she had read recently in a newspaper article that it was good for people to travel away from home, to discover how other people lived, staying in unfamiliar surroundings, sleeping in a strange bed, eating unusual and sometimes unpalatable food. Emma was just thankful she would not have to do it herself.

§

Alice was somewhat disappointed about her visit to Eliza. She had expected more practical help from a sister who had experienced love in all its stages; unrequited, misplaced and then replete. It appeared that although Eliza had been engaged to Robbie, she hardly knew anything about him that would assist Alice. There was Kate, of course. A chat with her might help matters so dear to her heart. She knew that Nathaniel had been propelled into proposing to Kate as he had heard she had received a proposal from someone else. But Kate had said that Nathaniel would have got around to it, eventually. She knew he had been stung with jealousy when he had overheard Jane and her father say something that day at Goodacre's. Maybe Alice could do the same thing with Robbie: produce a rival so that would make *him* jealous. But how was she to do that?

"And how did you get on at Eliza's?" asked Emma, noting that Alice had exactly the same hair style as before, and that she was home earlier than the stipulated time of nine o'clock.

"Oh, well enough," replied Alice, unlacing her boots. "She's got some new furniture and she's so house-proud. By the way, I saw Abigail on the train," she added, knowing this would interest Emma.

"And what was she up to?" asked Emma with some irritation. She still had not forgiven Abigail for the torment she had caused Eliza, although the latter, in her blissful state, seemed to have now put the whole matter behind her. The information that Abigail had been travelling to Ashton sparked Emma's curiosity. It was there she had bumped into Billy Lampson three years ago and had promised to deliver that letter to Eliza.

"She was going to St. Ann's Church; she's learning how to be a Catholic at some classes they have there," explained Alice, smiling as she saw the incredulous look on Emma's face.

This was news indeed to Emma and started ideas flooding through her brain, remembering what Mr. Burgess had told her at Eliza's wedding a month previously.

"Abigail is becoming rather partial to the Roman Catholic Church," he had said.

Abigail "becoming partial" to the Roman Catholic Church was putting it mildly, thought Emma. It seemed as if Abigail was becoming totally immersed in the Catholic faith. Maybe it was to please her aunt, and her father thought she was just a "bit partial to it" but was there another reason? Emma did not know a lot about the Catholic church, just that it was entirely different from theirs. She was aware of a few isolated facts: the clergy were not allowed to marry, and didn't those "Romans" always eat fish on Fridays?

Mr. Burgess had said Abigail was leaning towards Catholicism. He had attributed this inclination to his sister whose influence, no doubt, had begun to rub off on Abigail. Especially now, as she helped her Aunt Nan with church duties, cleaning and replenishing candles, washing the white cassocks of the choristers and so on.

"Not that I mind, you understand," Mr. Burgess had said.

Whether he minded or not was immaterial, thought Emma. He hadn't minded when his sister married a Roman Catholic, the old solicitor for whom she had been housekeeper for many years. She had married him on his deathbed and automatically inherited his house and money, the stipulation being that she convert to the Catholic faith. Emma had heard the story before, and evidently John Burgess had not objected to it, but perhaps he had had no say in the matter, being a younger brother. 'Partial' as Abigail now appeared to be towards the Catholic church, Emma couldn't help wondering if it had been tempered with a liking for someone in that church, although what she had seen of Father Dominic, a portly, middle-aged priest, did not substantiate this line of thought. But there had to be more to this than Aunt Nan's influence, especially since Abigail had always professed to dislike her aunt and her ways.

"And why does she have to go to Ashton to learn how to be a Catholic. Why can't she do it in Oldham?" was the obvious question from Emma.

"They don't have enough candidates in Oldham," said Alice, "and old Father Dominic doesn't like doing the classes. That's why she has to go to Ashton. Besides, Abigail said the priest there is young and ever so handsome. He's Irish and his name is Father Kevin."

So a young and handsome priest at St. Ann's, thought Emma. No wonder they were all flocking there to be converted. But at least if there was anything untoward going on, which Emma did not doubt, there was safety in numbers. The classes, according to Alice's information, were well attended.

"And, now I come to think of it," added Alice, "She was all dolled up and she smelled over-powerful of lavender."

This was the most illuminating information about Abigail that Emma had had for a long time and her detective instincts began to shift into high gear.

"And she's got titties on her like a sucking pig."

"Suckling pig," corrected Emma automatically.

"You know what I mean." Alice looked down at her own modest bosom as if wishing for more volume there, and seeing Emma's look of interest said, "She opened her coat to show me her new frock, and I've never seen anything like it."

Emma smiled to herself, and then started wondering again why Abigail was frequenting Ashton-under-Lyne. Her thoughts strayed to that important letter from Billy to Eliza, the one that had never been delivered even though Abigail had faithfully promised Billy she would give it to Eliza. At last, the vestige of a solution as to why Abigail was in Ashton that day came into her mind and rooted itself there. She had resolved to forget this whole debacle but none of them would ever forget the night that Abigail had almost died right in front of their eyes. It was a year and a half ago, but the memory of that horrific night came freshly back to Emma and as usual haunted her. A visit to Abigail might finally quench these negative thoughts. She thought she now knew why Abigail would go by train to the Catholic church in Ashton when she lived next door to the Catholic church in Oldham.

§

Emma called at the dark and dismal house of Abigail's aunt, the house that used to be the home and office of Mr. Edward Smythe, solicitor and maker of wills. His capacious mahogany desk, where he used to write his briefs, was still there. The house, spotless in beeswax and silver polish reminded Emma of a church, except that in the absence of fresh flowers which most churches displayed, there was a preponderance of dried flowers and wax fruit.

Abigail flushed under Emma's scrutiny of her and the surroundings, but after a few moments was quite forthcoming about the priest of St. Ann's. She explained that for the past few years she had been in the habit of delivering messages from one church to another, evidently part of the work for her aunt. Emma took full note of Abigail's top half, noting that she was obviously wearing one of those corsets that propelled a girl's bosom upward and outward, something girls of Emma's acquaintance did not wear. Certainly not mill girls. But then, Abigail was not a mill girl any more; hadn't been for some time.

"I take altar cloths, prayer books and rosaries," explained Abigail. "Whatever they ask me to do. The first time I went was because they didn't have enough wine for mass at St. Ann's and so Father Dominic asked me to take it from St. Mary's to St. Ann's. I took it in this bag," said Abigail, indicating a large hessian bag on Mr. Smythe's desk.

"Was that the first time you went there? The day you saw Billy Lampson and said you would give that letter to Eliza?" asked Emma.

"I think it was," said Abigail puckering her brow. "I can't remember exactly if that was the time, but around about then."

"So you've been lots of times to the Catholic church at Ashton?" asked Emma.

"I suppose so," admitted Abigail, sitting primly on the edge of her chair, fidgeting with the tassels on her bodice. "Aunt Nan always used to do the errands but she always sends me now. And Father Kevin is always so appreciative and thanks me special for doing it."

"How does he thank you?"

"He says he will always think of me favourably, even though I'm not a Catholic."

"Did he persuade you to convert to the Catholic faith?"

"Yes . . . and no. He would like me to, of course."

"He shouldn't be asking you to convert without your father's consent," said Emma. "I think I should go and see him." Abigail gave a little squeak of protest.

"I'm twenty-one; I can do what I like. And my father doesn't mind. As long as Aunt Nan is happy."

"And that's what really matters, I suppose," said Emma, in as convincing a tone as she could muster, although she doubted that Abigail would go out of her way to please her aunt. There was more to this. Emma was certain.

"I *do* live in her house, and I have to keep on the right side of her."

"Why were you all titivated up last Saturday, just for a class?"

Abigail blushed to the roots of her mousy hair. "He . . . Father Kevin, told me once I looked nice, so I like to keep . . ."

"Did you lead him on?"

"No, I never did. When I delivered the wine from St. Mary's he said, 'Let's make sure this wine is the right stuff.' And he took a swig right out of the bottle."

Emma winced. "Did you have a drink too?"

"You know I don't care for drink." Emma doubted this, knowing Abigail and her bragging about sampling her father's whiskey one Christmas. "But he poured some into a silver cup and said I was to drink it."

"And you obeyed, of course," said Emma, raising her eyes heavenward.

"But it was horrible, not like the wine we had at Christ Church in Chadderton, or the Madeira my Aunt Nan likes. It was sharp. No, I didn't like it one bit."

"Then what?"

"Then … nothing." Abigail waved a hand in her typical fashion and studied her finger nails.

That was her way of finishing most conversations recollected Emma, who resolved that on her next visit to Ashton-under-Lyne to see Eliza, she would stop by the Catholic church. She wanted to see this young, handsome priest for herself.

"What do you do here, when you're not helping your aunt?"

"I read a bit . . . and knit. Sometimes we play cards till bedtime."

"D'y see much of your father?"

"Why are you asking me all these questions? You're not my mother." Abigail made a valiant attempt to voice her annoyance, but hardly dared say those words as she had treated Emma in that capacity for the last few years, turning to her countless times for help and advice. A sniff from Abigail signalled that she didn't want to talk any more and that she was trying to generate some tears. Abigail was well acquainted with the wonderful effect of tears, but on seeing Emma's look of exasperation, also remembered that they were wasted on *her*.

Any further conversation they might have had was put on hold by the appearance of Aunt Nan, tall, lean and hard-looking. Emma had only met her once before, and kept to her previous opinion that the aunt wasn't young, but then, she wasn't old either and was nothing like her brother, John Burgess.

"Good afternoon to you, Miss Kershaw," said the tight-lipped woman, pulling off her gloves and laying them on the desk which seemed to be a repository for most things. "I trust you and your family are well."

"As best as can be expected," was the automatic answer from Emma who in reverse of the aunt, was now drawing on her gloves. "And I hope I find you in good health, Mrs. Smythe?"

These preliminaries having been dispensed with, the obvious discomfort of Abigail was certainly not conducive for Emma to dally any longer. They drifted towards the front door.

"Goodbye, Abigail," Emma threw the words over her shoulder as she vacated the dreary house. "Don't forget to call and see *us* some time."

§

Emma brimmed with purpose and was determined to see the priest at St. Ann's Church in Ashton-under-Lyne. She planned it after a visit to Eliza one Saturday afternoon. She now had the luxury of Saturdays off work at the Wharf Mill.

The deserted church smelt of incense and candles. At first, she could not find the priest. He was not in the sanctuary, and she feared he was otherwise engaged but soon Emma eventually located him in the vestry. He was indeed young with strong features, and unruly black hair.

"I'm Father Kevin. How may I assist you?" said the priest with a flashing smile, but his soutane spoke of a hurried dinner and the vestments not having been laundered for some time. Clearly, this was not the robe he used for Sunday mass. He self-consciously brushed the front of it and then ran his fingers through his hair. "You wish to attend our classes for new members, perhaps?" His dark roving eyes appraised Emma, at twenty-nine no raving beauty, but nevertheless a tidy and pleasant-looking young woman.

"I have come to see you about Abigail Burgess," said Emma, in her usual fashion of not beating about the bush. "And my church is the Church of England in Chadderton." Her tone indicated that she had no intention of attending his classes.

"Ah, Abigail," said the priest, brushing a lock of hair from his forehead. "A stray sheep."

"A stray sheep?" said Emma, thinking that was one way of putting it.

"Are you a relative?" he asked.

"Not exactly," said Emma, "but as near as can be. I've known her since she was about four years old. She used to live next door to us and has relied on me since her mother died." Emma hoped she had made her position clear and then came straight to the point. "Abigail got herself into trouble last year. You know what I mean? And I think you may have had something to do with it."

"You are referring to her condition as an unwed mother?"

"So you knew about it?"

"Abigail put her trust in me and I advised her what was the only solution—go to the Magdalene Home in Manchester until the birth, and then the child would be given up for adoption. Then she could return home."

Emma had heard about the Magdalene Homes for unwed mothers. They were not so much of a home but a laundry where girls were sent to work, some to await the birth of a child, some for other reasons. The work was hard, the life severe; some said it was even worse than being in prison. Emma had also heard that some girls did not return home, their families unwilling to have them back because of the shame they had brought on themselves.

"As you know, Abigail did not follow your recommendation. I advised her to wed the father, but she obviously did not want to, or could not."

He looked uncomfortable but was silent, not returning Emma's searchlight glare.

She continued: "The baby was … got rid of. How do you view that, in your doctrine?"

Again, no answer. Emma was sure she had found the perpetrator. She followed him into the nave of the church where he started lighting candles.

"Isn't it a mortal sin, to kill an unborn child?" she continued.

He was still silent. Emma thought he was not like their own parson, Vicar Whiteley, the Anglican minister, looking after his flock, advising them in his loquacious fashion, keeping them safe. Was Abigail safe now?

"I'm afraid I had no sway over Abigail in whatever she did." He suddenly found his voice.

"And now you encourage her to come to classes for entry into this …" Emma encompassed the interior of the church with a wave of her arms. "…knowing she had committed a mortal sin in the eyes of your doctrine."

"Our beloved Mother of God would forgive her."

Oh, would she, thought Emma. But aloud, "I think you had something to do with her condition, and because of your position here, you chose to ignore it."

"What are you getting at exactly?" The priest had his eyes riveted on the cracked tiles on the floor and then he slowly raised them to the saints in their niches, remaining deep in thought.

Emma pursued her quarry relentlessly. "She has no mother, just a father who loves his daughter dearly, but has no idea how to relate to her. I believe you took advantage of my young friend, Abigail, causing her to conceive a child. She almost died because of it. Did you know that?"

Emma perceived that Father Kevin *did* seem slightly disconcerted. Again, there was no reply from him. He crossed himself and then knelt down in front of a full-size statue of the Madonna, turning his back on Emma.

Her parting words were: "Some of your stray sheep might have lambs. And what would your merciful Mother of God do about that?"

Emma left the church looking back as she did so. Father Kevin appeared to be deep in prayer.

She was convinced she had found the father of Abigail's aborted child, but she was at a loss to know how to deal with it. Would he relinquish his priesthood if pressed, and who was to bring this about?

On the train back to Hollinwood station, Emma reflected on what she had been able to discover. There had been no fanfare: "You are a priest – some one who is looked up to, who hears confessions and directs his parishioners." He was just an ordinary human with ordinary human desires and foibles. How had he acted? Had he helped Abigail? She had never mentioned anyone helping her. That is why she carried out such a drastic step with a knitting needle that almost killed her.

Emma had more on her mind than the defrocking of a delinquent priest—let his conscience berate him. She could let Abigail know of her suspicions, and prevent any further involvement, but there was no point in making it public. What was she to accomplish by pursuing it any further? The one thing she had been avoiding would become a certainty: Abigail's father would know and she wanted John Burgess, above all others, to be spared that grief. She would tell her sisters, naturally, since they had been witness to Abigail's near-death experience. But other than that, perhaps she should let the matter rest. She couldn't help thinking, though, that a good place for Father Kevin would be a monastery, perhaps back in Ireland where he came from.

Chapter Twenty-One

It had been a hard winter, but the March wind was less biting when Mary-Ann took her first walk on the moors for several months. There was a pale sun and for once the air was dry although patches of snow were still showing from a blizzard in February. Mary-Ann was not the happy-go-lucky person she once was; she was sad and disturbed and she did not exactly know why. There had been the usual reprimands from Emma: "Don't go out walking today; it's still too cold; you have a cough," and so on, but she had to get out of the house. She missed Mary-Rose terribly and now there were only four of them at home: Emma with her never-ending rules and reminders; Alice who thought she knew everything just because she was in charge of a sub-post office. And, moreover, Alice had been wearing her heart on her sleeve because she was sweet on Robbie. It was embarrassing. No wonder Emma had said things like, "You're about as subtle as one of those coquettes in Paris," and Alice's tart reply, "What would you know about coquettes in Paris?"

And there was Jane who had nothing to talk about unless it involved music: scales, sonata and arpeggios. All that fuss and going-on when she had found out the great Franz Liszt had died two years ago and she had never seen him in person. Things like that did not matter to Mary-Ann who could never understand Jane's obsession with music, although she herself possessed a fine voice and had been in the church choir for several years. Mary-Ann missed Eliza, happily married in Ashton-under-Lyne and she missed Amy too, rarely at home from college in Manchester. It was now five years since Kate married. She now had three children, having given birth to another daughter, named Rose after the sister who had gone to America. Did Mary-Ann miss Davey, her husband? She had asked herself that question many times, but if she were totally honest with herself, she realised he was the person she missed the least. But he was her husband and no doubt there would be a reunion at some point, but she didn't like to dwell on it. She didn't want to go to America, much as she missed Mary-Rose, and yet, she didn't want to stay here either.

She meandered up the hill overlooking Chadderton, taking deep gulps of the bracing air until she started coughing. She looked down on the scattered chimneys of the mills, some shrouded in the swirling mist, some stark and clear, belching out smoke. She could just pick out the mill where she used to work, the Glebe, and could almost see the street where they lived which was nearby. Remembering what Emma had always said, she partly closed her eyes; those blackened chimneys looked like soaring cathedral spires, the village quaint and peaceful and not the bleak, grey place it was in reality once you were down there. She could see the canal with the huge bales of cotton waiting for the next dray to take them to the various mills. Further along the canal, Mary-Ann could see the Boat and Horses public house right on the bank of the waterway, a place she had never frequented but had heard plenty about.

The pale sun was suddenly doused by dark, scudding clouds, reminding her that she should be getting back down to the village.

It was eleven o'clock and she had the mutton stew in the oven in readiness for Emma, Alice and Jane coming home from work for their dinner. She made her way down the hill, passing along the canal bridge and wishing she could jump aboard one of those barges and be magically transported away from her unhappiness, but she wasn't sure where she wanted to go.

Mill workers passed on their way home to their midday dinner. What hordes of them there were, all earning their money at the looms or the spindles as she had done just over a year ago. Not for the first time did she consider that perhaps she had been better off then, when she didn't have to make decisions and deal with her conflicting emotions. She hadn't much liked the mill; it was an existence, but looking back, she must have been happy; she had been in good health then and was fancy-free.

§

Robbie was much impressed by Alice and her knowledge of Scottish poets, like Sir Walter Scott and Robert Louis Stevenson, whose verses she could recite with feeling, like a veteran actor. He found her gaucheness appealing. Even a year and a half in London had not given her sophistication or airs and graces. Robbie was becoming more and more attracted to Alice, but he was, however, extremely wary. He had been engaged once and it had come to naught. His wariness prevented him from committing this folly again, much as he was now drawing closer to Alice.

Alice, however, had no such wariness, although she had seen and heard enough about people who married without love. She suspected that was the case with Mary-Ann. Although Davey genuinely seemed to love her, he had gone away without his bride, and *she* certainly didn't seem heartbroken. In fact, she didn't seem to miss her husband at all and never talked about him. Alice knew she was not in this league. She thought about her favourite poem, the one about

Hiawatha and Minnehaha. How she longed for someone to love her like that.

Alice had to admit, it was all right working at Kendal's shop with its sub-post office—far superior to the mill where she had toiled for five years before running away to London. She had come to accept that her hopes for a stage career had quickly dwindled and were extinguished. For excitement and passion, the post office could not rival the stage, but at least it was more reliable than treading the boards. Her passion for acting and reciting poems would have to be reserved for Mrs. Goodacre's soirées which still took place every two or three months. And there was Robbie, a whole entity on whom passionate verse could be vented, especially now that he seemed to be taking notice of her.

She was thrilled to receive a letter from Robbie with an invitation. "I thought you might like to see a play," he wrote. "They are putting on a production of 'Twelfth Night' in Liverpool and I heard that after a few days there, it's going to Manchester. It will be at the end of the month."

This was exciting news. As usual when something unorthodox cropped up in their daily plans, Alice looked towards Emma, the unspoken question, as always—could she, should she, go? Even though she was now twenty years old, she still looked automatically to Emma for approval.

For once, Emma did not place any obstacles in the way of this unexpected outing. In fact, she thought she might like to go too.

"I've a mind to see some of this Shakespeare for myself," she said to Alice. "I'll know some of it, I'll be bound, after listening to your spoutings for years."

Alice was ecstatic. She was going to the theatre in Manchester with Robbie. It didn't matter that Emma was going too. She would have Robbie almost to herself. It didn't matter that Jane also invited herself. It was something to look forward to. Things were going in the right direction.

§

Jane had been to see Miss Partridge regarding the possibility of accommodation in London. As soon as she had heard of Jane's successful entrance examination to the academy, Amelia Partridge had wasted no time and had already written to her sister, knowing that she had been thinking for some time of employing someone to help with her three little girls.

"Of course, I've told her you are the perfect candidate," explained Miss Partridge to Jane. "She would like someone to live with them. They have just acquired a piano and she says she particularly wants the girls to learn to play."

And now Jane was on the train to London with Miss Partridge, who had arranged for them to visit her sister in the Easter holidays.

It was decided they should stay one night with Mrs. Blakiston, the sister who was not at all like her sibling, younger, though in some ways more mature and matronly. Affluence was in evidence around the home when Jane was shown around the tall, imposing house near Regent's Park.

Jane made the acquaintance of the three small girls, and felt comfortable with them. She worried a little about the arrangements as they sat down together for afternoon tea in the drawing room. The head of the household had come home early from work to see the proposed addition to his household. A wealthy ironmonger with a string of hardware shops, William Blakiston was curious about this Lancashire girl who had come all this way with his sister-in-law to see whether she would be the kind of girl they needed in his household. He felt that the unsophisticated girl, not yet eighteen, would be a welcome diversion from his three boisterous young daughters with their tantrums, tears and demands and also from his wife, a plain but wholesome woman, given to rather a buxom figure which plainly spoke of her various pregnancies, three of which had produced the daughters and three more that had ended in miscarriage. Jane found

Mr. Blakiston a rather austere figure, not joining in the conversation but eyeing her, taking in her neat appearance with her second-best frock, the one she wore to Goodacre's and the Blue Coat School, and her long auburn hair which, so far, she had not started putting up. Jane reddened under his scrutiny, but noted with pleasure the brand new Chappell grand piano in the large, elegant room.

"We do have a parlour maid and a kitchen maid," explained Mrs. Blakiston. "But I'd appreciate help with simple duties that concern the girls, like looking after their clothing, getting them up in mornings and taking them to school before you go to your college."

"And supervise their reading and prayers," interposed her husband. "And watch their manners."

"I can do that," said Jane and, wishing to dismiss the thing that worried her most, added, "Any cooking?"

"Just breakfast for the children and yourself, probably porridge."

Jane breathed a sigh of relief. Culinary work was definitely not her forte. "Is that all?"

"Of course, the main object—why we want *you*—is to teach our daughters the piano," said Mrs. Blakiston. "And in return for that you would have free board and lodging and use of the piano for yourself."

"Whenever I like?"

"When you aren't otherwise occupied, as long as it is to everyone's convenience. We are usually in the parlour of an evening, so the drawing room is at your disposal when the children are in bed. No late hours, of course."

"Of course not," agreed Jane fervently, thinking this was reasonable. With all she had to do, she would definitely not be keeping late hours. And it would be like having her own piano.

Then a thought occurred to her. "But can you wait 'til September when I start at the academy? It's only just the beginning of April."

"If you are the right person, we will wait until the middle of August; then you can get settled in before you start at your college." It seemed to everyone that Jane was the right person, certainly for the children with five-year-old Amelia (named after her aunt) tugging at her to come upstairs to see the rooms which had been prepared for the two visitors. Jane's was next to Amelia's room which she shared with her two sisters. Sophie, the eldest, at nine, seemed quiet and studious. Seven-year-old Charlotte was a replica of her mother, and appeared to be a talkative little girl. They obviously liked Jane.

Jane could hardly believe this arrangement, so unlike what poor Alice had had to endure during her foray into the London work force. But then, she had been in such haste, she had not had time to arrange anything beforehand. Granted, there would be restrictions for Jane, living in a strange house, but not like the ones she had at present when her practice time was confined to whenever she could escape to Miss Lamont's. She had long forsaken the humble harmonium, which Kate had so thoughtfully provided. Hadn't Emma accused her of looking a gift horse in the mouth? That's what it amounted to, in the view of down-to-earth Emma, who had never aspired to play music of any kind; who could barely comprehend Jane's remarkable flair and her need to express herself musically, just as she had never understood Alice's craving to recite plays and poems. Jane sometimes wondered why she was not in the least like Emma, so prosaic in everything she said or did. She wondered if Emma ever heard notes tumbling about in her head or words that forced themselves upon her lips. Jane doubted it, but she was acutely aware that Emma's military precision in everything she did had made all this possible. She had never appreciated Emma before whose greatest asset was her gift of nurturing, although at times she seemed interfering and over-protective. But Jane could hardly wait to get home to tell Emma everything and express her gratitude, something she was beginning to feel towards her oldest sister more and more.

§

Emma was kept awake wondering how Jane was faring in London. She would not, of course, have allowed her to go alone and she was relieved her worry was eased by the fact that Jane was accompanied by Miss Partridge. Mary-Ann's coughing also kept Emma from sleep.

She had appreciated having Mary-Ann available the last few months to help with the household chores during her recovery stage, and she had begun to hope that her sister would improve so much that she could help out at Goodacre's Ladies Department. Come September, Jane would be away in London and so they would need other help for the four hours a day Jane had been putting in. For the last two months, Kate's help had been non-existent since she had given birth to her third child. They had had to rely on her mother-in-law, but Caroline Goodacre was a poor substitute for Kate and most of the work was falling on Millie, who was supposed to be a full-time seamstress.

But now Emma's hopes for Mary-Ann were once again dashed. She had developed bronchitis. A week of taking the special linctus ordered by the doctor did nothing to alleviate the cough. That plus the Byssinosis was becoming too much to fight. The girl, once again, was pale and listless.

A letter from Mary-Rose cheered her somewhat. "They've had a very cold winter," said Mary-Ann, passing the letter for Emma to read.

"You'll be glad to know," wrote Mary-Rose, "that this past winter was not as bad as the one before we came when there was a severe blizzard on the East Coast."

They had certainly read about it in the newspapers: It was the 'Great Blizzard of 1888' and included New York, New Jersey, Massachusetts, Rhode Island and Connecticut. It had been one of the most severe recorded blizzards in U.S. history. Referred to as the Great White Hurricane, it paralyzed the East Coast with winds of forty-five miles per hour, snowdrifts of more than fifty feet, with railways and telegraph lines disabled. Two hundred ships had been grounded or wrecked and hundreds of seamen had died.

"Well, at least Mary-Rose missed that," said Emma.

"Thank goodness I didn't go," said Mary-Ann, trying to suppress a coughing fit. "It's cold enough here in the winter. But I do miss Mary-Rose."

The food that Emma had put into a small bowl was untouched. Mary-Ann's appetite had not improved. As usual, Emma regarded food as the panacea for all ills. But Mary-Ann did not respond to her ministrations, mostly lying on the sofa by the kitchen fire. It reminded Emma of how their mother had lain there for the months before her death. She was worried. She had every right to be, for when she came home from work a week later, she found Mary-Ann lying in her usual position, but she was motionless, and did not respond to Emma's greeting. Frantic fingers sought a pulse. It was rapid and feeble. Then Emma's head became cool. Her mind held nothing but that which was needed for the moment. Inscrutable as ever, like the Sphinx, she said to no one in particular, although Alice and Jane were the only others present. "Fetch Dr. Foster." Emma set about gently shaking Mary-Ann to try and arouse her, rubbing her wrists, patting her cheeks. Mary-Ann's eye-lids fluttered but she was not really awake. After the crash of the closing door, the house was as quiet as a museum as both sisters rushed out in search of the doctor; one to the hospital, one to his home which housed his surgery, to wherever he might be found.

Chapter Twenty-Two

Emma woke with a start. As always, her first thoughts were of Mary-Ann. It was six months since she had been taken from them. Emma seemed unable to emerge from the cloud of sorrow which had engulfed her since Mary-Ann had died in April, two days before her twenty-fourth birthday. In some ways, it affected Emma more than the death of her mother. She viewed Mary-Ann's death as a failure on her part. She had failed to look after her sister properly. And Emma had been the one to insist that Mary-Ann go walking on the moors to get as much fresh air as possible—that's how she had caught her death of cold, on top of her already weakened state of health.

With her father absent a great deal and since the death of their mother, Emma had always accepted she must shoulder the burden of being the eldest in the family; the eldest if you did not count Algy in London. He had stayed there, so he said, because of his secure job at the post office which he considered preferable to working in a cotton mill. But Emma had often thought that he had chosen to separate himself from the family because he was surrounded by so many girls, and felt stifled by them. She was fully aware, however, that, had Algy stayed with the family, he would not have taken up the nurturing role she had done, after the death of their mother.

She loved each sister, but was often apprehensive as she felt she had to act as both mother and father to them. She had always been concerned about the youngest, Jane, so gifted but also, in some ways, the most difficult. This trait in her youngest sister had worried and sometimes irritated Emma, but she had forced herself to overcome those feelings to encourage and cultivate Jane's gift without relaxing her own stringent rules too much. Alice, too, had been difficult and headstrong, but now she seemed to have reached equilibrium and was settling into a docile young woman. The others, too, had reached their destination in the scheme of things, but Emma was the architect of it all. Under her guidance, each had aspired to rise above their humble and impoverished background, even though Emma was sometimes accused of being too overpowering. Her father had told her from time to time she was too strict and demanding, but in her own mind she was just being single-minded and determined. And she had not always been successful in her methods. And she had had to remind herself from time to time, to be more like their mother, with her quiet words of encouragement or praise. She forgot about that sometimes. Now, with Mary-Ann's demise, Jane in London, and Alice's progress with Robbie, Emma could only foresee an isolated existence for herself, living alone at Bower Lane. She struggled with the realisation that their family was now whittled down to only two and even this would not last.

As Emma walked to work, she contemplated, not for the first time, that she was the only one of her family still working in a mill, albeit she was a senior weaver at the Wharf. Her mother had said it would be only for a little while when they moved north from London in 1872. Emma calculated it had been nearly seventeen years. Still, she had no complaints. She had managed to keep the family together; had fed and clothed them until they were old enough to shoulder some of the responsibility themselves.

Emma had baulked at Kate's suggestion that she should leave the mill and go to work at Goodacre's Ladies Department. What did she know about fashion? Nothing. In spite of having a fair knowledge of textiles, as an experienced weaver, the materials produced at the mill were not the kind used in dressmaking. In her supervisory position she did not want to forsake the work she knew inside out. She was aware that Mr. Leggate, the manager, relied on her and she valued his trust in her. There had been some unrest of late amongst the mill workers, goaded on, as they were, by the militant section of the work force. They were demanding a rise in wages, even though they had been told that, since more safety measures had been introduced, wages would be stagnant for the foreseeable future. Some of the mills had been on spasmodic strikes for weeks owing to the absence of a standard rate or scale of wages. Emma was thankful the Wharf Mill, so far, had not been among these. She simply could not understand why some workers had to continually grouse about everything. Emma was content enough to attend to her two looms, sometimes three, every day and get on with her job. She had told Kate that the ladies' department would have to manage with Mrs. Goodacre senior helping out.

But now she had to face the prospect of living alone. Jane was well into her first year in London. What she had witnessed between Alice and Robbie gave every indication that they would become engaged in the near future. Ever since that Shakespeare play, Robbie had come to visit as often as he could and romance was definitely in the air. Emma had liked the play well enough but couldn't help thinking a night at the Music Hall would have been easier on her eyes and ears. She had never held the same enthusiasm for the Bard that Alice seemed to have. Apart from the certainty she felt that Robbie and Alice would sooner or later be married, it was a sombre outlook and the house would be silent. It was doubtful whether Amy would return to Chadderton. She was in her second year at Queen's University and would spend at least another year there, and like many other students, she would probably take a teaching post in Manchester. But then, Emma knew she must hold the fort at Bower Lane, for might not her father still visit them every two months as he had done the last two years? So, too, would Robbie and Alice come from Birkenhead where they would live, once married. Jane had vowed she would come home from London whenever possible. Even so, with these thoughts, Emma dreaded the coming stillness of the house, the long, silent evenings where she would be the sole occupant. She could not get used to that notion. She had never feared solitude before.

Most of her waking thoughts were of Mary-Ann and the awful gap now left behind. In essence, she had lost both the twins—one to a horrible disease, and the other to a faraway land. It was unlikely that she would ever see Mary-Rose again. Davy had sent a rather stilted letter saying that by the time he had received the sad news of Mary-Ann, she had been dead for seven weeks. Obviously, there was no question of his coming back, the funeral long over. Emma wondered if he had ever fully expected Mary-Ann to join him in Massachusetts and if he had been surprised or upset at the death of his wife whom he had not seen for a year.

Emma was grateful that, at last, Alice had acquired some stability in her life. Working at Kendal's sub-post office and being courted by Robbie, she was less likely to approach anything in her previous slapdash manner. Emma no longer viewed Alice as an opponent, but rather an ally, which was just as well since they were the only two presently under the same roof.

§

A few weeks later, Emma congratulated herself that her subtle encouragement to Robbie to propose to Alice had produced the desired effect. He had hardly got the words out of his mouth before Alice had flung herself at him, gasping "Ye-e-e-s". They were now officially engaged which cheered Emma.

But her cheerfulness was short-lived when, a few days later, Alice arrived home from work and, kicking off her boots, announced, "Mr. Kendal has snuffed it."

"That's not a nice way to say it," chided Emma, who was saddened but not in the least surprised as he had been ill for so long, since that terrible accident when the main boiler had exploded at the Glebe Mill. Now there would be another funeral to attend. But this would be a bigger affair than the funeral of Mary-Ann. As well as the mourners in black attire, there would be black-plumed, prancing horses, black carriages and a lavish tea at the Albion Inn.

"I should go and see Mrs. Kendal and see if I can help in any way," added the ever-practical Emma.

"She's as right as ninepence," said Alice. "She's got her brother nearby and Lenny arrived from Newton-le-Willows this afternoon."

Nevertheless, Emma knew her duty as a long-time customer and friend of Mrs. Kendal, whose brother was Billy's father. She knew that Joe would not be as comforting as a female friend, and neither would her son, Lenny. He had distanced himself from his family for many years. "I'll go and see the poor woman tomorrow after work."

Alice was obviously not affected by the demise of her employer's husband. She hardly knew Mr. Kendal, but she felt sorry for his wife, even though, as a widow, Mrs. Kendal might find life somewhat easier.

She removed her engagement ring in preparation to helping Emma with the tea. She placed it carefully on the mantel piece, the usual repository for anything precious, and then rolled up her sleeves to fill the scuttle from the outside coal shed. Then she scrubbed her hands before cutting the bread, and buttered it whilst Emma sliced the ham and cut the fresh celery hearts. Just the two of them would sit down to a high tea at the hour of half past six o'clock. As usual, whilst doing some mundane chore, Alice's thoughts were on her fiancé almost fifty miles away in Birkenhead.

No one was more elated at the engagement of Alice and Robbie than Eliza. Finally, she was able to feel guiltless at her broken engagement to him. He obviously now realised things had turned out for the best and would be happy with Alice. Everyone was pleased that the young Scot was going to be a member of the Kershaw family after all. Eliza had strongly advised Alice not to mention that other, unwanted, engagement ring to Robbie. Let it remain where it was, forgotten. Robbie obviously did not want to economize on a new ring for his new fiancée or he would surely have mentioned it.

Enjoying the pleasures of courtship, Alice was, however, a little alarmed when Robbie casually mentioned the fact that his homeland called to him at times. It was nearly four years since he had left Scotland with a heavy heart, having lost all his family in the shipping disaster. He now seemed to be contemplating work on the Clyde where hundreds of men were employed in the great shipbuilding yards along the river.

"And what's wrong with the shipbuilding at Cammell Laird's in Birkenhead?" questioned Alice.

"Nothing at all. But don't forget, there's my family house in Scotland. It's tenanted but we could easily get possession."

That was something to consider, Alice thought, to have a house to call their own, but even so, she still wanted to live in Birkenhead and it should not be difficult for them to find a suitable house to rent.

"I don't think I'd like to go to Scotland," said Alice. "There was that horrific murder on Arran—the newspapers are full of it."

It was true; hardly anyone was unaware of the recent, grisly event: 'The Arran Island Murder'. Edwin Rose of Tooting, London and John Laurie from Glasgow were on holiday on the Isle of Bute, meeting on the excursion steamer to the Isle of Arran. The two men apparently formed a friendship, Edwin Rose expressing his wish to climb the famous and popular Goat Fell. The acquaintance evidently agreed and the new friends climbed the mountain on July 15th but only one came back—John Laurie. Three weeks later the badly mutilated body of Edwin Rose was found, his money and other belongings missing. It was concluded he had been pushed over a crag by his companion. John Laurie disappeared but was later found and charged with murder. Death by hanging was commuted by Queen Victoria to penal servitude.

"It's just like Mrs. Burgess's murder," said Alice. "Somebody was after money. John Laurie robbed that fellow and killed him. Mrs. Burgess didn't have any money on *her*, but she was killed anyway."

"Sometimes I think you should be working in a police station, not a post office," said Robbie. "It may not have been murder. Don't forget she died of a heart attack."

"Yes, but it was probably caused by that Frank Barrow," said Alice. "I hope they find him. He should be charged, but I don't think he should be hanged. It would be better if he got penal servitude. It sounds a lot better."

"Penal servitude is far worse," reasoned Robbie. "He would be sent away, probably to a barren island where he has to do forced labour and live on roots and dead rats."

"Perhaps," said Alice. "But you're right. We don't know if he did murder Mrs. Burgess."

"You've got murder on the brain again," said Robbie. "Forget about it. Think on pleasant things, like Scotland! Besides, the Isle of Arran is nowhere near where we'd be going."

"Even so, I don't think I would like to go to Scotland," said Alice. "If I have to leave Chadderton, I'd like to live in Birkenhead, near Pa."

Robbie was not going to relinquish his idea of going back to Scotland just yet, reminding Alice of a few things. "Don't forget it was due to Scottish inventors that wooden hulls of ships were replaced with iron and steel, and Scots engineers developed and refined the steam engine! And I do miss the bagpipes," he said, with a sidelong glance at Emma who pulled a face.

"The ones I've heard are as tuneful as the washboard in the scullery," she said.

"Perhaps Scottish inventions are something to be marvelled at," said Alice. "But we've got plenty inventions of our own here. And Cammell Laird's is just as good as those Clydebank shipbuilders."

Robbie just laughed. He loved Alice's red hair, her freckles, but not always her opinions.

But she was not unduly worried. There was no danger of their going to Scotland in the foreseeable future and their wedding was planned for next year. The smoking chimneys of Chadderton would be replaced by the clanking cranes of Birkenhead and Alice just loved the thought, for at least at Birkenhead, they were near the seaside, a place she had yet to visit.

And then, when Emma called them to the tea table, they resumed another conversation, discussing a topic that had been uppermost in today's newspapers: the arrest of a suffragette for her activities in London.

"If I had stayed in London, I should probably have become a suffragette," said Alice, smiling at the scandalised look from Emma and the amused one from her fiancé.

"Well, I wouldn't have been best pleased if you'd got mixed up with that lot, even though they *do* have the right idea," said Emma. "Heaven save us all from suffragettes!"

§

It was the middle of December. Jane relaxed on the train speeding northwards for the Christmas holidays. She regarded her companion on the seat opposite her, a fellow student by the name of Richard Gilchrist, who played the flute and was in his last year at the academy. She had been chosen by the Royal Academy to perform with him in Manchester. She knew the choice had been partly because both of them were from that area, but nevertheless it was an honour to be asked to perform at a concert that had been arranged by Richard's father, Sir Walter Gilchrist, who was a patron of the Hallé Orchestra.

The train had stopped at Coventry when Richard stepped out of the third-class carriage to try and procure something to eat from the station café, but he returned, saying it was closed. Jane took out her sandwiches, thoughtfully provided by Mrs. Blakiston and wrapped in a crisp white linen napkin. She offered her lunch package to Richard, who gratefully took a ham sandwich and then a sip from the bottle of lemonade while she took the cup. He might be the son of Sir Walter Gilchrist, thought Jane, but he didn't have refreshments provided for him by *his* landlady. She knew he could well have travelled first class but he had expressed his wish to travel with her. Sir Walter was sponsoring this performance to promote his son, who wished to join the Hallé when he finished at the academy.

"I do wish we were playing at the Theatre Royal instead of the Free Trade Hall," said Jane. "Franz Liszt played there when he was only thirteen, you know."

"The Free Trade Hall has far better acoustics than the Theatre Royal," asserted her companion. "And it's also the home of the Hallé orchestra. The Theatre Royal is more for pantomimes and variety nowadays."

Jane's assignment was to accompany this young flautist at a performance put on by musicians in Manchester, hardly on the same scale as Liszt. Still, it was giving her the opportunity to appear in public and she had won the coveted place over all her fellow students at the academy in London, not only because she was from Manchester but also, she had been assured by her piano tutor, because she was a competent accompanist and had already played in some student recitals with Richard.

Richard was two years her senior and was clearly in admiration of Jane. She was flattered by his attention but what she liked most was the reputation she had earned from other students and even some of the tutors. Everyone knew who Jane Kershaw was.

"I'm going to try for the Hallé once I've graduated," said Richard. "Do you have plans to return north once you've finished?"

It was far too early for Jane to have any plans beyond the immediate future. To her surprise, she had been homesick since going to London, so it was definitely within the bounds of possibility that she would return north, but to what? She had no idea yet.

Jane was excited over the prospect of performing with an advanced student, which could only bolster her own career. She was also relieved to be going home for the Christmas holidays. She had been away since September and it had seemed an age. The atmosphere in the Blakiston home had turned out not to her liking. Mr. Blakiston made her feel uncomfortable as he insisted on being present when she gave his three daughters music lessons. This was only three times a week. But she also supervised their practice most evenings and Mr. Blakiston was often there, in the drawing room, standing near the piano. Taking an interest in his girls, he called it, but Jane felt he was taking too much interest in her, leaning over her shoulder as she played a passage to her pupils. Sometimes he laid his hand on her shoulder, a gesture she did not like. And sometimes he was so close she could smell his Macassar hair oil, or even his breath.

However, now she was almost home and preparing to perform on the morrow with Richard. He lived on the other side of Manchester, probably in some large, elegant house, Jane was sure. Of course, Emma would accompany her to Manchester, primarily as a chaperone but also because she was keen to see her sister in performance. If the concert ended late, they would spend the night at Amy's student hostel at Queens University, but they probably would be in time to get the last train back to Chadderton. Amy herself was also going to attend the performance.

Jane had dreamt of this moment when she would be home again, but she had not accounted for the magnitude of it. As soon as she stepped from the train, she saw Emma, who enveloped her in a bone-crushing hug, sweeping her off her feet. Then outside the station, there was Kate holding the reins of the Goodacre trap. She jumped down and she too, without a word, almost squeezed the air out of Jane who could only gasp and shed a tear or two. But they were tears of joy and on the short ride to Bower Lane, words were exchanged, half finished sentences . . . what a lot of luggage, good thing Kate had brought the trap . . . Jane's hair was different . . . and that hat was so chic.

And there was Alice as soon as they arrived home, and it all started again. Alice was in love with Robbie and it was all romance and dreams from her, but she pumped Jane with so many questions, most of them were unanswered for the time being. Kate had to leave to see to her children and then there was the unpacking and giving of presents, saving some for Christmas, especially the ones from Aunt Clara. No wonder Jane had so much luggage.

"You've been to see Aunt Clara?" Emma was astonished, knowing Jane's last verdict on their stern and officious aunt.

"I couldn't spend simply every day at the Blakiston's," said Jane with downcast eyes, signifying to Emma that there was a reason Jane had felt the need to visit her aunt, something she vowed she would never do after their last stay at that inhospitable household.

It was just like old times, Emma doing the bread and butter, Alice flinging on the tablecloth and the clattering of knives and forks for the ham and cheese pudding. Jane could not wipe the smile off her face. She went up to her old room, the one she shared with Alice, putting her clothes away in the wardrobe, and her hat atop the high shelf. She would need it again the next morning when she and Emma took the train to Manchester. But in the meantime, it was heaven to be home. Jane stroked the faded blue counterpane on her bed. Just the same as when she left, and the old chintz curtains at the window, the ones Aunt Clara had put up when she came to their mother's funeral eight years ago. There appeared to be a new wash basin and jug on the dressing table. The one she remembered had been chipped, but then she recognised it was the one from Emma's room. She fingered the blue and white porcelain carefully. How sweet of Emma to put the newer one in here. She ran back downstairs to the kitchen. The best teapot was on the table and the best china cups from the cabinet in the parlour. She was getting the royal treatment.

During high tea, Jane regaled her two sisters with all that she had been doing in London. There had been little change since she had left home in September, except that Alice and Robbie were now engaged.

"It's a feather in your cap to be playing with this flautist fellow and you being allowed to come home early for the Christmas holidays an' all," said Emma.

"I think it was mainly because Richard Gilchrist and I are both from this area," said Jane. "There are other soloists taking part tomorrow, but they already live around Manchester."

"But you are the youngest," asserted Emma, who had read and re-read Jane's letters from London and was well acquainted with all the facts.

"Evidently I *am* the youngest, but Richard is only two years older."

"So you know him quite well?" As usual, Emma needed to know those kinds of details.

"Only because of the music. We've been practising this Hummel sonata for the last three weeks." Jane flexed her fingers. "I haven't practised for two days. I hope I don't make any mistakes tomorrow."

"How long do you practice each day?" asked Emma.

"I have my two classes a day for actual piano, then theory which I have to study, then I can practice a little before I go home if I hang around and wait for a chance. The older students have first call."

"But why can't you practice on the Blakiston's piano?"

"It's not always convenient for me to practice there. I have a few chores to do and sometimes I have not finished them before Mrs. Blakiston goes to bed, which is early."

Emma thought to herself that was not what had been agreed, but kept her silence.

The train rattled into Manchester the next day where they met Amy. After some refreshment from the basket that Emma was carrying, the two older girls went for a walk while Jane had her afternoon rehearsal with Richard and the other participants in the concert. She was surprised to find that the Free Trade Hall was, in fact, just across the street from the Theatre Royal.

"The Free Trade Hall is a much bigger place, more for orchestras and classical music," explained Richard. "It probably hadn't been built when Franz Liszt came." He would know these facts, thought Jane, with his father being connected to the Hallé. orchestra. But she was in awe at the grandeur of the magnificent concert hall.

Jane and Richard were not playing until the second half of the performance. In the intermission, she, Amy and Emma found the refreshment room and whilst collecting a glass of cordial she noticed a young army officer standing near the entrance of the room. He looked vaguely familiar, even from a distance. Suddenly, her heart seemed to miss a beat and she almost choked on her cordial. Could it be him, the one she had once looked up to, had dreamed of as the kind of hero she had read about in novels?

Emma noticed Jane's wandering eye and then she also spied the soldier, barely recognizable as the once popular schoolteacher who had suddenly blotted his copybook and left under a cloud. She watched with interest as Jane stared intently at the magnificently attired, confident young man. He was now so mature, and even more handsome than he had appeared at Christ Church School. Jane did some quick calculations as she manoeuvred herself nearer to where the subject was leaning nonchalantly against one of the columns in the huge room. He appeared to be with an older man, also in military uniform. She figured he must be about twenty-nine or thirty years old now.

She caught his eye and she could tell there was immediate recognition. He said something to his companion and then starting moving slowly towards her.

"Do I have the pleasure of meeting Miss Jane Kershaw, from Chadderton?" he asked, noting the same auburn curls, contained by a broad blue ribbon matching her dress of deep blue taffeta. It was the one she had worn when she was bridesmaid at Eliza's wedding last year, but it had not yet been seen outside Chadderton. She had wanted to put up her hair for this day, but Emma had persuaded her to leave it down. She was the youngest performer at the concert and Emma had wanted to make sure everyone knew it. Plenty of years ahead to have her hair swept up.

"Yes, how do you do, Mr. Hunter," said Jane, sweeping her free hand to grab the folds of her skirt, her best attempt at a curtsey.

"*Sergeant* Hunter, at your service, ma'am."

Goose pimples speckled her arms, and she felt herself under a surreal enchantment as she pictured him on the battlefields of the world. She could just see him in a Charge of the Light Brigade scenario except that had been in the Crimean War and, of course, he had not been born then. But he did look magnificent. He had obviously done well. Already the incident with young Jimmy Leighton was receding into a hazy corridor in Jane's memory. She found herself wondering whether Mr. Giles Hunter, of the East Lancashire Regiment, could fancy a girl of eighteen when he had once, perhaps, fancied a boy of nine.

"Sergeant?" said Jane, taking a sip of her cordial, and looking approvingly at the stripes on his arm. She hadn't noticed them at first; she knew little about army ranks but the array was most impressive. She finally found her tongue. "Did you ever get to India?" remembering the vivid stories of his uncle.

"I most certainly did; served two stretches with my battalion."

She listened attentively as he referred to a few skirmishes here and there but no major battles. She tried not to stare at him but he was a handsome fellow, looking unscathed, confident, refined, his hair brushed back in a debonair fashion and the once fair down on his upper lip now a full moustache. And then, Jane wondered, was that a battle scar on his oh-so-smooth chin, or had he cut himself shaving?

He took a good look at her dress of rich, rustling taffeta with puffed sleeves, sophisticated and fashionable but with a demurely square neckline. The sapphire blue was a striking contrast to the scarlet tunic of his dress uniform. He looked intently at her and could hardly believe this was the precocious school girl of twelve he had last seen six years ago. He remembered the occasion well. That snivelling little brat Jimmy Leighton had stolen the money for piano lessons from the church hall. He had gone after him, but it had back-fired and as no one believed his explanation, he had resigned from the school.

He acknowledged Emma and Amy with a formal bow. He remembered Emma well: tall and thin and also bossy. His memory of Amy was dim, one of a shy, retiring sort of girl who had not made much impression on him.

"Fancy seeing you here, Miss Kershaw, so far from Chadderton." His puzzled smile indicated clearly that he had not read the programme where her name was clearly stated as taking part in the second half of the concert. Emma wasted no time in clarifying matters.

"You'd better look sharp, Jane. It's nearly time for you to get ready to play."

She propelled Jane through the crowded room but not before Jane had a moment to say a gracious farewell to the sergeant. To Emma, his look of admiration was obvious as his eyes followed Jane leaving the room.

Jane found it hard to concentrate on the sonata. She ignored what she and Richard had discussed during the afternoon rehearsal, about taking the Allegro a little slower. She played it at a lightning tempo, but without fault from either of them. As they took a bow at the end of the Rondo, she scanned the audience for a glimpse of a scarlet jacket but it was impossible to pick anyone out. The concert hall was packed.

At the end of the performance, the applause was thunderous as she and other young musicians took their bows on stage. Again, she looked intently at the audience but could not tell a scarlet tunic from a scarlet gown.

Richard took his leave of her. "See you after the holidays, Jane. Have a good Christmas." He was eager to continue his acquaintance with Jane, but after this evening, little did he know, he stood no chance of being other than that, an acquaintance.

"What a marvellous evening," said Emma, after they had said goodbye to Amy and were travelling home on the train. "You and Richard were the best on the program."

"Well, you're biased," said Jane, but she was both pleased and proud at the comment. "But fancy seeing Mr. Hunter there. He's so marvellous, and that uniform . . ."

"Forget about him," said Emma. "Remember what he did?"

"We don't know the truth. Jimmy Leighton could have been lying," said Jane. "He could have taken the money, like Mr. Hunter said, and that's why he wanted to give Jimmy a thrashing."

"May I remind you he resigned from the school."

"It was so unfair. Well, he's now a sergeant in the army. And . . . he's so handsome."

"Yes, he's a fine-looking gentleman; probably more of a ladies' man now."

"Oh, will I ever see him again?" murmured Jane, more to herself than to Emma.

"Get him out of your mind, for goodness sake."

"Oh, but I don't want to. He's so . . . I'm sure he didn't want to hurt Jimmy, but he was so angry. Remember, Jimmy could be very naughty."

Emma agreed with her to some extent, but it was more to ease Jane's feelings than a firm belief. Also, she did recall that the piano lesson money, which was kept in a desk until the end of the day, had disappeared—a good enough reason for the teacher wanting to punish the boy who could have been the culprit as he was hanging around. She had heard the headmaster had tried to arbitrate the matter and the resignation of Hunter had been a mutual decision by both parties. Perhaps Hunter had merely chased after the boy to regain the money, but it had backfired. The money had never been found. No one had checked to see if was on Jimmy Leighton when Jane took him, bleeding, to the Kershaw's house. The truth would never be known.

But what was true for Jane was an aching longing, a yearning which she found disturbing.

Chapter Twenty-Three

1890

On a cold Saturday afternoon in January, John Burgess arrived unexpectedly at Bower Lane, bringing a book from his collection for Emma to read. She was surprised, giving a quick glance at the small volume before placing it on the mantelpiece. "The Last of the Mohicans" she said in an unimpressed tone, implying she had not heard of it. Her reading mainly consisted of newspapers and letters from Jane, Amy and Mary-Rose, although the latter's epistles were few and far between, and took many weeks to arrive.

"I thought you'd like to read Fenimore Cooper. He's so popular just now." A rather hesitant tone from the schoolmaster. "It's an adventure story, about two English girls who go to the wilds of North America to join their father who is a colonel in the army. They're kidnapped by native Indians."

Emma did not care to read about English girls being kidnapped. It would set her off worrying about Mary-Rose in Massachusetts and that would lead to dwelling on Mary-Ann who *didn't* go to Massachusetts and was now gone from this world.

"I've read about that Indian, Hiawatha," she said, trying to sound interested. She had not actually read it, just listened to Alice reciting it many times.

"Oh, this is nothing like Hiawatha. That's a poem. This is quite different."

Emma wondered why Mr. Burgess would want to lend her a book, just as he used to lend Amy books; but those were text books to help with her studies. She put two smoothing irons on the hob preparing to do the weekly ironing. She said nothing, certain that some further explanation for this unexpected visit would be forthcoming. It did, after an interminable pause, while he shifted his weight from one to leg to the other, declining her offer to take a seat. He loosened his coat.

"Emma, I've been promoted to the position of Headmaster at the Blue Coat School, and I will be taking up that position after Easter."

"Congratulations,' said Emma. "That's a marvellous promotion."

"It means I will be required to live on the premises as there is a house for the headmaster. It's a large house with four bedrooms, very comfortable, with every convenience."

"Why would you want to live in a great big house right next to the school?" She couldn't help her usual down-to-earth observations.

"I must. It's customary. The governing body and trustees maintain that a headmaster should always strive to follow the founders of the institution—to meet and uphold the traditions of the school. Therefore, the headmaster must live on the premises so that he has his finger on the pulse, so to speak." He looked at Emma earnestly, seemed about to say something, and then cast his eyes towards the floor.

Emma tested her first iron and shook out some linens which had been drying outside that morning. She started on a tablecloth.

He cleared his throat and started, hesitantly. "I've been thinking. It's time you left that old mill."

Emma wondered what the mill had to do with his promotion, but she said nothing.

He continued, but his speech was stilted, as if he had rehearsed it and not got it quite right.

"You've been at the Wharf Mill a mighty long time. I was wondering if you had given thought to leaving, doing something different? I thought you might like to live with . . . at . . . the headmaster's house . . . at the school. Your sisters are all well taken care of. Time to think of yourself now, Emma . . . As I said, it's a nice house. You would love it—I know. You'll be lonely when Alice gets married and goes to live in Birkenhead. And when your father comes, and Jane and Amy, they could come and stay at the house, of course . . ."

She didn't look at him and continued ironing; she wanted to make sure she was not mistaken in her understanding of this speech so far. She reasoned silently. There usually was only one reason why a man would ask a woman to give up her job to go and live with him.

Next came the sheets.

After a few minutes, John Burgess continued with his inventory of the benefits of the headmaster's house. Would Emma not like a detached house with a pleasing green lawn with a neat privet hedge, separating it from the school? Would she not like a water closet in the house instead of an outdoor privy? And so on.

This was quite a speech from the usually quiet, reserved man who only spoke at length when he was giving lessons at school.

But there was one thing he had so far neglected to mention. He seemed to be pondering the long list of benefits and seeking more. She cocked her head to one side, to indicate she was taking it all in, and fully expected him to continue.

But then he was silent. For Heaven's sake—was he asking her to marry him? Emma was confused. Was this what a proposal was supposed to sound like? From what she'd heard, none of her sisters had experienced anything like this.

"So, what do you think, Emma?"

How could she answer this man who, so far, had failed to communicate in a clear and defined manner?

"Is it a housekeeper you're wanting?" she asked, going over to the hob to change the cooling iron for the hot one. There was silence except for the thud, thud of the iron and the crackle of the fire.

For a man who taught English and Latin, John was suddenly at a loss for words. He had uttered the speech he had rehearsed and it obviously had not had the reaction he had wanted. He was now tongue-tied. He stared at the floor.

Her heart was in her mouth as she continued to pound that heavy iron, but she hardly dared look at him.

Had he finished, she wondered? Those sheets had never been so thoroughly and painstakingly ironed. Were all men like this, leaving something vital out? She thought of Billy and his poor means of communication with Eliza. She started putting the sheets and other linens away, using a stool to reach the high airing cupboard next to the fireplace. John hastened to help her, handing up the smooth linens for her to place on the shelves. As he helped her down, was it her imagination or did he try to hold on to her hand, ever so slightly? He released her hand, stepped back and took a deep breath, as if he was about to start speaking again, but no words came out. He just stood there stiffly to attention.

It was now late in the afternoon. Shadows were jumping up the walls from the fire before the lamps were lit as Emma put the ironing things away and started setting the table. "Alice will be home soon. I'd best get on with the tea. You'll stay for tea, won't you, Mr. Burgess? I'm sure Alice will be pleased to see you."

"Oh, please, call me John,"

Emma, always a stickler for etiquette, had never called him by his Christian name and it felt awkward now.

"I don't know what can be keeping Alice," said the slightly flustered Emma, while putting out the veal pie, the pickled red cabbage and the celery. She deftly cut the bread and after buttering it, finally produced the Victoria sponge she had made that morning, placing it on the table. She made a mental note to herself: get out of the habit of making a Victoria sponge every Saturday unless Pa and Robbie were coming. She simply could not get used to catering for only two people.

He seemed reluctant to leave and was slowly buttoning his overcoat. Emma checked the clock on the mantelpiece. "It's not like Alice to be late." She made sure the kettle was simmering on the hob.

"Being Saturday, I expect Alice has things to wind up after the busy week," said Mr. Burgess. "I must be getting along. I can't stay. My sister and Abigail will be expecting me. Please think about what I've said. I'll see you at church tomorrow."

Emma was feeling a little exasperated as she saw him to the front door. Had he missed something out of his discourse? But he said he would see her tomorrow at church, when matters might be made clear. He rarely attended Chadderton Church nowadays, being required to attend Sunday church services at the Blue Coat School.

Then a thought struck her. "What about Abigail? Is she going to live there as well?"

"No. she will remain with my sister."

He looked at her intently. "I have long admired you, the way you cared for your sisters after your mother died, dealing with their problems; how you helped my poor Abigail . . ."

Emma shot him a startled glance as he still lingered. Did he know the truth about Abigail? Emma thought it was a well-kept secret. Since that horrific and unforgettable event, she had come to understand Abigail's desperation, and also believed that no matter what, a girl should not be forced to bear a child conceived in ignorance. Emma had thought this through many times and come to the conclusion that Abigail had not had much choice in dealing with her predicament. Emma herself would likely have done the same thing, had she ever found herself in the same situation. But Emma, being who she was, would not have nearly killed herself, but would have brought about a satisfactory result. She looked at him as she had never done before. He was a tall, scholarly man, with prematurely white hair due to the horrible experience of his wife's untimely death and worry over Abigail's health. However, white hair or not, he was not an old man, and Emma estimated he could not be more than forty-five. His grey eyes were clear and steady, his cheeks unlined; in fact, Emma suddenly realised he was a handsome man.

She was opening the front door when he suddenly said, "Wouldn't you like to be a headmaster's wife?"

She smiled. This seemed to be getting more to the point. But, too late. Here was Alice bursting in.

"Mr. Burgess brought me a book," explained Emma to Alice who looked surprised to see their former neighbour who had not been to visit since Jane had taken her entrance examination to college.

"Good evening, Mr. Burgess, and how are you?" enquired Alice as he stepped out on to the street.

"I'm well, thank you, Alice." And to Emma, "I'll see you tomorrow at church."

§

Emma gave no further explanation to Alice for Mr. Burgess's unexpected visit. Previously, he had only ever brought a book for Amy or Jane and that was over a year ago. Alice had been puzzled. Obviously, Mr. Burgess had been having some serious discussion with Emma because she was unusually agitated. Alice knew only too well Emma was not going to divulge anything too soon, but Alice had plenty to say when she saw Kate after church the next day, telling her about the previous day's occurrence. They were both quick to notice that Emma had been singled out by Mr. Burgess and they were walking ahead, their heads together as if in earnest conversation, their eyes and ears for no one else.

"Y'know what this means, don't you?" said Alice.

"I hope it means Emma and Mr. Burgess will be getting married." said Kate.

"What it means is, we're getting Abigail for a sister."

§

If Emma had ever thought of matrimony, it had certainly never been for herself. But here she was, preparing for her own wedding. She had told John Burgess, now her fiancé, that she must see Alice and Robbie married first, so he would have to live in that big house all by himself until later in the year. Emma smiled to herself, remembering how in the past, the younger sisters had always speculated about what happened on a wedding night. She had always frowned upon this kind of banter. But now she smiled at their past conjectures and suppositions. She was about to find out for herself. She was more than ready for it.

"I'll wait as long as you like," John had said. "As long as you promise we'll be wed."

He had at last spelled it out on that walk home from church, just the way Nathaniel Goodacre had done to Kate seven years ago.

Now, Emma was in no doubt about his intentions albeit it had taken a while for him to actually pronounce the words he had found rather difficult at first. Now, seeing that Emma was becoming receptive to what he was trying to ask, he had become more eloquent.

"I've been wanting to ask you to be my wife long before this," he had explained. "I have loved you for a long time, but I knew you were devoted to your family and had never considered marriage for yourself. I started to pluck up courage once I could see that Alice was going to marry that Scots lad, and you'd be all alone. But then, when I was offered the headmastership, I knew it was the perfect time."

Emma had given one of her rare smiles once his intentions were clear and she was no longer under any misapprehension. She was nearly thirty and set in her ways, having accomplished her mission to see all her sisters well established with, of course, the one sad item for which she still could not stop blaming herself—the death of Mary-Ann. But suddenly, everything had changed. She started thinking about John Burgess in a different way. When she reached home, her heart was pounding, thoughts were tumbling through her head and she even forgot to put on her apron.

But the next day, she was rudely awakened from her euphoric state.

"Want to know what I just heard?" said Alice, breathless, after rushing home from Kendal's shop.

Emma knew she would hear it whether she wanted to or not, and poured boiling water into the waiting teapot before sitting down.

"Frank Barrow—you know, that fellow they think killed Mrs. Burgess, well, they've found him."

"And how d'you know that?"

"The baker who delivers to Kendal's told me. He knows because his brother-in-law is a policeman."

Emma, as ever, took this piece of news with a pinch of salt. "So they found him—here in Chadderton?"

"Oh, I don't know that, just that he's been found."

Emma thought this rather vague and, like most of the rumours that swept through Chadderton, originated either at the barbershop, a public house or the clerk's office at the Courthouse.

"Before you go gallivanting off to the police station, I can tell you that they won't be able to discuss it with you, so save your legs."

Even so, Emma worried that John Burgess, now her fiancé, would find this news disquieting and open up old wounds. There would have to be a trial and all that evidence would be raked over again, how John had found his wife dying in the cab when she arrived home. It was all too ghastly to dwell on yet again. She just wanted this nightmare to come to an end.

She thought again about becoming a headmaster's wife, with some pride and slight trepidation. But she was in love for the first time in her life and wanted this new, extraordinary life that was in front of her. The rest of the family were pleased and supportive about this change in their oldest sister's status. There was a lot of planning, particularly of Alice's nuptials, but Emma was determined *her* marriage ceremony was going to be a simple one. There would be two weddings this year, which would not be as complicated as the three weddings they had had two years ago of Mary-Rose, Mary-Ann and Eliza.

§

"So you heard that miscreant had been found, did you?" said Sergeant Wilkins, when Alice, in spite of Emma's admonition, decided to check up on events at the Victoria Street police station.

"So there'll be a trial now, won't there?" said Alice who was excited about the prospect.

"Yes, there'll be a trial, all in good time," said the sergeant, a mechanical smile on his lips. "He has yet to be identified by the cabbie who picked him up on the day in question, and that lass at the Big House. I think you know her."

"Oh, yes, Frances," said Alice, impatient as ever, and thirsty for knowledge of the procedure. She did think it an odd coincidence, though, to think that Frances, the dead woman's daughter, was the one who had spoken to Frank Barrow when she gave him the knives and scissors to be sharpened. Alice wished it had been herself. She knew Frances, like her sister, Abigail, was always in a quandary about something and had difficulty making decisions or stating her mind. "But I'm a witness, aren't I? I live next door and I was at home when Mrs. Burgess came home in the cab—dead."

"I've not been told that that. I know there were several people who were there at the time, so I'll have to check. But as soon as he's been identified, he'll be shipped off to Strangeways. And that's all I can tell you."

"Strangeways? That huge prison in Manchester?" asked Alice

The sergeant nodded, intent on his purpose of escorting her to the door, but Alice, inquisitive as ever, tried to evade his manoeuvres, wanting to delve into this matter some more. She knew that Emma's fiancé, John Burgess, had already been questioned by the police about this suspect who had been spotted on the Oxford Canal by Tinker Carberry.

Sergeant Wilkins found it hard to get rid of this young lady who should be in the police force, the way she carried on. But whoever heard of a woman constable?

"I'm sorry but I can't discuss this with you," he said, finally ushering her into the street and closing the door.

§

John Burgess was troubled when he came back from the police station. He had talked extensively to the sergeant and then he had been allowed to see the prisoner.

Emma gave him a questioning look. He knew he would have to explain, but this was so difficult. He began. At first it was disjointed but gradually he related to Emma, in a halting and hesitant way, his astonishing conversation with the prisoner.

"His name is not Francis Barrow, but Barreau. His father was French. His mother died when he was a baby, or so he had been told. But on his deathbed, his father told Frank that his mother was still alive—last known address Chadderton. Frank came up here from London to find her. She was a dressmaker. Her name was Mariah."

John seemed to have difficulty continuing. Emma could see he was overwhelmed by the enormity of the situation.

"Are you trying to tell me that his mother was your wife?" Emma remembered Mrs. Burgess telling her years ago that she had learned her dressmaking trade in London from a French couturier.

Burgess slowly nodded as Emma looked at him in disbelief. He continued. "The young man they have in prison told me he had lived all his life with his father, a French tailor, Jacques Barreau. The boy, Francis, grew up without a mother. They lived in Spitalfields, one of the main Huguenot areas of London, where a lot of French people went to live in the 17th century. His father, Jacques, did not speak English well and taught Frank to read and write in French although he went to an English school. His father would order materials from France and a few times they visited there. Frank said he found being bilingual was useful and lucrative. That's how he was mostly employed writing letters in French or English. He had learned something of his father's trade, but didn't like it much."

John Burgess took a deep breath. "Evidently this unmarried couple had a turbulent relationship, but he taught her the trade of tailoring and dressmaking, in the French style, and she became an expert. After she had the child, this boy Francis, Jacques accused her of having an affair with a college student who was giving her lessons in reading and writing . . ."

"That was you?" Emma could hardly believe what she was hearing.

He nodded. ". . . so Jacques Barreau left for France, with the baby. When he returned to London two years later, he found a letter from the woman he had abandoned. She had left it in case he ever returned. She wrote that because she had lost her child, she had finally decided to leave London with the student to go up north to a place near Manchester, called Chadderton."

Mr. Burgess took a long, apologetic look towards his fiancée.

"This unfortunate young man would not have tried to kill his mother. He was trying to find her, to make amends for all the wrong his father had done. He couldn't have done it," John shook his head despairingly.

He continued. "I brought her up here after Barreau took the baby and deserted her. He had treated her cruelly, and accused her of carrying on with me, when Mariah only came to the college to receive free lessons from a student, as I was then. She was only trying to better herself. She was a first-rate dressmaker but she could neither read nor write. I gave her free lessons at the college for several months. She was always fearful and apprehensive; she didn't appear to be in good health and she was always covered in bruises. She eventually admitted he had beaten her on several occasions. I never met him, but she told me he accused her of having an affair with her tutor; that was me. I was going to see him and have it out with him, but he disappeared with the child. Mariah was heartbroken. We searched for months but the father and baby had completely vanished, probably to France, where he often went. Believe me, we did everything we could to find her child and finally she said she wanted to come with me as I had graduated from the college and had a teaching post waiting for me up here. She had no family in London. I think they lived somewhere in Kent but she had lost touch with them since she took up with Barreau. Frank said his dying father told him his mother was alive, and confessed that it was his fault that she had left London."

Emma went to sit beside him. She leaned her head on his shoulder and took his hand in hers. "So his father only told the truth when he was dying?"

"Yes. And then Frank was determined to find his mother, with a view to getting to know her. Of course, he realised he was illegitimate as his parents were not married, but that did not deter him. He realised it was a delicate thing to do. From his discreet enquiries, he learned she now had a new life with a husband and two daughters; had done so for over twenty years. How could he make himself known to her without upsetting the family she now had? He took the job on the canal boat to get to know local people and learned, by talking to servants at the Applegate house, that Mariah had been there several times and was due to go again on that dreadful day. He waited for the cab to come round the corner and stopped it, getting in after telling the driver that he knew the woman inside. Of course, he didn't know her and was unprepared for her reaction on being told that he was her long-lost son. She had hysterics, saying that he was not her son, could not possibly be, and that he must be a robber. She reached into her case which was on the floor and took out some sharp scissors and proceeded first to stab him and then herself. He realised that this was hopeless. There was no calming her down so he took the scissors off her and jumped out of the cab. She was definitely alive when he left her. That this young man could have caused his mother's death is not possible. He says he did not attack her, that he would not have done so as he was looking for her to show that he cared and wanted to be united with her, as her son."

"Then he's in the clear," said Emma, dismissing it summarily. "He has nothing to fear."

"It will take some convincing of a jury," said John. "But when Tinker Carberry saw him down on the Oxford canal and told him he had been wanted by the police for several years, he readily agreed to come up here to clear up his name. He said he had nothing to hide."

Emma was mulling all this over. She found it incredible.

John Burgess continued his narrative. "Losing that child almost broke Mariah's heart. The loss of him so many years ago had such an extreme effect on her, I don't think she ever fully recovered. Of course, she had our two daughters, true, but were they the joy she had known with her first born? I fear not. I tried to be a good husband to Mariah, but she was a difficult woman to live with. Her obsession with her lost child took over her life. It was a passion she had never experienced with our two children who were always wayward and distant as if they knew their mother dwelled on her preoccupation with a previous loved child. I tried to be a guiding figure in their lives, but they seemed never to heed me. It was easier dealing with you Kershaw girls next door. Amy and Jane appreciated my tutoring, and even Alice, who thought she knew everything!"

He tried to smile at this, but Emma could see his anguish and her heart went out to him. His distress and his confusion were heart-wrenching.

"That means that Abigail and Frances are related to him," said Emma. "Do they know that the man suspected of causing their mother's death is, in fact, their half-brother?"

Burgess shook his head. "Not yet. I will have to tell them, but the police said I cannot do that until Frances has identified him as the fellow she gave the knives and scissors to sharpen. Otherwise, it may put her in a dilemma."

Emma, knowing Abigail and Frances too well, knew that she would be needed to help her fiancé deal with his daughters. He was distraught and seemed unable to stop going over his past.

"I had no intention of marrying Mariah when we first arrived as she was a few years older than me. I found her lodgings here in Chadderton, but there was talk around the village because I had brought her here so I decided we should be married; I confess I was never truly in love with her; but liked her and felt sorry for her. She was abandoned by that wretch who took her child. That's why she called our first child Frances, because she could never forget the baby she had lost who was called Francis."

Emma still could hardly believe what she was hearing. She had wondered about John's first wife now that she was to become his second. Emma knew he had been a good husband to Mariah and father to the two girls. But it was no wonder he had always seemed rather detached and sad and only came to life when he was engrossed in his books or imparting knowledge to those who wished to learn.

She felt like saying, "Do you still want to marry me? In view of all this?" But she could not bring herself to say it. She put out her hand to find his and found her fingers were crushed in a steely grip. He stared straight ahead.

"It's all my fault. If I had not allowed Mariah to come up here with me, she might, eventually, have been reunited with her child and all this would not have happened. But she didn't want me to leave her alone in London."

"You did what you thought was best," said Emma.

Then John Burgess seemed to collect himself. "I shall have to go to Manchester, for the trial." He put his arms round Emma. "Then we can start our new life. We belong together. You are my love, my life. I grieved for Mariah because she never found her son and now it's too late. But not too late for us, Emma."

They sat in silence, their hands clasped.

§

No one could have missed the headlines in the Oldham Chronicle: Frank Barreau had been acquitted.

John was relieved; it is what he had fervently hoped for. He looked exhausted, but relieved when he called to see Emma on his return from Manchester.

"It was harrowing," he said of the two-day trial. "The prosecution tried to prove Frank Barreau had come to Chadderton with the intent of not only finding his mother but of killing her as well. They tried to make out he had the motive, had a grudge against her because she abandoned him as a baby. Frank said that was not the case. His dying father confessed *he* was the one to blame for telling the boy that his mother was dead all these years—that it was his fault that she had left London."

"Did you have to answer a lot of questions?" asked Emma.

"Yes, all about my being at college in London all those years ago, and how Mariah came up here with me." He looked exhausted.

"Did they put Frances and Abigail on the witness stand?" Emma had so many questions.

"Just Frances, for a brief period. They asked what she said to him when she gave him the knives to sharpen. Abigail wasn't needed as a witness."

"But I was on the stand for what seemed like hours," said John. "But not as long as Frank Barreau, of course. He came across as sincere and honest. I think the Judge fully believed him and recommended the jury give a not guilty verdict."

"Well, he's free now," said Emma. "Will he be coming here, to see his sisters?"

"No. He talked to Frances and Abigail briefly in Manchester. He told me he finds them strange and unfriendly. Of course, they found it all most upsetting. He's going straight back to London. He works between there and Oxford."

Emma breathed a sigh of relief; thank goodness that dreadful business was finally finished. She thought only of John Burgess and his two daughters. Could they now put it all behind them and forget it?

§

Emma had not seen Abigail since before the trial. In fact, had not seen her since she and John Burgess had become engaged. It was time to go and seek out the girl to make sure she was all right after all that had happened. John had told her that both his daughters had been relieved that the trial was over and the prisoner released, but that they were still traumatized by the whole business, upset all over again by their mother's death.

But Emma thought it her duty to check on Abigail, especially as she had not seen her since before John had proposed. The finding of the wanted man and the subsequent trial had taken all the momentum away from the couple's engagement.

Emma had wondered whether Abigail was even fully aware and approved of her father's proposed marriage, not that it would make much difference to someone like Emma. But for once she was apprehensive about approaching Abigail, knowing the girl's hostility to change in circumstances, even though John had assured her that both his daughters were pleased about the forthcoming marriage.

Emma need not have worried. Abigail seemed to find the matter of little concern.

"If my Pa wants to get married again, that's his affair," she said nonchalantly, and could not help adding, "You're lucky, Emma, not to be left on the shelf."

Abigail had such a way of putting things, thought Emma, but she was so used to Abigail and her little ways, she did not take offence. Typical of Abigail, there were no congratulations forthcoming, or good wishes.

Nowadays, Abigail was Miss Prim and Proper. After Emma's earnest talk with her, to dissuade her from her leaning towards the

Catholic church, Abigail had declared she would not be converting to the Catholic faith. Aunt Nan had not turned a hair, but then, if truth be known and Emma thought she knew some of it, Abigail's aunt had probably been a somewhat reluctant convert herself, obeying the wishes of solicitor Smythe on his deathbed as a condition of their immediate marriage. The dying solicitor's proposal must have been a dream come true for the aging spinster. Even though she had not enjoyed the bliss of marriage, she had certainly benefited from a large home with income to match. To her, it was but a trivial request to convert to Catholicism for such benefits that would see her made for life. One thing Emma had heard via gossip, whether a Roman Catholic or previously as an Anglican, Nan Smythe was not a devout woman. But she was a practical one and not one to turn down an offer like that.

And Emma could see Abigail was becoming so like her aunt. Add thirty years and there you had a replica of Aunt Nan.

But was Emma being purely practical in her acceptance of a marriage proposal? In Abigail's view it certainly looked like that. But anyone knowing Emma more intimately, particularly her sister, Kate, knew that Emma's long-term practicality, ingrained in her since birth, had a soft side. She had never coveted the role of matrimony for herself, just being grateful some of her sisters had found security in that state, and the others, Jane and Amy were intent on their careers. Emma's knowledge of wedlock was scant, but she had witnessed some marriages that were successful and others questionable. It had always seemed to her a risky venture and one that she would never try. But now she realised she had a true, deep affection for her former next-door neighbour, which had surprised everyone, even herself.

Emma was gratified to hear all classes for potential 'recruits' to the Roman Catholic faith were now sent to Oldham Catholic Church where the ample-girthed Father Dominic presided. The young and handsome Father Kevin at St. Ann's Church in Ashton-under-Lyne had been replaced by an elderly priest, called from retirement.

"Religious conversion must be voluntary, without duress," Emma had told the penitent Abigail. "And now that you're going to stay a Protestant, don't be rushing to sign The Pledge or join the Band of Hope or anything like that."

Of course, she knew that was what those Methodists did at the chapel where, she had heard, Abigail had been seen lately.

Abigail said. "Don't worry Emma. From now on I'll be totally guided by you."

As long as that didn't mean she was going to be on their doorstep every day, Emma was satisfied. And Mrs. Smythe's house next to Oldham's Roman Catholic Church was a safe distance from the Blue Coat School. Abigail, just like all Emma's sisters, could visit whenever she liked, so long as she did not give them a shock and turn up bleeding profusely as she had done that time at Bower Lane.

Chapter Twenty-Four

1890

On a fine Saturday afternoon in December, Abigail Burgess walked up the hill towards the Blue Coat School and was surprised to see a familiar figure ahead of her.

Abigail fell into step with Jane Kershaw, relieving her of her small suitcase as she seemed to be also encumbered with a portmanteau and a music satchel.

"Home for the Christmas holidays?" asked Abigail, noting Jane's travelling dress of brown twill beneath a wool cape. A small felt hat perched atop Jane's abundant curls completed the outfit. Abigail guessed these items came from one of those big shops in London where she had heard there were bargains galore. But Abigail was wrong. Jane's attire was, in fact, modified clothing from Aunt Clara's house where she now lived. Who would ever have thought the old battle-axe and Jane would see eye to eye? But the gaunt house in Islington had become a haven since Jane had confided to her aunt that all was not well at the Blakiston's. Aunt Clara shrewdly guessed it had something to do with the suave, aloof father of the three little girls and had encouraged Jane to leave.

"Hello, Abigail," said Jane. 'We're both going to the same place?" More of a statement than a question.

"Going to see my Pa,"

"I'm going to see Emma, *and* your Pa." Jane never left anyone out.

It was the first time Jane had come home since Emma's wedding in the summer. She would divide her time between Kate's, Eliza's and Emma's this holiday.

"Strange, isn't it," said Abigail. "Emma is only nine years older than me and now she's my stepmother."

"Come now, Abigail. Emma is more like a sister. Surely?"

"I've got a stepmother—Emma," repeated Abigail. "And a sister—Frances. And you're one of my stepsisters."

"No young man then, Abigail?" asked Jane.

"Not for me. I'm not set on getting wed. Maybe it's not all that it's cracked up to be—tied to someone for life an' all."

Jane was not convinced. Abigail was not yet twenty-three and the way she dressed, with her furbelows, ribbons, and her hair done up in ringlets under that poke bonnet clearly indicated that she had not forsworn association with the opposite sex.

"Mind you, I'm glad my Pa's married. Seems to be happy with . . . her."

"Whether she's your stepmother, your step-sister, or your neighbour, don't forget you have a lot to thank Emma for."

"I suppose I have."

"We both have," said Jane.

"And you . . . at that college?" Abigail eyed the satchel Jane was carrying. "And maybe there's a young man you're fond of?"

"Absolutely not," said Jane thrusting from her mind the strong image of a scarlet uniform and a fair moustache. "Music is my life. One more year at college." Opening the gate to the headmaster's house, she paused to look down the hill before following Abigail along the path to the front door.

At the bottom of the hill, the houses looked like match boxes and the smoke-blackened chimneys were melting into the hazy dusk. Jane wondered about the folk down there. Would they be able to see those spires?

They would, if they had a sister like Emma.

THE END

Printed in Canada